DEATH ANGEL

ALSO BY LINDA FAIRSTEIN

Fiction

Night Watch

Silent Mercy

Hell Gate

Lethal Legacy

Killer Heat

Bad Blood

Death Dance

Entombed

The Kills

The Bone Vault

The Deadhouse

Cold Hit

Likely to Die

Final Jeopardy

Nonfiction

Sexual Violence: Our War Against Rape

DUTTON

LINDA FAIRSTEIN

DEATH
ANGEL

DUTTON
Published by the Penguin Group
Penguin Group (USA) Inc., 375 Hudson Street,
New York, New York 10014, USA

USA I Canada I UK I Ireland I Australia I New Zealand I India I South Africa I China

Penguin Books Ltd, Registered Offices: 80 Strand, London WC2R 0RL, England
For more information about the Penguin Group visit penguin.com.

REGISTERED TRADEMARK—MARCA REGISTRADA

LIBRARY OF CONGRESS CATALOGING-IN-PUBLICATION DATA

Fairstein, Linda A.
Death angel / Linda Fairstein.
pages cm.
ISBN 978-0-525-95387-6
1. Cooper, Alexandra (Fictitious character)—Fiction.   I. Title.
PS3556.A3654D4323 2013
813'.54—dc23
2013011909

Printed in the United States of America
1 3 5 7 9 10 8 6 4 2

Set in Janson Text
Designed by Spring Hoteling
Map by David Cain

For the friendship of the Davis family
One of Justin's greatest gifts to me

Allison, Susan, and Jordan
Peggy, Lizzie, and
Commissioner Gordon Davis

DEATH ANGEL

There is at Jerusalem by the sheep market a pool, which is called . . . Bethesda. . . . For an angel went down at a certain season into the pool, and troubled the water.

JOHN 5:2, 4 (KING JAMES VERSION)

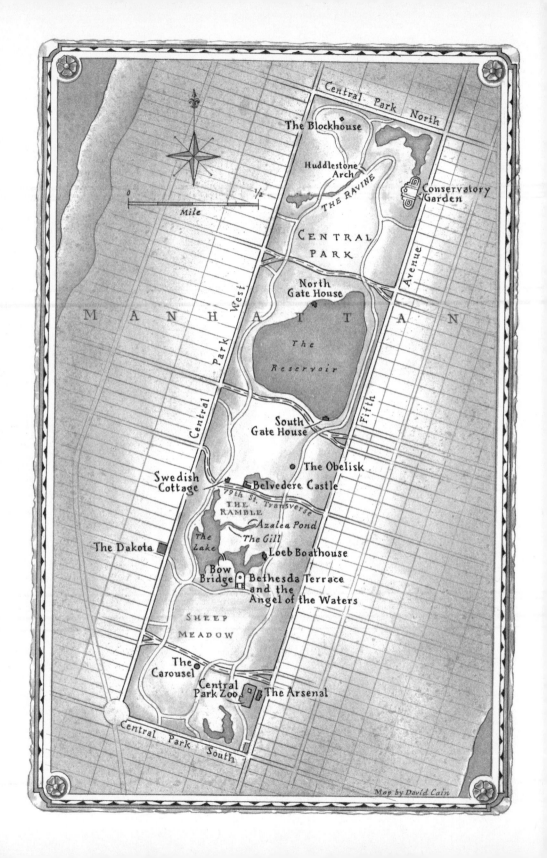

Map by David Cain

ONE

"Can you hold up those guys with the body bag, Loo?" I was jogging down the steps from the top of Bethesda Terrace, trying to catch up with Mercer Wallace, when the four cops and two techs from the ME's office passed me on their climb toward the waiting morgue van.

The lieutenant had his back to me, standing on the edge of the Lake and pointing at something across the water. Ray Peterson, the man in charge of Manhattan North Homicide, either couldn't hear me shouting because of the distance or wasn't interested in what I had to say.

I swiveled and backtracked up the broad staircase, hoping to overtake the crew carrying the corpse to the roadway on the 72nd Street transverse. But they had already reached the open doors of the transport vehicle by the time I hit the pavement and was stopped by uniformed cops who were stringing yellow crime scene tape across the gaping space between the elegant balustrades.

"Hey, Jack." After more than twelve years as a prosecutor in the Manhattan District Attorney's Office, I knew the morgue attendants almost as well as I knew my doormen. "It's me, Alex Cooper. Give me three minutes with her, please."

Jack picked his head up and turned toward me just as one of the officers brushed my hand off the tape. "In or out, ma'am?" the cop growled. "You want to ride with the body, that's fine. But you don't get back in here once you walk past this point."

I needed to talk to the lieutenant and be briefed on the findings along with Mercer, but I also wanted to see the girl whose remains had been found splayed beneath the northern abutment of Bow Bridge early this morning. I wanted to know what she looked like now, before her flesh met the cold instruments of the autopsy room.

Jack called out over the back of the young cop who was restraining me. "No can do, Alex. It's already a madhouse here between the regulars and the press scavengers. Feel free to drop by my office later on. She won't be on the table until tomorrow."

It was only 7:45, but it was obvious that police officers from all over the city were being bused in from their commands to form a perimeter around the roadways that led to the Terrace and the Lake, which was the very centerpiece of the Park. There was nothing more difficult to secure than a crime scene that had no obvious boundaries, in the middle of the most trafficked public space on the planet.

Mercer Wallace, a first-grade detective with the Special Victims Unit and one of my best friends, had picked me up at my home just a few blocks from the Park entrance. We had passed trucks from every major media outlet and watched as reporters and camera crews sneaked through the dense spring growth of bushes and plantings to get closer to the vista where death had intruded on this glorious spring morning.

"Alexandra, we're waiting on you." Mercer was shouting at me from beside the fountain at the foot of the steps.

I waved at him to let him know I'd heard him, then watched the van drive off before retracing my way down toward the Lake. I'd left the stern cop manning the tape barrier with more pushy onlookers to contend with than me. It was too early for the thousands of tourists who would flood the Park later on this June day, but the daily complement of joggers, power walkers, bikers, dog owners, Rollerbladers, and wildlife aficionados all seemed to be stopped in their tracks, trying to figure out the cause of the commotion below.

This time I took the two-tiered staircase—the eastern one— more slowly than my first descent minutes ago. I looked around at the stunning landscape and the water of the calm Lake sparkling with morning sunlight, but my eyes darted from tree to tree as figures—some in blue uniforms but mostly civilians in exercise gear—appeared on every path and in each leafy opening, like characters in a fast-moving video game. I wondered if the killer or killers were among them.

"Don't be looking for your perp, Alexandra," Mercer said. "He's long gone."

"How do you know?"

I joined up with him, and we continued on to the huddle of detectives clustered around the lieutenant. I recognized most of them from cases we had worked together—they greeted me by name—while those I hadn't met before acknowledged my presence with a "Good morning, counselor," the arm's-length term for a prosecutor—especially when she or he was treading on NYPD turf.

Mercer finished his thought. "'Cause she's been dead for weeks. Just washed up today."

"According to . . . ?"

"Johnny Mayes was here before we arrived."

Mayes was a brilliant young forensic pathologist. I nodded, understanding how well he knew his business.

"Thanks for coming over, Alex," the lieutenant said while he put out his cigarette against the side of the fountain before placing the stub in the pocket of his tattered brown jacket. No need to leave his DNA in saliva on a butt that would be picked up by Crime Scene investigators who were already scouring both sides of the shoreline for clues. "I wanted you to eyeball the kid before we moved her, but the paparazzi with the long-distance lenses were scrambling through the brush here. Had to whisk her the hell out before they grabbed one of the rowboats for a close-up."

"Got it, Loo. I'm here for whatever you need."

I'd been the prosecutor in charge of the Special Victims Unit for almost ten years. Our office had long had a system of assistant DAs "riding" homicides and major felonies—going out on calls with detectives 24/7—to try to make the legal piece of every valid case hold up in court. We went to crime scenes and station houses, hospitals and morgues—taking statements from suspects and witnesses, overseeing lineups, drafting search warrants, and generally lending our expertise on all matters likely to result in an arrest.

My specialty was a late entry in the field of criminal law. Sexual assault, domestic violence, child abuse, sex trafficking, and homicides related to these acts had been ignored by our justice system since American courts were created. But our office had lobbied for legislative reform and pioneered techniques to allow these victims— too long without voices—to begin to triumph in the courtroom in the late '70s and early '80s, a period when violent crime threatened to devour the island of Manhattan.

Lieutenant Peterson had already lit his next cigarette. "Don't know what we need yet. Don't know much."

"What else did Dr. Mayes say?"

Peterson started to walk along the path that led from the fountain toward Bow Bridge, which arched over the Lake to the Ramble. He repeated to me what he had probably just told Mercer, who was a step or two behind me.

"Doc says he doubted she was even twenty years old."

"No ID on her?"

"Pretty hard to carry your driver's license when you're naked, Alex."

I could see five men on the far side of the bridge—detectives, no doubt—all of them wearing booties and vinyl gloves. Four were standing at the water's edge, while one was crouching directly beneath the stone archway, his toes about to disappear in the water.

"Is that Mike?" I asked the lieutenant. His thick head of black hair was a giveaway, even at this distance, confirmed by his trademark navy blazer.

"Yeah. A rookie from the Central Park precinct caught the squeal. Mike was working a day tour, so I assigned the case to him."

Mike Chapman had come on the job shortly before I graduated from law school and joined the DA's office. He and Mercer had partnered together on many of the worst cases imaginable, remaining close friends after Mercer transferred to SVU, preferring to work with victims who survived their attacks.

The three of us started across the span, a familiar image in countless Park photographs featuring boaters and ice skaters. I couldn't help but look down at the water, as though some clue was about to float by just in time for me to spot it.

Mike ducked out and stepped back to talk to the other guys from the squad. I could see him shaking his head. He hadn't noticed our approach.

"Anything, Mike?" Peterson called out.

"Nothing, Loo," Mike shouted over his shoulder.

"Here's your minder, Chapman," Freddie Figueroa said, laughing as he pointed at me. My relationship with Mike was a source of great amusement to many of our colleagues, who couldn't figure how I tolerated his constant needling yet knew he'd covered my back in more situations than I could count. "You'd better come up with something fast."

"Hey, Coop," Mike said, flashing all one hundred megawatts of his best grin. "Hope you brought a crystal ball. This one will take more than your brains."

I started to walk to the end of the bridge, but he called me off.

"Stay there. Last thing we need is another pair of footprints in the mud. Did you see my girl?"

I shook my head. "Jack was ready to roll. The locals were about to surround him, so he took off."

"Hal's got plenty of close-ups if you want to take a look."

Hal Sherman, one of the masters of crime scene investigations, came up behind me. He'd been photographing each of the approaches to the Lake, on the theory that no one would know what angles were important until we had a sense of what had happened to this victim and where.

"Hey, Alex. Too quiet too long, huh?" Hal said, patting me on the back before he reached for his notepad. "That statue on top of the fountain, any idea what she's called?"

I looked across at the colossal bronze figure of a woman, raised high above the plaza and held aloft by four cherubs, with wings outstretched as she delivered her blessing over the Lake below.

"Sure, Hal," I said as he scratched the answer on a notepad. "She's the most iconic statue in the Park. She's called the Angel of the Waters."

Mike Chapman joined us on the bridge, pulling off his gloves and stuffing them in his rear pants pocket. "That name worked for her once upon a time, Coop. Now she stands up there with the best vantage point of all, sees everything that goes on here, but gives us nothing. I'd like to know everything that *she* knows."

"It's not even eight o'clock, and you're loaded for bear. Why take it out on an angel?"

"It's not the first body I've had in this Lake, Coop. We've got two cold cases—young women who have never been identified whose files are collecting dust in the squad room."

"How old are those runs that I don't even know about them?" I asked. "Are you figuring this one falls into some kind of pattern with the others?"

"I'm just thinking that statue may be an attractive nuisance. Maybe she blessed the waters a century ago, but now she's a magnet for murder. She's an angel, all right," Mike said, staring at the beautiful sunlit figure that towered over us. "A death angel."

TWO

Mike led Hal, Mercer, the lieutenant, and me along the path to the first pavilion on the north shore of the Lake. The large boathouse itself, where rowboats could be rented by the hour, was to our east. Four covered wooden sheds were scattered about the edges of the water as landing docks for rowers, a throwback to their Victorian origins.

We set ourselves up out of the direct sun, and Mike asked Hal to show me the digital photos he had taken when he first arrived.

"So the initial call to 911 came in at 5:49 this morning," Mike said. "Two guys out for a run on the pathway approaching Bethesda Terrace from below, to the west. One of them saw what he thought was the head and upper torso of a woman under the bridge, against the foundation, and stopped his friend."

"What time was sunrise?" Mercer asked.

"5:24. Plenty of light to see across."

"They touch anything?" I asked.

"Too spooked to get closer."

"What if she'd been alive and needed help?"

"Decomposition was evident, Coop, even from a distance," Mike said. "Hal, you got those shots?"

He cupped his hand over the viewer as Mercer and I leaned in.

The girl's face was mostly intact, but her skin was a ghastly shade of gray. Her head was to the side, one cheek hugging the concrete structure. The only eye we could see was closed and her mouth was agape, with stringy dark-brown hair plastered across her face. The area below her shoulder blade was discolored, and it looked like her bones were protruding through what once had been skin.

"Late teens is Johnny Mayes's estimate," Mike said. "No tats, no track marks. No surgical scars. Badly malnourished, lousy dentition, filthy nails all bitten down and cracked. I'm going with homeless."

"How long has she been dead?" I asked.

"Mayes figures it's been at least a month, but she was only left in the water for a day or two."

Mercer studied the photographs of the full body taken after the victim had been pulled from the water. "So, a dump job?"

Killed somewhere else and deposited in the Lake. Dumped here, by the murderer.

"Likely. But who knows where she's been all this time? That's a big problem."

"How'd she die?" I asked.

"Blunt force trauma. Check the photos of the back of her head."

Hal advanced the shots. Some object had crushed the skull with a couple of blows. Two different angles of injury suggested repeated applications of the weapon.

"Does Johnny know what might have caused this?"

"Lead pipe, maybe. Or a baseball bat. I'm hoping Derek Jeter has an alibi 'cause we're only two months into the season and he's hitting four hundred. Whoever did this has a pretty perfect swing."

"A tree branch?" I said.

"They got redwoods here I don't know about, Coop? I mean, why do you ask me a question and then take your own guess at an answer?"

"I'd like to stop by the morgue later," I said. I was fidgety and knew that I was annoying Mike before we'd even gotten out of the blocks. "I had a good chance to see what immersion in water did to a body when I helped with that girl who was murdered in France this spring."

"Save me, Jesus." Mike closed his eyes and shook his head. "Give me a break for a change, will you? Whose idea was it to call Coop in on this so early?"

The lieutenant looked at Mike, puzzled by his outburst at me. "What—?"

"I wanted her here," Mercer said. "It's going to be her case."

"We don't know that this is a sexual assault yet. Coop spent ten minutes with a lady in a lake on one of her holiday jaunts and—"

"It was a pond, not a lake, but go ahead, Mike. I made some observations that the French police found useful, so I thought maybe you would, too."

"Well, tell them to the medical examiner because he knows how long my vic's been dead and what killed her. You got any wild guesses on figuring out the 'who,' then stick around."

"Drain the Lake," I said.

"What?"

"Drain the Lake. That might give you her clothing, some form of ID, possibly the weapon. Maybe even other victims. If this fits together with your cold cases, maybe you get a bit closer to solving the whole thing."

Ray Peterson angled his head and looked at me.

"It's been done before. Draining the Lake, I mean."

"Who's going to sign off on that one?" Peterson asked.

"Don't confuse the Lake with the Reservoir. I'm telling you it can be done."

"You think I don't know that, Coop?" Mike said. "One of my vics was found when the Central Park Conservancy restored this hole ten years back, when all the DA would let you handle were petty thefts."

The Reservoir, above 86th Street in the Park, was originally built to hold the city's entire supply of drinking water, piped in by a complicated system from upstate New York and distributed throughout the boroughs via massive underground tunnels. The Jacqueline Kennedy Onassis Reservoir was now more than one hundred acres of exquisite scenery—no longer used to relieve New Yorkers' thirst—forty feet deep, holding a billion gallons of water.

The picturesque Lake, on the other hand, was only eighteen acres in area and just a few feet deep—also manmade by the Park's designers to replace the great untamed swamp that sat on the current site in the nineteenth century.

"Alex is right," Mercer said. "If the commissioner asks the mayor to do it, it'll happen."

Keith Scully had been commissioner for most of the mayor's tenure in office, and they enjoyed a strong respect for each other.

"I've got Scuba on its way here," Mike said. "Let's see what they come up with. You're over the top, Coop."

"Not if you believe this case is linked to your two old ones. About time you solved them, don't you think?"

"That wasn't my point. I was just saying the angel is falling down on her job."

"Missing persons?" Mercer asked.

"Figueroa's going down to look through files. We can't put up a photo or sketch of the girl until the ME cleans her up," Mike said. "And we're going to need a detail, Loo, to canvass the area around the Terrace and perimeter of the Lake."

"Yeah. Every morning for at least a week," the lieutenant agreed with Mike. "I'll start them at four A.M. and run it till ten at night. Creatures of habit, these Park people."

"Say it, Coop. Stop biting your lip and speak up," Mike said. "You look like you have that burning need to throw another rope out to rescue us."

"I'm not correcting the lieutenant. But today's Friday. A business day. You'll get an entirely different rhythm with any canvass you do over the weekend. Mercer and I had the same experience with our rapist who was targeting bikers up near the Reservoir."

Mercer nodded in agreement.

"Tomorrow and Sunday you'll have all the gawkers who hear this story on the news," I said. "But most of the working people who jog before going to the office have a different weekend schedule. People sleep in, dogs get walked later, businessmen who ran today at six are pushing a stroller at ten on Saturday. Your heavy days, the ones likely to yield value, will start on Monday."

"I guess I was right about your crystal ball."

"Who's going to be on top of the homeless parkies?" Mercer asked.

"I left that mess to Sergeant Chirico," Peterson said. "Problem with springtime is that they're all back out on the street. This place is so damn big you can find them anywhere, from the Sheep Meadow to the Blockhouse. Harmless and homeless, or toothless and ruthless. Takes all kinds to survive on the streets of this city."

"Detective Sherman!" one of the cops at the top of the steps yelled out to Hal. "You want me to send these guys down?"

Hal gave him a thumbs-up. "That's my Panoscan team, Mike. We'll do a couple of setups on each side of the Bow Bridge from this bank, and then a few from the foot of the fountain."

Just a few years in operation, the Panoscan was a vast improvement in crime scene technology. It would take only minutes to assemble a kit with a fish-eye lens to create high-resolution, 360-degree images. Things that may not have seemed obvious to first responders—clues possibly overlooked at a scene—would be available to Mike and Mercer by pointing and clicking on the panoramic image from their desktops.

"Great. Let's get out of the way, guys," Mike said, herding the rest of us back across the bridge to the footpath.

I waited until Peterson was a few steps ahead of us. "How come I don't know anything about your two cold cases, Mike?"

"There's a lot you don't know, kid."

"But you usually come to me with—"

"Bags of bones, Coop. Partial remains. That's what I've got.

From back in the day, before you hitched yourself to my star. No way to know who they are or how they died. No way to prove they were sexually assaulted."

"Throw in that woman from Brazil who was killed in the Ravine in '95," Mercer said, referring to a remote area in the northern end of the Park, "and the body in the Harlem Meer. Both cases colder than the iceberg that sunk the *Titanic*."

"So what are you two telling me?" I asked, although the picture was coming together for me without any more narrative. "Is this like those unsolved murders of young women out on Long Island, near Gilgo Beach? Some deranged killer sets up shop in the heart of the city's most populated public space and operates season after season?"

Mike and Mercer exchanged glances over my head.

"We don't know what it is yet. But we do know that it's been real stable here for the last couple of years," Mike said. "So nobody's going public with the bigger story, do you understand that? Not the district attorney or any of his flacks, or Scully has me walking a foot post in Bed-Stuy."

Mike stared at me until I nodded.

"Maybe there's nothing to connect any of these victims with one another. Maybe this poor broken body is a one-off. That's the approach we're taking for now."

"And so it's your idea just to make believe the Park is a safe place to be?" I asked.

"Safest precinct per square foot of any property in the city," Mike said. "I think the mayor's got the last word on what's a threat to his voters, Coop, and when he decides to tell them about that. There's a primary in three months and he's hoping it's a mandate for another term. You just figure out who this dead girl is, and I'll stay on top of the cold cases."

THREE

Judge Marvin Heller took his place on the bench at exactly 9:45 Friday morning. He ran his courtroom with an efficiency unique to the inhabitants of the Depression-era Criminal Court building that towered over Centre Street, shadowing the companion quarters that had been acquired fifty years ago to handle Manhattan's ever-growing docket of cases—now more than one hundred thousand a year.

I slipped into one of the seats in the last row of benches shortly after ten A.M., knowing that Heller had at least ten cases on the calendar he would call before mine.

I opened the Redweld and studied the notes I had made last night on a legal pad. I'd left the homicide team in Central Park to get on with their work and taken the subway downtown from 59th Street, at the south end of the Park, to Canal Street.

The morning train ride to Canal was, for me, like sitting in the middle of the biggest lineup any cops could stage. If I managed to grab a seat—and I much preferred that to the chance of being pressed against by a familiar *frotteur*, for whom New York's subway system was such a natural playground—it was easy to observe that most of the riders headed for the same stop were either lawyers or perps. The latter outweighed the former in number, and many of the recidivists who were frequent fliers in the system were as recognizable to me as my colleagues from the DA's office or defense bar.

I was far more comfortable in any criminal courtroom than on public transportation. The captain in charge of Judge Heller's court part bellowed out the name of the next defendant to appear: "Francisco Pintaro. People against Francisco Pintaro. Step into the well, please."

The young prosecutor made her way to the front of the room as her adversary walked with his client to the counsel table.

"Scoot over, Alex."

I looked up to see Eric Segal, who represented the accused rapist in my case, motioning to me to make room for him to sit beside me.

"What's up? Ready to drop the charges against my guy?"

"Not quite there yet. I hate to do that when they're guilty, Eric."

"How about a deal? Sweeten the pot a tad and maybe I'll tell him to take it," Segal said with a smile, lifting my right hand to peek at the notes I had made. He'd been a supervisor at Legal Aid for years, a good lawyer with a sharp sense of humor and a relentless style of cross-examination.

"No deal for Willie B. I'm hoping his parole officer on this case hasn't even been born yet."

"Tough talk for a weak case, Alex," he said, tracing the shorthand I used to make my points. "Hieroglyphics. That's all you've got on your pad, a bunch of hieroglyphics. You think you're going to whip my ass with those sorry points?"

Heller banged his gavel against his desktop and scanned the gallery for offenders, most of them farther up front than Eric and I.

"No talking in my courtroom. No talking unless you're addressing me, do you understand? And you, Mr. Pintaro, go to the restroom and pull up your pants so that the belt encircles your waist. I am not the least bit interested in seeing your butt cheeks every time you turn to your lawyer. 2:15 P.M. for a second call on this case.

Show some respect for this court, Mr. Pintaro, or you'll be held in contempt."

The captain called the next case, and people waiting on the hard wooden benches shuffled positions. Segal's client, Willie Buskins, was across the aisle, two rows ahead of us. When he spotted me, he began a stare-down—his typical attempt at unnerving me—narrowing his eyes and glaring at me in what he thought was his fiercest pose.

I glared back at him while I whispered to Segal. "Willie's not a candidate for a pass, Eric. He might as well have RECIDIVIST branded on his forehead."

Segal pointed his finger at Buskins and then waved it in a circle. Reluctantly, his client unlocked his eyes from mine and faced the front of the room.

"Don't you believe in reform, Alex? Willie's changed his ways. You going to ruin my whole summer with a trial?"

"Just half your summer. Heller will move this one along like a high-speed train."

Marvin Heller adjourned the parties in front of him for another month, and the captain announced our case.

"Meet at Forlini's at 6:30?" Segal said, rising to his feet and stepping back to let me out of the row. His wife had left him several months ago, and after making his way through half the young bunnies at Legal Aid, he reset his sights on the DA's office. "Cocktails on me."

"Rain check, Eric. I'm flying up to the Vineyard for the weekend."

I walked forward toward the waist-high wooden gate that separated the spectators from the well of the courtroom. Usually a court officer manned it to admit the lawyers when an unjailed defendant was present, but Heller had ordered one of the men into his chambers to refresh his water pitcher.

I stepped toward it and got ready to push it open, but Willie Buskins spun around and grabbed the gate with his left hand—a courtesy to me. As I passed in front of him, his back to the judge, he lowered his head and spoke the word "bitch," almost in my ear. The motley assemblage of thieves and assailants in the front rows heard Willie as clearly as I had and found the label much more amusing than I did. Marvin Heller would have had the officers walk Buskins back into the holding pen had he been aware of his remark.

"State your appearances for the record."

"Alexandra Cooper, for the People."

"Eric Segal, Legal Aid Society, for Mr. Willie Buskins."

"Be seated, both of you," Heller said. "I assume you two settled this matter during your little tête-à-tête in the back row, while I was trying to conduct business?"

Segal spoke over my apology to the court. "Always working for my clients, Your Honor. Rumor has it that Ms. Cooper actually has a chink in that armor she wears in court. I was just trying to find it before she tried to razzle-dazzle you with the law."

"I'm more easily razzled than dazzled, Mr. Segal. Is there anything to discuss?" the judge asked. Marvin Heller was about sixty years old, with thinning gray hair, wire-rimmed glasses worn low on his nose, and black robes that he carried with great dignity. "Or are we here to pick a date for trial?"

Eric Segal stood up. He smoothed his neon-striped tie inside his navy-blue suit jacket and then placed his hand on Buskins's shoulder. "I understand Ms. Cooper, whose case is hanging by a shoestring, plans to introduce some new forensic technique, Your Honor. I'd like to oppose that testimony before we open to a jury, sir. I'd like to request a Frye hearing."

Heller squinted and looked back at the notes he regularly kept in an oversized leather-bound ledger. "I thought this matter involved some sort of DNA identification of Mr. Buskins's, whose profile is well-known in the databank of convicted offenders."

Buskins grunted and started mumbling under his breath. He was thirty-six years old with a rap sheet that stretched back to his teens, and was recently released from prison after serving nine years for the rape of a neighbor in the Taft housing project.

"It is a DNA identification, Judge," Segal said, "but—"

"That battle's been over for almost a quarter of a century, Mr. Segal. What date suits you for trial?"

The Frye standard evolved from a 1923 Supreme Court opinion that limited the admissibility of scientific evidence to methods that have been generally accepted as reliable in the professional community, beyond what the justices called a "twilight zone" between experimental stages and well-recognized principles. The lawyers in my own office had fought and won that groundbreaking struggle to use DNA technology in 1989, opening the way for genetic profiling, which continues to revolutionize criminal justice to this day.

"May I be heard, Your Honor?" I asked. Eric Segal took his seat as I rose to my feet. He leaned over to Willie Buskins, probably urging him to keep his mouth shut.

"Something new, Ms. Cooper?"

"Actually, yes, sir. I'm planning to elicit testimony from a biologist at OCME," I said, referring to the Office of Chief Medical Examiner, "about a new technique called the Forensic Statistical Tool, or FST."

Heller squinted at me over his glasses, trying to write at the same time. "Another acronym, of course. Soon there'll be nothing left to the law but acronyms, DNA swabs, and every man's right to claim an exoneration the moment after he's convicted. We can just set up computers or lottery machines to make all the decisions. Judges will be irrelevant, won't they?"

Segal was quick to cut in. "There are those who say—mostly on the DA's side, Your Honor—that that day has already come and gone."

"Save the humor for your mates, Mr. Segal," the judge said. "Exactly what have you got, Ms. Cooper?"

"I'd prefer not to tip my hand in its entirety right now."

"Then a hypothetical. Can you give me that?"

"Certainly." As I began to speak, Willie Buskins turned his chair away from me and put his left elbow on the counsel table, resting his head on his arm. "Suppose the perpetrator of a crime is alleged to have used a knife to subdue his victim, Your Honor—although that's not the claim here. And suppose a knife was recovered near the crime scene and analyzed at the lab."

"So far I'm with you."

"When tested for DNA, the knife handle yielded a mixture of DNA."

"A mixture?"

"Yes, judge. Suggesting that not surprisingly, over time, the DNA of several individuals was deposited on the knife. Until recently, it had been impossible to determine whether the DNA of a specific person was part of that mixture because the sample amounts of skin cells scraped off the knife were so very small."

Heller was listening attentively. He liked the challenge of finding precedents and writing opinions that would lead to a new body of law.

"What has changed this possibility, Ms. Cooper?"

"The work of two forensic biologists at our own lab, Your Honor. Scientists named Caragine and Mitchell, who will testify at the trial."

"Only if they pass muster at a Frye," Segal interjected.

These two young women would blow Willie Buskins out of the water, I was convinced, having spent hours with them in their offices, trying to understand their painstaking work. The scientists in the 290-million-dollar lab that opened in Manhattan in 2007—the largest government forensics lab in the country—had analyzed more than forty-three thousand items for DNA results in the last year alone. The work of that department had been cutting-edge since its inception, and now had taken another dramatic leap forward thanks to Caragine and Mitchell.

"What's the FST, Ms. Cooper?" Heller asked.

"It's an algorithm for a software program—"

"Judge, how can you let a jury hear this kind of evidence?"

Segal said, flinging his arms to both sides. "I don't even know how to explain to my client what an algorithm is."

"On your feet when you're addressing me, Mr. Segal. And it seems to me that should Mr. Buskins decide to wake up and join us at these proceedings, I'd be happy to tell him that the scientists' fancy word is simply a procedure for solving a problem in a finite number of steps."

Heller lifted the gavel and slammed it down with such force that it sounded like a cannon had been fired in the courtroom. Buskins still didn't pick up his head until Eric Segal poked him in the ribs.

"Go on, Ms. Cooper."

"This new program can analyze a DNA mixture—it has analyzed the evidence submitted in Mr. Buskins's case—and determine the probability that it includes the defendant's profile."

"So you're talking statistical probabilities here?"

"Yes, sir. A year ago, before FST was developed, the lab comparison would have yielded no result. The People could not have gone forward with a prosecution. Now we can deliver a likelihood—"

Segal pushed back and stood up. "You can't convict someone on a likelihood, Your Honor."

"Let her finish."

"A likelihood that Mr. Buskins's DNA is in the mixture recovered—when compared to the DNA of random people. If it were a low value in the mixture, then we might not be able to establish the defendant as the source, whereas a higher value could certainly include him as a donor."

Willie Buskins hadn't used a knife to threaten the fourteen-year-old girl who was the victim of the rape behind Taft Houses. He had wrapped one of his powerful arms around her neck to drag her off her bicycle, using the pink two-wheeler with purple tasseled handlebars to make his escape, leaving her curled up behind the garbage Dumpster in which he'd dropped her clothing. Although he had not ejaculated during the attack—leaving none of the more traditional DNA source of a rape suspect in seminal fluid—he had left trace evidence on the handlebar of the child's bike. On the right side, there was a low likelihood of Buskins's DNA in the mixture, but the left one suggested that he was the donor of the skin cells—985,000 times more likely to be so than the DNA of four random people tested in comparison.

Buskins had been granted bail, despite his criminal history and my loud objections, because the fourteen-year-old—who had been snatched from behind, after dark—had been unable to be certain of her identification of the attacker.

"Look, Judge, even if you believe in this voodoo, it's not generally accepted by the scientific community. It's only used at the New York City lab."

"Is that true, Ms. Cooper?"

"Not at this point, Your Honor. OCME has conducted more than half a million test runs in the last two years, and now the protocol has been approved by the New York State Commission on Forensic Science, so it has in fact gained use in labs across the country."

When Willie Buskins muttered, "Bullshit," I knew it was exactly what Eric Segal would have liked to say to the judge, too. Fortunately, Heller hadn't heard the thug.

"All right. Let's mark this for hearing and trial on the Monday following the July 4th holiday, shall we? Will you both be available?"

"Yes, sir," I said, and Segal nodded in agreement.

I waited until he escorted his client out of the courtroom before I made my way down the aisle and into the long corridor on the thirteenth floor.

Before I reached the elevator bank that led to the interior entrance to the New York County District Attorney's Office, the men's room door opened. Willie Buskins must have been waiting for me in there, stepping forward boldly to walk almost at my side as I passed by.

I picked up my pace and turned to the row of elevators, headed for the first open door, not caring whether it was going up or down.

"Just seein' how fast I could make you move, Ms. Cooper," Buskins said, holding the heavy doors open while I pressed the button to close them, laughing so hard that the gold jackets on his two front teeth—the ones his victim had described—were exposed to me. "Don't you play dirty with me at that trial. I've had mines, Ms. Cooper. Mess with me and I'll see that you get yours."

FOUR

I was standing at Laura Wilkie's desk, in the cubicle in front of my office. She had been my secretary since I had taken over the unit, and was as loyal as any person with whom I'd ever worked.

"I understand the Boss wants to see me, but I'd like you to take this down first." I dictated to her exactly what Buskins had said and done in the courtroom, and the behavior that followed.

"You've got to do something about this, Alex. Want me to send a copy to Judge Heller?"

"No. Just get one up to the DA's squad, for their threat file. I'm sure Buskins is all mouth and not about to do anything stupid before trial, but his words did rattle me and I'd like to have it all on record."

"Will do."

"And put through assignments, please, for doctors Caragine and Mitchell, for a Frye hearing on July 8th."

"Got it."

"Nothing from Mike or Mercer?"

"All quiet."

The phone messages and requests from assistants in the Special Victims Unit to meet with me would wait another hour.

"I'm off to brief Battaglia."

Paul Battaglia had been Manhattan's elected district attorney for six terms—twenty-five years—and was the only person most voters remembered in that role. He had grown the legal staff to more than five hundred lawyers during his long tenure and was responsible for many innovations in crime fighting. He never tried to micromanage his supervisors, but he had an unquenchable desire to be the first to know every important fact in a case or on a matter of personnel.

The gatekeeper to his office was my good friend Rose Malone—a superb executive assistant whose discretion, memory for detail about almost everything that had transpired under her watch, and great good looks made her the DA's most valuable asset.

"It's your lucky day," Rose said with a smile. "He's in a particularly upbeat mood. Whoever he met with at breakfast gave him a box of Cuban cigars. You can go right in."

Battaglia was sitting at the head of the conference table, flanked by Pat McKinney, chief of the trial division. Although my relationship with McKinney had been a rough one for many years, he'd been unusually gracious to me since we'd worked together on a major international scandal earlier in the spring.

"Good mor—"

Battaglia's elbows rested on the arms of his chair, his fingers templed below his chin, with a fat cigar stuck in the middle of his mouth.

"Practically midday, Alex. I'm having lunch with the commissioner, and I don't have a damn clue about what happened in the Park last night."

"I'm sorry, Paul. You weren't here when I went up to court." And McKinney was rarely in his office before late morning, either because he couldn't tear himself away from his harebrained girlfriend or because his shrink appointment ran overtime.

"What does it look like?"

I pulled out a chair at the opposite end of the table and sat down. "Dump job. The body was found in the Lake, but they don't think she was killed there. I was only in the Park for half an hour, but the guys haven't come up with much yet or they would have left me a message."

"Is she anybody?" Battaglia asked, thinking—no doubt—of which part of his constituency he would have to work. Priest, preacher, rabbi, councilman, community group—someone to whom he would need to express interest and give assurances that his best people would be on the case. "Do we have a name on her?"

Of course she's somebody. Somebody's daughter, I wanted to say. *She is somebody's broken and battered child or sister or aunt or girlfriend. There's most likely a relative who is going about the ordinary business of his or her daily life but will soon get the news that a loved one has been murdered.*

"No name. Chapman thinks she's probably homeless."

"Raped?"

"We won't know till after the autopsy. Her skull was bashed in. No clothes on, but that could be for a variety of reasons. She was in the water for a couple of days at least."

"Do you want to keep it?" McKinney was directly above me in the chain of command. On many occasions he had tried to strip me of cases I wanted to handle. If the homicide victim had been sexually assaulted or killed at the hand of an intimate partner, it fell to my unit and Battaglia usually backed me.

"I'd like to, Pat. Obviously, I don't know what we've got, but chances are once we confirm an ID, a lot of the people we'll need to talk to—the girl's friends—are the population we're good at dealing with." My colleagues in sex crimes work specialized in vulnerable young women.

"I spoke with Lieutenant Peterson a few minutes ago," McKinney said. "He's not thinking this will be a quick fix. Needle-in-a-haystack kind of thing. Catch a lucky break is all they can hope for. You in for the long haul?"

"I'd like to be."

"Then it's yours."

"Thanks."

Battaglia asked me a dozen more questions to which I had no answers before he dismissed me with a wave of his half-chewed cigar.

The rest of the day flew by with phone calls and staff meetings. Most of the lawyers seemed eager to get out in time for weekend travel, and I was one of them.

I was going to my home on Martha's Vineyard, catching the last flight out of LaGuardia at nine P.M. with Vickee Eaton, who was Mercer's wife and a second-grade detective assigned to the Office of the Deputy Commissioner of Public Information at One Police Plaza.

At five, I dialed Vickee's cell. "Do we have a plan?"

"Our office has been totally swamped with calls about the homicide in Central Park."

"Does that mean we're grounded?"

"Not a chance. Scully and the mayor did a stand-up at City Hall an hour ago. Bare bones. Not many facts to go on. And they put out a hastily done sketch of the girl. If anyone recognizes her from this one, I'll be amazed. No more to be said by my guys till there's a new development."

"Does that mean you expected me to make the plan? 'Cause I totally dropped that ball. We can take a cab to LaGuardia."

"Girl, I just want to be sitting on your deck in Chilmark with an ice-cold glass of your best white wine when that full moon is straight overhead," Vickee said. "Mercer's picking me up behind One PP at six sharp. Meet me here. He says a quick dinner at Primola with Mike and they'll have us both up to speed on the day's happenings in the Park and get us to the airport in time for the flight. You cool with that?"

"Beyond cool. See you shortly."

I locked up at a quarter to six, leaving behind all my case folders for a change. I couldn't remember taking off for a weekend in months without having to grind through a closing argument or prep witnesses without a break to relax.

The lawyers who hadn't cut out earlier in the day were coming out the doors of both buildings in hordes, like a fire alarm had gone off. Most of the young ones had getaway bags on their shoulders, heading to Hamptons share houses or the Jersey shore. I crossed behind the Federal Courthouse on Worth Street, cutting through the building next to Police Plaza to the parking garage, where Vickee and Mercer were already waiting for me in his SUV.

"Are we good to go?" I asked, climbing into the rear seat.

"Nothing to stop us now," Vickee said. "One more phone call to Logan before Mercer's sister wrestles him into bed and I am airborne."

Vickee and Mercer's four-year-old, Logan, often came with us on our Vineyard escapes, but this time his mother wanted the chance to sleep late while her husband and son did some male bonding.

"Did you spend the day in the Park?" I asked Mercer as he turned under the Brooklyn Bridge exit ramp and nosed onto the uptown FDR Drive.

"Only another hour after you left. Peterson's been really territorial about this one. He's calling it a plain and simple homicide—"

"Like there is such a thing."

"And he didn't want any other units there with his own guys except for a uniformed detail doing a grid search of the area around the Lake."

"Around the Lake?" Vickee said. "That's the whole park. How do you limit how far they go?"

"You don't. The ring just grows larger every day the men don't come up with evidence to link to the body."

I glanced across the river at the enormous glass box that covered the antique carousel that had been restored and opened on the Brooklyn waterfront last year. It was where I had celebrated my thirty-eighth birthday in April, a most bittersweet end to a difficult day.

"You hungry?" Mercer asked.

"I don't think I've ever eaten dinner this early. But I didn't have much for lunch, and you can bet there won't be much stocked up in the house, so I'm glad we're stopping."

Mercer Wallace was one of the handful of African American detectives to make first grade in the NYPD more than a decade ago. He was five years older than I, and although his solid six-foot-four-inch build made a fierce impression on the bad guys he chased, there was an exceptionally gentle quality about him that won him the trust of the most traumatized crime victims we encountered.

After his mother died in childbirth, Mercer was raised in Queens by his father, who was a mechanic at Delta Air Lines. He had married Vickee ten years back, but she had left him shortly thereafter because she'd been emotionally torn—as the daughter of an NYPD detective—by the toll the job took on most marriages and a terrific fear that it would overwhelm her own. After a shooting that almost cost Mercer his life, she came back to him, and they remarried and started life over again with Logan. To Mike and to me, their relationship offered a model of stability—of trust and of love—that neither of us had been able to imitate.

I listened as they talked to each other, Vickee reciting a checklist of things that were part of Logan's routine from the time he opened his eyes in the morning till the end of a long day. How much milk in the cereal, who was expected for a playdate, what parts of the house were off-limits to the kids, what she'd prepared for Mercer to heat up for dinner—everything sounded so enviably cozy and normal.

"You with me on this, Alex? I guess my wife thinks she's been raising this boy by herself the last four years."

"She'll get real by the time I return her to you Sunday night."

Mercer parked illegally on Second Avenue in the 60s, throwing his laminated NYPD plaque on top of the dashboard. Primola was one of my favorites—an upscale Italian restaurant with consistently good food, where the regular customers are showered with attention by an efficient and cheerful staff.

Mike was seated at the bar, sipping on his vodka as he chatted up the bartender. Giuliano, the owner, greeted us more quickly than

Mike did. "*Signorina* Cooper. *Detectivo—buona sera.*" He called out to the headwaiter, "Dominick, give Ms. Cooper table one, *subito.*"

The four of us made ourselves comfortable at the round table in the front window and ordered our drinks. Vickee and I decided to stay light with a glass of white wine.

"Tell us everything," I said to Mike.

"It was a really frustrating day. I'm hoping we get a jump after the autopsy tomorrow. That's set for two P.M., and I'll be there. Not much to go on so far."

"I'm glad you'll stand in. I never got a chance to swing by the morgue today."

"Did you catch Scully's clip on the news?" Vickee asked.

"I heard it on the radio coming over."

"Did the search turn up anything?" I said.

"Yeah. About ten minutes after you took off this morning, one of the rookies walked out of the bushes." Mike pulled his handkerchief from his pocket and held it up with his knife centered inside it, the white cotton cloth draped around it. "He had his pen hoisted up and a pair of white panties—like maybe the biggest size they make—hanging off the pen so he didn't mess them up. 'These must have come off the dead girl,' the kid says proudly."

"But she's so thin."

"That's only half the point. Within minutes, four other guys nosing into four other bushes come out with white panties in the air. Some with polka dots, one with glitter, one with lace—and a bright green thong, too. There was so much white cloth waving in the air, I thought the NYPD was surrendering to Hannibal."

"What does that tell you?" I asked. "The underwear, I mean."

"Springtime in Central Park, Coop. It tells me that all the young lovers with no place else to go try to find a sweet spot between there and Strawberry Fields to get it on late at night. It tells me that the lab will be up to its eyeballs in analyzing jism from intimate garments that have nothing to do with our homicide. But you can't chance to ignore a single one of them."

"Do you have any idea how big that Park is?" Mercer asked.

"Yeah, actually. We got some stats today," Mike said. "843 acres, and we haven't even done a thorough job on one of them so far. And they're all being trampled by the press-hounds who are hoping to beat us to a solution. You've got entire countries—like Monaco— that are smaller than Central Park. It's only 489 acres, the whole thing."

"It's not a country," I said. "Monaco, I mean. It's a principality."

Mike rolled his eyes. "Another factoid from the vast archives of a Wellesley College scholar."

"I wasn't correcting you. I was just—"

"I know you weren't, Coop. You were just being yourself. Hey, Dominick," Mike called out. "What are the specials? We've got to get these broads to the airport."

Vickee and I split a tricolore salad and an order of orecchietti con broccoli rabe, while Mike and Mercer both started with the penne pasta special followed by veal chops. Murder was never an inhibitor for Mike's appetite.

"Obviously, you know you can call me if anything develops be-fore we're back," I said. "Vickee will be getting constant info from DCPI. Are you working all weekend?"

"I was supposed to anyway. Today was my first day back on. I'll start at the canvass in the morning both days, be at the ME's office tomorrow afternoon."

"Can I canvass with you on Monday?"

"Suit yourself."

Mercer put his drink down. "Alex was really helpful to us on the Reservoir rapist case. People that didn't want to be bothered break-ing their jog for a tough old cop like me were willing to talk to her."

"Didn't I just say she could come along? By then, Scully will have announced the formation of a task force, right?"

Every major case that wasn't solved immediately and might ben-efit from the collaboration of some of the special agencies within the NYPD wound up being run by a task force. Mike and his superb team of detectives who worked the Manhattan North Homicide squad would rather keep this case—like all their others—to themselves, taking it down methodically and strategically with the vast experience and knowledge that made them such pros.

"Undoubtedly," Mercer said.

"So Peterson's holding Monday afternoon for a crash course on the geography of the Park. Scully already has a promise from the parks commissioner, Gordon Davis, to lead the session himself."

"Davis is a big deal," I said. "He's one of the mayor's favorite players."

"No kidding."

Central Park seems so integral to the life and landscape of Manhattan that most people assumed it had existed in its present form naturally and forever. Instead, as the city grew from its commercial roots and settlements on the southern tip of the island in the 1600s, landowners and merchants became increasingly aware that the open land north of 59th Street was likely to be overrun and strangled by the growth of this nineteenth-century metropolis—which had spread without any thought for a public park in its master plan. At last, in 1857, legislation was finally passed to enable the creation of this glorious enterprise, known first as the Greensward.

"So what's the deal with the Park?" Vickee asked. "I had to make a lot of notifications today, not just to Davis's office. It's a public-private joint enterprise, isn't it?"

"Yeah. The Department of Parks and Recreation is responsible for setting all policy—that's why Gordon Davis is in charge. He's a mayoral appointment. But it's a monster to maintain. The budget is almost fifty million dollars a year, just for the Park. So when the city was in financial trouble in the '70s and the Park was deteriorating from neglect, some philanthropic New Yorkers created the Central Park Conservancy. That's the private fund-raising piece, which does most of the heavy lifting now. They come up with eighty percent of the money to run the place. So we have to make nice with them, too."

"You're right, Mike. I feel that task force coming on strong," Mercer said.

"I get the sense that if this poor girl had been dumped behind a bodega on the Lower East Side," Vickee said, "there wouldn't be quite this frenzy, no matter who she turns out to be."

"Homicide rule number three," Mike said. "Never kill anybody in a landmark location. It always ups the ante."

"Amen to that," Mercer said.

"Did you talk to Battaglia about keeping the case?" Mike asked me.

"Yes. Both he and McKinney are fine with it."

"Then I've got a present for you. When you and Vickee take a break from gossiping this weekend," he said, handing me a thick brochure, "you can get familiar with the Park. I realize we all think we know it, but I'm talking about the ball fields and waterfalls and streams and glacial rocks and all the other hideaways that we'll have to look at. Study up."

I started to unfold the map on the table in front of me.

"This whole thing is the vision of two men," Mike went on, "who planned it down to the number of trees and rocks and foot-paths, gates and promenades and terraces. Nothing between 59th Street and 110th Street is there naturally. Nothing. And none of it was left to chance. These two guys—Olmsted and Vaux—they were geniuses."

Mike tapped his glass to tell the waiter he wanted a second drink.

"Who?" Mercer asked.

"Frederick Law Olmsted and Calvert Vaux, the two dudes who created Central Park."

"They were landscape architects. They won a major competition to design the Park. And it's not Vaux," I said, pronouncing the name as Mike had, rhyming with "so." "It's Calvert Vaux—sort of rhymes with 'hawks.'"

Mike slammed his hand on the table, sloshing my wine over the rim of the glass. "What is it about you that you can't stop yourself from telling me I'm wrong? Telling me I'm wrong with more regularity than I bet you have when you go to the bathroom?"

"What did I do? The commissioner will correct you on Monday if I didn't do it now. You might as well go in on top. Let him know how smart you are."

"This morning it was about the lake that you had to tell me was a pond. Now I call Monaco a country and you say it's a principality. The architect's not Vaux like 'so,' he's Vaux like 'hawks.' I haven't seen you in more than a month, and I was actually beginning to look forward to hanging out with you on this one. Not anymore, I'm not. You wanna know why you're spending a weekend alone?"

"She's not alone, Mike," Vickee said, getting to her feet and fanning herself with her napkin as though the heat was too much to take. She smiled and patted me on the head. "Alex will have me. I'll show her what my cougar talent can do to spice up her life. Is the restroom down those stairs in the back?"

I nodded.

"You're alone because you are so damned critical and picky and self-righteous."

"I'm nothing like that, am I, Mercer? I—I just corrected the pronunciation thing. I didn't mean anything by it." I started to reach for my drink, but my hand was shaking so visibly that I rested it in my lap.

"You are so doomed to be alone in your ivory tower, blondie. Waiting for King Louis the twenty-something of France to return and rescue you."

"Back off, Mike," Mercer said, catching the dig at my relationship with a Frenchman—Luc Rouget—that had recently splintered and left me with a heavy heart. Luc and I were trying to figure out whether to pick up the pieces, and how to do that with an ocean between us. "That's over the line."

"No, it's not. When Coop's unhappy, she thinks we all need to be unhappy with her."

"I'm not unhappy."

"Get honest with yourself. You're miserable. And have you figured out *why* Pat McKinney and the district attorney were so agreeable about giving you this case? Isn't it strange that your weasel-faced supervisor didn't try to pull it out from underneath you today, like he always does?"

Mike sucked in more vodka before he answered his own question. "They want you to fail, Alex Cooper. This case, this woefully sad murder that is going to play out in the media all over the world, has all the earmarks of a dog. I expect it'll be barking at me from now till the day my pension vests, like the rest of those ice-cold cases from the Park. McKinney wants you to fall on your face so he can grind his shoe into the back of your neck. They're all looking for you to fail for a change, and just maybe, they found the case that will accomplish that for them."

FIVE

I picked at my salad while I waited for Vickee to come back to the table. I was determined not to go downstairs to splash some cold water on my face, for fear I would lose my composure if I were alone.

Mercer tried to lighten things up by making small talk, but that didn't engage either Mike or me. "Remember that Preppy Murder case?" he said. "Robert Chambers, the scumbag who killed a friend of his behind the Metropolitan museum in '86? That's the only murder in the Park I can think of except for the Brazilian jogger in '95. And the two kids who stabbed the homeless guy to death in '97. The squad had both of them in custody within hours, just like they did with Chambers. I don't know why you're so pessimistic."

"Robert Chambers's friend was Jennifer Levin. Eighteen years old. Nice girl. Trusted the bastard and walked into the Park to her death, hand in hand with him. But she had ID in her jacket pocket, a loving family that threw themselves into helping the cops, and twenty kids who saw them together an hour before she was killed," Mike said. "Not happening here. It's not like that at all. If this girl's been dead two or three days already—or more likely, as Johnny Mayes said, at least a month—how come nobody's even reported her missing?"

Mike's father, Brian Chapman, was a much-decorated detective who had worked many of the city's most high-profile cases before his son came on the job. Chambers had been one of his perps.

"Mike, I'm sorry for being so rude. I really am."

"Forget it, Coop. My mother says 'rude' is my middle name. It's the part about being miserable that I hate to see. Get over it."

Foolish advice coming from Mike. He had been engaged a couple of years back to a great girl named Valerie Jacobson, who had survived breast cancer only to be killed in a freak skiing accident. Mike had internalized his grief so completely that he'd never been able to fully open himself to a relationship ever since.

"Want me to check on Vickee?" I asked Mercer, looking for an excuse to break away.

"No, she's just making a call to Logan, I'm sure."

Mike took three plastic bags from a case he was carrying and put them on the table. "Just so I'm not holding back anything, I'll be dropping these things at the lab. Back burner, of course. We picked up a lot of crap today: used condoms and a lead pipe that could have crushed someone's skull; a few kid-sized baseball bats that might have done the same; bits and pieces of tiny sailboats that had been smashed on the Lake—every kid in walking distance of the Park has one of those—and all the dirty laundry, underwear in every size and color you can imagine. The ME's going to give us a small conference room. We'll get a wall-sized map of the Park and put pins where everything was found. A field guide to the detritus of Manhattan's park people."

"What's in the bags?" Mercer asked.

"Some of the few things that didn't seem like pure trash. Stuff that a few of the guys found off the pathway, at the northernmost tip of the Lake, between the shoreline and the bridle path. Could be where the body went into the water. You never know." Mike pushed the three bags across the table, toward Mercer and me. "I'm dropping it all off for prints and swabbing."

I was so cowed by Mike's outburst that I was afraid to ask

questions and have him pound at me again. Mercer picked up the first bag to examine and then handed it to me.

"Look, Alex. It's a miniature castle. Could be something a kid dropped out of a stroller or backpack. Nice find."

"You know what I think it is, guys? I think it's Belvedere Castle." My voice was tentative, but I was certain about the distinctive shape of the structure.

"That's the one just above the 79th Street Transverse?" Mercer said.

"Exactly." It was one of the most distinctive lookouts in the Park, perched high above Turtle Pond and designed in the style of a medieval castle. It had always been a favorite destination for my older brothers when we visited the city as children, and I knew its outline well. For decades it was home to the National Weather Service, and is still the place where meteorological instruments record the amount of snow and rainfall in the Park's center for every weather report around the country.

"Pretty rich kid to have a model this perfect," Mike said.

I removed my cell phone from my tote and snapped a photograph of the figurine. "Maybe the Conservancy shop sells this kind of thing, but it is pretty ornate, and it looks like it has some age to it."

Mercer held up the second bag, and Mike spoke before we all jumped in. "The Obelisk, right? Cleopatra's Needle."

"Look at the detail in those carvings," I said. It was a safer thing to point out than the fact that the Obelisk—twin of the fifteenth-century-BC monument that stands on the Thames embankment in London—had nothing to do with the Egyptian queen, who was born centuries after their creation, except that she had moved the striking pair to Alexandria to commemorate Caesar's death.

I took a picture of the obelisk while Mercer read from the tiny reproduction plaque carved at its base that it was installed in the Park, on East 81st Street, in 1880.

"I'd guess that these are part of a very valuable collection," I said. "Someone with an entire miniature reproduction of Central Park. They don't look like ordinary street garbage to me, and they don't look like kids' toys."

"Yeah, we're checking the burglary squad and some of the antique shops, and the Conservancy is putting a notice on its Facebook page. It's probably got nothing to do with my girl, but you never know."

The third item was something different altogether. It was not the same scale as the others, a single figure almost as tall as the nine- or ten-inch obelisk. It was made of a different substance, too.

I lifted the bag and turned it over gently in my hand, admiring the beauty of the small form.

"She's an angel."

"The Central Park angel? The Angel of the Waters?" Mercer asked, reaching for her while I took another photograph.

"No, she's clearly not that," I said.

"Could have been a lucky break," Mercer said. "Murdered girl, thrown in the Lake, clutching a statue of the Bethesda angel. Might have tightened up the search a bit."

Not only was the little angel entirely different in shape from her world-renowned counterpart, but her arms didn't reach out to bless the waters in front of her, nor were her wings lifted and spread. She was very old, a figurine molded from clay or bisque, chipped and worn over the ages. Her clothing was painted, highlighted by some sort of gilt. Her skin was painted, too—the color of ebony.

I held the bag up to the light to look more closely at her. I knew the Bethesda angel in the Park quite well. She had a finely chiseled nose, slim and straight. Her lips were narrow, and her short hair—only slightly wavy—was parted in the middle to frame her face. She looked like a young beauty from a Botticelli painting. This dark form in my hand had a handsome face with rounded cheeks outlined by long ringlets of black hair that reached her shoulders. Her eyes had been colored the deepest brown, her nose short but wide, and her lips quite full. It seemed to me that these idealized figures had been created in the same time period—different in function and spirit, perhaps, but each representing the beauty of her race.

I couldn't help but wonder whether these two angels—one white, one black—both had a connection to the dead girl who had been found so very close to them.

SIX

"I had hoped to skip town before the first tantrum," Vickee said, returning to the table as the three of us were finishing our appetizers. "Sorry for taking so long. You'd think it was life-threatening to run out of Cocoa Puffs."

We rushed through our dinner, the others doing most of the talking while I tried to think about how much of my stress I'd been imposing on everyone at work. I had not known Vickee as long as my two closest friends—Nina Baum, who had been my roommate at Wellesley College, and Joan Stafford, a playwright who split her time between Washington, DC, and the city—but she was a straight shooter and a terrifically loyal pal, so I expected to get some tough feedback over the weekend.

I told Giuliano to put the bill on my tab as we were just about ready to leave. Mike asked him if we could go down to his office to check out the Final Jeopardy question, which had been a habit of Mike's for as long as I'd known him. Crime scene, cheap bar, morgue, or my apartment, there was no setting in which he didn't stop everything until someone around him—often Mercer or me—put down twenty dollars as a bet on the night's big answer.

I was the last of the four of us down the narrow steps to the basement office. Mike used the clicker to turn on the small television propped on a high corner shelf. His timing was never off, and within a minute of finding the right channel, Alex Trebek revealed the large game board and announced that the final category for tonight was "MEDICINE."

"I owe you twenty," Mike said, pointing a finger at me. "See me after payday next week."

"It's not like you to throw in the towel," Vickee said.

"It's the Benjamin Cooper theory. Coop'll slam-dunk this one 'cause her old man taught her as much about medicine as she knows about the law. Just watch her double down."

My father, the son of Russian Jews who had fled political oppression to come to the States, had started his medical practice as a cardiologist. Soon after leaving med school, he and his partner fashioned a half-inch piece of plastic tubing into a device that had been adapted for use in almost all surgery worldwide involving the aorta. The Cooper-Hoffman Valve not only changed our modest family circumstances and allowed me a very privileged upbringing, but also, more important, changed medical procedures in his field for the entire profession.

"The usual twenty," I said. "You're up, Mercer."

"What does she do if she knows the answer, Mr. Chapman?" Mercer asked. "Is she supposed to keep her mouth shut and lose, like you do with my four-year-old when you play checkers, to make him feel better?"

"That would help," Mike said, chewing on the olive from his drink.

When the commercial was over, we had all bet the minimum and waited for the answer to be posted. "Term for rare condition of individuals who share the same brain."

Trebek read the answer aloud twice.

Mike turned away and started to walk out of the room. "What is Alex Cooper and a jackass? That would have been my answer."

"I'm sorry, sir," Trebek said to the first contestant.

"Not me," Mike said. "I'm not the least bit sorry."

"We don't call them Siamese twins anymore," Trebek chided the player. "Politically incorrect, don't you think?"

I was relieved that I didn't know the proper term either. Vickee looked to me for guidance, but I just shrugged my shoulders.

It was Trebek who announced that the question was "What are craniopagus twins? Craniopagus is the word we were looking for to describe twins joined at the head, who sometimes actually share the same brain."

"No winners tonight," Vickee said. "Time to get ourselves on the plane to paradise."

I tugged at the bottom of Mike's blazer as I tailed him up the stairs. "I promise to come back on Sunday with a new attitude if you'll be a bit kinder. How's that?"

"Works for me."

I could barely hear him. He wouldn't turn around to look at me, just hit the landing and kept on walking through the growing crowd of Friday night customers, straight to the bar.

Vickee put her arms around Mike from behind and kissed his cheek.

I said, "See you Monday," and walked out with Mercer.

It took less than twenty minutes to get from the door of Primola to the terminal at LaGuardia. We said good-bye to Mercer and checked in, boarding half an hour later.

The short flight—fifty minutes from takeoff to landing on a crystal-clear night—was right on time. It was always hard to talk over the noise of the two turboprops, so I closed my eyes and thought about Mike's tirade while Vickee worked on a memo about the day's press inquiries. One of the minivan cabs drove us from the airport to my home on a hilltop in Chilmark—an old farmhouse on a lovely piece of land, surrounded by ancient stone walls and overlooking the water.

The caretaker had readied the house for our arrival. Vickee had been here many times, so she carried her tote upstairs to the main guest room while I went into my bedroom and changed down to a T-shirt and leggings.

She was in the kitchen five minutes later. "Nightcap on the deck?"

"The perfect complement to a full moon."

Vickee opened a bottle of chardonnay while I put ice cubes in a glass and filled it with as much Dewar's as it could hold. I grabbed shawls for each of us to wrap around our shoulders in case it got chilly, and we went out onto the deck in bare feet, carrying our drinks.

We clinked our glasses together, and I stretched out on one of the lounge chairs. Vickee stood on the edge of the deck, looking off at the horizon, where the only lights in the distance appeared to be from the gas dock across the water in Menemsha.

"This is about as close to heaven as I expect to get until I die," she said, coming back to pull up a chair beside me.

"It's a pretty special place. I can come up here carrying all the aggravation and anxiety that the job imposes, and by the time I wake up the tranquility and peacefulness of this island have overtaken me. It's like I'm a different person." I sipped the Scotch so that it didn't overflow the glass. And then I laughed. "I guess that's the fix Mike is hoping for."

"Mercer'll tune that boy up, too. He needs his own attitude adjustment," Vickee said. "One of the things I like best is sitting out here in the dark and seeing all these millions of stars. Folks in the city don't know what they're missing."

She was right. The bright lights everywhere in big cities made it impossible to glimpse the total brilliance of the night sky. Here, the deep navy background looked like a velvet ceiling with sparkling white lights dangling from it.

"Can you see the North Star?"

"Help me out."

"That's the Little Dipper," I said, pointing to the familiar outline within Ursa Minor, the Little Bear, one of the prominent constellations of the Northern Hemisphere in June.

"Got it."

"The two stars that form the lower half of the cup, or the dipper? Make an imaginary line straight up above them, and that really bright one, that's Polaris, the North Star."

"Is that the brightest star in the sky?"

"Most people think so, but there are forty or so that beat it out," I said. "Don't tell Mike I knew that."

"I'm too much of a city girl. How *do* you know that anyway?"

I picked up the pace of my sipping. "I bought this house with Adam Nyman. I don't have to tell you that story, do I?"

"I know it all too well." Vickee reached over and put her hand on top of mine. "I didn't mean to make you sad, Alex."

I'd met Adam when I was in law school at the University of Virginia. He'd been a med student there, and then a resident on duty when I was thrown off a horse on an afternoon I should have been studying constitutional law. Instead I wound up being treated in the ER. Our affair led to an engagement twelve years ago, and we bought this house together, planning our wedding for the great lawn that Vickee and I were looking out over. On the long night drive to get to the island, Adam's car was sideswiped. He crashed to his death from a bridge on the highway in Connecticut, a heartbreak from which I knew I would never fully recover.

"You didn't make me sad at all. It's wonderful to think about Adam." I stretched my neck back and looked for more stars. "He taught me all about the constellations. We'd take a night swim in the ocean and then come lie down on the lawn, right below here. I can show you Lupus, the Wolf, if you look to your left. And that's Boötes, the Herdsman. He circles and circles the North Pole, keeping all the celestial beasts together."

"But they're not the same all the time, are they?"

"They change every month," I said. "You know, the zodiac."

"So this is just June?"

"The month Adam and I were supposed to get married," I said, squeezing Vickee's hand. "It was a sky just like this one the night he was killed."

"It must be so hard to—"

"It's actually wonderful to have such intense memories, such happy ones. I see Adam in the stars whenever I look up. That's a good thing, I promise you."

Vickee's cell phone rang, and she ran in to the kitchen counter to pick it up. She came back to the screen door and it was obvious she was talking to Mercer. "No, I just forgot to call is all. My bad. We're sitting outside, and yes, we'll go to sleep soon. Love you very much. G'night."

She came back out and extended her cell to me. "You want this?" she said. "I just got chewed out for neglecting to call my man. Did you forget to say good night to anyone?"

I smiled at her. "No, thanks. No one's looking for me now."

"It must be almost morning in France."

"I see where you're going with this, Vickee, but I haven't spoken to Luc in more than a week."

"Mercer says he still calls you all the time. That he wants to try again."

"I don't know that we can ever put what we had back together. I think a lot of it was smoke and mirrors. The whole picture was my total escape from the darkness of the work we do, and yet I'm thoroughly invested—emotionally and professionally—in that work."

"But you loved him, Alex. I thought it was the real deal."

"I thought so, too. It's pretty easy to love someone when he's not around all the time and most of what you see is the fantasy. It's much more impossible if you can't trust him."

"But he was a victim, too. Surrounded by a bunch of vultures."

"And he didn't tell me the truth about that either. Mike could have been killed because Luc was holding all the cards about his business dealings so tight to his chest. That sickens me."

Vickee got up to help herself to another glass of wine. "Ready for a refill?"

"I think this should be enough for me."

"Since you brought Mike's name into this, I want to talk to you about him."

I held out my half-empty glass to her. "About that refill, Vickee, why don't you bring it on? Although I'm not sure there's enough Dewar's on the island to go there."

She came back and handed me the refreshed cocktail. Then she settled onto the lounger, her legs pulled up beneath her, facing me square on. "What is it with you and Mike, Alex? Mercer and I keep thinking you two get halfway to hooking up and then it blows wide open, like tonight."

"We've never been halfway to hooking up. Are you crazy?"

"You know the man's a little bit in love with you."

"In love with me?" I threw back my head and gulped more Scotch. "Tonight he compared me to a jackass, which is one of the milder things he's had to say about me."

"Mike met you when? Same time as Mercer and I did, back when you were fighting the ghost of Adam, right after his death. You were so young and fresh, but there was this rift down the middle of your soul—we could all see it like it was a crimson tear in your chest—that I never thought would heal."

"I don't expect it ever will."

"Then there was this parade of—well, unsuitable guys. Totally unavailable men," Vickee said, working up steam. "Guys who cheated on you, who were never there for you, who didn't seem to care about the world you live in every day."

"Luc wasn't like that."

"Then give him another shot, if you think he's so stand-up. But keep him arm's length from Mike for a while, 'cause if we hear him call you 'darling' one more time, I think Mike or Mercer will flatten his nose."

"What's wrong with 'darling'?" The alcohol was getting to me.

"It's so saccharine. It's like he might confuse you with the last woman in his life, so he uses the generic greeting. 'Darling' this and 'darling' that. Mike was ready to take him out."

"While you're at it, anything else you want to drop at my feet while I'm feeling really low? I haven't got any fight in me tonight," I said.

"Look, half your office and half the blue bloods at One PP think you and Mike have already done the deed. There's no reputation to save. You might as well give it a try."

"Done *that* deed? Slept with each other? Was it good for *them*?" I said, mild annoyance beginning to trump my amusement. "Because if it's ever happened, I have to say it's pretty much slipped my mind. And if that's what my troops and your bosses spend their time handicapping, the crime rate in the city should be off the charts."

"Lowest it's been in forty-nine years. That's how come I can concentrate on your love life. What's to lose?"

I stirred the ice cubes with my finger.

"Alex Cooper. You're slow on the uptake. I asked what you've got to lose?"

My head was beginning to spin. "Maybe the best friend I've ever had, although that didn't seem to be the case the way he talked to me tonight."

"You've thought about it, though, right?"

"Of course I've thought about it." Mike Chapman was six months older than I. Although we had taken strikingly different paths to public service, we both had a passion for doing justice that was pretty much identical. A Fordham University grad, he had majored in history, but his career path took a dramatic turn when his father dropped dead of a massive coronary two days after he turned in his gun and shield. "Mike's smart, he's funny—sometimes even when I'm the butt of the joke. He's the best in the world at what he does . . ."

"And he's almost as handsome as my man," Vickee said.

"He's like a brother to me, not a lover."

"You've got two brothers already. You don't need a third."

"How fast before Paul Battaglia tells me I can't work any more cases with Mike? That I can't have him on the witness stand with defense attorneys badgering him about how he only got confessions because I demanded that he give me that kind of evidence?"

"So work cases with Mercer," she said, looking at me over the top of her glass. "Is it the cop thing?"

"What do you mean?"

"Well, that you come from this really wealthy family, that you live off your trust fund in a lavish apartment with a compound on Martha's Vineyard, that you like all these fine things that none of us could ever hope to have."

"That's about the most insulting thing you could say to me. You think it's about money?"

"I don't want to think that."

"My grandfather was a fireman, and I absolutely adored him. My mother's a nurse. My father's parents were impoverished immigrants, and my father was the first in his family to go to college. He's brilliant, I'm happy to say, and created something that he was lucky enough to make money from. And by the way, that's what allows me to devote all my time and whatever intelligence I have to public service."

"Could you marry a cop, Alex? Really?"

"I could marry my plumber if I was in love with him," I said, thinking better of another sip. "And I happen to have a very cute one. Of course I could marry a cop."

"Think of it," Vickee said, closing your eyes. "You and Mike could be like Nick and Nora Charles. Fancy digs, car and driver, over-the-top furs."

"Asta. I really ought to have a dog."

"Solving crimes with a cocktail in each hand while the NYPD stands by helplessly. Give him a shot, Alex. Like they say on the street—YOLO."

"YOLO?"

"You only live once."

"That's the wine talking, Mrs. Wallace. You need to remember to take something for that headache you're going to wake up with."

"No waking me up, understand? First morning I've had in months without my little Dinosaurus Logan crawling in beside me. Would you mind if I slept out here?"

I stood up and took both of our glasses to head for the sink. "It's so much more comfortable upstairs," I said as she put her feet on the wooden decking. "And be sure to hold on to the banister tight."

Vickee grabbed my arm to steady herself, then embraced me in a hug. "I hope I didn't come on too strong. Remember I walked away once from the best guy I've ever known. Don't you do that before it's too late to fix."

"Say it all right now before you go to sleep, because the next forty-eight hours are a no-picking-on-me zone, okay? Sleep as late as you want. It's almost midnight."

I turned out the lights and went into my bathroom to wash up. My cell phone started to ring the moment I reached for my toothbrush. I went back to the nightstand to pick it up.

"Coop? Did I wake you?"

"Nope. Vickee and I are just headed to bed."

"You sound—sort of cool," Mike said.

"And you sound sort of intoxicated."

"I am. Way drunk. Left my car near the restaurant and walked home."

"And I'm as cool as I sound."

There were a couple of moments of silence.

"I just called to tell you I was totally out-of-bounds tonight. I pounded you like a mean son of a bitch, and I want to apologize."

"Then I'm glad you called. Apology accepted."

"We've got to find an hour to talk next week. I've been wanting to do that."

"Looks like you'll have the chance."

"Not the Park, Coop. Something that has me tied up in knots."

"To do with me?" My heart started to race. Maybe Vickee and Mercer had lit a fire under Mike, too.

"No, not exactly. Well, not directly."

"Oh."

Mike made a halfhearted attempt at a laugh. "I've got my first stalker."

"No, seriously."

"I am serious. And it's a problem, because it sort of involves you," Mike said. "I just wasn't prepared to see you this morning. I wasn't ready to talk about it."

"What involves me?"

"Remember just before Christmas last year, when I had the detail on Judge Pell?"

"Yeah. One of the hedge fund guys she sentenced to heavy time in that fraud case hired a hit man. It wasn't my case. What's this got to do with me?"

"Things got out of hand," Mike said, taking care not to slur his words.

"How do you mean?"

"It got personal."

"You and Jessica Pell?" My head was reeling as I sat down on the edge of the bed. "How'd you let that happen, Mike? She's old enough to be your mother."

"Hey. She's only five years older than we are. Mercer's age."

I was stunned. It was such a professional boundary violation that I couldn't imagine that neither of them had nipped temptation in the bud. "Well, age was the nicest of the things I could think to say about her, actually. Jessica was only appointed to the criminal court because she'd had an affair with that asshole deputy in the mayor's criminal justice office, and the next best thing he could do for her other than leave his wife was put her on the bench. She's half a psycho, Mike."

"That's the half that's after me, Coop."

My emotions had overtaken any attempt at rational thought. Vickee had tried to put me on a path to rethinking my love life, but Mike was otherwise quite engaged.

"This is TMI, Detective Chapman. Your love life is way too much information. I'm going to wish you and Jessica pleasant dreams, and I'm going to hang up the phone. Unlike me, you're not alone on Friday—"

"Stay with me, Coop. I am one hundred percent alone," Mike pleaded with me. "It was just a few—a few—"

"Dates? Or were you doing on it overtime so the taxpayers like me could protect Jessica?"

"Coop—"

"I know you have trouble saying the word 'sex,' Mike, but are you talking about a physical relationship with Jessica Pell?"

"Yeah. I mean, not for a long time. Maybe a month or two, and I'd only see her once a week. After the detail was over in mid-February."

I was speeding through the events of March and April, wondering how I had missed any signs of this when Mike and Mercer and I had been working together. Jessica Pell cut a striking figure, in and out of her judicial robes. It was hard not to notice her when she entered a room, and difficult to be in her way when there was something she wanted.

"I am off the clock, my good friend, and you are totally over the line. So don't be offended but we're about to be disconnected."

"Coop, I'm calling because Jessica's dragging you into the story."

"Oh no she's not."

"She's been calling the squad 'round the clock since I refused to see her again. She spoke to Sergeant Chirico on Monday. Made up this whole bullshit story about her life being in jeop because *you* used your influence to pull me off the bodyguard assignment for our last big case."

The timing for that intersection of their personal drama and our last case would have been about right. I was sorry I had thrown the rest of my drink down the drain.

"He knows better than that. What reason did she give?"

"She told Chirico that—I'm just saying what the judge told him—that you were jealous of her 'cause you had a thing for me . . ."

"A thing? What did I have for you, Mike? Is a 'thing' something sexual? 'Cause if you can't even say the word, I doubt you're much good at getting it on. Explain this one to me."

"I know it doesn't make sense, Coop. All you are right now vis-à-vis me is pissed off."

"Dead on."

"So just to make trouble for me, Judge Pell says you had me assigned to work with you, expressly to end my relationship with her, which also ended her protection by the department. And by the way? That's when the attempt on her life was made."

"Tell me Manny Chirico didn't fall for this, did he?"

"He's solid as a rock. And he's trying to keep it away from the lieutenant till we can figure out how to defuse Pell."

I was usually good with stalkers, but I had no business in the middle of this mess.

"Jessica's goal is to meet with Commissioner Scully if Chirico doesn't do anything to discipline me by the end of next week, Coop. She wants me out of the homicide squad," Mike said, referring to the most elite unit in the department. "The judge wants Scully to flop me back to uniform, and if he believes her for a minute, that's exactly what he'll do."

SEVEN

All week, in anticipation of our Vineyard trip, I had counted on the fresh evening breeze to help knock me out for a good night's sleep. Now I was practically frantic, thrashing around in bed as Mike's conversation trumped even my thoughts of the dead girl lying in the morgue without a name on her toe tag.

I'd made some stupid decisions in my love life, but how could Mike have let himself get involved with a head case like Jessica Pell? Street-smart, flamboyant, always keen to be the center of attention, and crazy enough that some people thought she had written the threatening letters to herself to remain in the spotlight.

And if she was looking to ruin Mike's career, perhaps Jessica had already made the same run at Paul Battaglia in order to derail my prospects, too. I replayed this morning's scene in my mind—McKinney and Battaglia rolling over and giving me the case in the Park without argument, whether or not it proved to be a sexual assault or intimate partner violence.

Now Mike's comments at dinner were really stinging. If Jessica Pell was behind the DA's decision to undermine me, then he was right that this case was the dog that could be my downfall. That was the way Battaglia liked to move mountains—without leaving fin-gerprints, if it were possible to do so.

I rolled over onto my stomach to try to relax myself, but my at-tention came back to Jessica Pell herself. What the hell had I ever done to cross her? She'd been a prosecutor in the Bronx DA's office for four or five years before flaming out there by mishandling three child abuse cases. Then she'd gone to a firm that did nickel-and-dime defense work, mostly DWIs and low-level drug possession. It was her affair with one of the mayoral deputies that launched her career on the bench. Jessica never played well in the sandbox with other women, but I hadn't ever exchanged more than ten words with her outside the courtroom.

I crunched the pillow under my head and turned onto my side. Whatever sleep I managed was in between thoughts about how I could help Mike navigate his way through this difficult morass that threatened his career and both our reputations. I struggled to re-member who in my office had approved my assignments of Mike during our last few cases. They couldn't go through to the NYPD without a supervisor's signature.

By seven A.M., my restlessness having barely abated all night, I saw no point in remaining in bed any longer. It was a glorious morning, and I slipped into the outdoor shower, looking out across Menemsha to the sailboats on the Vineyard Sound in the distance.

I dressed in jeans and a shirt, put the top down on my red Miata, and drove three miles to the Chilmark Store to pick up *The New York Times* and fresh muffins for Vickee and me. I took my first cup of coffee onto the porch of the store, sat in one of the rockers, unfolded the *Times* to read the story of the Park murder, pleasantly distracted by the parade of islanders, many of whom I was seeing for the first time this season—fishermen, lobstermen, waitresses, construction workers, house painters, schoolteachers, and landscapers—for whom this small general store was the same lifeline it served as for me.

I knew Vickee wouldn't be awake for another couple of hours.

Back at the house, I walked the perimeter of the property, enjoying the spring plantings that had started to bloom and added such color after the long, bleak island winter.

I tried to distance myself from the train wreck that had become Mike Chapman's life, but nothing in my spectacular view contributed to calming me. I went inside to organize my dresser drawers and closets. There were shirts and sweaters of Luc's that he had kept here—an array of sherbet-like colors in cashmere and cotton that reminded me of his warmth and affection as soon as I held them in my hands. I would need to wrap them and mail them back to him in France.

At around ten o'clock I had ground a bag of coffee beans, certain that the noise would awaken Vickee.

She stumbled downstairs half an hour later, expressing her delight in a morning without a wake-up visit from Logan.

We took our coffee on the deck, read the papers, then walked down and dangled our feet in the pool, deciding on a plan for the day.

"You seem fidgety, Alexandra. Did I upset you last night?"

"Nope." As much as I didn't want to withhold anything about Mike from Vickee, I assumed that what he had unloaded to me was in confidence. I expected that Mercer would be one of the first friends he would tell. "What do you want to do today?"

"Eat. Best option on the island."

We had a lunchtime regime that was both obscenely fattening and wonderfully delicious. It started at the Bite—a tiny shack off to the side of the road in Menemsha where the Quinn sisters served up the best fried clams I've ever eaten. Then we walked farther down the road, bought a dozen of the freshest oysters the local ponds produced every day in season from Larsen's Fish Market, and ate them on the dock, and ended our feast with an ice cream cone at the Galley, waiting for the line to go down at the hugely popular takeout place.

I kept Mike's secret all day, checking my voice mail too often for messages that never appeared and texts that weren't sent. I kept it through our bike ride to the Aquinnah Cliffs and back, enjoying the bright sunshine as we cycled home into the wind. And I kept it through dinner at the always crowded State Road—amazing seafood hauled in by island fishermen and salad from the chef's own gardens— when we were finally ready for another meal at nine P.M.

It was my turn to be the designated driver, so I didn't open a bottle of wine until we got home at eleven. "I'm going to the hot tub, Vickee. Put on your bathing suit and come along."

"No wine in the hot tub."

"You know what? I have taken enough advice from you in the last twenty-four hours to do me for the foreseeable future. You be the lifeguard. I want the water temp to be a hundred degrees, and I want my wine. Feel free to stay behind."

"Well, maybe a little wine. I'll join you in five."

I changed into my suit, grabbed a towel along with the wine bottle and glasses, and walked down through the dewy night grass to the corner of the pool with the Jacuzzi, dialing it up to a very warm temperature. Vickee wasn't far behind.

"Did you talk to Mercer?"

"Phone tag all day and evening."

"He didn't tell you anything about Mike?"

"I'm saying we didn't talk."

I tested the water with my toe, turned on the bubbles, and sat down inside with my glass.

"Then bury this till you hear it from Mercer, okay?"

"What?"

"Mike's getting jammed up. Big time."

"Mike who?"

"Last night you had me engaged to the guy. Now it's 'Mike who?'"

"*Our* Mike?"

The warm water and cold wine were taking the edge off. So was confiding in Vickee.

"You must have known—you and Mercer—that he was involved with a woman a few months ago?"

"I'm not all up in his business, Alex. What woman?"

"Jessica Pell."

"You're talking hot," Vickee said. "Good for Mikey."

"Turns out it's not so good for him at all."

"Why? 'Cause you were expecting him to have saved himself for you all these years? You're twisted. So I'm not handing you a virgin. Is that your issue?" Vickee tipped her drink in my direction. "You've been some places I wouldn't exactly suggest you claim on your résumé, babe."

"I have no quarrel with you there." I steadied my wineglass on one of the granite pieces of the pool's coping and refilled it. "What I mean is that Pell went all bunny-in-the-boiling-pot on Mike when he ended their brief romance. Puts me smack in the middle of it by saying I pulled him off her bodyguard duty 'cause I was jealous."

"Always knew those green eyes would get you in trouble, Alex."

"Be serious, Vickee," I said, lifting myself up onto the side of the hot tub and wrapping a towel around me. "She's made a beef to Sergeant Chirico, and probably to Battaglia, too. Pell wants Mike transferred out of homicide. Out. Gone. Stripped of his shield if she has her way. Back in uniform. Maybe the rubber gun squad."

Vickee's mood changed immediately. She got to her feet and wrapped the towel around her like a sarong. "I've got to call Mercer. This can't be happening."

I turned off the Jacuzzi settings and lights, and we practically ran back to the house. Vickee grabbed her phone from the counter. "I'm going upstairs. I promise you I'll get Mercer on this. Maybe he can spend tomorrow with Mike. Try to find a solution."

"Why don't you call him from here?" I said, longing to hear Mercer's response, but Vickee was halfway up the stairs.

"Doing it my way, Alex. I need some privacy."

I went to my room to shower and get ready for bed. I felt shut out of everything. I was so disconnected from what had been going on in Mike's life, and excluded from the intimacy that was a hall-mark of Mercer and Vickee's marriage.

It was another night of tossing and turning for me, an early trip to the store for newspapers, and what seemed like an eternity until Vickee came down the stairs at eleven o'clock and carried her coffee mug out onto the deck.

"Good morning," she greeted me. "I hope you feel better than you look."

"Not so much. Any luck?"

"Mission accomplished. Mercer is going to make an intercept at church. Figured he could corner Mike when he comes out of Mass with his mother," Vickee said. Mike tried to take his widowed mother, who was devoutly religious, to Sunday Mass every week. "Take her home first and then find some quiet time together to talk, while Mike's in the mood to atone."

"Nice. Thanks."

"What are you doing, working out here when we're supposed to be thinking no further ahead than our next meal?" she asked, see-ing several sheets of paper spread out over the table, held down by rocks so they didn't blow away.

"Just trying to keep my overwrought little brain occupied," I said, lowering my sunglasses to avoid the glare. "Did you see these things at Primola, or were you on the phone when Mike showed them to us?"

"I didn't see anything Friday night," Vickee said, lowering her-self into a chair and pulling the closest page toward her.

"It's a printout of the shot I took with my cell. Looks like an antique model of Belvedere Castle, doesn't it?"

"I'm not so familiar with Belvedere. Does it have something to do with the dead girl?"

"Who knows? Mike says cops were just picking up everything in sight."

"Well, Logan would have a swell time with this, wouldn't he?" she said. "Just throw a few of his little knights on the parapet up here. And this one? Ah, it's the Obelisk."

I pushed the third printout over to her, and she picked it up to study the image.

"An angel," Vickee said, pushing her sunglasses on top of her head to look more closely. "A dark little figure, isn't she?"

I nodded.

"Mike didn't say this was part of this other stuff, did he?"

"No," I said, pointing out the differences in scale and substance to her. "Just somewhere northwest of the Lake. She's unusual, isn't she?"

Vickee sighed. "Not if you grew up in my neighborhood, Ms. Alex. We've got our own angels, just like we've got our own devils."

"Well, it's an odd find in Central Park in the West 70s. Forget the murder case, this precious little object just makes me wonder about the child she belonged to."

"Exactly where did the cops pick it up?" Vickee wasn't joking around now. "Where does the bridle path cross near the Lake?"

I pulled the large map Mike had given me closer to us. "There, right below the transverse."

"So 78th Street? 79th? Not far from Central Park West?"

"About there. What are you thinking?"

"That maybe this angel's a relic from Seneca Village. Maybe that has something to do with the girl—or the man who killed her."

"What's Seneca Village?" I asked. "Where's that?"

Vickee sat back to tell me. "It used to be right close to that area, say 80th Street up to 89th Street."

"Near Central Park?"

"Not just near it. It's inside what became the Park—a stone's throw from where this figurine was found. There was no Park when the village existed, in the mid-1800s. Seneca was the first significant community of African American property owners to be created in Manhattan."

"I've never heard of it."

"And it wasn't a ghetto, Alex, but a stable settlement of working-class people."

"Houses—and . . . ?"

"Houses and schools, all seized by the government in 1857. An entire thriving village simply destroyed to create the great Park."

No doubt the state had authorized the legal doctrine of eminent domain to take the private property for public purposes.

"Your landscapers—those Olmsted and Vaux guys—they just displaced two hundred fifty people and knocked down their houses."

"I had no idea."

"Not many people do," Vickee said, holding up the picture of the ebony statuette. "They even destroyed three churches that served the little village. And one of them was called All Angels'."

EIGHT

"How do you know about this?" I asked. "I mean, maybe it's nothing—our victim's Caucasian—but what if it's related to the perp or the scene?"

I picked up my cell phone and dialed Mike's number. It went to voice mail immediately, and I left a message for him to call me.

"It's called black history, Ms. Cooper. Just like that graveyard you stumbled into near City Hall. And this place has a special connection to my family. So you know that Logan is named for my great-granddaddy Logan Bateman?"

"I do. He was a carriage driver for a wealthy family that lived on Fifth Avenue."

"That's right. Well, one of *his* great-greats—I don't know how many greats, girl, but Big Logan, as we called him, was born in 1893—and one of his ancestors was a man named Epiphany Bateman, born in Tuskegee."

"Who gained his freedom before the Civil War."

"Long before that," Vickee said. "Epiphany made his way to New York, where he established himself as a bootblack. He did well enough to buy one of the first lots of land, in 1825, in what became known as Seneca Village. Epiphany was a trustee of the African Methodist Episcopal Zion Church—"

"Built right in the Park? Or what became the Park?"

"Just where that playground is now on 85th. Dig down, you'll find the pew that Epiphany Bateman sat in every Sunday. It's all in the family Bible. The Mother AME Zion Church, Alex, was considered the wealthiest black church in America at that time. These folk even built their own schools for their kids. Colored School #3 is what it was called."

"And All Angels'?" I asked.

"That was the third church in Seneca Village, built closer to 1850. The community was so upscale that whites began to move in, German and Irish immigrants mostly. All Angels' was the only one of the three churches in the community that was integrated, so Epiphany moved his family over to worship there."

"Does Mercer know all this?"

Vickee smiled at me. "Well, that depends on whether he listened to my father when he'd tell all those family stories. I got no guarantee of that."

"When these villagers were moved out of the Park, Vickee, did they set up another community? Are there lists of the family names in church or city records?"

"So the dead girl is white. You're looking to make the killer a scion of Seneca, are you, Ms. Alex?"

"I'm looking for long shots, Vick. Are there names?"

"The families all scattered, sadly enough. Some of my ancestors moved down to Little Africa."

I gave her a blank stare.

"C'mon. Don't you know? Little Africa was a small black community on Minetta Lane in Greenwich Village, but the people of color were later forced out of there. Some stayed on the Upper West Side, like the rest of my relatives, and some moved on to the Bronx."

"You started me on this track. The black angel, could it really be a relic from a church that's now buried beneath Central Park?"

"Columbia University anthropologists did a dig a few years ago. Talk to them. They found dinner plates and cow bones and teapots, and a few crosses from one of the churches. Of course there are relics. It was a vibrant community for the thirty years of its existence. Then it was just razed to the ground and covered with plantings and grasses."

Vickee's phone rang, and she grabbed it. "Hey, babe. Everything good?" She listened while Mercer told her something and then she replied, "I'll tell her. And Alex is real interested in Seneca Village. She thinks you ought to have the Rothschild anthropology team from Columbia look at the black figure—in case angels are part of the theme here, and in case one of my long-lost relatives is still wilding through the Park. See you tonight."

"What's going on?" I asked.

"So Mike's just dropping off his mother after Mass. He's agreed to spend the afternoon with Mercer, and he said he'll open up about Jessica Pell. That's all good."

"Thanks a million."

"And Mike said he forgot to tell you last night, but the autopsy was negative for any signs of trauma in the vaginal vault. No semen. Sexually active, it appears, and never pregnant. Plus, so long in the water, there's nothing on the body for DNA. Dead end there."

"Mechanism of death?" I asked Vickee, whom I assumed had heard it from Mercer.

"Depressed fracture of the skull."

A blow or blows of such force that the smooth outer bone of the vault was cracked and depressed inward.

"Nothing from the canvasses, I guess," I said.

"We'd each have heard about it from someone by now, don't you think? Let's get some clothes on and go for a run on Black Point. And leave your phone right here. Be off duty for an hour or two."

I hated to run, preferring to get my exercise stretching and doing pliés in a ballet class I tried to attend on Saturdays when I was in the city. But Vickee had started her regimen when she was training at the Police Academy and kept her well-toned body in shape by jogging five miles a day.

"On the beach, no less? We can't run in sand."

"Stop whining. It's packed as hard as concrete when the tide's out. Let's go."

In five minutes we were on our way to Black Point, one of the many gated beaches that lined the spectacular south shore of the Vineyard, where the Atlantic surf pounded the island. Massachusetts was one of only two states that allowed ownership of property down to the mean low water mark, so even in the height of the season, only owners with keys could access the wide strips of sandy seashore that were punctuated every few miles by handsome public beaches.

There were only three other cars in the parking lot. We made our way over the dunes, where the sight of the seemingly endless ocean with its variety of blue and gray and aqua waters roiled and pounded against the sand.

We dropped our bags near the entrance and stretched, warming in the sun that was almost directly overhead.

Vickee's body—she was an inch taller than my five-foot-ten—cast a long shadow as she took off to the east. I satisfied myself by staying well behind her, trying to keep a steady pace.

I was drawn to the ocean view. Many years ago I had scattered Adam's ashes on this beach—his favorite place to be with me—and I always felt connected to him here, whether I sat high on the dunes as the sun went down or swam in the waves, soaking up his spirit.

And I glanced down from time to time while I ran, not looking for beach glass like a child, but one day expecting to see the shimmer of a small diamond on a gold band. It was here, after Valerie's violent death, that Mike had thrown the engagement ring he'd bought for her into a surf that appeared to be as full of rage as he was, though I tried in vain to console him.

Vickee and I stayed at the beach for most of the afternoon—reading crime novels, napping, and gossiping. We went back to the house to shower and pack up, stop for an early supper at the

Chilmark Tavern, and drive to the airport. In the morning, my caretaker would bring the car home for me.

The flight back was also easy. We hugged good-bye and each took a cab to our homes, Vickee to Queens and me back to Manhattan.

It was only nine P.M. when I unlocked my door and went inside. I poured a drink for myself and went into the bedroom to play back my messages.

The first one was from Mike, who had obviously chosen to avoid talking to me by not calling my cell. "Hey, Coop. Thanks for putting Mercer on to me. It helped to open up to him. And when you come to the canvass in the morning, Sergeant Chirico wants you to hang with him, not me. Just in case word is out about Jessica Pell, he doesn't want to add any fuel to the fire. G'night."

Seconds after that message had come in at eight, there had been a second call. No one spoke, but from the background noise it sounded as though the caller was standing on a city street. I walked to my large window, which offered such a grand vista twenty stories above the sidewalk, just reassuring myself of the normal traffic below.

It was a hang-up, but the number registered on the caller ID wasn't familiar to me. Even though there was no name displayed, the number had been captured on my dial because it was one that I had apparently phoned at some previous time.

I reached into my desk drawer and pulled out the emergency numbers for the DA's office, running my finger down the pages, scanning for those with a 646 area code. At the very end was the list of judges who had agreed to make themselves available to take nighttime calls when our assistants needed a signature on a search warrant.

Of course I had phoned that number in the past. When I had worked the Reservoir rapist case with Mercer, our big break came from a tip I received in the early hours of the morning.

It was Jessica Pell who had placed the hang-up call tonight. Judge Jessica Pell, who was going to try to take me down with Mike.

NINE

At six A.M., standing on the corner of Fifth Avenue and 72nd Street, I texted Sergeant Chirico, asking where to meet him. It was an overcast morning but expected to clear. Already, hundreds of the people who would use the Park this day were pouring into it on foot, bikes, blades, and pedicabs before the seven A.M. auto traffic would be allowed.

"I'll wait for you in the parking lot behind the boathouse," he replied. "Know it?"

"Yes." It was three blocks north of where I would enter, just off the east drive.

As I walked toward it, wearing slacks and a blazer in an attempt to look casual but professional, I passed more cops than I ever remembered seeing in one place at any time. My keys and ID were in my pants pocket, and I carried only a pen and a thick notebook.

All along the roadway that was still barred to vehicular traffic, cops were trying to stop every jogger, biker, and dog walker—having started before sunrise almost two hours ago—to ask whether they had seen or heard anything out of the ordinary on any of the mornings the week earlier.

Many people seemed eager to stop and answer questions, some

expressed annoyance but complied, and a few didn't slow down for a moment, just waving off the cops who tried to approach them.

"Good morning, Sarge. Thanks for letting me be here."

"No problem, Alex. I know you've done it before."

"Is Mike—?"

Chirico cut me off. "He's out on the Point. I don't think you're likely to see him."

"The Point?"

"It's that long piece of land at the southern tip of the Ramble that juts into the Lake. It sits directly opposite Bethesda Terrace— straight in front of the angel—and due east of Bow Bridge. The Point is wooded and remote. There won't be many people around, but Mike's got a secluded spot where he can take in all the action around the Lake, in case our killer is the kind of guy who wants to watch our operation."

"So is there a rush to judgment here, Sarge? Punishing Mike before you know what happened?"

Chirico shook his head at me. "You know me better than that. I'm trying to cover his back. He's out there with the squirrels and the chipmunks and the red-throated warblers till I can talk this Pell woman down off the ledge."

"So Lieutenant Peterson doesn't have a clue?"

"Sure he does. He just doesn't want to give Pell the satisfaction of thinking it rises to the level of needing his attention," the sergeant said. "You've got to ease up, Alex. Otherwise people will start to think she's got real ammunition. Let's get going."

"Just so you know, she called my apartment last evening. Hung up when she didn't get me at home."

"I'll make a note. But you ought to tell the DA."

My heart sunk. "I'm sort of hoping he doesn't have to find out."

"Where's your backbone, Alex? This broad's on a mission. And your common sense? If she hasn't told Battaglia yet, I'd be mighty surprised. He's got more sources than the pope," Chirico said. "Let's get my team in place."

The sergeant called out to the sixteen young cops—three women and thirteen men—who were gathered in small groups in the parking lot, waiting for orders. "Listen up!"

The clusters came together around Chirico, who introduced them to me and to Tom O'Day, the park ranger who was going to accompany us to our canvass site.

"We've got our assignment, guys," the sergeant said. "We're going up in the Ramble this morning, and our goal is to stop everyone who will talk to us, to see if they saw or heard anything unusual last week."

He passed around a small paper with a headshot of the dead girl, after she'd been autopsied and cleaned up at the morgue. "Show them this face. She might have been homeless, and a lot of homeless men and women hang out in the Park, so it gives us another chance at getting her ID'd."

"What's the Ramble, Sarge? I work on Staten Island," one of the cops said. "I've never set foot in this Park."

Manny Chirico turned to O'Day to field questions. He pointed over his shoulder to the winding wooded path that led uphill behind the boathouse.

"This is actually the most complex area of Central Park, in terms of its topography," O'Day said. "It was all pretty much a swamp when the Park was laid out. But the designers wanted New Yorkers to feel like they could escape from the city, so they brought in mountains of soil and boulders to create this woodland walk."

"This is man-made?"

"Entirely, except for some glacial bedrock that was laid down twenty thousand years ago," O'Day said. "We're going to climb up this web of pathways—there are all kinds of steep angles and sharp turns—"

"I'm a straight-line kind of guy myself," the cop said, growing an audience of comrades for his wisecracks.

"Then you've pulled the wrong assignment. There's only one straight line in this entire Park, Officer. It's the Promenade on the

Mall, taking you from Bethesda Terrace back toward 59th Street. Just that one. I'm about to lead you into thirty-eight acres that look like you might as well be in the Adirondacks. If you've never been here before, you won't believe you're in the city."

"A guy like me could get lost," another cop said.

"Good point," O'Day said. "See the streetlights? Every one of these lampposts has a location marking on it—four numbers that tell you exactly where you are."

He stopped at the foot of the path and pointed to the small plaque affixed to the post. "See that? 7500. The next one up there will be 7502. The first two numbers tell you what street is our parallel outside the Park—that would be 75th Street—and then they go in order, even numbers only when you're east of the center of the Park, from double-0 to 02. Above 100th Street, they're tagged with the last two digits, so the first post at 101st Street becomes 01-00."

"Where's 7501?" the same guy asked.

"Just off 75th Street on the west side. The numbers over there are odd, like everything else about the west side."

We started to walk, two at a time, up the incline, which began as an asphalt path but soon became gravel and dirt. Within minutes, the sights and sounds of urban New York were far below us, as we were shaded by overgrown trees and serenaded by what sounded like varieties of songbirds.

Tom O'Day stopped all of us at the first fork in the trail. "Some of you are going to head that way, up to the Gill."

"What's the Gill?" a female officer asked.

"It's a stream. Runs out of Azalea Pond up above us, by 77th Street. It twists and turns with a few cascades, then takes a pretty steep drop down a gorge into the Lake."

"Even the stream is artificial?"

"Yes, ma'am. Same pumped-in-from-upstate water that runs out of your tap. But you'd never know it."

"So the body that was found in the Lake could have been thrown in the water up here and floated down?"

"Not a prayer," the sergeant said. "There would have been quite an accumulation of postmortem skin tears and discolorations. Wait till you see this stream—and the boulders in it. Tom, why don't you tell them who's likely to be around?"

"Sure. At this hour of the day we get your more adventurous runners. Guys on the clock prefer the roadway or Reservoir trail, not just because of how steep it gets here but because the ground is so rough, with tree roots and rocks in the way. They rarely stop for anyone. Your dog walkers are the friendliest by far.

"There are plenty of tree-huggers here. See this—this mini forest? All of it brought in more than a hundred years ago, to look subtropical and exotic. You got tupelos and American sycamores, cucumber magnolias and sassafras. The place is dominated by black cherry and black locust 'cause they self-seed so aggressively."

"But they don't talk," the Staten Island cop said. "So what do I give a shit about the trees?"

"Because the people who study the trees, kid, are extremely observant," Chirico said. "They can tell you the difference between the leaves on a Kentucky coffee tree and on a scarlet oak. I listened to them all weekend. They'll be able to tell me if you were on this path last Wednesday, and whether or not your nose was running like it is now."

The cop wiped his nose with his handkerchief and stepped back.

"And then there are the birders," O'Day said. "Another super-friendly bunch. And also great eyes for detail. There are more than 275 species of birds that drop into the Ramble and forty that stay here—we're part of the Atlantic Flyway."

"What's that? The Flyway?" It was the female officer again.

"The migration route that birds follow from Canada down to Mexico. They like a line that doesn't have high mountains in the way, and plenty of food to eat. They love it here."

"Birders are also keen observers," Manny Chirico said. "Keep in mind that many of them have binoculars and cameras with them to take pictures of rare birds—to prove that they saw them and that kind of thing—so be sure to ask about that. And lots of them do sketches, so check if they have a pad with any relevant drawings."

"The Ramble had a certain reputation once," a serious young cop said. "Is that still an issue?"

"You mean the gay thing?" the sergeant asked.

"Yeah. Like in the '60s and '70s. Wasn't there a lot of gay bashing up here?"

Tom O'Day answered. "Since the beginning of the twentieth century, the seclusion of this part of the Park made it especially popular for gay men to cruise. And then, you're right. It was the perfect place to beat and rob them. Very few gays were open then, so many of the crimes never got reported."

"But now it looks like just a remote nature reserve," I said.

The ranger smiled at me. "It's still a haven for gay sex. Maybe it's the retro feel of sneaking off into the woods instead of hanging out in a bar. Anyway, by the time you each set up a post, you'll be overrun by my Ramblers."

"Okay," the sergeant said. "Start in pairs and see how it goes. Try not to let anyone give you the brush-off. Everything's in the details, so have your memo books ready and take it all down. And guys? Canvassing is tedious work. Maybe the most tedious. So expect a lot of rejection before you make any headway."

Within seconds, at the fork in the path by the antique *luminaire*, or lamppost, numbered 7528, all sixteen of the cops had vanished from sight. The overgrown foliage and the curving pathways provided perfect camouflage. We were in a wilderness aerie, climbing and climbing away from the city streets but able to see the tips of skyscrapers that ringed the entire Park.

Manny Chirico was wearing a brown linen jacket, chinos, and a polarized pair of Ray-Bans. He looked more like a *GQ* cover model than a homicide sergeant. "Stick with me, Alex."

"Okay, but what are we going to do?"

"Walk every square inch of this park within a park—I'd get them to turn over every boulder if I could."

"I thought the groundskeepers here were meticulous."

"They are," Chirico said. "The rules are zero tolerance for garbage and graffiti. But we're talking about physical evidence."

"You like the Ramble for finding the perp, or for thinking the crime scene is here?"

Manny's expression suggested he was as frustrated as one might imagine. "Like it? We've got four sergeants, Alex, and each one is assigned an area adjacent to the Lake to supervise and hope to find a weapon or a piece of clothing or a real clue. Me? I pulled the short straw of the northern border. You think I wouldn't rather be talking to half-naked sunbathers on Bethesda Terrace than crawling through the Ramble? Everybody else has wide-open spaces with some trees and bushes around them. Me? I got such a tangle of rocks and streams and tree stumps that I'll be lucky if I don't find three more bodies under the dead leaves."

"Well, you put on a good show for the kid cops," I said.

"Let's start at Azalea Pond."

We wound around more pathways, over short rustic bridges that spanned the gorge, until we came upon an opening just after lamppost 7736. There was a large pond surrounded by bright fuchsia azaleas in bloom, with several benches—empty at the moment—and vines and creepers everywhere underfoot around the water's edge.

Chirico was taking detailed notes, and both of us were snapping photos with our cell phones.

"Ever been up here before?" he asked.

"Not this far. It's spectacular."

"Glad to see it through your eyes. To me, there's a perp behind every bush."

Chirico's walkie-talkie crackled, and he held it up to talk. It was still more reliable than a cell in some of the Park's more remote locations. "Go ahead."

"Sarge? I'm Jerry McCallion. Staten Island, remember? Read me?"

"Yeah."

"Got a man who thinks the deceased looks like someone he knows."

"Keep him there," the sergeant said. "Where are you?"

"7616."

"Give me five."

I tried to keep up with Chirico as we wound our way down the path. Several of the teams had engaged a variety of morning walkers, showing the copy of the dead girl's photo and asking for help. Most of the cops shrugged their shoulders and shook their heads as we passed by, suggesting they had come up empty so far, despite cooperative citizens.

Manny Chirico introduced both of us to the man who was waiting beside the cop. "I want to thank you for talking with us, sir. Do you think you can help?"

The man was holding a cocker spaniel on a leash. "I was out of town all last week, so I can't be useful in that regard. But this girl does look sort of familiar to me."

"Someone you know?" I asked.

"She might have gone to school with my daughter."

"What school is that?"

"Brearley." The man was referring to one of the most prestigious private schools in Manhattan. Something in the girl's life had taken a dramatically bad turn if this man wasn't mistaken.

"May we talk to your daughter?"

"Sure. But she's in Hong Kong for the summer, on an internship."

"Is there a Brearley yearbook at your home? We're pretty anxious to identify this young woman."

We took all the man's information and told him there would be a uniformed cop at his door within the hour to follow up.

He started to walk away and then turned back to us. "Did either of you see *The Wall Street Journal* on Friday?"

We both shook our heads.

"Google just acquired a company called PittPatt. It's out of a project at Carnegie Mellon. Recognition software called Pittsburgh Pattern that was developed from an army grant after 9/11. Supposedly one could take a photograph of a crowd, highlight a single face within it, and compare that face automatically to images on Facebook and social media sites."

Chirico was writing as fast as he could manage. The well-dressed dog walker had just gone from promising information about his daughter's once-schoolmate—even though our corpse didn't look much like a Brearley girl—to giving us an entirely new state-of-the-art way to identify an unknown victim. He handed Manny his card and walked off.

The next hour and a half continued to be frustrating. There was a woman who had seen a commotion—a couple fighting—and placed them near the beloved statue of Balto, the Alaskan husky who helped save the people of Nome during a diphtheria epidemic in 1925. She babbled for twenty minutes before recalling that the argument she witnessed had been on Saturday and not earlier in the week.

An elderly man with a canteen slung over his shoulder had stopped midpath to remove from harm's way three young red-eared sliders—a turtle species that lived in the Ramble—and carry them deeper into the woods. He remarked to two cops that he had heard screams on his morning walk almost exactly one week ago. He engaged them for more than ten minutes before they realized he was also obsessed with a meteor headed for earth and the shrieking noises that it emitted.

By nine A.M., everyone with purpose—people with day jobs—had finished their Park jaunts, and now there were the more casual visitors.

Manny and I were poking among leaves along the banks of the gorge when his radio crackled again.

"Sarge? I'm Officer Resnick, from your detail." I could hear a woman's voice. "I got a birder with something interesting."

"Where are you? Can you make me?"

"Yup. I'm at 7322."

"73? That's way south of us. You must be almost at the Point."

I picked up my head. That's where Mike had started his morning.

"Just about the tip of it. I got a great shot of the Lake from where we are."

"Will your witness stay?"

"She says yes. We're waiting for her sister, who took a picture with her camera. There's a detective here who's giving me a hand."

Manny Chirico turned off the radio and wagged a finger at me. "We'd better hustle. But promise me, Alex, you'll stay out of Mike's way. Let's not add to the problem."

"Well, apparently I *am* the problem. I don't intend to stir it up, you can be sure."

Although we were only the equivalent distance of three city blocks from where the message had originated, the complex series of twisted trails and narrow bridges made it almost a fifteen-minute walk.

Mike's back was to us as we approached. The young police officer lifted her arm when she spotted us coming, and beside her was a gray-haired woman dressed in sensible clothes with low hiking boots, whom I guessed to be about seventy-five years old.

"Hey, Mike," I said, following in single file behind Manny Chirico.

"Coop. Sarge." He acknowledged both of us but didn't make eye contact. "Meet Helen Austin."

"How d'you do?" Austin said, stretching her arm out to shake hands with us. There was an old-fashioned manner to her speech, as well as her dress.

"Ms. Austin studies birds here. She was just showing us a great horned owl until your gentle tread scared him off."

"What is it, Mike?" The sergeant's annoyance was palpable.

"Helen?" Mike said to her. "Would you tell my boss what you saw?"

She held her head high but shook it from side to side. "I'd prefer you repeat it."

"Ms. Austin was out here last Wednesday morning. She hikes here every Monday, Wednesday, and Friday. She leaves her house on West 76th Street at nine, and her sister meets her right at the tip of the Point at 10:15."

"Like clockwork," Helen Austin said. "You can set your watch by us."

"Last Wednesday, the sisters had just joined up when a man came toward them from between this stand of trees. Am I right so far?"

"Indeed."

"He startled them."

"That was clearly his plan, Sergeant," the woman said. "To startle us."

"He stood in front of them on the path and exposed himself, and—"

"He didn't expose himself, Detective," Helen Austin said. "He was already exposed. Fully dressed, in a long-sleeved black T-shirt and dirty blue jeans. With his privates already hanging out for all the world to see. And then he began pleasuring himself just inches away from us."

"Pleasuring . . . ?" the sergeant asked.

"Masturbating, Sergeant. Hoping to shock the two of us, I'm sure."

"Were you able to do anything?" I said.

"Of course, young lady. My sister needs a walking stick. She's older than I," Helen Austin said—pausing for effect, I thought. "She lifted the stick and smacked the fellow right between his legs. Not bad for a couple of old spinsters, don't you think?"

"You know what they say about a bird in the hand," Mike replied. Helen Austin was as taken with his warm grin and sparkling eyes as the rest of us usually were.

"Well, it wasn't in his hand very much longer, I can tell you that."

"Can you describe him?" the sergeant asked.

"Better than that. My sister snapped a photograph," Austin said. "She'll be here any minute."

Not every pervert went on to become a homicidal maniac, but the canvass had already yielded a potential offender in the Ramble.

"Might as well tell them," Mike said to her.

"He was an African American gentleman—well, 'fellow' is more correct than 'gentleman.' In his midthirties, I'd say. Light skinned. Close-cropped hair, a mustache, about six feet tall."

"Would you be able to recognize him, do you think?" I asked.

"Take it easy, Coop. She just told you they've got a photograph," Mike said. "You interrupted the most important thing. Helen?"

"Not that I wanted to be looking at his private parts, but there was a tattoo on his right hand, with which he was holding his penis. That's the most disturbing part of this. I've seen plenty of impolite young men before. But there were two words tattooed, just below his knuckles."

Helen Austin drew a line across her own hand, suggesting the position of the inked letters. "The words printed were KILL COPS."

Manny Chirico and I exchanged glances. The harmless masturbator who liked to shock unsuspecting birders might have much deeper felony roots.

"Jailhouse art," the sergeant said. "That tattoo information and a photo will be a huge help to us, Ms. Austin."

She was peering over our shoulders, and I turned my head to see whom or what she had spotted. It must have been her sister who was approaching.

"Come quickly," she called out. "These police people are asking questions about our interloper last week. I told them you managed two photographs of him."

The sister took her time on the rocky path and approached us with an enthusiastic greeting. She asked me to hold her stick while she removed her camera from her cross-body bag and handed it to Manny Chirico.

"They should be the last two images, sir. I haven't touched them. We tried to tell one of the rangers about the incident on our way out of the Park, but he wasn't much interested."

And that of course was Wednesday, two days before the body was found in the Lake.

The sergeant opened the viewfinder and was trying to bring the images up. "I'm sorry, Ms. Austin, but there's no photograph of the man's face, is there? I can't find it."

"I'm not sure I got much of his face," she said. "I was so rattled I was lucky to get the bottom of his chin, down to his knees."

Chirico rolled his eyes and passed the camera to Mike.

"Be patient, Sarge," Mike said, laughing at Manny's short fuse. "Let me zoom in and see what's here."

I stood closer to Mike and watched as the image enlarged. But Helen's sister must have been moving when she hit the button to take the photo because it was too fuzzy to see clearly.

Mike's smile vanished when he brought the second shot into view and framed it on the camera's small screen. "You were close about the tattoo, Helen. Just a few letters off, but they make a hell of a lot of difference."

"What is it?" Chirico asked.

Mike passed the camera over my head. "What the jailhouse tat says, Sarge, is KILL COOP."

TEN

Ten minutes later I was sitting between Mike and the sergeant on the porch of the Loeb Boathouse, overlooking the Lake. It had been closed off to tourists, and Lieutenant Peterson was using it as a mini command center because of its unspoiled vista of the Bow Bridge and the area surrounding the place where the body was found.

"I'm not the only Coop in the world, you know. That might not be referring to me."

"You've made more than your share of enemies," Mike said.

"Just following in your footsteps, I think." He'd yet to be alone with me this morning, so there had been no mention of Judge Pell.

"The Alexandra Cooper Wing at Dannemora. Everybody doing twenty-five to life, sitting around in their therapy sessions making voodoo dolls of Coop and her team at SVU."

The sergeant put his finger to his lips to quiet our bickering. He was on the phone with an analyst at One PP, in the tech information hub known as the Real Time Crime Center. The Center was a rabbit warren of computer screens and technicians—a modern effort to centralize all the information gathered by the NYPD.

Every arrest report and detectives' steno pad contained valuable nuggets of detail. One database recorded descriptions of birthmarks and scars; another was the source for dental irregularities—missing teeth, grids, gold or silver caps; and yet one more listed unusual gaits—limps, if suspects had them, as well as how pronounced or severe they were.

The tattoo database had become one of the most regularly used. Frequently, based on things victims had told me about their attackers, I called to request a search of a particular body part—like the left shoulder blade or the back of a man's neck—for a certain word or symbol. With a few keystrokes by a good detective analyst, a single phone call could lead to a suspect with a criminal history, and a subsequent arrest.

"Kevin? It's Manny Chirico. I'm up in Central Park and I need a check of your tattoo base."

He waited while his contact got ready to take the information.

"Can you enter the word 'kill'?" Manny asked.

Chirico put his hand over the receiver. "He says 'kill' is really common in gang art. The search will pull up lots of kills."

"Great. All Coop needs is an angry banger."

I was trying to think of guys I had put away recently who had been gang members.

Chirico whistled. "Okay, 276 hits with the word 'kill.' Now try 'kill cops.'"

The answer came within a minute. "Twenty-three. I guess we're not too popular, are we? Now search for 'kill Coop.'"

It took two or three minutes for a response because the officer must have tried entering the words several times.

"No luck, eh? Thanks for trying." Chirico looked at me and said, "Got a blank on that one."

"I'm sure you're overreacting," I said.

"A guy jerking off in the Park? He's one of your boys, Coop," Mike said. "Either he got the ink after he did his time and that's why he isn't in the database, or he hasn't gone to trial yet. But he's definitely part of the SVU posse."

"Let me call Laura."

I dialed my secretary. "Good morning, Laura. I trust you got the voice mail that I'd be spending most of the day in the Park."

"I did. That's what I told Rose when she called looking for you."

"Battaglia wants to see me?" I said, wincing as I looked from Mike to Manny. "Tell him it will have to hold till tomorrow."

"That's what I said. No blowback so far. Need anything?"

"We do. I'd like you to go back through all the unit indictments for the last five years. Pull out screening sheets on convictions of any male, black, twenty-five to thirty-five, that I had anything to do with. Review the pending cases, too. And see if you can match our list against parole—make sure we know all our offenders who've been released within the last year. Double-check anything that took place in a park—Central or any other city park. Will that keep you busy for a few hours?"

"It's a slow day, Alex. I don't mind at all."

"Thanks. Call me if you need anything. We'll be working with the parks commissioner most of the afternoon."

I hung up and asked the sergeant what to do next.

"That Reservoir rapist that you and Mercer put away," Chirico asked. "What kind of time did he get?"

"Four victims, so he's doing the better part of two hundred years."

"Yeah," Mike said, "but did he run with a gang? Maybe he's got somebody on the outside who has it in for you."

"That's a lot of 'maybes' to check when you're a prosecutor who specializes in violent felons. Why don't you see how many con- victed offenders named Cooper are in jail?"

"We can do that, too," the sergeant said. "We've got an hour till we get our briefing from the parks commissioner. That's a good time to let everyone know about the Austin sisters' perv. In the meantime, while we've got some privacy, would you two like to tell me anything I should know for my dealings with Judge Pell?"

I stepped out onto the patio of the boathouse restaurant and leaned against the railing. "I seem to be the last to know, guys, so feel free to fill me in."

Mike was running his fingers through his hair, which he always did when he was nervous. "I really don't want to do this right now, Sarge. I've sort of sandbagged Coop on this."

"I'd say we've all been sandbagged. You don't have time to waste," Chirico said. "You ever appear before this woman?"

"I don't know. Maybe I testified in a hearing once or twice. I fucked up, Sarge, is all I can say. The lieutenant had me on the detail 'cause Pell claimed she was getting threats."

"Claimed?"

"I never heard the threats. There were some notes—typed—that came in the mail to her office. One with white powder."

"Like anthrax?" the sergeant asked.

"Like talcum pretending to be anthrax."

"Who from?"

"Supposedly it all involved a Wall Street trader gone too greedy. She presided over the case and sent him up the river for ten years. A piker compared to Coop."

"And the threats?" Chirico asked.

"The guy hired a hit man. The letters started coming to Pell in December, and the chief administrative judge called in Battaglia and the chief of detectives immediately. They put security on her 24/7."

"I know we only let them have you two nights a week," the sergeant said. "Who else?"

"They pulled a female detective from Major Case, and two guys from the DA's squad did most of the work. Between Christmas and the end of February, there were no more threats and nothing unusual happened. Scully ended the detail."

"Then what?" I asked.

"Then I got really stupid. Is that what you're waiting for me to say?"

"I guess so."

"Pell was smart, tough, funny. Kind of quirky."

"All the things you find resistible in *me*."

"And sexy."

"Oh."

"Yeah, she wasn't always mooning about some guy who was out of reach."

"So you got in bed with her," Chirico said.

"But it was after my assignment was over." Mike put his hands in the pocket of his chinos. "On my own time."

"And it ended because . . . ?" the sergeant said.

"Don't make it more dramatic than it has to be. The thrill was gone, Manny. It was just a fling. She gives off a lot of 'crazy' the minute you get close. I wanted out."

"And how did I become your exit valve?" I asked.

Mike picked up a stone from the patio and skipped it across the smooth surface of the Lake below us. "It was that last week of April. Things were wild with Luc here and that murder case. I was working it with all my free time since I couldn't do it officially because of my friendship with Luc and you."

"I'm grateful for that. Seriously."

"I must have told Jessica that it was your birthday. That I might be spending it with you. I was using that as an excuse 'cause I knew I wanted out," Mike said, his fingers back in his thick shock of black hair. "I think it's what really set her off. Made her believe it was all about you. End of story."

"Except that somebody tried to kill her right after that?" Chirico asked.

Mike spoke the words slowly: "So she says."

"How? I mean what was the attempt?"

"Pell has a house in the Hamptons. Claimed she was followed into her driveway late at night by two masked men in a car who got out and tried to jump her as she was opening her side door."

"Anything forensic to back it up?" the sergeant asked.

"No evidence. No neighbors home to hear noise. No tire tracks. Just a lot of broken glass and one hysterical judge," Mike said. "And she admitted she broke the glass herself because she was too nervous to get the key in the lock."

"So what does the prisoner who hired the hit men have to say about it?"

"It would have been awfully hard for him to pay off the hit men if they'd been successful, Manny," Mike said. "The schmuck had a heart attack and dropped dead in state prison last winter. You know any hit men who work without an advance and no insurance for the final payment? That's why I think she's off her rocker."

ELEVEN

"What are you doing, Coop? We've got most of the police force saturating the Park," Mike said. "You look like you're ready to undress."

"I am only half ready, but maybe it makes sense to do it all the way." I held on to the railing and stepped out of my driving moccasins and onto the seat of one of the chairs, hoisting myself up to the top of a dining table. Then I pulled off my cotton crewneck sweater. "Hold my belt for me, will you, Sarge?"

I unbuckled it and whipped it out of the loops.

"What do you think—?"

"C'mon, Mike. Off with your blazer." I crossed my arms and looked at my watch. "We've got fifteen minutes. Ready for this? I bet you're quick about it, aren't you? No foreplay. Not too much small talk."

Manny Chirico got my point first and started to nod his head, laughing with me. "I'm trying to quench the rumors, Alex, not stoke the fires."

"Be careful what you wish for, guys. The rumors about Mike and me pale in comparison to his—his—"

"Stupidity, Coop. You can say it."

"Stupidity it is. Thanks for that, Mike. And apparently half the department and everyone in my shop from Battaglia on down—you might as well throw in your mother and mine, too—think that we've been in each other's pants, Mike. So maybe if we just get it on in broad daylight—"

"Keep your voice down, Coop. You're sounding wacky."

"I figure you like wacky. I can do wacky, too, Mike—you know that. I can do over-the-top crazy as well as Jessica Pell, I promise you that. In fact, I feel it coming on," I said. "Here we've got the other half of the department watching us, in this beautiful setting all around the Lake, so maybe we can defuse the gossip and let people know that *we* know that *they* know about us. Whaddaya say? Get naked right now. Who knows? You might even enjoy it."

"Why's that?" Mike asked. "Because you think so many others have?"

"Legions. More than I can count."

He grabbed me around the knees and pulled me toward him, folding me over his shoulder in a fireman's carry to plant me on the ground next to Manny Chirico. "I give up, Sarge. She's all yours. I can't handle her right now."

"At least I tried. I thought a little comic relief would beat blowing my top. Besides, I'm better for your sorry reputation than Pell is, don't you think?" I picked up my sweater and knotted it around my shoulders. Then I waved my arms at the cops who had stopped in their tracks to watch the commotion I'd tried to create. "Back to work with all of you."

"Where's the big meeting?" Mike asked. His phone rang, and he walked toward the exit to answer it.

"At the Arsenal," the sergeant said, turning to me. "That's where the commissioner's office is."

"64th Street. We can walk from here," I said. "Would you mind telling me what you're going to do about Judge Pell and her—well, her story about Mike? I hear she gave you a deadline."

"Better you don't know, Alex. I'm working on a plan."

The boathouse parking lot had become a staging area for different teams sent in to relieve officers walking the grid. Chirico and I threaded our way through them, stopping to examine plastic toys, fragments of cloth, and all the other objects that had been recovered in the search.

"That was the lab," Mike said when he caught up with us. "You know those two miniature statues and the angel I dropped off on Friday night?"

He was directing his conversation to the sergeant, not to me.

"Yeah."

"No forensic value. I thought maybe one of those metal sculptures could have been the weapon. Either one of them is heavy enough to have cratered the girl's skull. But no luck."

"Any DNA?" Chirico asked.

"Smudges and overlays. Nothing there."

"Do you mean smudges or mixtures?" I asked. "You know I'm doing a Frye hearing on mixtures in two weeks. If there are only three samples in a mix—"

"I probably would have said 'mixtures' if that's what I meant, Coop, don't you think? Those items are hopelessly smudged, okay? And coated in mud on the parts that aren't smudged."

"Seventy-two hours and the clock is ticking," Chirico said, leading us on the roadway—closed off to traffic for the next three days of police activity—to the southeast. "I really hoped to turn up something this morning."

The three of us knew the age-old policing rule that homicides went cold after forty-eight hours. Modern forensics had breathed new life into old investigative styles, but outside crime scenes were always the worst, then and now. It was rare to have fingerprints on any surfaces, weather wreaked havoc on evidence of every kind, and boundaries were often hard to fix.

"Seventy-two since we found her, Sarge," Mike said. "And she was killed weeks before that."

"Miracles happen."

"Rarely on my watch," Mike said.

"That's not the way the judge tells it."

"Are you going to let that subject be or what, Coop?"

"I thought this relentless approach would resonate with you, but I guess I'm wrong," I said. "Do either of you know anything about the parks commissioner?"

"My City Hall sources tell me he's a great guy," the sergeant said. "Brilliant lawyer, passionate about civic causes—don't you remember, he's on the Public Library board?"

"No wonder the name sounds familiar," I said, thinking back on the murder of a rare book conservator we'd worked more than a year ago. "Gordon Davis. A very elegant man. Witty and charismatic. African American, almost as tall as Mercer. Light skin with piercing green eyes."

"You talking Match.com or the parks department?" Mike asked.

"Did I leave out the part that he's got a fabulous wife who's a law professor? Just saying he's a man you notice," I said. "Now, the strange part is why anyone would create a public park and build an arsenal inside it, storing all that ammunition right where you're inviting everyone in the city to hang out."

I knew I had hit a ground ball to Mike. If there was a question about military history that Mike was unable to answer, I hadn't yet come upon it. The staid Arsenal building, dark brick and turreted, was a Fifth Avenue landmark. With hand railings carved in the shape of muskets, it had a façade as serious as the zoo directly behind it was whimsical.

"There's a lot I don't know about the Park, but that part I do," Mike said. "There are only two structures left inside the Park—between 59th Street and 110th Street—that predate the Park itself. The Arsenal was opened in 1851, far north of most of the residential population of the city, to hold all the munitions for New York's National Guard. A pretty short-lived purpose, once the plan changed."

"So it was only an Arsenal for ten or fifteen years?" the sergeant asked.

"Yeah. Then they had to move all the dangerous explosives out of the area. It actually became the first building of the Museum of Natural History, before the one we have today. Now it's headquarters for the parks commissioner and the zoo."

"What's the other building? The one that's even older than that," I asked.

"The Blockhouse."

"Yeah, Peterson mentioned that. But I don't remember it."

"Do you know where the Cliff is?"

"Inside the Park?" I asked. "No."

"Up on 109th Street, on the far west side, at the edge of a very high precipice. The Blockhouse is the last remaining fortification built in 1814 to defend against the British. It's a great-looking stone stronghold, but I wouldn't advise a visit at night without a police escort."

"Why?"

"'Cause it's in such a remote area—roofless now and hopefully securely locked."

"Have we checked it out, Sarge?" I asked. "What if someone got into it?"

"It's happened before," Mike said. "Not murder or rape, but a great place for kids to use a makeshift ladder and scramble inside. I'm not thinking any individual could get a body out of the Blockhouse and down to the Lake without running into someone. They're more than thirty city blocks apart."

"Good place to hold a hostage till you figured out what to do with him or her," I said. It was fast becoming obvious that the Park was a small city within Manhattan, with more places to hide out than I had ever imagined.

Chirico tipped his head my way to assure me he'd have it checked out.

The roadway led us directly down to the Central Park Zoo. A harem of California sea lions was rafted together on top of their pool, basking in the sun to the amusement of scores of tourists. Chirico led us around to the front steps of the Arsenal. He and Mike tinned the guard with their gold badges and we were admitted to the lobby for our meeting with Commissioner Davis.

The anteroom was full of detectives from Manhattan North Homicide, Major Case, and the Central Park Precinct squad. We milled around, trading ideas about what had brought the dead girl to such a brutal ending, until the secretary guided us into the conference room.

There was almost a spark of electricity when Davis entered. He introduced himself, instantly engaging and vibrant. "Good afternoon, ladies and gentlemen. Welcome to the People's Park." Davis was the only one standing. The rest of us were seated around a long rectangular table. "What many have called the most important work of American art in the nineteenth century."

Lieutenant Peterson thanked Davis for taking the time to talk with us.

"I'll tell you whatever you need to know about this place, and you make sure to solve the crime before tonight. Deal?"

"It doesn't look like murder's bad for business, Commissioner," one of the detectives said. "I almost got trampled by a pack of tourists getting in here."

"Almost forty million visitors a year, including the folks who use the Park every day."

"Not exactly a crime wave when you got one dead body in forty million," Harry McAvoy, a senior Major Case detective who'd been on the job almost thirty years, said half under his breath. "I don't get the big deal here."

"I've been asked to give you the lay of the land, and to make all our experience available to you," Davis said as he walked to an enormous map hung on the far wall. "For management purposes, the Park is divided into ten sections, and each section has five zones. I'd advise you to break down the same way for this week's work. Each of our sections has a supervisor, and every zone has a gardener. Those are the guys who have to drop their pruning tools to pick up a candy wrapper. So if anything is out of place or unusual, it's your zone gardeners who are likely to have spotted it.

"Then we've got roving crews that move between the zones. Tree experts, turf and soil monitors, rodent control—"

"You oughta step that one up a bit, Commish," McAvoy said.

"I have a few emerald boa constrictors in the zoo who could take care of most of the city's rats in a couple of nights, Detective. Anytime you want to borrow my snakes for an evening tour of duty, give a call."

"We're looking at 843 acres, am I right?" the lieutenant asked.

"Yes. Six percent of Manhattan's total size. Seven bodies of water, including the Lake and Reservoir; twenty-one playgrounds; nine thousand benches, which would stretch seven miles if you put them end to end; and twenty-four thousand trees. You'd be very smart to use our ground crews and our rangers—they've walked every inch of this place and can tell you things you couldn't begin to imagine about it."

All the guys had questions and started shouting them out. "Got any suggestions about where to do a quiet kill?"

"We spend a lot of our time ensuring that kind of thing doesn't happen."

"Well, it just did, sir, so if you can cut to the chase."

I guessed Gordon Davis to be in his early sixties. "You're all too young to remember what happened to this Park in the 1970s."

"Seen it myself, Commissioner," Lieutenant Peterson said.

"During the fiscal crisis of those years," Davis said, "it was city services that suffered the most cuts. All of the parks—in every borough—were in an advanced state of deterioration. There were mobile task forces that cleaned them on a weekly basis. Weekly—can you imagine what this place looked like under those conditions? The parks were not only filthy and unkempt, but vandalized and virtually abandoned to the poor and the criminal element. The Sheep Meadow—which actually had sheep grazing on it until 1934—"

"I think I stepped in some sheep shit yesterday," one of the clowns from Major Case said.

"I expect that stuff is petrified by now, Detective. But don't be surprised if you come up with animal bones," Davis said. "Every now and then, when the earth turns over after a big storm like Hurricane Sandy or kids dig a new spot off the beaten track, the remains of the sheep and pigs who lived here before the city fathers took it over come to the surface.

"As I was saying, though, the Sheep Meadow had become a dust bowl in the '70s, petty thefts and muggers forced the closing of Belvedere Castle, and there was more graffiti covering Bethesda Terrace than there was grass on the ball fields."

"What turned it around?" Manny Chirico asked.

"The public-private partnership," Davis said. "The establishment of the Conservancy and its ability to fund-raise at a time of such fiscal austerity. Just to be clear, the annual budget for Central Park is forty-six million, eighty-five percent of which comes from the Conservancy, not the City."

"Didn't one individual give a fortune to Central Park just last year?" I asked.

"The largest monetary donation in the history of the city's park system," Davis said. "John Paulson, an investment banker, gave one hundred million dollars to thank the city for all that the Park meant to him throughout his life. As a teenager, he told us, he used to hang out at the statue of the Angel of the Waters—which was bone-dry back then. He called that statue the heart of the Park. Most of us who work here think it's the heart of the city—and I'm expecting you gentlemen to make that right again."

"Did he give you enough money so we can drain the Lake?" Mike asked.

"We're starting by dredging it first, Detective. Those efforts begin tomorrow."

"So in the meantime," one of the Major Case guys asked again, "give me a hint, Mr. Davis. Where would you go to off somebody?"

I didn't think the commissioner brooked fools or comics, so I thought he wouldn't take that question seriously. He turned to Peterson and asked if there had been any progress in identifying the victim.

"No, sir. We had a possible lead this morning—a man who thought the girl might have gone to Brearley with his daughter. But we have the yearbook now and we've made contact with the young lady in the picture and she's alive and well."

"Are you still thinking your victim might have been homeless?"

"That's our best guess, so far."

So although it first seemed the commissioner was ducking the question about where might be a good place to kill someone, he was instead building to an answer in a most logical way.

"Since this Park was created, it has always been a magnet for the homeless. In the 1860s they were called 'tramps' and 'bums,' and they migrated to the new Park in droves. In the Great Depression, the poor pitched tents and made shanties around the Reservoir and on the margins of the parks. In every period of economic downturn, the disenfranchised find their way into the Park. So it wouldn't surprise me if that's why your victim found solace here."

But there are so many different reasons for why people are homeless, so many kinds of psychological and emotional distress, and not all of them have to do with financial needs. Until we knew why she was here—if homelessness was the reason—we'd have no idea with whom she might have come in contact, if her killer was not a total stranger.

"Places to kill someone," Davis said to himself, turning to the map behind him, his hands tucked in his pants pocket. "Starting from the south, one could get lost in the nature sanctuary just off the 59th Street entrance, which is pretty dense and has no formal paths. I've always thought the arches get a bit spooky after dark—Greengap or Driprock or Willowdell—but, hell, they've been used in a thousand movies and crime shows. Way too obvious."

The Davis deadpan made it impossible to tell whether he was serious or joking around, but most of the men were furiously writing down the names of Park sites—obscure to most of us but clearly Davis's home territory—in their memo pads.

"The polar bear den at the zoo is a natural—but then, this girl wasn't mauled, was she? Literary Walk is one of my favorite places. Your victim would have to be a writer, though, if put to death somewhere between the statues of Sir Walter Scott and William Shakespeare."

"How many statues you got in here anyway?" McAvoy asked.

"Thirty-six. But they don't make good places to hide." Davis's long slender fingers moved deftly over the map. "Simon Bolivar, Hans Christian Andersen, Alexander Hamilton . . ."

"How many of the statues are women?" I said, smiling at the commissioner.

"Two, young lady. Alice in Wonderland and Mother Goose."

As a kid, I had always wondered why there weren't any women important enough to be commemorated in the City's great park. "I could nominate a few real ones."

"I'd appreciate that," Davis said. "Back to crime scenes. Strawberry Fields—makes me sad to think that the guy who killed John Lennon spent the whole afternoon before the shooting enjoying himself in our Park. The Ramble? That's as good as it gets for being remote. Like a world apart, but it's hiding in plain sight. You've got glacial erratics . . ."

"Erotic what?" Same guy, Major Case squad.

"Erratic. Something like yourself. Glacial rock deposited thousands of years ago on top of bedrock that's entirely different in composition. One of my recurrent nightmares is a tourist being crushed by one of those glacials toppling off its base. We wouldn't find him—or her—for years. The Great Lawn, if you don't mind an audience. The Loch, the Ravine, the North Woods, the Harlem Meer. What do you think, gentlemen? This Park is probably the size of four or five of your precincts—and yet there's only a fraction of the crime in here. I can think of dozens of places to kill someone, although I can't imagine depositing the deceased in the Lake, as this guy did."

"I'll bite," Manny Chirico said. "Why not?"

"Because it's clear she's going to be found. A few of the spots I've mentioned, it could be forever before somebody came upon her. In any of the grottoes, under one of the waterfalls in the Ravine—hell, if you're dumping her in a body of water, she's a lot more likely to bottom out in the Reservoir, which is enormous."

"So the killer wants to be caught," I said.

"No killer wants to be caught, Coop. Did you drop out of Psych 101 in favor of English lit?" Mike's friends laughed with him. "If they wanted to be caught, we'd be out of business and schmucks would just be lining up at the courthouse to throw themselves at you. Norman Bates had his mother up in the bedroom for how many years? You didn't have to look far, but he didn't want to be caught. Bonnie and Clyde? They left bodies in every bank from Louisiana to New Mexico, in plain sight. No desire to be riddled with bullets in a police ambush. Son of Sam? Murder after murder, they're all strangers to him, and he's nailed by a parking ticket. Psychobabble at its best, Madame Prosecutor. If he wanted to be caught, where the hell is he? And Commissioner Davis didn't say anything about what the killer wanted for himself; he said the killer wanted his *victim* to be found. He left her in the heart of Central Park, in the heart of this city."

"A man who listens to me," Davis said, cocking his head and turning on his most electric smile. "A rare and wonderful thing. I'm guessing you two are married, the way you talk to each other."

Mike blushed while he protested, and half the guys in the room guffawed.

"Just lovers," I said to the commissioner. "Not married yet."

The room went instantly quiet. McAvoy scoped his team—some bemused and others smirking, homicide detectives looked from one another to the lieutenant—and I was paranoid to read into all of the glances that each of them knew about Jessica Pell's threat to bring Mike down. Manny Chirico acted like he was ready to gag me.

"May I ask you something about Seneca Village, Commissioner?"

"Sure, Ms. Cooper. What would you like to know?"

"You may have heard about some objects that were recovered near the Lake on Friday."

"Actually, I don't know anything about them."

"Well, one was a figure of an angel. It appears to be quite old—I can show you a photo after the meeting—and she's black. A detective told me about Seneca Village, and I was wondering if this artifact might have come from there."

Davis put his finger to his lips, and his brow wrinkled as he thought. He took a few minutes to describe the short history of Seneca to the group.

"I wouldn't have any idea about the source of your object, but there's no access to the area of the village right now," he said. "The last excavation was in 2011, by the archaeologists from Columbia."

"Digs?" I asked. "They opened the area?"

"Very carefully executed and supervised, Ms. Cooper. They used ground-penetrating radar to study the village, using it to detect what was a rich trove of artifacts."

"What did they find?" Peterson asked.

"Most significantly, the walls of the home of the sexton of one of the churches in the village. All Angels' Church."

I slipped my phone out of my pocket and tried to avoid distracting the others by holding it in my lap to pull up the photo of the ebony angel.

"They found remnants of clothing, some ceramics, butchered animal bones—really a fascinating record of the kind of life these people led. Most of the dig is preserved on video. Radar allowed the scholars to keep it very narrowly confined so they neither destroyed any remaining structures nor disturbed the five cemeteries that remain under the Park."

"Cemeteries under here?" someone murmured. "That's creepy."

"But now, Commissioner, could someone access those areas today?"

"That wouldn't be possible, Ms. Cooper. After the dig, the soil and plantings were completely restored. The men who work in that zone would have noticed any attempt to interfere with the ground cover. Why?" Davis asked. "These objects you're talking about, do you think they're connected to the murder?"

Peterson moved to the front of the room, next to Davis. "We'll get back to you on that, Commissioner, once we've gotten further along with our investigation."

"But why did you ask, Ms. Cooper?" Davis wasn't easily put off.

"It's like what you said about the girl's body."

"What? That the killer wouldn't have put her in the Lake unless he wanted her to be found?"

"Yes. You've got half the NYPD doing a strip search of your Park. There's no garbage, of course. We get that's a cardinal sin. So they're not wasting any time picking up candy wrappers and soda bottles. But they find three objects—each of which looks antique, and each of which is not a child's toy or a broken sailboat—three objects that appear to be of substance and of value, on the shore of the Lake, just dozens of yards from the girl's body. We've got no other leads at this point, so perhaps you should take a look at them."

"I'm happy to do that," Davis said. "Maybe your killer wanted them to be discovered."

"Or maybe," I said, "maybe it's our victim who's talking to us."

Mike stopped shaking his head and picked it up to stare at me.

"Could be the dead girl," I said, "who's leaving us a sign. Could be she's the one who wanted something to be found."

TWELVE

I knew that would get Mike's attention. Like most good homicide detectives, Mike developed a special bond with his victims. It started at the scene of the crime, when he saw the body at its worst, with the reveal of all that the murderer had done to take a human life. How much force, how many blows, what kind of injuries and how many of them were needed to cause death or were just an additional outpouring of some interpersonal venom.

He was there for the autopsy, when the brilliant pathologists coaxed more of the story from the bones and the tissue, the trunk and the limbs of the deceased.

And then he stayed on it, with fierce determination and a unique skill set—part from his father's DNA and the rest from his own training and experience—until he could see that some measure of justice was done.

The detectives hammered Commissioner Davis with questions for another hour. We took notes of every mention, interested as always to see in how many different directions each one of these investigators could go with the same information.

The meeting broke up at two o'clock, most of the men as anxious to grab lunch as they were to get back to work.

Davis had invited Peterson, Chirico, Mike, and me to come to his office and had instructed his assistant to call out for sandwiches.

While he returned some of the calls that had come in during our session, Sergeant Chirico took me aside, steering me by the elbow into an alcove outside Davis's office.

"It doesn't help things if you start going rogue on me, Alex. Jumping up on the table in the boathouse to threaten to take your clothes off, letting go with a line about being lovers in front of the whole gang . . ."

"Look at the faces of your men, Sarge. I don't think Judge Pell's wrath is a well-kept secret. And according to Vickee, DCPI might as well put out a press release confirming that Mike and I are a couple. Whatever plan you think you have, I'm guessing it's too subtle. I think you need to fight Pell's fire with fire."

"How?"

I exhaled. "I don't know. Let me think about it. You just can't let her win this battle."

"Alex? Manny?" Peterson called from down the hallway. "Where are you two?"

We walked back to the commissioner's office in silence, past the handsome murals of nineteenth-century soldiers in formation, a reminder of the original purpose of the building.

Davis asked to see the three photographs I had taken of the vouchered items. He studied the angel with intense focus. "All I can suggest is sending someone to the Columbia group with this figure, to see if it looks like anything they uncovered in the dig."

"Will do," Mike said.

"And these miniature statues of the fort and the Obelisk, they're really interesting. Do they have any maker's marks?"

"I left them at the lab the other day, just to see if they might have any forensic evidence on them. But that was a negative. So once the mud is off them, we can check for that."

"What I need to do, Detective, is introduce you to the head of the Conservancy. This is the kind of thing that looks unusual enough that she or someone on her staff might be familiar with it."

"That would be great," Mike said, steno pad in hand to take down her information.

"Her name is Mia Schneider. My secretary will give you her number. But she's out of town for another two days, and no one knows the Park's history as well as she does."

"Then I'll pick them up tomorrow and be ready when she's back on Wednesday or Thursday."

"I can do better than that," Davis said. "Wednesday evening is the annual Conservancy fund-raiser. It's held in the Park—in the Conservatory Garden. It's a pretty spectacular way to see Central Park. My wife and I have a table. Why don't you be my guest, Detective? I can introduce you to anyone connected to the operation that you might need to know."

"Thanks, sir, but I can't—"

Gordon Davis's eyes twinkled as he talked. "Sure you can, can't he, Lieutenant? Hell, you can even bring your—Ms. Cooper here."

"We're not really involved," I said. "I was just joking."

Davis liked being mischievous. "I've got a sense of humor. I can roll with that."

"It's a good idea for you to go, Mike," the lieutenant said. "Alone."

"Sure," Davis said. "After all, what if one of the zookeepers is the killer? Or a trustee? Might as well get to know the players. See them in their natural habitat."

"Loo, I think the commissioner's right," Manny Chirico said. "No disrespect, Loo, but I think Alex needs to go with Mike. I'll explain my reasoning later."

Chirico clamped his lips together and nodded at me. If he didn't have a plan to deal with Jessica Pell earlier, he was developing one now.

Mike planted his left hand on his hip, and the fingers of his right hand began working his hair. "Bad idea, Sarge. Let's save the dirty laundry for when we get out of the commissioner's office, but me and Coop? Not happening."

Davis pointed a finger at Mike. "I'm expecting you, Chapman. You and Ms. Cooper. Don't disappoint me."

"I know Coop looks very *Downton Abbey* on the outside, Commissioner, but this broad is totally *Homeland.* There's a Carrie Mathison inside her, obsessed with me like I'm Nick Brody, waiting to burst out," Mike said, faking half a smile, "and I'd just hate to see it in full bloom at your fund-raiser."

"Black tie, Detective. Cocktails at six, dinner at seven." Davis said, dismissing us. "Anything else right now, Lieutenant Peterson?"

"Thanks, sir. Thanks for your time."

Davis's secretary gave us a small office so that we could eat our sandwiches. I carried them in, and Mike slammed the door behind me.

"Deal breaker. I don't own a tux, Loo."

"It's a good opportunity, just like Davis says. Rent one."

"I've got to spend a hundred bucks to go to fund-raiser for the squirrels and wildflowers?"

"Use some of the dough you made on all that overtime guarding Judge Pell," the sergeant said before biting into his roast beef sandwich.

"Whew, Manny," Mike said. "We're into tough love now, I guess."

"Don't let it ruin your appetite, Mike. I've been thinking about how we deal with Pell and—"

I tipped my chair back and shook my head so the sergeant could see me. I didn't want him blaming—or crediting me—with his strategy.

"I just think we're smarter to draw her out. That's why I think it's a good idea to send Alex with Mike to the Park on Wednesday night. To let them keep working together. If that smokes Pell out into the open, all the better for us. Any other way, she wins."

I munched on a corner of my turkey wrap.

"And if this gets to Scully?" the lieutenant asked. "It's the mayor who appointed Pell."

"For all the wrong reasons," I said. "And it's the same mayor who appointed Scully, too. That's the good news."

"So far I'm in charge of dealing with Pell," Chirico said. "We'll try it my way. What's the rest of the day?"

"I'm heading back out to see how the canvass is going," Mike said.

"Me, too. I mean, not the same place you'll be, but that's what I'm going to do," I said.

"Tomorrow morning I'll pick up the statues and bring them down to the office. Your photography unit can document them, and you can set someone on tracing them."

"I'll be free as soon as Battaglia finishes with me."

"What does he want?" Mike asked.

"I can only guess, but I think it has to do with a pound of my flesh."

Peterson and Chirico were finishing their lunch and ready to leave. "I've had two teams working since yesterday morning on circulating the girl's photo to some of the homeless shelters. I'd better get a buzz on that," Peterson said. "And I'm calling SVU. We might as well bring Mercer back in on this, along with some of their other senior people."

Mercer had been in Homicide for years before asking for the transfer to Special Victims. He liked the rapport he developed with survivors of sexual assault, helping them triumph in the courtroom and restoring their dignity. Mike preferred work that did not involve hand-holding the victim. He saved his compassion for the dead.

Mike and I walked out behind them. "Are you going back to the Point?" I asked him.

"Nah. I've had my excitement for the day. I'm going to try the other side of Bow Bridge. See what the shoreline looks like over there. You?"

"Bethesda Terrace." It was where all the gathered information was being centrally reported to one of the sergeants from Intel. "Best place for me to keep up to speed."

We fell back behind the bosses as we walked out of the Arsenal. "How late are you staying?"

"Don't know. It's getting close to the longest day of the year. Till it gets dark, I guess."

Many of the Park regulars had evening rituals—jogging, biking, blading, dog walking, in the hours after work. If there had been any kind of confrontation between our victim and her assailant that started at dusk or in early darkness, these would be the people who might have snippets of information.

"So how about if I pick you up at Bethesda at nine tonight? We knock off and have dinner?"

I turned to look at Mike, puzzled by his offer. He was running so hot and cold, frazzled by Pell's threats and frustrated by the lack of progress in the case, that I still didn't know how read him. "Me?"

"Is there anyone else in earshot?"

"You must have started at five A.M. today. You know they won't pay you OT for this?"

"Like I'm in it for the big bucks, blondie? It's my case, remember? And it's Mercer's idea to have dinner."

"Then I'll see you at nine," I said. "Thanks for including me."

Mike called out to the lieutenant and caught up with his two supervisors. I walked behind the building and headed north again, cutting across paths until I got to the foot of the Promenade on the Mall, walking that single straight line right to Bethesda Terrace.

The rest of the afternoon and evening was uneventful. Tourists were curious about the massive police presence, so it seemed as though as many people were stopping to ask us questions as there were to answer them.

Most of the Park regulars were willing to be helpful, pausing to express concern, ask who the dead girl was, and offer advice of every kind. Police noted descriptions of men who had shouted obscene comments to women joggers, men who had come on to college students in bikinis spread out on blankets on the Great Lawn, and men who had been rowboating on the Lake.

The cops had me spend an hour with an NYU professor who encouraged me to study Dreiser's *An American Tragedy* to see if there were any clues in that classic about the drowning of a poor working girl—knocked out of a rowboat in a lake—by the boy-friend who'd found a richer prospect he wanted to marry.

By the end of the day, we had thousands of generic descriptions of unpleasant men who frequented the Park. We had nothing that remotely pointed to a killer.

Shortly after nine, Mike pulled up in his car on the roadway adjacent to the Terrace.

"How do you do this grueling legwork day after day?" I asked him. "I'm beat."

"Beat is good," he said. "As long as you're hungry, too."

"Thirsty."

"Even better. Mercer's holding a table for us at Patroon."

"Now I'm hungry and thirsty. Nothing could make me happier."

We headed east, down to 46th Street between Lexington and Third Avenues, where my friends Ken and Di Aretsky owned one of the classiest restaurants in the city. Patroon featured the best steaks in town, and a grilled Dover sole that was off the charts. Ken was as nice as anyone in the business, providing a clubby atmosphere that ensured relaxation as much as it did fine dining. And he had been a great resource for Luc Rouget when my Frenchman had tried to open a fancy restaurant in New York earlier this year. Mercer and Mike were taking me to one of the places that I was most comfort-able, most pampered.

Mike was moving swiftly down Fifth Avenue. There was no traffic, and we had the lights with us. "You know why those two dudes—Mr. Olmsted and your buddy Vaux—you know why those guys beat out all the other landscapers who entered the contest to design the Park?"

"I just assumed they had the most experience."

"What experience? This was the very first landscaped urban park in America."

"So what then?"

"There were thirty-three official entries," Mike said. "But your guys were the only ones who insisted that the Park—to work as an artistic pastoral landscape—had to be completely separated from the city streets. No coal wagons or fire engines or dust carts wandering through it."

"That makes sense."

"It was their plan—Olmsted and Vaux—to sink all the transverse roads, the ones that cut east to west from Fifth Avenue to Central Park West, below the road surface."

Of course Mike was right.

"Four huge transverse roads and they're all below the surface of the Park grounds," he said. "That's ingenious. No commercial vehicles at all on Park drives, and nothing that even obstructed any of the views. Pretty damn clever."

"It is. But you're thinking about something. About the case."

"Yeah."

"That most dump jobs would involve a car, right?"

"Yeah. That if our girl was killed somewhere else—'cause there's no sign of a struggle near the Lake, and no drag marks around it—then she's likely to have been killed somewhere else in Manhattan and then dumped from a car."

"And since there are no transverse roads anywhere near the Lake, the closest place a car could have stopped is where you just picked me up, on top of the grand staircase at Bethesda Terrace."

"And the Park is closed to traffic from seven P.M. to seven A.M., so that pretty much means if the killer came by car, he would have been hauling the body in broad daylight, at the height of tourist season."

"Impossible."

"So where did he come from, Coop?"

"How I wish I knew."

We were silent until we reached the restaurant and parked several spaces away from the front door. Annie, the hostess, greeted us with her characteristic enthusiasm, and Stephane, who had been maître d' from opening day, escorted us to the tiny elevator.

"Mr. Wallace is waiting for you upstairs," Stephane said. "*Comment ça va*, Ms. Cooper? I haven't seen Mr. Rouget in quite some time."

I swallowed hard. "You know it's his busiest time back in France."

"*Bien sur.* I hope you're managing well without him."

"Fine, thank you."

The door opened onto the fourth-floor landing. Patroon was one of the only restaurants in the city to boast a rooftop dining area. The fresh air on this late spring night was exhilarating, and the crowd around the bar made it all so cheerful and refreshing.

Ken was sitting at a corner table with Mercer. They both stood up as we approached, and we exchanged kisses.

"You didn't happen to TiVo *Jeopardy!* for me tonight?" Mike asked Ken.

"Give me a break, Mike." Ken looked dapper, as always, with his custom-tailored suit, a Turnbull & Asser shirt, and horn-rimmed glasses. "I didn't know you were coming in until after the show was over. I'll buy you a drink instead."

"That's a good way to start. At least it will cover my wager. Mercer? Did you see it?"

"Yes, I did. And I lost."

"What was the category?"

"Russian literature."

"I'm screwed again. Make it a double, Ken."

"The answer was something about a Russian nobleman and poet whose great-grandfather was African."

"Who is Doctor Zhivago?" Mike said.

"And he would be a fictional character," I said. "Like Alice in Wonderland, Mother Goose, and Norman Bates."

"You don't know either, really?" Mike said. "Two nights running? That's not possible."

"Don't humor him, Alex," Mercer said. "He can deal with it."

"Alexander Pushkin. Peter the Great adopted a young Ethiopian boy as a member of the royal family. I guess that was better than enslaving him. Anyway, he was the poet's ancestor."

Ken knew our drinks and sent over a round for the table. Mike and Mercer ordered the porterhouse for two, I asked for the grilled sole, and Mike piled on all the sides he could think of—fries, onion rings, crispy brussels sprouts, sautéed spinach, and a salad for each of us.

I sipped the Scotch and leaned my head back, knowing it was hopeless to look for the same stars I had seen over the weekend. The city sky was just a milky gray.

"You're coming into the case," Mike said to Mercer.

"I know. Peterson called the office this afternoon. Told me to meet you at the lab in the morning."

Mike asked him to take the small black statuette from there up to the Columbia archaeology team to see if he could get a provenance on it.

We spent the next hour telling Mercer everything we'd learned about the Park and how unsettling it was not to be able to figure out how the body wound up in the Lake.

"And the girl? What's her name?" Mercer asked.

"Don't know," I said.

"I understand that. I meant Mike's name for her."

Mike always gave his victims a name. It was another way for him to humanize them, even when we didn't know their identities. Sometimes he'd gotten heat for his bad taste, like the time a hooker was found in a cardboard shipping container on the sidewalk in Hell's Kitchen. Foxy—his sobriquet for the fox in the box—found its way into the *Post* coverage of the case. He'd become gentler in the years since that embarrassment.

"There's only one thing to call her," Mike said. "Till someone puts a name to that sorry face, she's Angel."

THIRTEEN

"Is anyone in there with him?" I asked Rose on my way into Battaglia's office.

"No, he's alone."

I had spent the first two hours of the morning returning yesterday's calls and setting up a case file for all the reports from the squads and foot soldiers taking note of everything that happened in the Park. Then Battaglia arrived at 10:30 and called for me.

"If I scream for you, Rose, come bail me out."

She continued filing the DA's massive amount of incoming mail rather than make eye contact with me.

"Good morning, Paul."

"Morning," he said, turning away from the computer screen where he'd been checking the stock market's opening activity. "How long are we going to drag this thing out?"

He reached for a match and lit the cigar that was clenched between his teeth.

"I'd like to think until we solved it, but I imagine the department will give it one week of going through the Park with a fine-tooth comb and then back off."

"It's one thing to put all this manpower into a case if it looks like we can make it. It's quite another to have you all out there spinning wheels and getting nowhere."

"I wish I could agree with you."

"What?" He cupped his good ear and turned it to me. "Now, what's all this crap going on with you and Chapman? Jessica Pell called me at home on Sunday."

"She's crazy."

"She's not so crazy that she doesn't know what's going on before I do. You swore to me a couple of years ago that you and Mike were just buddies. I wouldn't have let you work cases with him if I thought you two had crossed that line."

"I told you the truth then and it's still the truth today. Even though it's none of your business."

"That time I heard you, Alexandra," Battaglia said, removing the cigar from his mouth to articulate more clearly. "Everything that happens in this courthouse is my business."

"But—"

"I won't have you trying murder cases with your main witness on the stand, and some high-powered, high-priced mouthpiece cross-examining him, asking whether he held a gun to the suspect's head because his demanding girlfriend won't let him back in bed if he doesn't come home with a confession." Battaglia stabbed at his desktop with his forefinger. "Are you or aren't you?"

"Am I what?" I was standing in front of the DA, flushed with anger and defiance.

"Are you in bed with Mike Chapman?"

"I was stupid enough to answer you once. Now you'll have to decide for yourself whether it matters because I'm declaring that subject off-limits for discussion between us. You've got five hundred lawyers in this office. Are you policing all of their bedrooms, Paul? 'Cause that is one monstrous job, if you're up to it."

"I'm not policing anything. You've got the high-profile cases, Alex. You live in the glare of the lights, if you can."

"You put me in that position years ago, Paul. I can live with that, and with whatever I choose to do."

"Where are you going?"

"Back to work."

"Consider yourself lucky that I did this one-on-one. I left McKinney out of it. I'm not trying to hurt you, Alex. There are things I just need to know."

"How fortunate can I be? There's your man McKinney, who left his wife and kids for one of your least-talented lawyers—the laughingstock of the trial division, really—whom you only hired because her mother, at the time, was a major television news reporter. See what that got you, Paul? The mother lost her job because of some on-air tirade, and you're stuck with the harebrained kid, who sits in the chief's office all day drinking tea and mooning at him. Shall I move on to the next bedroom?"

"Don't walk out on me," Battaglia shouted as I headed for the door.

"I'll be back as soon as I have case news to report. If it's gossip you want, I'm pretty much up to speed on that, too. My sources are even more reliable than yours."

I swept past Rose's desk and back to my own. Laura was in my office, helping Mike unwrap the two metal miniatures of Park landmarks.

"Hey, Mike. Everything okay?"

"Yeah. Mercer's on his way to Columbia, and the lab cleaned up these little beauties for me."

The castle and obelisk had both been given a bath. Mike handed me Cleopatra's Needle, and I turned it upside down. Engraved on the bottom was the name of the silversmith who had designed the objects and the year in which they were made: Gorham and Frost. 1910.

"Laura, have you tried to call information?"

"The company doesn't exist anymore, Alex. I've called and checked online."

"Surely these must be part of a larger set."

"Could be any of the structures in the Park that existed by that time," Mike said.

"And they must be extremely rare. I can't imagine they were lying around the Park very long or they would have been picked up. By a groundskeeper or a thief. They're really quite beautiful."

"I've called the Conservancy," Mike said. "They're going to check records to see whether they can connect them to any exhibits they've ever had. Our best bet may be the Schneider woman, when we see her tomorrow night. Gordon Davis says she's a walking history of the Park."

"Shall we take them up to be photographed?"

"Yeah."

"We'll be back in half an hour, Laura. Hold the needy at bay for me, please."

Mike and I had enough case-related things to discuss to keep away from the personal. I didn't tell him about Battaglia's comments, or about my answers.

After we left the photo unit, I said good-bye to Mike at the elevators.

Back at my desk, I went through the list of parolees that Laura had assembled, but none matched the description of the man in the Ramble yesterday morning. I busied myself with the flood of anonymous tips that accompanied this kind of case, and with catching up on the cases of the other lawyers in the unit.

My posse of close friends—Nan, Catherine, Marisa—made a point of coming by at lunchtime with salads, to see if they could take any assignments over for me.

At the end of the day, having heard nothing else from Mercer or Mike, I went home and ignored the television, ordering in from my local deli. I drew a deliciously scented hot bath and relaxed for the evening.

This was the rhythm of many major cases I'd worked. Things started off with a frenetic unfolding of evidence and information and, if not solved immediately, settled into peaks and valleys of developments. I was glad to have this night alone to myself.

The first time the phone rang it was close to 10:30. I was in my den, in a bathrobe, enjoying my drink.

The incoming number was Mercer's. I was hoping he had information about Seneca Village.

"Hey. Good to hear from you."

"Not so good as you think, Alex."

I sat up straight and dropped the book I'd been reading onto the floor.

"What is it?"

"An attempted rape."

"Damn. How's the victim?"

"She's going to be okay. I'm with her at the hospital now."

"Did they get the guy?"

"Not yet. And it was after dark, so she's not sure she can make an ID."

"Thanks for the heads-up, Mercer." He was good to call me so I could arrange for someone to handle the new matter first thing in the morning. Even though there was no arrest, someone in the unit could get started working with the victim. "It's more than that," Mercer said. "The attack was in Central Park."

"What the hell—? What's going on?"

"Don't know. I just don't know."

"But the Park is flooded with cops."

"Not the north end. Most of the police presence has been south of 80th Street since Friday."

"Where did this happen?"

"Up north. At the foot of the Ravine, at about 106th Street. Just under Huddlestone Arch."

And yesterday Gordon Davis had remarked on how spooky the arches get after dark.

"So because it's only an attempt, I take it there's no seminal fluid. No DNA."

"Very little to go on, Alex. Medium-complexion black man. Average height, average weight. The only thing our vic is sure of is that the guy had a tattoo on his hand. Two words—not pictures—but she couldn't make them out."

Kill, I said to myself. I didn't want to speak the whole expression out loud. A rapist on the loose with KILL COOP inked into his skin.

FOURTEEN

"I'm Alexandra Cooper. I work with Mercer," I said to the woman who was sitting in a small office near the Emergency Room at Mount Sinai Hospital. "I'm with the DA's Office Special Victims Unit."

By the time I was off the phone with Mercer, the police car he'd sent to pick me up was in front of my building.

"Look, I just want to go home, okay? I don't have anything else to say."

"I know it's late and I know you've been through an ordeal, but I'd appreciate it if you could answer a few more questions for me."

Flo Lamont was still in a hospital gown, waiting while the advocate who was part of SAVI—the hospital's Sexual Assault and Violence Intervention program—brought her a clean T-shirt with which to leave the hospital. Her legs were jiggling nervously as she listened to me.

"I want to go over what happened to you one more time, in a little more detail."

The uniformed cops had gotten all of Flo's pedigree information. The nineteen-year-old African American woman lived with her mother in Schomburg Plaza, a high-rise complex just across

110th Street from the Park. She worked in the shipping department at Macy's.

"You're not gonna find this dude, you know? I don't see why it matters."

"Mercer's really good at what he does," I said. "He might surprise you."

Flo looked up at her detective and then looked him over, up and down. "But the guy didn't do anything to me."

"That's not exactly how I'd describe things," Mercer said, although that's the way many victims described an uncompleted attempt to commit this brutal crime. "And it's only because you fought him off that he didn't finish what he set out to do."

The 61—the complaint report that the first uniformed responder scratched out—was only two sentences long: "At the T/P/O—time and place of occurrence—an unknown M/B threatened Flo Lamont with a lead pipe and attempted to have intercourse with her. Lamont resisted and attacker fled."

Those few words were enough to send someone to state prison for fifteen years if he was apprehended. But it was the detail missing from the summary of the elements of the crime that might determine if we would ever connect this assailant to Flo's case.

The rookies who'd encountered Flo, after a young couple looking for a secluded place to hang out heard her screams, asked her hardly any questions at all. She was sobbing and shaking, so they put her in their patrol car and made the short trip down to Madison Avenue and 100th Street, to the Sinai ER.

Those cops were required to turn the case over to Special Victims detectives, who had the expertise to do more in-depth questioning in a compassionate manner, which is part of what made them qualified for such sensitive work. Although Mercer wasn't catching new cases because of his assignment to Angel's homicide, his boss wanted him to go out on this one in case there was any connection between the two.

"You gonna tell my mother about this?" Flo asked, massaging her left shoulder with her right hand.

"You're nineteen," Mercer said. "We don't need to tell your mother anything."

"Them cops kept asking me why I was in the Park after dark. Like I was doing something wrong."

"We know you weren't doing anything wrong," Mercer said. He pulled up a second chair and sat opposite Flo, so he could talk to her eye-to-eye. "I'm going to ask you why you were in the Park, also. But only because that's where this crime happened. I have to know why you were there and what you were doing—just like I'd ask if this had happened in a school or in an office building. I'm not accusing you of anything."

"The Park is like my backyard. I been going in it to play since I was a kid."

"I grew up in Queens, right near a big park. Not as nice as this one, though nothing is. I spent half my life in that park."

Flo picked her head up again and looked at Mercer. She was trying to use her street sense to see whether he was someone she could trust or not. I needed him to get her to lose her attitude so I could jump in and retrieve some more facts.

When the cops had asked her what she was doing in the Park at 9:30 at night, Flo's answer to them had been "Nothing."

"Most of the time, when I went to the park to do sports," Mercer said, "it was daytime. When I went there at night, it was usually to meet up with friends. How about you?"

"Sometimes I go there to get away from people. Just like to be by myself."

"Was tonight one of those nights? You wanted to be alone?"

Flo nodded her head up and down.

"I have plenty of times like that. Who were you getting away from?"

"A guy."

"Your boyfriend?"

Flo sneered and suppressed a laugh. "Sometimes."

"You want to tell me his name?"

"No chance. He have nothing to do with this."

"Fair enough."

She checked Mercer's face again to see if he was sincere about that.

"Were you with him before you went into the Park, or were you coming from home?"

"With him. Hanging out on 110th."

"Till he said something stupid to you, and you got mad and crossed the street."

Flo tilted her head. "Now, how you know that?"

Mercer smiled at her. "'Cause he's a guy. That's what guys do half the time. Hanging out on a beautiful night with a nice girl, and we blow it. Say something, do something stupid. Am I right? Then you headed off to—I don't know—someplace that's special to you two. Someplace you go to be together 'cause you knew he'd follow you eventually. Try to make it right."

Flo stopped bouncing her legs. She was completely fixed on Mercer.

"I don't know about making it right," she said, leaning forward to play with Mercer a bit, "but I know he'd want to get him some before he went home for the night."

"His loss," Mercer said. "Totally his loss. So where were you headed?"

"You know the waterfall?"

"All three of them."

"The big one. The one closest to where I came in."

Among the most beautiful creations in the Park were the three waterfalls in the Ravine, north of 102nd Street. They looked as natural as any country scene or wilderness preserve but were completely man-made. They were so carefully engineered more than 150 years ago that each was designed to be entirely different from the others. The rocks were set at different distances so the sound of the water cascading was unique to each site, depending on the height of the drop and the size of the boulders below.

"I know it. Is that your spot?"

"Yes," Flo said. "Leastways it was until tonight."

"You were just going to hang out by the waterfall?"

"There's actually a little ledge inside it. You know, behind the fall?"

"I didn't know that. Did you, Alex?"

Mercer would draw me in now, getting ready to turn his witness over to me.

"I had no idea."

Flo was happy to show off her knowledge. "You just get like a little wet passing in, but then you can sit and look out. Kind of a cool thing. It's like a little cave, almost."

"A cave?" My interest was as piqued as Mercer's. "You can go inside it?"

"Not really. It's sort of a dug-out space behind the waterfall. I used to hide out there with my friends when we were kids. Me and my boyfriend—like two of us could just fit there for a while. You know, like sitting and talking is all."

I wondered how many cave-like places there could be in this massive Park, with all the rock outcroppings and formations that had been styled to build up the ground surface.

"Did you tell the cops that you were on your way to the waterfall?"

Flo frowned at me. "They was so not interested in me once I told them I went in there alone. They didn't need to know nothing else."

"We want it all," Mercer said.

There was a knock on the door, and one of the young advocates introduced herself and handed me a clean T-shirt and a pair of hospital pajama bottoms for Flo.

"Why don't Mercer and I step out so you can get dressed? I'm sure you'll be more comfortable out of that gown."

"I want my own shirt. I wanna go home in my own clothes."

"We need your clothes," Mercer said, trying to calm the reagitated young woman. "They're evidence."

Mercer had showed me the three items he had collected from the RN who'd done the forensic exam. The yellow cotton halter top had been ripped off Flo by its thin strap. Her shorts were torn as well and covered in dirt, just like her underpants.

"It's after eleven o'clock, Flo. Will your mother be waiting up for you?" Mercer asked.

"No. She don't wait up."

"I'll drive you home. She won't see you this way."

"What do my clothes prove?"

"For one thing, the tears in the fabric show the force this man used. And the fact that you were on your back, rolling in the dirt—"

"But you ain't never gonna find this guy, so what's the difference what I say?" Flo stood up and started to take off the gown. The cuts and scratches on her back, from where she had rolled on the ground on stones and twigs, were deepening in color. They were more intense than the digital shots that had been taken in the ER, so we would need to get another set, showing the progression of the bruising, within the next twenty-four hours.

I followed Mercer out of the room. Within seconds Flo called out to us that it was okay to come in.

Mercer held the chair out so she would sit down again. "Alex and I have worked these cases together for a very long time. The men who do this? For the most part, Flo, they're pretty damn stupid. They get away with it once or twice, but not for long."

"And what really makes them extra stupid," I said, "is that once they attack one or two women, they get really comfortable doing it the same way. They think that if it worked for them once, it will work that way every time. I know you didn't tell those two cops much—"

"Why should I? They acted like I was some kind of whore."

"This will be the last time they do anything like that," I said. "I promise you."

"So it's the detail we want to get from you, Flo," Mercer said. "Sometimes, just the way a guy does things, the words he uses—we can maybe tie him to another case like yours, one where a girl wasn't as smart as you were or as brave."

"Talked crazy is what he did. Grabbed me and threw me down. Total crazy badass guy."

"Start from where you walked into the Park on the corner of 110 and Fifth," Mercer said. "Were you alone?"

"I was by myself, if that's what you mean. But there were lots of people around at nine o'clock, inside the Park and out."

Flo walked us from the entrance to her route on the pathway that took her halfway around the Harlem Meer, the latter word being Dutch for "lake." She told us that she hadn't encountered anyone she knew, and that she wasn't alone until she turned off the wide walk to head for the Ravine.

"Do you know where Huddlestone Arch is?" Mercer asked.

"Yeah. That's where this guy was waiting for me, when I came out of Huddlestone."

"Did you see him up ahead?"

"Nah. It's like a little tunnel, you know. All dark inside till you come out the other end. I was looking back over my shoulder half the time."

"For that fool who let you walk away?" Mercer said.

Flo laughed nervously. "Yeah. For him."

"Did you hear anything?"

"Not at first. I mean, just the sound of the water kind of whooshing through."

"Then what happened?"

"I heard him before I saw him. I heard him, like he was talking to his dog. Nothing strange about that. He was calling to his dog, like, 'Here, Buster. Come back to me.'"

Who did I know with a dog named Buster? It sounded familiar to me, which was a minor distraction from Flo's story.

"Then he was like blocking the end of the tunnel, asking me if I saw his dog."

"Did you?" I asked. "Did you see the dog?"

Flo looked at me as though I was off base. "Dog? That boy didn't have no dog."

Both Mercer and I knew what was coming next.

"But I turned to look behind me and that's when he grabbed me."

"Grabbed you how?" I asked.

"Yoked me," she said, hooking her right arm across her neck. "Yoked me and bent me over backward so my knees gave out and I fell on the ground, all the time him pulling me off the walkway in between the trees."

"And—?"

"That's when he started yelling crazy stuff at me. Calling me 'bitch.' Telling me I was gonna burn in hell for what I done. Telling me my sister was a devil," Flo said, shaking her head and rubbing her shoulder.

"Your sister?" Mercer asked.

"I don't have a sister. That's what I'm saying 'bout crazy. Then I see his penis."

"Did he let go of you to unzip his pants?" I said.

"Nope. He never let go of me. His pants was already unzipped. He was hard by the time he threw me down."

Perhaps he'd been masturbating in the bushes, like he'd done when he approached the Austin sisters.

"What did he do then, Flo?"

"More crazy talking. He was mad at me for fighting him. That's when he ripped my halter. Tore the thing clear off."

"What kind of crazy talk?" I asked.

Flo kept stroking her shoulder and upper arm, which clearly bothered her. "All about the devil and stuff. But then he wanted *me* to say things. But I didn't want to say 'em. He was all like sitting on top of me, so I couldn't move, and my back was aching from rolling on all those rocks and branches."

"Tell us the words, Flo. Tell us, please, what the man wanted you to say."

"Don't put this in your report, okay?" She was almost squirming in her chair now.

Mercer coaxed her just to repeat what had happened. We knew it wasn't her choice of words; it was her assailant's.

In a voice not much louder than a whisper, Flo said, "'I'm a ho.' He wanted to hear that. Two, three times maybe. He wanted me to tell him how big he was and how much I wanted him inside me."

Tears started to streak down her cheeks as she spoke, and at that moment the whole image began to come together for me.

"He made me use the F-word, saying I needed him to do that to me. But I wasn't saying it loud enough for him," Flo went on. Then she paused and looked at Mercer. "It was almost funny, what crossed my mind. I was so scared my boyfriend would be coming along and he'd see me half naked, saying that to another man, and he'd think I'd gone off and done that to spite him."

The modus operandi that Mercer hoped we might take from Flo's story was coming together. The faked approach that stopped most walkers in their tracks, helping another park person to find a lost dog; the dog's name, Buster; and the same man, a rapist, then demanding that his victim call herself a whore and compliment his private parts and prowess—I actually knew that MO.

"You're almost there," Mercer said.

"It was 'cause I wouldn't talk louder and I wouldn't hold still that he got so mad. Took the piece of pipe out of his back pocket and threatened to bash in my face with it."

He told his victims he'd make them so ugly no man would ever look at them again, beating them to a pulp with a twelve-inch lead pipe.

"He held it right up to my cheek so I could feel the cold metal, so's I knew he wasn't fooling around. That's when I saw he had some words tattooed on his hand," Flo said, touching her cheek with her fingertips. "Looked like two separate words, but it was too dark to read what they said."

"What words did he use when he had the pipe in your face?" I asked.

"He said—he said he'd make me so ugly that no man would ever look at me again."

"I'm glad you didn't let him do that, Flo," Mercer said.

"So then this couple must have come up through the arch. I was thrashing around and screaming again 'cause this maniac was ripping at my shorts, trying to get his business all up in me. And this couple—they was Hispanic, and the guy was really heavyset and tough-looking. I yelled to them for help. That's when the dude got off me and started running, without even zipping up his pants. The Spanish guy is the one who picked me up and walked me out to the cops. He's why I didn't get raped."

"That's what I know." Flo exhaled and sat back in her chair. "That's what happened to me."

"Thank you for giving us all that detail, Flo," I said. "I promise you we're going to find this man. We're going to get him before he does this to anyone else."

She trusted Mercer, but she was pretty well convinced that I was just bluffing. She rolled her eyes and looked up at me. "Now, how you gonna do that, Miss District Attorney?"

"Because you just told me who the crazy man is, Flo."

"No, ma'am," she said, standing up, "I have no idea who he is. I just want to go home now, if you don't mind."

She stepped past me and opened the door to walk out of the room.

I closed it behind her and leaned against it. "There I was, racking my brain to think of all the guys I sent upstate. I never thought of the ones that beat *me*."

Mercer smiled. "You're serious? You know this guy?"

"Crazy-ass dude is right," I said. "Raymond Tanner. Raped

three girls in St. Nicholas Park, looking for his imaginary puppy named Buster."

"Back when? How'd I miss this?"

Tanner's MO was as distinctive a signature as his fingerprints.

"While you were hospitalized, Mercer. After the shooting."

"You tried the case?"

"And lost. Not guilty by reason of insanity. Raymond Tanner should have been behind bars for the rest of his life."

FIFTEEN

I was at my desk at 7:30 on Wednesday morning, pacing in front of the window. Papers were strewn all over the desktop—notes and sketches from Angel's investigation—and on the floor, my Raymond Tanner files.

"You've got to calm yourself, Alex," Mercer said when he arrived fifteen minutes later with coffee and Danish. "The whole department will be on this guy's tail before noon."

"Impossible. I've been up all night. There's still no one picking up phones in admin at the Mental Health Unit at the Fishkill Correctional Facility."

"Scully's on top of it. We pulled photos of Tanner and the entire case folder is up at One PP."

"How come he isn't all over the news this morning?" I asked. "How come there isn't a manhunt for him already?"

"The commissioner first wants to check that Tanner isn't tightly tucked away in his cell at Fishkill. That could put a hitch in your theory."

"I hope Scully has better luck than I do. I've checked our files. We haven't even had a first letter about a fitness hearing yet. This whackjob is supposed to be in a secure facility till I'm in a rocking chair. He's as dangerous a psychopath as they come."

"How'd you treat him in your closing argument?"

"Like the beast he is."

"Well I guess he's had a few years to work on his body art, thinking of you the whole time. That could explain the tattoo."

"Does Scully agree we should look at him for Angel's death?"

"Whoa, Alex. Slow this one down. What's your thinking? Tanner's never killed anybody, has he?"

"Not that we were able to link him to. Where do I start? He likes young girls—teenagers. I know what you're thinking, that Angel is white but Flo is black. Black and white—he's done both."

"Nothing young about the Austin sisters," Mercer said.

"He was just gaming them, I bet. Shock value, but they're not his type. He's at his best in a park setting, though. That's for sure. The three we tagged him for last time were farther uptown in St. Nick's, but he's clearly into Central Park now—as per the Austin sisters as well as last night's attempt. He's an ambush kind of attacker— the foliage in the Park gives him perfect cover to hide and to escape. He carries a lead pipe, and Angel had her head busted open with a weapon like that. No DNA, so maybe she was resisting the assault and Tanner went wild, like he started to do when Flo pushed back."

"Possible."

"Tanner's got a thing for the devil, so maybe he's sending a message to the Angel of the Waters. Not bad for openers, is it, Mercer?"

"Nice circumstantial picture. But that's all you've got and maybe all you're likely to get, so let's keep steady. Stick to what we know."

At 8:01 I sat down and dialed the number again. This time a man answered, identifying himself as the director of the mental facility at Fishkill prison, about an hour and a half north of New York City.

"I'm Alexandra Cooper. I'm bureau chief of the Special Victims

Unit of the Manhattan DA's office. I'm calling to check on one of your prisoners. His name is Raymond Tanner."

"How do you mean, Ms. Cooper? Check on— In what way?"

"I prosecuted Tanner for three rapes. The verdict was NGRI. Last I knew he was institutionalized at Clinton," I said, referring to a maximum security prison tucked away on a bleak stretch of land near the Canadian border. "Our computer system tells me he's under your roof now."

"I don't know all our men by name. I may have to get back to you."

"Tanner's memorable, sir. Three rapes of teenage girls in a park in Harlem, and a suspect in more than five other similar assaults. Has a psych history of auditory hallucinations, regular communications from Lucifer himself."

"Many of our prisoners are in touch with the devil, Ms. Cooper. Directly or indirectly. Let me take your number and call you after I pull the file."

I repeated the number twice. "My purpose is to find out whether Tanner is still in your custody or back at Clinton." I decided not to include a third possibility—that he had fled the prison system and was out on the street. "We're investigating a matter about which he might have information. There are two officers on the highway coming to interview you, so I just wanted to give you the courtesy of a heads-up. Thanks so much."

"And who would those two officers be?" Mercer asked as I hung up the phone.

"I just figured that if I told him he'd lost a prisoner, I might not get a call back so fast. But if Tanner's in the wind and cops are on their way up to speak with him, this guy is far more likely to freak out and tell me to put the brakes on our team."

"And so far you beat the commissioner's office to that call. Drink some coffee. You need all the caffeine you can get to fuel that competitive streak, Alex."

"I would so love to deliver Tanner to Scully," I said, taking the lid off my second container. I scooped some papers off the floor and handed them to Mercer. "See what this bastard did? I'm hoping there's something in these folders that will tell us where he hangs out."

It was eighteen minutes later when the prison administrator called back.

"Ms. Cooper? I don't know how far along your detectives are, but if you can reach them on the highway, it might be good to stop them."

"Why? Is there a problem with Raymond Tanner?"

The three-second hesitation said it all. "We're trying to locate him for you."

"For *me*? Don't your people want to know where he is?"

"Of course we do."

"What are the choices? His cell, the yard, the infirmary, the mess hall? Or could he be back at Clinton?"

"We're working on that, Ms. Cooper."

"I never received notice of a parole hearing or any action suggesting his release was imminent. Are you with me on that?"

"Yes. Yes, but—"

"I'd suggest you get past the 'but' as soon as possible."

The faceless administrator with the mild-mannered voice was slow to respond. "Raymond Tanner has been a model prisoner, Ms. Cooper."

"Sociopaths often are. I assume you're not taken in by that fact."

I'd had a murder case in which the defendant, a parolee, had tutored the warden's children and given piano lessons to his wife. It was part of the well-documented manipulative character of some of the worst homicidal maniacs.

"He's participated in all his compulsory therapeutic programs."

"There is no known therapy for recidivist sex offenders, sir. That's meaningless to me."

"Nine weeks ago, Ms. Cooper, Raymond qualified for two-day passes."

"He *what*?"

"Raymond qualified for work release. Two days each week, he's on an early morning bus to the Bronx and he's back here by late the next evening."

I wanted to reach through the phone line and throttle the administrator, who sounded as though he'd taken horse tranquilizers.

"Right now. Right this very minute, do you know where Raymond Tanner is?"

"Most certainly. He should be at his job today. He's training in food services at a nursing home in the Bronx."

"Give me that name and address, please. And the person he stays overnight with while he's away. We'll need that, too."

"Not without a subpoena."

"Hardball, is it? I'll have one for you shortly."

"Why, Ms. Cooper? Has Raymond done something?"

"What's your worst nightmare about one of your prisoners, sir?"

My rigid attitude was met by silence.

"One more thing, if you'll tell me," I said. "Do you keep a record of your prisoners' tattoos?"

"Yes. Yes, these days we do."

"So tell me about Raymond Tanner, please."

"Give me a minute to examine the file," he said. "Yes. A lot of graphics on his chest, his back, his upper arms."

"Anything to suggest violence?"

"I can't interpret these drawings, Ms. Cooper. Someone will have to do that for you."

"How about his hands. Anything on his hands?"

"No images," he said. "Looks like just words."

Just. Just words. "Is one of them 'kill'?"

"Could be that. It's rough and hard to read, like so many prison tats are. Could say 'kill.' And it looks like the other word is 'coop'—oh, Coop—as in Cooper? Now I see your worry."

"I'm not worried a bit, sir. Tanner's obviously had more than enough time to find me, if that was his primary goal. But I think you ought to be." I thanked him and hung up the phone.

"Tanner's out?" Mercer said.

"No hearing, no notice to us. Model prisoner and all that bullshit."

"Let me call Peterson. He should be the one to give Scully the news."

"Nan opened a grand jury investigation for Angel on Monday. I'll ask her to go in again at ten and start one for Flo." Prosecutors did not have subpoena power. That request for evidence or testimony could only come from one of the six grand juries that sat five days a week for an entire month.

"When did the work release start?" Mercer asked.

"Nine weeks ago. And Dr. Mayes said Angel may have been dead as long as a month or more. Add that point to my list of circumstances."

"Will do."

I switched places with Mercer so he could make the calls, while I went to tell Pat McKinney about the case against Flo and the fact that Raymond Tanner was at large.

I walked toward McKinney's office, but it was still early and he wasn't in yet. I reversed myself and went into the executive wing to tell Paul Battaglia.

The district attorney had heard about the attempted rape in the Park on news radio while being driven down to work. He was waiting for details from me when Rose announced me.

With great skill, Battaglia cross-examined me through the facts of Flo's case. I also explained to him that Tanner might be a person of interest in Angel's case.

"Does Mercer like that idea?"

"It's too early for anyone to know enough to disagree, Paul, don't you think?"

"Never too early for some people to disagree with you, Alex," Battaglia said, striking a match as he clamped a new cigar between his lips and drew on it. "Nice work last night. Now tell Mercer to find the guy before he hurts someone else."

"He's on it."

The morning was a frenetic choreography of phone calls and updates. Lieutenant Peterson put Mercer directly through to Commissioner Scully, Gordon Davis called to ask for the facts of Flo's case, Mercer spent twenty minutes trying to reassure Flo neither her name nor any statements that could identify her would be made public, and the press had started its feeding frenzy with courthouse reporters sniffing around Laura's desk for an inside scoop.

To get away from them, Mercer suggested we move down the hall to the conference room adjacent to Pat McKinney's office. We spread Raymond Tanner's long criminal history out on one side of the table and covered the other with Angel's case, including all of Hal Sherman's photographs of the scene.

I worked the landline and Mercer his cell, with bursts of interruption from Laura as calls continued to pour in.

"I'm switching through the administrator from Fishkill, Alex," Laura said. "He says you spoke with him this morning. I'll put him on this line, okay?"

I signed off with Nan, who was on her way from the grand jury with subpoenas, and picked up the prison admin call.

"I owe you an apology, Ms. Cooper. On Raymond Tanner."

"What is it?"

"I'll give you any information you want."

"My subpoenas are ready."

"Mr. Tanner's first work release date was April 3rd."

"That was more than two and a half months ago," I said.

"He did return regularly for the first six weeks of his release. But it appears he went AWOL in the middle of May."

My temper was ready to flare. "So you have no idea where Raymond Tanner is as we speak, is that correct?"

"I do not."

"What's the name of the nursing home where you placed him?"

"Sunrise Services on Gun Hill Road." His answers were coming faster now. "But he hasn't shown up there in a week."

That fact didn't surprise me in the least.

"And the residential address?" I asked.

"He stays with his grandmother on the Concourse. The exact number is here on my desk."

"For your information, sir, both his grandmothers were dead before he was born."

The chief administrator couldn't resist one last shot. "I'm not the one who lost the trial, Ms. Cooper."

"And I didn't let a prisoner escape," I said. "We'll talk again, I'm sure."

The fact that Tanner was at large, and was undoubtedly Flo's attacker, would ratchet up the media attention on him and everything we were trying to get done.

Mercer and I were focused on our work when Mike arrived, shortly after eleven. He was carrying four large paper bags, grocery-store size, that appeared damp on the bottom and lower half.

"Good morning, Coop. Morning, Mercer. Peterson told me you had a late night."

"And a productive one. Alex has the life history of Raymond Tanner laid out along that side of the table. You need to check him out."

"What's in your bags?" I asked.

"So that dredging-the-Lake idea of Gordon Davis's may be the shot we needed." Mike made himself a space at the end of the table with his back to the door, gloved up, and opened the bags one at a time to display their contents.

The first item was a sweatshirt—a navy-blue hoodie that zipped up the front. "Size medium. Unisex, I'd say."

Then he removed the second piece of clothing, which was a pale-pink T-shirt, with a fitted body and cap sleeves. "This one's a small. A ladies' small," he said.

Third was a pair of khaki-colored cargo pants, as damp as the first two pieces. "Also small, and nothing in any of the pockets."

From the last one he extracted a dark-green plastic bag with a red tie—the large size, for lawn and trash.

"Check it out, guys. Tell me what you think I've got," Mike said, tossing each of us a pair of gloves to put on before either of us touched any of the items.

"I'd say it's the basic uniform of a homeless person."

"Very good, Coop. Female variety."

The pink tee was the only nod to feminine dressing. I picked it up to look it over, front and back, for markings. Inside on the seam was a label from Target.

The hoodie and cargo pants were traditional gear for young people living on the streets. Their styles allowed kids and young adults to be gender neutral, and the hoods made it easy to conceal most of the face if they didn't want to be recognized. Trash bags were the homeless equivalent of sleeping bags—a bit of protection from the wind and weather when one settled into the sack for the night.

"Where did this stuff come from?" Mercer asked.

"The crew started dredging yesterday, from the western side of the pond."

"Did a lot of things surface?"

"Not so much as you'd think because of how fierce they are about making sure there's no garbage in or around anyplace. When they picked up again this morning, these things were all clumped together, about fifty yards from the far side of Bow Bridge, snagged on some rocks on the little island in the middle of the Lake."

Mercer was doing his own check of the pockets of the pants and sweatshirt.

"I thought you'd want some photos now," Mike said. "Then I'll take them to the lab to have them dry out. Then to the morgue to see if they look like they'd fit Angel."

Mike and I both had our backs to the door when Pat McKinney came in. I was leaning on the table, making notes on a legal pad, while Mike was giving me the names and contact information for the men who had found the items.

"Hey, everybody," McKinney said. "Big score last night, Alex. And good call, Mercer, for bringing her up to the precinct. Maybe this won't be a lost cause after all."

I was glad that McKinney had eased up on me lately. The office was such a tremendously collegial place that it had always been jarring to have someone who ranked between the DA and me ready to backstab me for no apparent reason.

I turned my head to talk to him. "You want the details on the attempted rape? And Mike just came in with these clothes that were found pretty close to the body in the Lake."

McKinney walked toward us and looked over my shoulder. I straightened up to tell him the story about Raymond Tanner, along with the news from Fishkill. Mike filled in the blanks about the search in the Park.

When McKinney stepped back toward the door, Mike and I returned to our conversation and my note-taking.

"If you ever get that three's-a-crowd feeling, Mercer, my door's always open to you," McKinney said.

Neither Mike nor I moved a muscle. I wrote across the bottom of my pad in big letters, all caps: IGNORE HIM.

Mercer shook his head. "There is so much spite in your soul, Pat, I sometimes wonder how you don't choke on it."

McKinney gave one of his fake chortles. "It's not spite, man. Who zings me more than Detective Chapman?"

"Mike's funny, Pat. You're just small-minded."

"Willy Shakespeare, was he petty?" McKinney asked. "Isn't he the wordsmith who said, 'Pell hath no fury like a woman scorned'?"

I scribbled again and pushed the pad to Mike as soon as McKinney was halfway into his quote.

Mike never picked his head up but repeated the play and playwright's name I had written down as though they had just come off the top of his head. "That would be Willy Congreve, Pat. *The Mourn-*

ing Bride. Lots of people think it's Shakespeare, but then lots of people are ignorant, like you."

"See, Mercer? He gives as good as he gets," McKinney said on his way out the door. "Now Chapman's mastered seventeenth-century literature? Just goes to prove, like Battaglia says, that he's spending way too much time with Alexandra."

SIXTEEN

"Get me out of here for a while," I said to Mercer after Mike left for the lab. "Anywhere."

"I'll drop you at home. Nan Rothschild, the head of the Seneca Village anthropology team, wasn't in yesterday. I'm going back to talk to her about the black angel."

"Home actually sounds good."

"I had you out awfully late, and you've got to meet all those bigwigs at the Conservancy tonight. Get a nap," Mercer said. "And a hairdo."

"Do I look as bad as all that?"

"You look tired, Alex. And anxious."

"I'm both."

I told Laura to make excuses for me and walked out with Mercer. He drove me home, letting me off in front of my hair salon. I took his advice and tried to relax while my head was massaged and my shoulder-length hair was swept up into a fancy knot that would complement the style of the outfit I was going to wear.

I napped for an hour, awakened by Mercer's call.

"Feeling better?" he asked.

"Almost human, thanks to your suggestion. Did you meet with Rothschild?" The world-renowned urban archaeologist had helped the police before with a site near City Hall that dated back to the period of the Revolution.

"Yes. And she's as fascinated with that little figure as you are."

"Has she ever seen it? Or one like it?"

"She's never seen this one, but there are a few carved antique angels that have been excavated from the site around the churches. And her team will compare ours, trying to date it and see if it's made of similar materials."

"Any reason to find an artifact like that near Bow Bridge?"

"She's as baffled as we are."

"The site she excavated, at Seneca Village, could anyone else have had access to it besides her team?" I asked.

"That's one of her concerns. The holes that were made were very carefully figured by ground radar, and there were multiple entrances, well guarded at the time. But there are always scavengers around a dig site, and Rothschild can't swear someone didn't get in. Unless it's a completely random object, which is why she's interested in having an expert study it."

"And that will take—?"

"Longer than you're likely to want to know. But she gave me another lead."

"What's that?" I asked, looking at my watch. Mike was going to pick me up at 5:45, and I still needed to dress.

"So Vickee gave you her family history of All Angels' Church, right?"

"She did. One of three in Seneca Village."

"I had no idea—and I bet Vickee doesn't either—that All Angels' was founded by another church. By a church that's still standing on West 99th Street and Amsterdam today."

"What do you mean?"

Mercer went on to explain. "There's an Episcopal church called St. Michael's that was built on the Upper West Side in 1807—one of the very few of Manhattan's houses of worship that's been located on the same site for more than two centuries."

"I've never heard of it," I said, thinking back to a bizarre series of murders we'd investigated at old religious institutions. "But it's been there even longer than St. Patrick's Old Cathedral."

"Exactly. I'm standing inside the place right now, looking at a whole bunch of antique Tiffany stained glass windows."

"What was a fancy church doing way uptown when that part of New York wasn't even populated then?"

"The deacon's filling me in. He says in the old days these parishioners were all rich members of Trinity," Mercer said, referring to the historic Episcopal church—one of the first in the city—that opened in 1698 on lower Broadway, a world away from St. Michael's by the primitive street conditions and means of travel of that period. "When those folk started building summer homes along the Hudson River, this church was created to be like an annex to Trinity."

"And then?"

"St. Michael's is known for its social ministries. So the deacon tells me that when an African American community was growing in Seneca Village in the 1820s, it's this very church—still standing—that helped to create All Angels' Church. This is like the mother church to the one in Central Park. So when two hundred fifty people were thrown out of their homes so the Park could be built, a few of them came back to St. Michael's."

I was growing excited by the possibility that there might be a living link, a way to connect the artifacts found in the Park.

"Is there someone who can look at our statue? Our black angel?"

"There is, although the deacon hasn't ever seen anything like it here. But I'm sticking it out till all of his flock finds a way back to the soup kitchen for dinner tonight."

"Why?" I asked. "What's that going to do for us?"

"Seems they do a lot of ministering to homeless youth at St. Michael's. The deacon thinks the dead girl looks familiar to him. Wants me to talk to some of the young people who might have crossed paths with her. Maybe we can get an ID out of this."

SEVENTEEN

I opened the door when the bell rang and burst into the broadest smile I'd managed in a week.

Mike had one hand braced against the door frame, the other in the pocket of his pants. He looked smashingly handsome in the rented tux. "Bond," he said, in his best imitation of Sean Connery. "James Bond."

"And I'm shaken—as well as stirred. You look so good, Detective Chapman. Come on in."

"Don't want to be late, blondie. Is my tie right?"

"It's crooked."

"Well, why didn't you say that?"

"The new me, Mike. I'm not going to be critical of anything you do."

"Jeez, kid. How will I know it's you?" he said. "D'you know how to do a bow tie?"

"Sure," I said. He pulled the knot out of his tie and I stood nose to nose with him. "You have to start with one side a little longer than the other."

I crossed the longer tab over the short one and looped it through, telling him about Mercer's call as I did. He stared at me while I spoke, taking in the makeup and how the hair was swept off my face without uttering a word. My thumbs and forefingers formed a bow and then wrapped the longer end around again. When I finished making the knot, I pulled both ends to make sure it sat right against the pleats of Mike's shirt.

"Better?" he asked.

"Much. It's straight now." I stepped back to get my evening purse, shawl, and keys.

"You look—" Mike started to say something to me but interrupted himself.

"What?"

"You don't look like a hard-ass prosecutor is all."

I was wearing a white satin top—sleeveless—with sequins and flower-shaped beads that covered the bodice. The floor-length white silk crepe skirt was narrow, with a slit on one side that reached practically to midthigh. The strappy high-heeled sandals made me almost as tall as Mike.

I had expected a compliment, but that would have been out of character, too. "I can change into black leather and chain mail, if you prefer."

"That's how I think of you, Coop, but this will do fine for tonight."

"Then let's party," I said, closing the door behind us. We went downstairs, through the lobby, and onto the street to Mike's car.

It was 6:30 when we walked through the ornate wrought-iron Vanderbilt Gate on Fifth Avenue near 105th Street. I took Mike's arm to descend the wide staircase into the Conservatory Garden, one of the most magnificent sanctuaries within the Park.

It was the perfect evening for a lawn party. It was warm with a slight breeze, and the sky would be light for another two hours. Volunteers lined the path at the bottom of the steps to greet guests and give them their table assignments. The stunning green lawn that was the centerpiece of the Italian garden was covered by one enormous tent—large enough to hold tables for the five hundred guests who were pouring into the Park. It was bordered on both sides by an *allée* of pink and white crabapple trees.

"Let's find our host," I said, looking for Commissioner Davis among the crowd of well-dressed, prosperous-looking New Yorkers.

"Follow me," Mike said. He had spotted several waiters winding through the crowd with bottles of champagne.

He lifted a glass for each of us from one of the trays and extended them so that they were filled. I took one from him, and he clinked it against mine.

"To our truce," I said.

"For as long as it lasts. And to Angel."

We walked the length of the tent, seeing no one either of us knew, and then Mike kept walking around the path, past the twelve-foot-high jet fountain that pumped water into the air.

"Where are you going?"

"That spot where Tanner attacked the girl last night? It's right out back this way."

The rear of the Conservatory Garden wasn't far from the Huddlestone Arch. "Let it be, Mike. You're not here to walk a crime scene."

"Just nerves. Just want to check out the landscape. See how Tanner likes to work."

"I can tell you almost everything about that."

"Then talk to me."

Mike doubled back and we started to stroll around the side of the tent, watching the Park's loyal supporters fawn over the colorful display of tulips that lined the walk.

"There's Gordon Davis," Mike said.

We could see his head above the crowd and made our way toward him. He was encircled by a troupe of admirers who were listening to him describe the efforts that had gone into creating the perfect floral display for this evening.

"Ah, my new friends!" he said as we approached. "Meet Alex Cooper and Mike Chapman. You two clean up nicely."

Davis started introducing us around. "Hello, Professor," I said to his wife, a petite, attractive woman whose silver-streaked Afro matched the strands of glitter in her dress.

"Please call me Peggy." I let Mike do the meet-and-greet while the professor and I talked about the class she taught at NYU Law School.

Shortly before seven o'clock we were all asked to find our tables and be seated. I was between Commissioner Davis and Mike, who had a stocky matron on his other side. She appeared to be already in her cups and happy to be placed next to such a good-looking dinner companion.

Fifteen minutes later, Mia Schneider was at the podium to welcome the guests. She looked to be in her early fifties, a very handsome woman with a fine sense of style—a look that stood out in a tent full of well-heeled people. She had a good sense of humor and a quick intelligence and seemed to savor her role as doyenne of an organization that does so much for the Park and the city.

Gordon Davis leaned over to tell Mike and me that he had asked Ms. Schneider to stop at the table to meet us before she settled in for dinner. While we waited for her, we tried to answer all his questions about last night's assault. The timing of two major crimes wasn't a gift to the organizers of tonight's event.

I watched Mia make her rounds—stopping for handshakes and kisses from her admirers, working her way to us. She greeted Mike and me enthusiastically and we stepped away from the table, with Gordon Davis, to talk about our investigation.

"You don't have to tell me anything that's not in the newspapers," Mia said. "But I love this Park and I need to know you're going to restore our sense of well-being here."

"We're working hard to do that," I said. "The case last night, the victim told me that there's some kind of ledge behind the waterfall in the Ravine. That you can actually sit on, behind the fall. It made me wonder, with all the boulders in the Park, if there are actual places that one could hide in."

"You mean caves or grottoes?" Mia asked.

"Yes, anything like that. I assume we're talking with two people who know the Park better than anyone in town."

She and Davis looked at each other. "Pretty much so," she said.

"More places than you can count," Davis said. "But most of what once were caves have been covered over."

"How many were there?" Mike asked.

"Olmsted and Vaux created dozens of them. It was part of their master plan to design something entirely unlike the city, unlike the enormous swamps they were replacing."

"Some of them were natural, Gordon," Mia said. "Don't you remember that story about the cave near the lower end of the Reservoir that workmen found when they were clearing the dense underbrush?"

"Recently?"

"In 1857, Mike," Mia said, laughing. "We've got a load of clippings from the papers and magazines going back to the origins of the Park. That one was natural, but many more were landscaped in."

"Do you have the original plans?" I asked. "Would they show these caves?"

Davis shook his head. "There were years and years of original plans, some rejected by the City Council, many others modified over time."

"Modified why?"

Davis crossed one arm over his chest and held the other up, his forefinger to his mouth, as he thought about an answer. "In some instances the changes were made because of expense. Occasionally, there were accidents that made the designers reboot."

"What kinds of accidents?" I asked again.

"Remember the Park was constructed before Alfred Nobel invented dynamite. So it was gunpowder that was used to break up the bedrock under the surface, shape some of the boulders that were brought in, and manage the glacial rock that needed to be moved," Davis said. "More gunpowder was used to create the illusion that this

Park was a natural woodland—more gunpowder than was used at the Battle of Gettysburg."

Like everything else about military history, that fact got Mike's attention. "So men working with it—with vast quantities of black powder—were killed."

"Exactly. That changed plans and designs, too."

"Some of the grottoes or caves that were first left open to the public were closed over after time," Davis said. "Animals—I'm talking about sheep and goats—wandered into them. People, bums mostly, camped out in them. They've all been closed over."

"But can you get us the site information of where they are, open or closed?" I said.

"Between our two offices, I'm sure we can give you a good idea of where they were," Mia said, patting me on the arm. "You're not thinking of *Beauty and the Beast*, are you?"

"No offense," Mike said, "but we're beyond fairy tales."

"I was referring to the TV show."

"I've never heard of it," I said.

"Me neither."

"Very cult in the '80s, when you two were still kids."

"Don't go there, Mia," Davis said, wagging a friendly finger at her.

But it was clear that she was irrepressible and spirited. "I can't believe you don't know this show. You can get it On Demand. It was about a relationship between this man-beast guy who lives underground in Central Park, with a sort of Utopian society of outcasts. He falls in love with a prosecutor—"

Mike reached back to the table for a wineglass that had been filled as we sat. "Hold your tongue, Mia."

"Wait. So she's this spunky assistant district attorney—"

"I don't do 'spunky,' " I said, laughing along with her.

"Well, you can get it on DVD. It's funny, really. And the Beast—"

"No, thanks," Mike said.

"He's very noble, I promise you, and a heartthrob. Played by

Ron Perlman. He lives in this world with mystical waterfalls and labyrinth tunnels."

"In the Park?"

"Yes. In the Park. I think," Mia said, "that's where so many people get the idea that there are underground caves here. Urban myth, Mike. We'll make sure you know about anything that might have resembled a cave."

I still wasn't convinced that there weren't more places to conceal oneself in the Park, and that the psychos like Tanner didn't know them intimately.

"The police found some interesting objects near the Lake, Mia," Davis said to her as his wife signaled him to return to his seat. "Can you describe them to her, Mike?"

"I can bring them to your office tomorrow," he said.

"Fine."

"I've got photos of them on my cell phone," I said. "It's in my purse, on the chair."

I reached for the phone and pulled up the images. The statuette of the angel meant nothing to Mia Schneider, but she practically gasped when she saw the silver-plated reproductions of Belvedere Castle and the Obelisk.

"Where did you get these?"

"I'm not the one who found them," Mike said. "But a couple of the detectives spotted them underneath some bushes, on the far side of the Bow Bridge. You've seen them before?"

"Yes. Yes, I have," Mia said. She was even more animated, pressing the zoom command to enlarge the images. "The Conservancy mounted an exhibition of the Dalton collection about ten years ago. I'm sure these must be part of that set. I can't imagine anything else like them."

"I can show you the pieces tomorrow," Mike said. "But where's the Dalton collection and what is it?"

"Do you know who Archer Dalton was?"

"One of the robber barons," I said. "Made millions. Was it rail-roads?"

"Exactly."

"Coop knows the millionaires," Mike said. "I'm better on perps."

"Sometimes there's an overlap, Mike. They weren't called robber barons for nothing," Mia said. "Shortly after the Civil War, when he was a very young man, he got into the train business. Cornelius Vanderbilt, Mark Hopkins, Leland Stanford, and Archer Dalton all made their fortunes that way. Dalton's Northern Atlantic Line built a piece of the first transcontinental railroad. He and Vanderbilt were great rivals. The gate you walked through tonight is from Vanderbilt's mansion on Fifth Avenue at 58th Street, where it stood when the Park was opened."

"And Dalton?" Mike asked.

"He was an outlier in that crowd. Didn't want to be part of what became known as the Four Hundred."

"Four Hundred what?"

"The social elite of New York. The number supposedly referred to the people who could fit inside Mrs. William Astor's ballroom. That didn't interest Dalton at all. So when the Dakota opened its doors in 1884, Archer Dalton left his Fifth Avenue digs and all the swells behind him, and was the first tenant to rent apartments there, on Central Park West. He took the entire top residential floor—the eighth—at the time, and when it eventually became a co-op, his granddaughter bought all the apartments on eight that faced the Park."

Mike whistled. "Pretty piece of change that must have been. What happened to her?"

"She's still alive, and still in the Dakota," Mia said.

There was no more famous residence in Manhattan than the Dakota, then or now. It had been home to the rich and prominent from the start, and was the fictional setting for the movie *Rosemary's*

Baby, the classic novel *Time and Again*, and a Jack Reacher caper, as well as the tragic backdrop for the murder of John Lennon.

"It was she—Lavinia Dalton—who loaned us the collection for our exhibit."

Mike looked at me. "Then we can go see her tomorrow."

"She's not well, I'm afraid. Lavinia's close to ninety, and she suffers from dementia. I can call her nurses, and if she's having one of her better days, I'm sure they'll allow you to go by. But I wouldn't expect to get much from the visit."

"I want to know about these silver pieces," Mike said. "How they got out of her house or wherever she kept them, and when."

"Why don't we sit down?" Mia said. She asked Gordon Davis to go over and join her guests—undoubtedly high rollers all—while she took his seat to give us some of the background. "I can get you started on the story of the silver.

"Lavinia was an only child, and to say that Archer Dalton doted on his granddaughter would be a gross understatement. She was raised in the Dakota, too, of course, which meant that Central Park was her front yard. She adored everything about the Park."

"Who wouldn't?" I said.

"As a gift to his son—Lavinia's father—on his tenth birthday, Archer Dalton had commissioned a set of railroad trains. A train set like any other little boy might receive," Mia said, holding out her hands, palms up, while she grinned impishly, "except they were all of Papa's Northern Atlantic models, and they happened to be crafted in silver."

"By Gorham and Frost," Mike said.

"You're good," Mia said, pointing at him. "So in honor of Lavinia's birthday—her tenth, too—Dalton commissioned another unique gift from the most celebrated silversmiths of the time. He had them build miniatures—in silver—of all the important landmarks in the Park that existed by then and had an architecture firm reproduce the landscape, to scale, to place them on."

"That must have cost a fortune," I said.

"Archer Dalton had a fortune. Several of them. Fortunes, I mean."

"And where was there space to house this?" Judging from the size of the two pieces I'd seen, the layout must have been enormous.

"There was an entire room in the family apartment devoted to the train set and the Park," Mia said. "Lavinia has always been one of our most generous donors, so I saw the set the first time I went to court her. You think there are treasures at Versailles or Blenheim Palace? This collection is staggering."

"So why would anyone have broken it up?" Mike asked.

"I'm shocked to think that happened," Mia said. "It took me a decade of begging, from the time I first came on the Conservancy board, to convince Lavinia to let us mount the exhibit. You've got to go to the apartment and talk to the staff. I'll have to get her attorneys in, too."

"Who represents her?" I said.

"The only person she trusted with her affairs was a wonderful lawyer named Justin Feldman. But he died last year."

"I knew him well." I thought of my beloved mentor and friend, biting down on my lip to stem the wave of emotion that swept through me. "Lavinia must have been very wise to have had such good counsel."

"I'll find out who's looking out for her now and let you know."

"How many pieces made up the collection?" Mike was attacking the mixed green salad while he talked.

"If I remember correctly, there were something like fifty-three or so. These two, and of course the Carousel, the Arsenal, the buildings that later became Tavern on the Green."

"That was a restaurant," I said, remembering the sprawling banquet space. "What had it been before?"

"It was a series of barns where the sheep were housed," Mia said. "There was a miniature of the Blockhouse and the original horse stables. Then there were copies of the statues that had been erected up to that time—Alexander Hamilton, Daniel Webster—"

"Alice in Wonderland?" I asked.

"She came way later. But Beethoven and the Indian Hunter—I remember those. And the monument to the *Maine* was one of the most spectacular, as it is in real life."

Mike added his historical military details. "The tribute to the two hundred sixty sailors who perished in Havana when the *Maine* exploded in the harbor, sparking the Spanish-American War?"

"That's more than I knew about it," Mia said.

The oversized memorial dominated the southwest entrance to the Park and was a striking landmark for New Yorkers. High atop the two-story base was a gilded figure of a triumphant Columbia— the quasi-mythical name given to female figures representing America—leading her chariot of horses and sea creatures.

"Was Dalton's copy of the memorial gilded, too?" I asked.

"Twenty-four-carat gold leaf."

"That must have been a standout."

"In the case of Archer Dalton," Mia said, "all that glittered was indeed gold."

"And Lavinia," Mike asked. "Did she have a favorite?"

"She adored the Carousel, of course. Each of the horses was decorated in vibrant colors, like the ones in the Park, with enamel. And they actually moved up and down as the piece spun around.

"But Lavinia loved the Bethesda angel best, she told me when we were spending time together planning the exhibit."

I didn't know whether to be surprised by the coincidence of a body found near the angel or to accept that the magnificent figure was a natural to be anyone's favorite.

"She liked to play near the Lake and the fountain when she was a child. And that early stubborn feminist streak in her enjoyed the fact that the statue, designed by Emma Stebbins, represented the first time a woman was commissioned to create a major piece for New York City in the nineteenth century."

"I so want to meet Lavinia," I said. "I hope there's a spark of her spirit left."

"You must ask to see the angel when you go to visit," Mia said. "Archer insisted on placing jewels in the figure's eyes. He stopped short at sapphires, but there are blue topaz or some semiprecious stones that bring the sculpture to life. Almost haunting, in fact."

"You mentioned calling her nurses and lawyer. What about her family? Isn't there family?" I asked.

"It's a terribly sad story, Alex. But there is no family."

"She never had children?"

"When Lavinia was nineteen, she eloped with an Englishman— a viscount, in fact—who had all the charm in the world, and his title, but absolutely no money. Within a year, Lavinia had become pregnant, and the viscount had managed to have her move a fair amount of money into his name. But he had also fallen in love with a stage actress, very scandalous in those days. He abandoned Lavinia, and she came home to her father. She also took back the Dalton name and raised her son as Archer Dalton the third."

"What became of him?"

"Lavinia raised Archer by herself till he went off to Groton and Yale. He actually married and divorced twice, then lived the bachelor life for while, before settling down for the third time with a young woman Lavinia was very fond of—a terrifically bright Vassar grad—and they had a baby girl together a couple of years later. They went off on a ski trip to Chamonix, leaving the child at home with Lavinia and the nanny. The small plane they'd chartered to fly in from Paris crashed in the Alps. Archer and his wife were killed instantly."

"That's tragic," I said. "I'm almost afraid to ask about the baby."

"I know it happened before you were born," Mia said, "but surely you've heard of the Dalton kidnapping case? 1971?"

"Baby Lucy?" Mike said. "That's *this* Dalton family?"

"That story was as big in its day as the Lindbergh kidnapping was in 1932," I said. "Was it ever solved?"

One round of waiters was removing the salad plates while a second group behind them placed the dinners in front of each of us.

Mia shook her head. "I was a teenager when Lucy disappeared, and I don't think there were parents in New York who didn't clamp down on their kids, no matter their age or how rich or poor they were. The child was snatched right out of her home, so it seemed."

"Out of the Dakota?" I asked. "The place looks like a fortress."

"Charlie Lindbergh was taken out of a second-story window in a country house with no other homes around for miles. How the hell do you get someone out of the Dakota?" Mike asked. "Did Lavinia ever talk to you about it?"

Mia Schneider reached for her wineglass. "Once, Mike. Only once. Before I went to meet with her I had my office pull up all the clippings about the case. I got to know the story pretty well, although I had no intention of bringing it up. One day we were having lunch at the apartment, in the dining room overlooking the Park, and Lavinia asked me if I knew—if I remembered—the story of Baby Lucy."

We were both riveted on Mia as she recounted the crime.

"The child had just celebrated her third birthday at the end of May, and this happened a week or two later. Lavinia had gone out for the day, but when she came home and went into the nursery to see Lucy, the room was empty."

"Weren't there servants?" Mike asked.

"Too many of them. The driver had been with Lavinia, of course. There was a cook, a laundress, two housemaids, a butler, a secretary, and two nannies. One of them had put Lucy down for her nap, and when she went in to check on her an hour later, the child wasn't in her bed."

"What did she do?"

"Nothing. For three hours she did nothing, which gave someone a pretty good head start."

"Why?" I asked. "How could that be?"

"Because it had become fairly common, when Lucy woke up, for her to go into the kitchen to get a snack from the cook, or follow the laundress around, or put a little apron on and help the house-maid dust the big empty rooms day after day. There were staff quarters one flight above, and I'm told children used to love playing there on rainy days. Lavinia loved all the attic spaces as a child, she used to say. I'm sure Lucy was no stranger there either."

"Poor little rich girl. It sounds like the staff thought she was just in some other part of the apartment," I said.

"The entire eighth floor of the Dakota, Alex," Mia said, stretching her arms out to either side. "More than twenty rooms, with more ways in and out than in an amusement park funhouse. Staircases and elevators for the residents, and other sets just for the servants. Staff quarters, as I said, mostly all above the apartment, on the ninth floor of the building. A gym and a playroom under the roof, and croquet lawns and tennis courts behind the building."

"And then there's Central Park out in front. You'd hardly have to force a child to want to go into the Park," Mike said. "Most of the servants must have been suspects."

"All of them were. Their families, their boyfriends and girlfriends, too. Even the staff in the rest of the building—doormen, handymen, janitors. But Lavinia refused to fire any of them unless they were charged with the crime, which never happened. I think one of the housemaids and the social secretary are still with her today."

"Charlie Lindbergh's body was found a couple of months after the kidnapping," Mike said. "Dumped in the woods not very far from where he was taken, if I'm right."

"Yes," I said. "A blow to his skull, possibly from being dropped when the guys were trying to carry him down the ladder."

"But Lucy was never found, was she?" he asked Mia.

"Never. Not a trace."

"Ransom notes, like Lindbergh?"

"Lavinia told me that was one of the most painful parts of the case. Because she was so wealthy, all kinds of lowlifes jumped in and began to demand money for Lucy's return. Vultures of every sort."

"Did the police deal with them?" I asked.

"She had great respect for the way the NYPD handled the case. They ran down every lead, although the detectives and the FBI agents involved never believed it was the work of strangers. It would have been too hard to penetrate the Dakota, and too unlikely not to encounter one of the staff inside the apartment, as vast as it is."

"Did anyone hold out hope that Lucy was alive?" I had seen those stories countless times in the newspapers—of children taken from a parent by an angry former spouse, from a hospital crib by a psychotic visitor, from a deserted bus stop by a child molester who raised his victim in the basement of a home, sometimes in chains for years.

"Only Lavinia," Mia said. "She has never allowed anything in the nursery or playrooms to be touched. It's quite disturbing to see, actually, but the staff continues to honor her wishes. She told me she would wait the rest of her life for that child to return home, although the police made it clear to her that they believed Lucy had been killed. None of the attempts to demand ransom for Lucy led to any plan to bring her back to Lavinia. All hoaxes, she suspects."

The story had killed my appetite. Mia told us she was going back to her guests and would send Gordon Davis to join us. "I'll get in touch with you tomorrow," she said. "I'm curious to know how those two silver pieces got out of Lavinia's home, and if the rest of the collection is intact."

"So am I," Mike said.

"Thanks for coming tonight. Please enjoy the rest of the evening."

"That's all we need," Mike said. "A connection between the Baby Lucy case and our Angel. It'll give the press the feeding frenzy they thrive on."

"Last week you told me there were other cold cases from the Park, Mike."

"No three-year-olds. Nothing like that."

I leaned back with my wineglass and tried to make small talk with the commissioner. He, too, knew the Dalton kidnapping case well, but had not been in charge when the silver exhibition was on display so had not known about the fabulous Park pieces.

We spent the rest of the evening being introduced to Conservancy members, reassuring them about the quality of the investigation, as we listened to clever speeches and appeals for support.

At eleven o'clock, as the gala appeared to be breaking up, we said our good nights and followed the crowd through the tent and up the staircase to Fifth Avenue. Mike had parked nearby, and we walked to the car.

We cruised down Fifth and Mike made the turn onto my street in the low 70s. The Drifters were singing "Up on the Roof" and my eyes were closed as I sang along. As we approached the driveway, I was jolted forward when Mike suddenly applied the brakes, then sped up and drove straight ahead past my entrance toward the traffic light to turn downtown.

I reached up to rub my neck. "I think they call that whiplash. What's your problem, Mike?"

"It looks like your problem tonight. The black Lexus parked in your driveway?"

"I didn't see it. Wasn't paying attention, I guess."

"The license plate read 'JSC 421,'" he said.

"Justice of the Supreme Court of the State of New York."

"Looks like Jessica Pell is on your doorstep."

EIGHTEEN

"Of course she can find out where you live," Mike said. "All the judges get that handbook with the bureau chiefs' contact information in it."

"And I suppose it's obvious she knows where you live, too. Why the hell can't she just be your stalker and leave me out of this?"

"We can't go to my place either. If she gives up waiting for you, she's likely to show up ringing my bell."

I sat up straight and swiveled to look at Mike. "Don't tell me. Pell's actually been to the coffin?"

Mike's studio apartment, just ten blocks from mine in a walk-up building that had fallen into disrepair ages ago, was so small and dark that he had given it a grim nickname. It was rare for him to let anyone into this little bit of personal space that he called home.

He blushed and took one hand off the wheel to comb it through his hair. "Did I tell you how pushy she is?"

"That's it. I'm going to call her tomorrow. Or go up to her courtroom and blow this thing open. It's insane."

"Don't go off the reservation, Coop."

"According to her threats, you've got two days left before she uncorks it. Pell doesn't get to call the shots, as far as I'm concerned."

Mike made another turn and was heading west again.

"Where are you going?" I asked. "We're a little overdressed, but I didn't eat any dinner. We could split a sandwich at PJ Bernstein's."

The classic New York deli—a dying breed—was one of my favorite neighborhood retreats.

"Better than that. I've got a room with a view," Mike said. "Trust me."

"I'm actually thinking you didn't just say those last two words."

Mike looked over to make sure I was smiling. "This is business."

He parked on East 63rd Street, in front of a consulate near the corner of Fifth.

"The Park?" I asked.

"The Arsenal."

I was more than puzzled but followed Mike down the steps from the sidewalk and up another flight to the front door of the old building. He dialed a number on his cell and someone answered.

"It's Mike Chapman. Yeah, Detective Chapman. I'm at the front door with my partner."

Six minutes later—while we talked about everything except Mike's purpose in bringing me here—a night watchman opened the three locks and let us in the lobby.

"Thanks a lot. This is my partner, Alex Cooper."

The startled guard was surveying my outfit but not looking me in the eye.

"I've got all my stuff upstairs. Okay if we go on?"

"No problem if you know the way. But—but her shoes . . . ?"

"Undercover. Coop works undercover. Vice squad. Like a hooker, you know? She'll take them off. Not to worry."

The sleepy-eyed man just shrugged and pointed to the elevator.

There were five stories in the building, but the elevator only went as high as the fourth. When we exited, Mike led me into a stairwell. "I'm taking you to the best-kept secret in the city."

"Should I be flattered," I said, hiking up my skirt so that I could follow Mike up to the landing on the fifth floor, "or is this just totally weird? And why do you have things here?"

"'Cause I spent most of last night in the same place."

"Up on the roof?"

"Just like the Drifters. Hearing that song is what made me think of bringing you here."

Mike pushed against the door, which led to a terrace that was landscaped like a patio on a Fifth Avenue penthouse. There were flowers and plants surrounding the entire space, and a small greenhouse on the far corner.

I stepped out into the middle and slowly made a 360-degree turn. The entire skyline of the city was around and above me, landmark buildings easy to distinguish with twinkling lights that set off structures against the dark sky. When I looked down, it was across the green treetops of the Park that stretched all the way uptown.

"This is amazing," I said. "How did you know it was here?"

"Commissioner Davis told the lieutenant that on the north and south ends of the Arsenal the rooftops had just been restored, and that this one provides a great vantage point to look over the southern end of the Park. They rent it out for cocktail parties, if you're interested. Peterson sent me up here yesterday for a few hours with night vision goggles, just to see if anyone was running around in the woods," Mike said. "I pretty much stayed till morning."

"I don't blame you."

"Wish I could have seen as far as the Huddlestone Arch."

"Impossible, obviously. Did you find anything interesting?"

"I had really good equipment. Best I could do was about a couple of hundred feet away. Lots of warm bodies, though, all through the night. Some couples, some alone, some walking around, and some just curled up sleeping, even though the Park's officially 'closed' from one to six A.M.," Mike said. "Another flight, Coop. C'mon."

"Flight to what?"

"The part that's a secret."

We went back into the hallway and out another door, which left us in a four-by-four space with a metal ladder made of thin round rungs heading straight above us about twenty feet.

I looked up but wasn't anxious to make the climb.

"Can you do it, Coop?"

"Some other time." I had mild vertigo and was wary of anything that involved heights.

"Take off those ridiculous shoes and be daring. I'll stay below you in case you panic."

"I'm not the panicky type." I unstrapped my sandals and left them on the cold stone surface beside the ladder. I put my foot on the first rung and steadied myself as I moved slowly, hand over hand. When I got to the top, I looked over onto the small area that was perched, like a giant birds' nest, above the terrace we'd just been on. "Maybe I am panicky. There's nothing to hold on to."

"The brick wall. Just hold on to that."

I looked down and Mike was right behind me. I grabbed on to the old bricks that formed the top of the wall, and swung my leg—grateful for the slit in my skirt—over the side, planting my bare feet on the paved surface.

"There's a purpose to this, right?" I asked. I was playing with the strands of hair that had come loose from the carefully styled twist on top of my head. "Something worth the cleaning bills?"

"A piece of history."

"I prefer my history in a book. I'm less likely to kill myself that way."

Mike came right up behind me. He pulled off his bow tie and removed the jacket of his tux.

"Look at this. Only a few hundred people have ever been up on this turret since the building was constructed." He went to a small metal box tucked in a corner of the roof and opened it, removing a logbook with a pen attached to it by a long chain. "Check out these names, and then sign yours and date it."

The names of the last five mayors of the city were there, along with Gordon Davis and his predecessors. Members of the Conservancy, a handful of Park devotees, a few politicians, one NYPD detective from the night before, and now I would join that short list. I picked up the pen and wrote my name.

Then Mike took me by the hand and led me to the western side of the roof. "Look down. Look over there."

I could see the zoo and the whimsical Delacorte Clock, which chimed on the half hour throughout the day, playing familiar nursery rhymes to the delight of young visitors.

There was a large storage bin along the side of the brick wall. Mike lifted the lid, propping it open while he removed his night vision binoculars, and then came back to my side.

I held them up and looked out into the Park, but it was all a blur.

"I must be doing something wrong. How do I adjust these?"

Mike stood behind me, practically touching his chest to my back, while he reached both arms around me and showed me how to focus the lenses and turn on the night vision feature. I was tempted to lean back against him and close my eyes, but he seemed intent on getting me to see.

"Better?"

He stepped away from me and rested his hands on the edge of the brick wall.

"Better than what?"

"What can you see?"

"Penguins. I can see dozens of penguins," I said with a laugh.

"Don't bullshit me, Coop. They're inside for the night. Those must be all the dudes from the Conservancy in their tuxes."

"Monkeys? I do see them, like they were ten feet away."

"Yeah. Japanese snow monkeys. They have their own hot tub down there."

I moved the glasses slowly across the treetops and then down among the branches. I could clearly make out people walking through the Park while many others were sitting on benches or rocks, enjoying the very mild night.

"Too bad you can't see the Lake from here," I said.

"That's exactly what I thought last night. Another season, before the leaves blossomed or after they fell, it would be a clean shot."

I spent several minutes scanning the Park. I could see the skating rink and the Dairy, the long, wide stretch of the Mall between the leafy green borders, and the top of an occasional statue that peeked through.

"What are you doing?" I asked Mike. I had turned my attention to the buildings that made a perimeter around the Park, starting with the Plaza Hotel on the southeast corner. 59th Street was a mix of residences and fancy hotels, and I was looking up and into windows from my unique perch on this isolated tower.

"Checking my messages."

"Any news?"

"My mother says hello."

I was crazy about Mike's mother, a devoutly religious woman who doted on her son, the youngest of four and the only male child. She was born in Ireland and still had a healthy trace of a brogue from County Cork.

"I've got to get one of the photos that was taken at the party and send her a picture of you in your dress clothes," I said. "Wait—put your tie and jacket back on and let me take one up here."

"Send her a snap of a penguin, Coop. Anyway, she said the Final Jeopardy category was baseball."

I had moved along to the magnificent all-glass façade of the Time Warner Center, which was catty-corner across Columbus Circle from the Maine Monument. The shops and restaurants on the lower floors had closed, but lights still sparkled all the way up to the top.

"I'm in." I had grown up in a household with four men who loved baseball—both my brothers, my father, and my grandfather—and I knew almost as much about it as Mike and Mercer did.

"Here's the answer," Mike said. On the rare occasions when he knew he wouldn't be anywhere near a television set, Mike asked his mother to leave three messages for him. One with the category, second with the answer, and third with the winning question. "'First president to throw out the ball on opening day.'"

I had just rounded the corner to Central Park West, looking up at apartments that had sweeping vistas over the Park and toward the east.

"Are you peeping or what?" he asked.

"Trying to. It's amazing how many people are up and active at this hour. And I don't know which president threw out the first pitch."

"1910. It was the fat man," Mike said. "Who was William Howard Taft? Washington Nationals beat the Philly Athletics three-nothing."

"Interesting. Take twenty bucks off what you owe me."

"What's got your attention, Coop?"

My gaze was arrested when I reached the frame of the Dakota, made to be the city's first luxury apartment building, on the corner of West 72nd Street and Central Park West. Designed by the same firm that created the Plaza Hotel, now over my left shoulder, it had a completely distinctive slhouette. There were high gables and roofs with a profusion of dormers and niches, referred to in architectural terms as German Renaissance style, although the interior was decidedly French in character.

"The Dakota," I said. "Can you imagine what it must have been like to have lived there in the 1880s? I mean, civilized New Yorkers didn't live north of 59th Street then. I think the building got its name because the Upper West Side of Manhattan seemed as remote as the Dakota Territory."

"Is it petty of me to be happy when you're wrong, Coop?"

"Not petty. Just mean. I know you delight in it."

"My dad was one of the guys on John Lennon's homicide. 1980."

Brian Chapman had been a legend in the department, and had

worked so many major jobs that some guys joked that his investigative skill and wisdom in homicide cases had been passed through his DNA to Mike.

"He spent a lot of time at the Dakota after the shooting. Told me the architect who created the place had a real attachment to the names of the new western territories and states. Can you see the Indian?"

"What Indian?"

Mike moved behind me again, encircling me with his arms and guiding the binoculars. "Can you find the entrance to the building? That big wide space on 72nd Street."

"Yes."

"Okay, go up higher, right under the tip of the roof."

His body was against my own now. As I lifted my head back with the glasses, my ear brushed against Mike's cheek. My heart was racing, and I knew it wasn't because of the architecture of the grand old building.

"See it?"

"Yes," I whispered.

"It's a Dakota Indian. Bet you never knew that."

"I didn't," I said softly. I wasn't thinking about the unusual façade.

"You're looking for Lavinia Dalton," Mike said. "That's why you're so quiet. Long past her bedtime, Coop."

I nodded my head.

"Let me see," he said, taking the binoculars from me and standing next to me to study the behemoth structure. "You know what's really interesting?"

"What?" The night was warm, a precursor to summer just days away, but I had goose bumps on my bare arms and neck.

"Did you see the great big windows in all the apartments?"

"Um," I mumbled.

"Then look up at the row of tiny ones—the windows hidden just under the ledge of the roof."

"Eyelids."

"What do you mean?" Mike asked.

"Turn around and look at the buildings that line the Fifth Avenue side," I said. If I thought I had briefly engaged Mike's attention, I had lost it for the moment. "See? Small windows on the highest floors, like slits of eyelids rather than eyes wide open."

"Yeah."

"Everywhere you can see, those top-floor apartments were used by the servants of the rich tenants down below."

"But why would they take the best views—the most prime real estate on the highest floors—and use it on servants' quarters?"

"It wouldn't happen again today," I said. "But before penthouses became fashionable, back one hundred years ago when these buildings were put up, rich people were reluctant to live closest to the chimneys that puffed out black soot and rooftops where maids hung laundry. That's where they housed their workers."

"Wait a minute," Mike said. He had scoped the prestigious addresses of Fifth Avenue and gone back to the Dakota. "So think about Lavinia Dalton's apartment. Her building looks out directly over the Lake, over the Angel of the Waters, right?"

"Yes."

"I mean, they're both a bit north of 72nd Street," he said. "If you were in the Dalton apartment, or even a flight up in the dormers, you'd be at a perfect height and ideal vantage point to see what was going on at the Lake."

"And at a lot of other places in the Park."

"You're shivering, Coop." Mike put the glasses down and reached for his jacket, wrapping it around my shoulders. "Why didn't you tell me you were cold?"

"I'm not cold, really," I said. "Something just—I don't know—just chilled me."

"It makes no sense that the Dalton apartment and the pieces of silver have anything to do with the dead girl, does it?"

"Don't know." I was beginning to fade, a combination of exhaustion and feeling emotionally spent. My back was to the stone wall, while Mike faced out at Central Park West.

"When we get into the Dakota, we should ask to check out the servants' quarters."

"Sure. But you're getting ahead of yourself," I said, pulling the jacket tighter around me. "Have you studied the Panoscan photographs yet?"

He put the binoculars down on top of the wall and looked at me.

"No, but I get where you're going."

The Crime Scene team had used the new equipment to do a 360-degree shot from the point at Bow Bridge where Angel's body had been found. "I imagine, in addition to everything else it shows, that it will point you directly back to the Dakota."

"Course it will. Good thinking, Coop."

"Am I off duty now?"

"Is that what you want to be?"

"Totally. And I think you can take me home, too. If Jessica Pell hasn't given up on confronting me by now, the doormen will have to run interference. I'm really tired, Mike."

"Let's not go yet. It's kind of—I don't know—kind of magical up here."

"But it's so late, and we have a lot to do tomorrow."

"You're right, Coop. It's so late, and I still haven't apologized to you properly. And you're cold."

"I told you I'm not cold. I'm—I'm nervous, I think. That's why I'm trembling."

I was looking around everywhere, at everything, except into Mike's eyes. He touched my face with his right hand and aligned it with his own. We had flirted with this moment more times than I could remember clearly.

"There's something I want to do, Coop. And I'm nervous about it, too."

"Then we're even."

Mike smiled again, and I closed my eyes for a second.

"YOLO," I said, smiling as I channeled Vickee's heart-to-heart with me.

You only live once.

Mike Chapman grinned with all his dazzle and brought his lips to meet mine. He kissed me. His touch was tender and warm as he lifted my chin and pressed his lips against mine, holding us in that position for several seconds, although it seemed like an hour.

Then he took his hand away and stepped back, running his fingers through his hair. "Are you okay with this?" he asked.

I let the tuxedo jacket fall to the ground. "Very okay."

He came toward me again. "Do you mind?"

"Mind what?"

"The pins. The ones holding your—style?—whatever it is—in place. I have no idea what they're called, but could you take them out of your hair?"

I was breathing fast, fumbling a bit as I reached up and started pulling out the pins that held my formally arranged twist in place.

"It's just not you," Mike said, taking them from my hand and putting them in his pants pocket. Then he tousled my hair so that it fell to my shoulders, loose and long, curling softly around my face.

"Now is it me?" I asked, smiling back at him.

"I'll tell you in a minute."

We kissed again, and this time we embraced and caressed each other till I needed to stop for air. "This is crazy, isn't it?" I said. "Good crazy, but crazy."

"You still want to go home, Coop?"

"I'm not sure about anything. But if we're going to—if you're going to—well, can you stop calling me 'Coop'? It's not the most—well, feminine name for me."

"I can't do Alexandra or Alex. Those names are for everyone else to use. 'Coop' is my own. I'm not the least bit confused about your gender identity."

I wanted the night to last forever. We were alone together in our own aerie, apart from everyone in the world, in the middle of the most beautiful park in the most exciting city—visible to any of the ritzy neighbors who wanted to look out their windows from high above but unidentifiable to all.

We kissed several more times, laughing and whispering to each other, as comfortable as I would expect to be in the arms of my best friend.

"Taking it slow, right?" Mike said when I pushed away and turned around, inhaling the fresh night air, trying to comprehend what was happening to us.

"Slow would be good. It would be smart."

"You don't always have to be smart, you know?"

"Yes, I know. But don't you think we have to talk about some—?"

"Shh shh shh shh shh. Plenty of time for talk, Coop. Will you stay here with me for a few hours? Watch the sun break through?" He was behind me, kissing the top of my head and stroking my arms. "I've got a blanket in with my supplies. We can just sit down and lean back, use my jacket for a pillow. Just sit and hold on to each other."

"I'd like to do that. Fall asleep with your arms around me."

There was no street noise, no sirens or garbage trucks, no one to burst into this night's fantasy. We spread the blanket and stretched out. It was as though we were all alone on the island of Manhattan.

NINETEEN

Shortly after dawn crept over the horizon, Mike somehow steered me over the brick wall and onto the narrow rungs of the ladder, cautioning me not to look down as I stepped one foot below the other. He dropped me off at home at 5:45. The doormen were used to the odd hours of my comings and goings, but I looked terribly bedraggled in my well-worn evening outfit of twelve hours earlier.

I showered and ate breakfast, passing up the temptation to nap in order to get to the office early. It was 7:30 when I got off the elevator and went to unlock my door. I was startled to hear Mercer's voice call out to me from the far end of the hallway.

"C'mon down to the conference room after you open up," he said.

"Anything wrong?"

"I got a girl here. I'm hoping she can make an ID."

I threw down my handbag and tote and hurried down to the conference room, which had become the default headquarters of the Park investigation.

Mercer intercepted me outside the closed door. "You all right, Alex? You look like you haven't had any sleep."

"I haven't. I spent the night with Mike. The whole night."

"You *what* now, girl?"

"I don't mean that way, Mercer. And I am getting such mixed signals about what everyone—including you and Vickee—think I ought to do with my love life. Forget it. We went to the Conservancy dinner, and we found out about the silver miniatures and about their connection to a kidnapped baby who's never been recovered—dead or alive. I was busy, and it looks like you were, too."

"Sure enough, St. Michael's Church is a mainstay for the homeless. It's on the list that the team is working off—shelters and such—distributing pictures and stopping in for questioning. They just hadn't reached here yet."

"So who've you got?"

"Calls herself Jo 'cause it could be a guy or girl's name—she tells me—and she's gay. Claims she's nineteen, but I'd guess younger. She's afraid we're going to turn on her and send her back home. Jo's a runaway from somewhere down south. The accent sort of gives up that much."

"Does she know Angel?" I asked.

"I'm not sure whether or not she's bluffing. Came into the church soup kitchen for her meal last night, and one of the deacons asked her—like everyone else coming through—to talk to me. She looked at the photos and the sketch and thinks she's spent time on the streets with Angel. The church took her in for the night, and I had Uniform do a fixer out in front in case she tried to leave. But there she was waiting for me this morning, maybe looking for some meal money and a witness fee. She's a gamer, Alex. I don't want her to work us over."

"Understood," I said. "Take me in."

Jo was sitting at an empty space at the conference table. She was eating a bacon-and-egg sandwich that Mercer had bought her, washing it down with a bottle of juice, a large cup of coffee, and soda cans for later on.

I introduced myself and although she glanced up at me, Jo kept on eating. She had an androgynous look, small and very thin, with short-cropped hair clipped in a boyish style and bright dark eyes that darted back and forth between Mercer and me as we talked.

Jo had run away from a family that didn't accept her sexual identity, and a town in Alabama in which hostility against LGBT youth was a point of pride for many citizens. She had taken money out of her mother's wallet for the bus fare to New York and left home while both her parents were at work one March morning. She had chosen Manhattan, as thousands of runaways do every year, because of its reputation for open-minded acceptance and a large network of gay youth. There was also a plethora of information available online about underground life and survival techniques for people who come to the big city with no place to stay.

I pushed one of the morgue photos—a picture of Angel after she'd been autopsied and cleaned up—across the table to Jo. "Did you know this girl?"

"Yes, ma'am. At least I think I did."

I went right to the facts we needed. "Do you know her name?"

I shouldn't have been disappointed when Jo said she did not. "It was just a hi-and-bye kind of thing. We weren't friends or anything like that."

"Do you remember where you saw her the first time?" I asked.

"Uh-huh. I do, because it was the night I got to New York. I had no place to sleep, so a girl I met at the Port Authority told me about Uncle Ace's house. She taught me how to jump the turnstile and all that."

Estimates were that about four thousand young people between the ages of thirteen and twenty-five are homeless on the streets of New York every night. The city has, at best, two hundred fifty shelter beds to offer them. "Uncle Ace" is the name for the A, C, and E subway lines—the longest ride in the city—stretching from the northern tip of Inwood to the farthest end of Far Rockaway. It frequently served as a refuge for kids who wanted to get off the mean streets of the city.

Mercer told Jo we'd been calling the dead girl Angel. He asked how they had met on the train that night.

"You know the way it is."

"Not exactly," I said.

"I was the new girl. There were four others who were riding with my friend, and one of them was Angel, or whatever you want to call her. When you've got no roof over your head, you've got to sleep for as long as you can whenever you can. And somebody in the group has to stay awake, making sure no cops come along to bother us. Or no perverts either."

"So you spent the night together?"

Jo scowled at me. "Not how you think. She wasn't a lesbian. Your girl was straight."

Most of the counselors we worked with told us that 40 percent of the country's homeless youth are LGBT, unable or unwilling to stay at home or in foster care, free to take risks and experiment by moving out into the world, even without a roof over their heads.

"Did you have a chance to talk to Angel?" I asked.

"Lots of chances. She was nice to me. She was a good person. Taught me lots of ways to take care of myself."

But in the end Angel was unable to keep herself safe.

"Did she ever tell you where she was from?" Mercer asked. "Why she left home?"

"I didn't care where she was from. Most of us don't like to talk about that because we don't ever want to go there again, and you never know when someone is going to snitch on you."

Jo sat back and gulped some of her coffee. "She didn't have much of a home. Her mother died when she was ten, and that's when her father started abusing her. Sexually abusing her."

Sexual and physical abuse were the next most common reasons for teens to leave their families. Mercer and I saw these kids more regularly than we would have liked.

"You must have spent a lot of time together for Angel to tell you something like that," I said.

"Not really. No reason not to be open about that stuff. We all need each other to survive is how I look at it. It was two nights on the train, that group of us."

"Where did you go during the day?"

Jo put down her container of coffee and stared straight ahead. "Not saying."

"It's nothing Mercer and I haven't heard before. I can promise you we're not looking to get you in trouble."

There were few decent ways for the homeless population to provide for themselves. The older guys had the can-recycling business pretty well locked up, scouring garbage pails on the street for empties to return to stores. Begging worked for men with no legs and women who panhandled with babies in their arms. Healthy teens were more likely to shoplift than to recycle or to beg.

"I tried to get work," Jo said. "I left home with a résumé that I kept in a folder with my backpack. I would have waitressed or worked in a grocery store or a Walmart. But it's hard to find a job when the economy sucks."

And harder when you don't have a place to shower or clean clothes to wear to work.

"What else did Angel help you with?" I asked, hoping for more connections to get us into her world.

Jo took a minute to answer, perhaps wondering whether to give up the information. "She's the one who took me to the museum."

"What museum?"

"Natural History. The one with the dinosaurs and all the dead animals behind glass."

Another link to Central Park. The great American Museum of Natural History was merely five blocks north of the Dakota, facing the Park.

"What did you see at the museum?"

Jo looked at me as though I was clueless. "We didn't go there to see anything. We went there to sleep."

"To sleep? But where?"

I thought of the huge hallways in the museum, filled during weekdays with schoolkids on field trips and on weekends with families and tourists enjoying the treasures housed there.

"After two nights on the train, I spent a week on the streets. I couldn't hardly sleep 'cause it's pretty dangerous to do that. Angel? I ran into her again in Port Authority, and she took me to the museum. The bathrooms there are gigantic, but the stalls are really narrow. So once you lock the door of the stall, you can lean your head against the side of it and sleep till the end of the day when the janitor comes in to mop. Everybody on the street knows about the history museum."

Desperation, like necessity, was the mother of invention.

"Didn't you ever try to get into a shelter?" I asked.

"Not at first. I knew there weren't a lot of beds available, and I was mostly afraid they'd try to send me back home, all those social workers and stuff."

"Covenant House? Did you ever go there?"

"No, ma'am," Jo said. "Y'all got any cigarettes?"

"We'll get you some as soon as we're done," I said. "Why not?"

Again the look that caught her frustration with me. Covenant House had been in business rescuing teens for forty years and had 70 percent of the beds for them in the city.

"It's run by the church, Ms. Cooper. The Catholic Church. I'm not real comfortable with that, any more than they are with me."

"Did Angel ever talk about Covenant House?"

Jo thought about it and answered in the negative. I knew the detectives had started their search to identify Angel at the revered institution that had long ago weathered its own sex abuse scandal, but was hoping that Jo could make a link to a different point in time, several months back, when she first met the dead girl.

"Did she ever mention any other shelter?" Mercer asked.

"She took me to a church once. I think it was way downtown. But there were no beds. And it might have been Angel who told me about Streetwork."

"You know Streetwork?" I said. "Was she ever there?"

It was a brilliant program run by Safe Horizon, the country's largest and best victim advocacy organization. The nonprofit had done groundbreaking work with survivors of domestic violence and established cutting-edge centers for child advocacy. The DA's office worked closely with the well-trained staff, and Streetwork was their latest initiative to reach out to the city's disenfranchised and home-less youth—making contact with twenty thousand of them a year.

"I don't know the answer to that, ma'am," Jo said. "I wasn't ever there when she was."

"Did you use any of their facilities?"

"Yes, I did. I went for meals sometimes, and to take a shower. And once when I got all depressed and tried to cut myself, it was that girl—that Angel—who told me to go to Streetwork for, like, psych services."

I could see Mercer scribbling a note to double-check with the team to see whether they had checked out both of the shelter loca-tions Safe Horizon operated, as well as the drop-in centers for counseling.

"Did you ever have a phone or a laptop since you left home?" I asked. "Do you have either one of those now?"

"I sure don't, ma'am." Jo smiled for the first time. "Besides, I wouldn't have anyplace to plug them in, would I?"

Walk into any of the Apple stores in New York and look for the section of the store with the older devices, not the trendiest new stuff. Any hour of the day or night there was bound to be a gaggle of homeless kids—obvious by the condition of their clothing and the beat-up backpacks—just hanging out to charge their cell phones and get back on the street.

"So how many times would you say you saw Angel between March and now?" I asked. "How did you keep in touch with her?"

Jo reached for a package of strawberry Twizzlers from the bag of snacks that Mercer had bought for her and ripped it open. I didn't think of them as breakfast food, but she was still hungry. "I didn't say I kept in touch with her. If I ran into her—which I did maybe ten times in all—she'd be kind to me, like I said."

"Apart from the train, Jo, where did you see her?"

"The Park. Me and my girlfriend spent a couple of nights with her in Central Park."

I tried not to show my excitement.

"Do you know that Angel—that this girl in the photograph—was killed there?"

"No, ma'am. There's a story going 'round that someone drowned in the Park, in one of the lakes, but I didn't know it was her."

"We don't have a real name for her, as you know, and we don't know how to find her family."

"That would be a waste of time anyway," Jo said. "Her dad is all there was, and frankly I don't think he'd care."

"There must have been someone in her life—a teacher, a friend back home, the people she hung out with here."

"She didn't really hang out that much. She didn't really trust most people she met."

"Sounds like she trusted you," Mercer said.

"My girlfriend says Angel—whatever you're calling her—got along best with people who were wounded, just like she was."

"Wounded?" I asked.

"Not like bloody and all," Jo said. "Folks who'd been hurt hard along the way, sort of like I had. People who had handicaps—physical ones and mental, too. She had a kindness for them, likely grew out of her own pain."

"Is she the one who took you to the Park?"

"No, ma'am. Nobody needs to take a homeless person to Central Park. Everybody knows how to work it there."

"Work it?"

"If you've got nowhere else to sleep, you go to a park. Small ones, big ones. There's parks everywhere, in any city. Me? I like Central Park best. So many places to be where nobody bothers you."

"Don't the police—?" I started to ask.

Jo blew me off. "Old guys, they sleep on benches out in the open, but most of the kids I hang with go deep in the woods. Hard to find us, and cops never give us a hard time."

"Isn't it dangerous?"

"So was being at home for me, and for—well, Angel. This is much easier," Jo said, reaching out to pat the filthy blue bag beside her. "Me and my girl, we have a favorite tree we like to sleep under. And I got everything I need in my backpack. Did you find her—Angel's—pack?"

"No," I said. "Something special in it you can tell us about?"

"No, ma'am. Just we all keep everything we own in these. At night, it's my pillow. Nobody could get to it without waking me up."

"Can you describe her backpack?"

"Nope. I had no reason to notice. She just had one, like we all do."

"What else did she have?" Mercer asked. "Do you remember anything else, anything about her clothing?"

Jo thought for several seconds. "A dark hoodie, last time I saw her. Cargo pants. Maybe a month ago or so is when I remember being with her, she had two shirts. Real pretty ones with ruffles and such."

"Where did she get them?" I asked. "Did she have any money? Did she have a job?"

Jo looked out the window and hesitated before answering. "She told me she lifted them."

"Shoplifted?"

"Yeah. From Macy's."

The idea that Angel had stolen things gave me a new source of hope. "Do you know if she was ever arrested?"

"She never said. But I don't think so. She was good at swiping food from bodegas," Jo said, remembering something that made her happy. "Last time I saw her she had one of those big jars of peanut butter and must have been five of us that ate dinner and breakfast off her."

"Where in the Park did Angel stay, Jo?" I asked. "Where is your favorite place, and where was hers?"

She looked back and forth between Mercer and me. "I'm not telling you where I go. I don't want any trouble."

"You won't get in any trouble," I said. "I promise you. We want to find the man who killed Angel. We want to give her a decent burial. This isn't about you, Jo."

"Did she have a spot?" Mercer asked.

"Yes, sir. She was staying in a place they call the Ravine. You know where that is?"

"I do," I said. "Up near 110th Street."

"I'd never seen anything like it. Me and my girlfriend couldn't believe we were in New York City. Angel said the woods were so thick there and it was so far off the road, down this big hill, that nobody would bother us. So we slept there, I think it was two nights."

"Was Angel with anyone else?"

"Two other people."

"Tell us about them," I said. "Anything you can remember."

"Guys. They were both guys. One was a tranny," Jo said. "A white kid, maybe sixteen, from Long Island, who'd been beaten up pretty bad when one of the men he came on to found out."

A wounded transsexual who sought shelter with Angel sounded just right.

"The other one was African American. Old, like maybe my grandfather's age. Skin color dark like yours," she said to Mercer, "with his hair all white. I don't know where the tranny is now, but the old guy is Vergil. Folks call him Verge. Everybody in Central Park knows him, even the cops."

"Knows him because he's done bad things?" Mercer asked.

"Oh, no. 'Cause he's lived there forever. Verge looks out for people. He knew Angel's story, about her being abused and all. It's Verge who made her leave the Ravine. Told her that bad stuff had happened there. He said there was a guy going around at night attacking people."

Raymond Tanner? Could he have been Verge's concern? Tanner's work release had started in April and by mid-May he'd been AWOL. We needed to find Verge as soon as possible.

"When he made her leave the Ravine," I said, "do you know where Verge took her?"

"Yeah. Yes, I do. We went together. Me and my girlfriend, and her and the tranny."

"Where to?"

Jo hesitated again. "Verge took us to the Ramble. He said we'd be better off there."

Again I kept a poker face.

"The Ramble covers a huge part of the Park," Mercer said. "Can you describe where you were?"

Jo held her hands out to the side. "Verge said it was called Muggers Woods. That's what I remember 'cause it sounded like a bad place. He said it used to be that way a long time ago, but not so much anymore. And it was perfectly fine."

"Do you know it?" I asked Mercer.

"As of yesterday I do. It's far north of the Point, way back off the paths," he said to me. Then to Jo, "Does Verge have some kind of problem? Is there a reason our girl was with him?"

Jo smiled. "Yeah. Verge is real slow. I had an uncle like him, my mama used to call retarded. But fortunately people don't use that word now. He's simple, is what I'd say. Can't read, and sometimes he talks nonsense."

"What kind of nonsense?"

"Verge talks like a child, really. Likes to spend his time at the zoo, panhandlin' for money. Speaks about the animals like they're his friends. Says his family used to have a house in Central Park. Silly things like that."

I leaned forward when Jo mentioned a house in the Park. "Does Verge say he lived in that house?"

"Oh, no, ma'am. He talks about it like there were houses there a hundred years ago. I told you it's nonsense."

"Not so crazy, Jo," Mercer said. He didn't stop to tell her about Seneca Village, but I knew that's what he was thinking.

"Did you find her notebook?" Jo asked.

"Not yet," I said. "Tell us about it."

"Lots of us write in journals. Especially the girls. You know when you sleep outdoors, it's always good to keep a book by you, 'cause then the cops think that you're a student. But it really doesn't have anything to do with that. Like my girlfriend, she makes lists. People she misses and people she doesn't, stores where she lifted things so she can pay them back someday when she gets a job, which churches serve food and what times of the day."

"And you? Do you write?"

"Mostly about places I've been on the street so I can tell other people about them—what's good and what's bad. Angel, she mostly wrote descriptions of folk. What their problems were, what she tried to do to help them. Sometimes she even sketched their faces. She could draw really good." Jo paused for a few seconds. "She wrote in it every night, the times I was around her. You find that notebook, and you'll pretty much find her life."

"Did she let you read any of it?" Mercer asked.

"Not exactly. She showed me her drawings every now and then. Even made one of me with my girlfriend."

"Was she afraid of anyone, Jo? Did she ever confide in you about that?"

"Just her father is all she told me. She told me nobody could hurt her as bad as he did."

"How about Verge?" Mercer asked. "Did you ever see him get violent, get angry with anyone?"

I was sure he was thinking, as I was, about someone who knew the remote places of the Park so well and had attached himself to a vulnerable young woman. We needed to find to out who and where he was as quickly as possible. We needed to know whether he had a criminal history.

Jo rolled her eyes at Mercer. "No way Verge ever got angry. I told you he wanted to protect Angel. He's got this thing he carries with him all the time, this little thing that he told her would make her safe. I guess that didn't work."

"What kind of thing?" I asked. "Was it a weapon of some kind?"

"No, ma'am. Nothing like that. I only saw it once, the last time we were with her," Jo said. "It was some kind of cherub, some little creature that was painted mostly black with gold trim."

Mercer was already reaching for the folder with the photographs of the ebony statue.

"Did she tell you that Verge gave her the cherub?" I asked.

"She never told me how she got it," Jo said. "But there can only be two ways, don't you think? Verge either gave it to her, or she stole it."

TWENTY

"Your head looks like it's spinning and 'bout to fly off your body," Mercer said.

"We've suddenly got so many directions to go in that I don't know where to start."

My paralegal was making the short walk to Canal Street to buy clean clothes—T-shirts, pants, and underwear—for Jo. She had welcomed our invitation to shower in the restroom and was playing the vending machines for snacks and chips like they were Vegas slots.

"Where's Mike?"

"Don't know. He was going to check the Panoscan from the center of the crime scene to see what the views were from Bow Bridge. We're waiting to hear from the head of the Conservancy to see if she can get us into Lavinia Dalton's apartment. Now we need to find Verge."

"I'll call Manny Chirico about that. Get him ID'd, picked up, record checked, and tease everything he knows out of him—good guy or not. And I'll go back at Vickee."

"About what?" I asked.

"Whether she knows of other Seneca Village descendants. If there are family names that survived the generations, and whether Verge is one of them, walking around with that little black angel."

"Maybe St. Michael's Church has records about All Angels'," I said. "And you've got to set up some system to keep a daily tab on Jo. She may pick up more information out there from her homeless buddies, and we have no way to reach her."

"A little respect and a lot to eat will go a long way with her. I'll set up a twice-a-day check-in. She can stop at a fixer in the Park or wherever she is, and she'll have my card so any cop anywhere can loop me in."

"I'll hunt down Mike and push the visit to Dalton, but first I'm going up to Jessica Pell's chambers to have a face-off with her."

"Not a good idea, Alex."

"It wasn't a great one of hers to stake out my driveway last night. Today's Thursday, and her big threat was to take Mike down by tomorrow. I'm not expecting a physical confrontation. Her court officers and law secretary will be right outside the door."

Mercer laughed. "I have no doubt you'd win if it was mud wrestling, but Pell's on a mission."

"So am I," I said, with renewed anger because of the tenderness of last night.

"I'll wait for Jo to clean up, then take her where she wants to go and get on top of Verge. But you have to promise me you'll stay away from Pell, you hear?"

"I'll do my best, Mercer."

After we separated and I thought through Mercer's admonition, I told Laura that I had to watch one of the assistants on trial. I respected the judgment of my friends, but it was my own conscience that was nagging at me.

I walked up to the DA's squad on the south end of the ninth floor. Ever since the office had been established, the NYPD had staffed it with a team of detectives—more than forty of them—whose assignment was to work with prosecutors on investigations and witness interviews. Some of them took turns guarding Battaglia, and all were available to work with us on serious matters.

The small cluster of cubicles known as the wire room was one of the most sophisticated operations in law enforcement. Several detectives whose specialty was electronic surveillance were geniuses at installing video equipment pursuant to search warrants the lawyers obtained. I had partnered with them on scores of undercover operations—from a dentist who was abusing his sedated patients in his office to child molesters who had lured adolescents to meets at hotel rooms. They were the teams who had mastered the art of setting up wiretaps and bugs, bringing down everyone from financial scammers to drug dealers with international cartels.

The door to the equipment-filled room was open, and three of the guys had headphones on and were listening to playback.

"Got a minute?" I asked Artie Scanlon, who was seated closest to me.

"Sure. What do you need, Alex?"

"I have a witness coming in—total sleazebag—and Mercer Wallace won't be there to second me. Would you wire me up? The inconsistencies are all over the map, and I just don't want to get burned by being alone."

"Easy enough. Got a case number, or is it something I've been working on already?" Scanlon stood up and reached on a shelf above him to pull down a small recording device that could be concealed inside the front of my silk blouse.

"One thirty-nine," I said. It seemed as good a number as any.

"Do you need video? I got a camera that will fit over the button of your shirt," he said while he checked the batteries in the audio device.

"I just need the voice, thanks."

Scanlon handed me the tiny microphone and showed me how to clip it onto my bra. I turned around so that he could attach the control package to the rear waistband of my slacks.

"Flip that switch to activate when you're ready to start and you'll be good to go."

"Thanks, Artie. I'll have it back to you within the hour."

I returned to my desk to pick up a file folder so that I looked like I had a legal matter to discuss with the judge.

"Mike wants you to call him," Laura said.

"Will do when I get back. Have to go up to the fifteenth floor on a case."

"I told him you'd get back to him right away. He thinks you two can get into the apartment of a Mrs. Dalton this afternoon."

"Fine, Laura. Please just tell him I'll meet him wherever he wants at two." I reached for my blazer on the back of the door, to cover the bump on my waistband.

"I would have had your case file ready, Alex. Which one is it?" Laura was efficient and loyal and always ready to cover my back.

"Not to worry. Just something Battaglia asked me to do. I'll be back in half an hour."

I raced down the staircase and crossed the seventh floor to get to the elevators that fed into the main section of the courthouse. When the doors opened, defense attorneys and perps, girlfriends and rent-a-baby toddlers stepped back to make room for me.

Jessica Pell was in the middle of a calendar call when she saw me enter the crowded courtroom. She sat bolt upright and adjusted her robe over the lacy white camisole that showed beneath the opening.

I waited for a break between cases before I approached the court officer. "I don't have anything scheduled today, but I'd like a brief appearance before the judge."

"No problem, Ms. Cooper. I'll tell the clerk to fit you in next."

I waited while Pell listened to a bail application on a burglary case. She appeared to be distracted by my presence, trying to keep an eye on me while she responded to counsel. I sat in the front row and flipped on the recorder when the clerk called my name.

"Do you have a case before me, Ms. Cooper?" Pell asked, the right side of her mouth twitching occasionally when she addressed me.

"A matter to discuss, Your Honor."

She rose to her feet and told the court officers she wanted to recess and take me in the robing room.

"I'd like this on the record, Judge Pell," I said, well aware that she was not about to let me talk in open court.

Pell directed her question to the stenographer, pointed one of her long fingers—nails painted a deep burgundy—at the machine on which all the proceedings were memorialized. "You didn't get that, did you? I'd like you to strike it if you did."

The stenographer held up the narrow strip of paper with one hand and drew an X across the part where I had spoken.

"Follow me, Ms. Cooper."

She came down from the bench, and one of the officers led us into the robing room, closing it behind us to ensure our privacy.

The corner of Pell's mouth continued to twitch. "What problem brings you up here, Ms. Cooper?"

"You, Your Honor. The problem I have with you."

"You're joking, right?"

"Not for a minute. There are a few things I was hoping to put on the record."

"Not until I hear them first," she said, walking behind the desk to put some distance between us. I had no doubt the microphone would pick up our conversation just fine in the empty room.

"I can begin by asking what you were doing at my apartment building last night."

She put her palms on the desk as though to steady herself.

"I beg your pardon?"

Pell was stalling while she thought of what to say.

"Midnight or a little later. Waiting in your car at my front door."

"That's absurd. I don't know anyone in your building. I don't even know where you live," she said, throwing her hands in the air. "Listen to me—trying to defend myself against your ridiculous statements as though I had to. I was at home, Ms. Cooper. Now, take your accusations out of my courtroom and keep your mouth shut."

"And what should I do with the photographs, Judge Pell? The pictures I took with my cell phone?" She was as easy to bluff as a six-year-old. "The JSC 421 plate."

She lowered her voice, gritting her teeth and pointing her

finger at me as though it was a talon. "You are about to find yourself in contempt, Ms. Cooper."

"The photos, Judge. What would you like me to do with them?"

She was pretty close to snapping. "Do you have any idea of the kind of pressure I'm under? Do you know that I have been threatened and harassed and stalked, and I have been trying to get your goddamn office to take me seriously?"

"And you thought that a house call to me would accomplish that?"

"It's not about you. There—there's someone else who lives in your building."

"You just told me you didn't know where I live."

"I don't have to tell you anything," the judge said, unable to control the pitch of her voice. "You're the one who's responsible for putting my life in danger, Ms. Cooper. It was you who pulled the detail off me, even before the death threats landed on my desk."

"I had nothing to do with whoever was guarding you, for whatever reason. So you made up some bullshit story to tell Paul Battaglia because Detective Chapman came to his senses and got out of bed with you?" I asked.

"None of your business, you jealous bitch," Pell said.

"Jealous of what? I've never slept with Mike Chapman." Last night's kiss had given urgency to my idea to confront Jessica Pell while I could still speak the truth.

"That's a lie."

Not yet it isn't. "So you told the district attorney that you blamed the security lapse on me, right, with absolutely no regard for the truth of the situation?"

"Our conversation is none of your business, Ms. Cooper."

"You are going to be so screwed, Judge, when the results of the handwriting analysis and the DNA on the envelopes in which your so-called death threats arrived are released to the *New York Post*."

"Why—?"

Her anger was changing to fear as I started to talk about the evidence. "I've talked to Commissioner Scully about this."

"What I reported to Chapman's supervisor was in full confidence. If I had gone to Commissioner Scully directly, Mike Chapman would be looking for work by now."

"He is too well respected in the department for anyone to take you seriously for very long," I said. "Scully gets—we all get—that you are completely strung out, Judge Pell. That having been dumped by the deputy mayor was a—"

"You're outrageous, Ms. Cooper. I—"

"Was a form of public humiliation you might not have deserved. But Mike Chapman doesn't deserve anything like it either, nor do I. So I happened to stop by the lab this morning, and I can promise you that finding your DNA in the mixture of the fingerprints on your so-called death threats will undercut anyone's belief in the crap you're trying to sell and may—most thankfully—get you bounced right off the bench."

"You don't know what you're talking about."

"Most of the time I actually do, Judge. And I'm presenting witnesses at a hearing in ten days in front of your colleague, Judge Heller, about the admissibility of FST—fragmentary mixtures of DNA. So I'm pretty much up to speed on the science of it, and that—along with the comic book antics of your imaginary hit men—well, I'd say the likelihood of your reappointment to the court is about as promising as an encore hookup with Detective Chapman."

"You're going to pay for this, Alexandra Cooper."

"Threaten me again, Your Honor, why don't you? I have a fierce loyalty to my friends and to the colleagues I respect, and I'm not about to let you bring one of the best detectives in the city down because you think you've been seduced and abandoned."

"Even if my DNA is on that stationery, I can explain that to Scully and the analysts. My relationship with Chapman has nothing to do with the legitimacy of the threats I've received." Jessica Pell looked like a caged animal now.

"Legitimate, my ass. Which headline will come first, do you think? JILTED JUDGE FEIGNS FEAR?" I asked. "Or PELL PENS POISON EPISTLES?"

Jessica Pell was ready to bring our conversation to an end. She came out from behind the desk and started to walk past me to the door.

"You've got quite a mouth on you, Ms. Cooper."

"Just warming up, Judge." I took a step back to get out of her way. "I think the ultimatum you gave to Sergeant Chirico was that he find some way to discipline Mike Chapman by the end of this week or you'd go to the commissioner. So I guess if you haven't withdrawn your complaint by noon tomorrow, we get to take our gloves off and get down and dirty."

Jessica Pell stopped in her tracks. "What exactly do you mean by that?"

"I've asked the lab to rush the results of the analysis of your letters. And I hate when law enforcement officers leak information, Your Honor, but they'd make such a great story for the Sunday papers—along with the photo of your car parked in front of my building last night. It will be hard to find someone to believe you after that."

The judge pivoted to face me, lifting her right arm to take a swipe at my face. I turned my head to try to avoid the slap, but two of her nails caught the edge of my cheek.

"They won't believe this either," she said. "But you deserve it, and a kick in the gut to go with it. I suggest, Ms. Cooper, that the prosecution rests."

My face stung, and I could feel a trickle of blood run down the side of it. Before I wiped it away, I reached for the battery pack on my waistband and held it in front of Pell's nose.

"I have the feeling the sound of you hitting me will come through loud and clear, Your Honor," I said. "And actually, I'm very well rested."

TWENTY-ONE

"Did that snow monkey get a piece of your cheek, or did you cut yourself shaving this morning?" Mike asked.

It was 1:30 in the afternoon, and for the first time in days, clouds were moving in over the Park. We were standing at the foot of the Bow Bridge, where Angel's body had been found.

"Must have been a cat," I said.

"Want to tell me about it?" he asked, hands on hips as he kept up the usual tone of our patter in front of the group of cops standing behind him.

"Nothing to tell. I just scraped it on the edge of the kitchen cabinet when I reached for a coffee mug."

"I know you can't cook, Coop, but not even a safe cup of brew?"

"Danger everywhere," I said. There was no point telling him about my tête-à-tête with Jessica Pell unless my efforts failed. "What's here?"

"I checked in with Hal Sherman this morning, to see the Panoscan."

"They filmed it right from this spot, didn't they?"

"Exactly. It's interesting, but I don't know that it gives us much."

Mike was looking due north, and I took my place next to him. We were even with East 73rd Street, though much closer to Central Park West.

"To the north," he said, "all you can see is the Ramble. It's tree covered and so steep that anything—or anyone—up there would be obscured from viewing this place or being in sight range. There could be a connection, of course, or it could be where the killer came from—"

"And the body, too."

"Yes, and the body. But the foliage is too dense to see through."

He turned to his right and I did the same. Above the tree line, the upper floors and rooftops of the prestigious addresses of Fifth Avenue—the Gold Coast, as it has often been called—dominated the view.

"See how many of them have the little eyelid windows you were talking about?" Mike said.

"All the old buildings do."

"The staff sure had the best views, if nothing else."

Then we took in the southern perimeter, just as we had from the Arsenal roof the night before. Finally we were facing west, staring directly at the façade and roof of the Dakota, with a completely unobstructed view.

"I froze the Panoscan right there," Mike said, "and zoomed it in. You can see everything so clearly from this point."

"Did you catch anyone looking out the windows?" I asked, jokingly.

He held out his arm, pointing at the apartment. "I swear there's a shadow—a shadow the size of a person—framed in the window on the ninth floor, right above where Dalton lives."

"Really?"

"Hal is going to try to enhance the shot for me. Probably not a big deal, though. There were sirens and lot of police activity by the time the Panoscan team arrived. I'll bet half the buildings on both sides of the Park had people rubbernecking from their windows."

"I guess so. Anything else?"

"That's it. Just wanted you to see it from this perspective."

When I called Mike before I left the office, he told me that Mia Schneider had arranged for us to visit Lavinia Dalton. Her nurses would admit us at two and allow us to see her briefly, if she was up to it, and to look around the apartment, especially in the room that housed the collections of silver.

We left the other cops behind, crossing the bridge and climbing the steps of Bethesda Terrace to exit the Park on 72nd Street and Central Park West.

"You okay, Coop?"

"Very okay." My head was down, and I could feel the color rising from my neck to my forehead. "You?"

"Don't get all sappy on me, kid. It was just a kiss."

"Not spunky, not sappy," I said. There were still uniformed cops everywhere along the walkways of the Park. "How long does the lieutenant think this police presence is going to last?"

"Tomorrow's one week since the body was found. Scully's going to pull most of the units out of here by the weekend."

"'Cause she's nobody?"

"Because the sight of so much blue in the green Park is off-putting to the tourist trade. The mayor wants business as usual. He gave us a week to get our killer, and we failed."

"But Raymond Tanner's out here somewhere."

"Don't whine, Coop. You know how I hate that."

"Remind me what else it is you don't like," I said, waving at two policewomen I'd worked with a few months back.

"There'll still be an undercover team working on the homicide, and with all the media Tanner's had in the last twenty-four, I expect he's anyplace but Central Park."

"He likes it here. Comfort zone and all that."

"Tanner also likes his freedom. There are lots of parks in the five boroughs," Mike said. "Did Mercer have any luck with names from Seneca Village?"

"He called Vickee before he left my office. She had some old family papers from the church, but nothing with names on it. He's figuring to get Verge by tonight and take it from there."

The entrance to the Dakota was on 72nd Street, a two-story-high passageway through to the inner courtyard around which the massive building had been constructed, protected by a manned gate house. It was in front of this very spot that John Lennon was gunned down.

Mike gave his name to the guard, and we waited until he got the okay to admit us.

"To the right, please. Elevators in the far corner, to the eighth floor."

We walked across the cobblestones, both of us dwarfed by the sheer size of the walls around us. Inside the lobby, we waited for the doors to open and deliver us to the door of the Dalton apartment.

"Good afternoon," Mike said, extending his hand with the blue-and-gold shield in its leather case. "Mike Chapman, NYPD. This is Assistant District Attorney Alexandra Cooper."

I said hello to the young woman, who was dressed in a traditional housemaid's uniform, a black dress with crisply starched collar, cuffs, and apron.

"Come in, please," she said. "We've been expecting you."

Mike and I followed her through the entryway into a living room that was at least fifty feet long, with ceilings almost twenty feet high. The Oriental carpet was patterned in deep burgundy and navy blue, the sofas and club chairs were in subdued colors also, and the elegant but slightly faded décor appeared not to have been updated in several decades.

Beyond that was a formal dining room, walls painted a deep

yellow and cabinets at both ends displaying sets of porcelain din-nerware and crystal wineglasses that looked fit for a king.

The next two rooms were small parlors, both facing the Park like the ones we had just come through. They were all designed *enfilade*, so that each time the housemaid opened the next pair of doors, the migration from one room to the next flowed naturally. You could see over your shoulder to the front door and, if all were opened at once, ahead to the end of the floor. Off to the right—the side away from the Park—was an entrance to each, which I presumed fed into a corridor that paralleled the grand spaces.

"Miss Dalton is resting in the dayroom," the maid said. "The nurses will assist you from here."

She pushed the two door handles and stepped back. The first person I saw was a nurse, dressed all in white, who was arranging chairs around a single bed, where Lavinia Dalton was sitting upright, another nurse beside her.

The room was lighter and more cheerful than the others, and though the day was overcast, the narrow bed was in front of a large window, positioned so that Lavinia could see the Park laid out below her.

Mike took the lead again in introducing us to the nurses, and I watched as Lavinia cocked her head and smiled at the sound of his voice. We were invited by the nurse to move closer and sit down, and the elderly woman smiled with what seemed to be delight at the arrival of visitors.

Lavinia Dalton was very well cared for, by all appearances. She still had the bones of a once-beautiful face, with light-blue eyes that sparkled as brightly as her smile. Her hair was thick and white, cut short and carefully coiffed. She was wearing a silk dressing gown and still showing off the Dalton jewels—a large diamond ring, several gold charm bracelets with discs the size of silver dollars, and sapphire studs in her ears to match the color of her eyes. Her back was supported by three pillows, and I recognized the classic design of the thousand-thread-count percale Porthault sheets that were more costly than Mike's monthly rent.

"Miss Dalton," Mike said, "Alexandra and I came to say hello to you."

He had seated himself closest to her, reaching out to take her hand, capturing her attention as he did with so many women who were instantly engaged by his charm and good looks.

"Archer," she said to him, her bracelets jangling as she clasped his hand in hers.

"No, ma'am," the older nurse said. "This is Mr. Mike."

"How do you do, Miss Dalton?" Mike said, beaming back at her. "You're looking very pretty today."

"Thank you, son. I'm so happy to see you."

"What kind of day have you had?"

"I don't know," she said. "You should ask the nurse."

"You're having a very good day, Miss Dalton. You've enjoyed your lunch, and now you have new friends come to visit." The older one spoke again, while the other left the room.

"We've just come from Central Park," Mike said. "That's why we thought we'd visit you."

"I love the Park." Lavinia Dalton lifted her head from the pillow and looked out at the view. She had a clear shot of the western end of the Lake and the great vista overlooking the Bethesda angel. "Perhaps we should go for a walk."

"Not this afternoon, Miss Dalton," the nurse said. "It looks like it's going to rain."

"We need the rain."

The old woman was right, but I didn't know whether that was because she knew we'd had a dry, sunny spell or if she was just making pleasantries.

I turned my head at the sound of footsteps. A very attractive woman in her early sixties came into the room, dressed in a cardigan sweater and pleated skirt. Her long blond hair was held back off her face by a headband.

"Good afternoon, Detective, Ms. Cooper," she said, addressing each of us. "I'm Jillian Sorenson. Mia told me that you would be coming today. I'm Miss Dalton's secretary."

She was all business, stern and unsmiling.

"Thanks for having us in on such short notice," I said.

"Jillian," Lavinia said to her, "Jillian, is Archer coming today?"

"No, Lavinia. But you've got lovely guests who are here to see you."

We went back and forth with Lavinia for several minutes, and although she was talkative and good-natured, it was obvious her memory was compromised.

I asked Jillian Sorenson if we might talk to her in another room, and Mike and I retraced our steps to one of the small parlors.

"We don't want to upset Miss Dalton," Mike said, "but we do have some questions to ask."

"Why not start with me?"

"Well, because we'd like information about things that go back quite a long time."

"I've been with the Daltons since the late 1960s," she said. "That's why Lavinia knows my name, even though she can't call the nurses by name these days and she's unlikely to remember she just talked to you now if we reenter the room in half an hour. There's still a good amount of the long-term memory intact."

"Will we upset her," I asked, "if we talk about her family?"

"Most likely."

"And you—?"

"I went to Vassar with Archer Dalton's wife, which is how I found out about the position as Lavinia's assistant," Jillian said. "It was a tremendous challenge for a first job because she was such a vibrant social figure in those days. Hard to keep up with her."

She was a few inches shorter than I and spoke with a clipped upper-crust accent. I was guessing her roots were on the Philadelphia Main Line.

"I imagine it was," I said. "Do you live in the apartment?"

"When I got out of college, I did live here for the first six years. I have my own home, but for the nights Lavinia isn't doing well, I do keep a room here."

Mike seemed to perk up. "So you were on the staff when Lucy was kidnapped?"

Jillian Sorenson's back stiffened. "I thought your interest was in the silver, Mr. Chapman. I hope you don't intend to bring Lucy's name up in front of Lavinia."

"It is about the silver, but—"

"And I wasn't considered staff," she said, responding rather archly, "like the other servants were. I was in charge of all Lavinia's business and philanthropic correspondence. I was treated like family, and I lived in the family quarters."

"Were you working here when Archer Dalton and his wife were killed in the crash?" I asked.

"Yes, I was. Lavinia had me fly to Zurich to identify their bodies," she said, "and arrange to bring them home. It was devastating for me, of course, because we'd been so close."

"And when Lucy was kidnapped?"

"Why don't you read the old newspapers, Ms. Cooper? And the police files?" Sorenson said, snapping at me. "There were nine of us working here that day while Lavinia was out. And each of us was interrogated and fingerprinted and questioned time and time again. My photograph was in all the newspapers, which proved rather an embarrassment to my family."

"An embarrassment for them versus a tragedy for Lavinia Dalton," Mike said, shifting his arms like a set of scales.

"I'm not minimizing the horror of Lucy's disappearance—of her death, although that's a word I'd never use in front of Lavinia. But we all paid a dreadful price for being here that day," Sorenson said, her arms crossed as she clenched them with her hands. "Even my fiancé was dragged through the dirt by the tabloids."

"Why—?" I started to ask.

"Because those reporters who thought the Dakota was impene-

trable by strangers and assumed the kidnapping was an inside job
were looking for a mastermind smarter than the butler. My fiancé
was an investment banker. They figured he might have typed some
of the ransom notes, which dictated how the money was to be paid
and delivered, Ms. Cooper. He ended our engagement the day before
we were to be married."

And my fiancé had been killed in an accident the night before
my wedding. I understood her anger and pain.

"So if you two are here to play sleuth all over again about one of
the largest manhunts in police history, you've come too late. Neither Lavinia nor I have anything to say about Lucy," Sorenson said.
"If you have questions about the silver collection, however, I'm
happy to tell you everything I know."

This was not the reception I'd been counting on based on Mia
Schneider's story last evening.

"Is the collection here?" Mike asked.

Jillian Sorenson paused before she answered. "Yes. May I assume this has something to do with last week's murder and not
Lucy's kidnapping?"

"I can promise you it's not about Lucy," Mike said. "That's all I
can tell you."

"May we see the pieces?" I asked.

"I told Mia I'd show them to you," Sorenson said. "You'll have
to come this way."

Instead of retracing our steps through the parlors and dining
room, Jillian Sorenson led us out into the hallway that seemed to
run half the length of Central Park West. Doors lined both sides of
the wide corridor.

"These doors," Mike said, "what do they lead to?"

Sorenson wasn't happy to have more questions, but she did her
best to answer them as we walked along.

"As you might know, when the Dakota was built, it was meant
to have sixty-five apartments, places in which rich people could live
as comfortably as in their private mansions, but with far more

services available. They were all rentals at that original time, not offered for ownership until decades later."

The dark corridor was lined with photographs, large nineteenth-century prints commemorating the construction of the Transcontinental Railroad, interspersed with superb portraits of Lavinia's forebears posed with presidents and potentates.

"No two apartments," she said, "were alike, so there is no single floor plan that matches another one. Archer Dalton rented six of the large apartments on this floor and broke through to combine them."

"Six?" I said. "He could have housed an army."

"That was his plan. He hoped his family would grow in generation after generation—which never happened—and he counted on a large staff being one of life's necessities. The rooms that face the Park are all the major ones, as you've seen, including three master bedrooms."

"Lavinia's?" I didn't dare say the names of Lucy and her parents.

"Then a sitting room, then young Archer's, and then the nursery for Baby Lucy." Jillian Sorenson did it for me.

"So the nursery was the last room in the south corner," Mike said. He was back to the kidnapping, seeing how easy it would have been to sneak the child away without calling attention to yourself, if you were familiar with the extraordinary maze of doors and hallways.

"On the other side," Jillian said, gesturing to the rooms on the right, "are the kitchen, the laundry rooms, my old bedroom and office, some of the quarters where the more important senior staff could sleep."

"And the rest of the staff?"

"Some were day workers who slept downtown in their own homes, like the laundress and the kitchen workers—except for the cook. Others had quarters upstairs, which was quite common in those days."

Mike winked at me—a nod to the eyelid windows under the eaves of the building.

"So no view on that side," Mike said, "where your room is?"

"No view of the Park," Sorenson said, "but the Dakota is a real novelty. Since it's built around a courtyard, it has fresh air and brightness from both sides. It's quite cheerful from these rooms really, with large windows and lots of western light all afternoon."

Halfway down the hallway was a wall that split the block-long corridor in half. We had to zigzag around it to get to the bedroom wing. It provided a natural barrier between the more public rooms and the intimate spaces, which might also have proved of good use to the kidnappers of Baby Lucy.

"Mia Schneider told us that Lavinia refused to allow any change in Lucy's room," Mike said. "That she expected the child to come home, and wanted things to be exactly as they were when she was taken."

"That's true, Mr. Chapman. And I'm not permitted to show it to you, if that's where you're going with your statement."

Jillian Sorenson was either rigidly professional, or the events of forty years ago had filled her veins with ice.

"Why is that?" Mike asked.

"That's as Lavinia wishes it to be."

"In case you didn't notice, Lavinia's not too sure what day it is."

"There are some things, despite your rudeness, Mr. Chapman, that she still feels very strongly about. I don't intend to satisfy your curiosity with a peek at the nursery."

There were only three doors left on each side before we would reach the south end of the floor. Jill Sorenson stopped in front of the second, on the courtyard side, and opened the door.

"These are the police officers Mia told me about," she said to a woman standing inside the room, back against the window and hands clasped in front of her, who had clearly been waiting for us. "Bernice, this is Ms. Cooper and Mr. Chapman."

"Pleased to meet you," she said, with the vaguest hint of a Scottish brogue in her voice. "Bernice Wicks, at your service."

The woman, dressed in the same formal maid's outfit as her

junior counterpart who had admitted us to the apartment, seemed to be just a few years younger than Lavinia Dalton. I wanted to tell her to sit down and relax, not stand ready to cater to us.

Jillian turned on the overhead lights and the Dalton silver shined like it was reflecting off a room of mirrors.

"May I help you to something to eat or drink?" Bernice asked.

"No, thank you," I said.

The room was practically the size of the living room, and although there was not much sun streaming through the western-facing windows today, there was so much silver, one needed almost to blink from the glare.

Directly beneath our feet, for half the length of the room, was the fabulous reproduction of Dalton's Northern Atlantic railroad cars. The tracks were laid out in a complicated array of figure eights and long straightaways. There was a handsome model of Grand Central Station, which anchored the set, and then every kind of train car, from a fancy locomotive to passenger cars, coal car, tankers, milk trains, and finally a caboose.

Around the room, in display cases and mounted on shelves, were other pieces—undoubtedly designed for Archer Dalton by Gorham and Frost. There were wine buckets and punch bowls, trophies and loving cups, and in one enormous glass-fronted cabinet a silver dinner service for twenty-four people.

"I asked Bernice to meet us in here because she has looked over this collection since she started with Lavinia. Isn't that right?"

"That's right, Miss Jillian." The woman exuded a warmth entirely lacking in Sorenson.

"No need to stand here on our account," Mike said as I looked beyond the train set to the extraordinary copy of Central Park that was laid out on the far side of the room.

"I'm happy to do my bit."

"Don't you want to get off your feet?" Mike asked, pointing to a fine old leather couch against the wall.

"Thank you, sir. But I'm heartier than I look."

"How long have you worked for Miss Dalton?"

Jillian Sorenson knew exactly what direction Mike was headed. "Bernice came to work for Lavinia, as one of two housemaids, in 1968. She's been extremely dedicated to us and refuses to accept retirement. Isn't that right, Bernice?"

"Retire to what, Miss Jillian?" she said with a hearty laugh.

"So you were here in '71?" Mike asked.

"We're the only two from that time still in the household," Jill said. "Lavinia respected each of us and took our part while we were being investigated and our reputations cut to shreds. We'll always be here for her, Mr. Chapman."

"Did you live here at the time of the kidnapping, Bernice?"

"Not full-time," Bernice said. "I had to take a job because my husband had just passed—not even forty years old. My daughter was nineteen at the time and able to look after my son, who was only fourteen when I started here."

"Bernice stayed in one of the little rooms upstairs when we required her to sleep over, once or twice a week, if there were big dinners or affairs."

"And my Eddie was allowed to sleep over, too, if need be. How he loved Mr. Archer's train set, and it certainly made Miss Lavinia happy to have a boy to play with them."

Bernice was as determined as Jillian to keep our attention on what we had come to see.

I guided myself around the train tracks, toward the mock-up of the Park. Jillian walked along the wall and turned on the lights overhead.

The entire layout was a dazzling re-creation of the landmark park, every prominent feature instantly recognizable as I knelt down to study the Maine Monument at the southeast entrance.

"We've only seen two of the pieces before today, Ms. Sorenson," I said. "They're quite impressive, but this really takes your breath away."

Her grim expression gave way, at last, to a smile. "They do

exactly that, Ms. Cooper. Archer Dalton paid a king's ransom for these back in the day. The value now is so many millions of dollars that it's rather shocking."

"This collection belongs in a museum," Mike said, pinching the nape of my neck as he walked around me.

"And someday it will be in one," Jillian said. "But for now, they're exactly where Lavinia wants them to be. Is there something particular you're interested in?"

Mike squatted on the east side of the Park setting and was looking methodically at each of the pieces.

"We thought you might be missing a few pieces," I said, "and that you might help us figure when and how they became separated."

"That's ridiculous. Another kidnapping is what you think? Silver treasures this time? Bernice is in and out of this room every day, Ms. Cooper. She dusts and polishes all the pieces. Bernice?"

"All accounted for, Miss Jillian. No mystery here."

"Are you pointing fingers again, Mr. Chapman?"

At that very moment, my eyes stopped on the statue of the Obelisk. It was standing behind the miniature of the Metropolitan Museum of Art, exactly where it was supposed to be.

"Mike," I said, "the Obelisk—"

"Check. And the castle is here, too," he said to me. "So how many of these sets were created, Miss Sorenson?"

"Only one. The trains for Archer, and the Park for Lavinia," Jill said. "One of each."

"Do you mind if I pick this up?"

"Not at all, Detective."

He turned the obelisk over to examine its base. "No markings here, Coop. No Gorham and Frost hallmark. Nothing engraved."

"I don't understand how this can be," I said.

"Miss Jillian, don't you want to tell them about the originals?" Bernice Wicks asked.

Jillian Sorenson looked at her as though she was shooting daggers with her glance.

"What do you mean, Bernice?" Mike asked. "I thought there's only one set."

"What she means, Detective—and I hope you don't need to repeat this to anyone—is that these collections—the train and the Park—are the maquettes for the originals."

"Maquettes?" Mike asked.

"Scale models," I said. "Prototypes. Artists use them all the time when they're creating sculptures and things."

"Damn," he said. "I really do need to work on my French, Coop."

"What's the big deal?" I asked Jillian Sorenson.

She seemed rather chagrined by Bernice's revelation. "When the collection is photographed for antique journals, we've not had to tell them about the originals. It's only when museums or galleries—or an appraiser—sends a scholar to study the pieces. It's not public knowledge that they're just models."

"Would people care?" Mike asked.

"Of course they would. And it's necessary for us to keep the interest in the collection heightened, for its eventual placement or sale when that time comes. Its uniqueness, its rarity, will be a significant factor," Sorenson said. "Several years ago, though, the insurance for keeping these two sets in the apartment became prohibitive, so we replaced them with the maquettes—at the insistence of our insurance brokers. In truth, the models are so well done it would be hard for anyone to know."

"And you arranged that?" Mike asked.

"She certainly did," Bernice said. "We all helped, but Miss Jillian did it without disturbing Miss Lavinia for a minute."

"Lavinia wouldn't have heard of the exchange," Sorenson said, with a hangdog expression on her face. "Damn the insurance, she would have told me."

"And where are the originals?" I asked.

"In storage, Ms. Cooper. With a lot of other items that form the Dalton heritage."

"I think there's been a breach of security, either here," I said, "or at the storage facility."

Jillian Sorenson bristled at the suggestion, and Bernice Wicks took a cue from her colleague. Neither wanted to hear another accusation.

I took my phone from my pocket and brought up the photographs of the Obelisk and Belvedere Castle. I let her hold the phone and look at the close-ups of them.

"They've got the Gorham and Frost markings on the bottom. They must be the real thing."

"I don't know what to say, Ms. Cooper. It's a most unlikely scenario."

"And more unlikely that there is a third set of Park statues commissioned by Archer Dalton."

As Jillian Sorenson passed the phone back to me, it vibrated in her hand. She was shaking her head in denial that anything she had supervised could have gone wrong.

I answered the call and heard Mercer's voice.

"You and Mike need to meet me," he said. "The Park anticrime unit has found Verge."

TWENTY-TWO

The black man with a scowl on his face was sitting in a child-sized chair in the front of the marionette theater of the Swedish Cottage inside Central Park, just above the 79th Street Transverse.

He sported a pure white Afro, very few teeth, and a T-shirt with the unpleasant statement I LOOK MUCH SEXIER ONLINE.

We were in the rear of the room. Mercer had his back to the man and was talking to Mike and me. "Vergil Humphrey. Sixty-three years old. From Queens originally. Hasn't been in trouble for a while but has a history of sexual battery in Florida, including a felony conviction there, for which he did serious jail time."

"Jo thinks he's harmless," I said. "What do you have on the victims?"

"From the statutory charge, looks like he had a thing for thirteen-, fourteen-year-olds."

I put my head in my hands. "And living in the Park with hordes of teens who are struggling to find a safe haven."

"Verge tells me he volunteered for chemical castration before his release, six years ago," Mercer said. "I have a call in to the Glades County prosecutor to check it out."

"Is that a real fix, Coop?" Mike asked.

"It's usually a ploy for an early parole. An antiandrogen drug that's supposed to interrupt any inappropriate thoughts by shutting down the ability to maintain an erection."

"What I meant is, does it work?"

"I'm not a believer. I suppose it can, but there isn't enough evidence. Very few states have legislation that allows it. I don't think it stops the urge to molest; it just may change the outcome."

"How?"

Mercer answered him. "Say the perp is still attracted to teenagers. Finds a target but he can't perform, so maybe he gets frustrated and takes out his anger on his victim."

"I see. Can't rape her, so he beats her up," Mike said.

"Or he sexually abuses her in some other way."

"No seminal fluid. No DNA."

"You're thinking of Angel," Mercer said.

"She's too old for him," I said. "Guys into thirteen, fourteen don't usually do nineteen, twenty. Pervs get fixated on an age that works for them. If they prey on six-year-olds, they're not usually drawn to twelve-year-olds."

"The professional world you have chosen to inhabit is totally demented, Coop. Besides, what if our girl looked younger than she does now in a refrigerated box?"

"Jo says Verge was her friend, her protector," I said.

"Still could be the way he gains the trust of his vics."

"How'd you find him?" I asked Mercer.

"Like Jo told us, all the cops know him. Came up here to live with his sister when he got out of jail in Florida. Wasn't too friendly a place to be a convicted child molester, so he moved back up north. When his sister kicked him out of the house, he started living in parks, working his way to this one."

"What do the cops say about him?"

"That he's no trouble at all. Friendly guy, sort of simple. He's good to the homeless kids, and the troublemakers seem to leave him alone."

"Good to the kids," I said. "That's the part I don't like."

"You'd have had cases against him already if he'd been assaulting them," Mike said.

"Really? In your experience, Detective, is law enforcement the first place kids on the run from their families who stay alive by petty theft and sleeping in public bathrooms and using false identities turn to? You know better than that. We hardly ever get complaints from the homeless. That's why they're such easy targets."

"That's why a disproportionate number of them wind up dead," Mercer said.

"What's all this talking behind my back?" Verge called out to Mercer.

The three of us walked to the front of the room, and Mercer gave him our names. The scowl vanished, and Verge started speaking with us.

Mercer had shown him an eight-by-ten color photograph of Angel after the autopsy, and we gave it to him again. "I told the man I met this girl. I'm not good on time, but I'd say maybe a month or two ago. The girls like me," he said with a practically toothless smile.

"What do you know about her?" Mercer asked.

"I know she's dead. Least she looks dead in that photograph, and your cops have been turning this Park upside down looking for the man who hurt her."

"Have you given them any help, Verge?"

"Haven't asked me for any."

He spoke clearly and directly, though there was a childlike affect to him.

"Well, that's why the three of us are here. To see what you know," Mercer said. "Can you tell me her name?"

"Haven't got the slightest idea of that. I'm not good on names anyway, and there are too many kids out here to be remembering all of them."

"But this girl was special. Someone told us today that you were protecting her. That you helped her leave the Ravine and move down to this end of the Park."

"I've done that for lots of people."

"Why is that?"

"I don't like the Ravine, the north end of the Park. It's too quiet up there. Besides, I grew up down here."

"You grew up in Queens, didn't you?" Mercer said. "Not the Park."

"I did. But my people are from the Park."

"What do you mean, Verge?"

"We had a house here, right here in Central Park. Right about 84th Street."

"That you lived in?"

"No, Detective. Long before you and I were born." Verge leaned forward toward Mercer and tapped on his forehead with his finger. "People think I'm touched when I say that, but it's true. I can prove it to you."

"I get it, sir," Mercer said. "Seneca Village."

Verge leaned back and roared with delight. "Now, how do you know about that?"

"My wife's family came out of Seneca. She'll be so happy to talk to you."

"Maybe we're kin, your wife and me. Maybe we're related."

They talked about the history of the former African American community for several minutes. Verge had no idea what had become of other residents, but the tales had come down through his family, and he relished speaking of them to someone who didn't think he was making it all up.

"How well do you know the Ramble?" Mike asked.

"Better than almost anybody. I can show you places you've never seen," Verge said, turning his head to me. "You're so quiet, young lady. Can I take you for a walk?"

I knew I didn't look like a teenager, but I thought of his criminal background and got goose bumps from the idea of letting a sexual predator like Verge Humphrey walk me through the wilderness.

"Sometime I would like that," I said.

Mercer had established a relationship with Verge that got the older man talking. Mike was interested in getting information without any more stroking.

"When did you move back up from Florida?" Mike asked.

"Who said anything about the Sunshine State?"

"I heard you lived there for a while," Mike said.

"For too long," Verge said. "Got myself in trouble there, but you probably know that already."

"What'd you do?"

"I'd like the young lady to step out, if you don't mind. It's nasty, what they say about me."

I started to walk back to the far end of the room. Verge's voice carried throughout the space, though I busied myself with e-mails on my BlackBerry to look as though I had no interest.

Mercer eased Verge into a conversation about his criminal conduct. He admitted exposing himself to young women, starting back in his teens. He had several juvenile arrests in New York, but nothing that showed on his adult record.

"I stayed out of trouble for a good long time after that."

"Did you go to school in Queens?"

"I dropped out of high school," Verge said. "Got a job nearby here, in the same parking garage where my daddy worked. Worked there for nearly fifteen years. Right over on Amsterdam Avenue."

Right under his father's nose every day, just a couple of blocks west of the Park.

"What happened after that?"

"When he died, I started having problems again."

Verge took Mercer through the typical progression of a sex offender. Exposing himself to potential victims before he worked up the wherewithal to attack, climbing fire escapes to look in windows for women undressed or undressing, and then actually grabbing victims from the street to sexually abuse them.

Although their voices were subdued, I could hear the conversation, and all the excuses that Verge offered for his behavior.

After a couple of close calls with police in Queens, his mother shipped him off to Florida in 1980, to live with his oldest sister. His behavior escalated there until he was finally caught and convicted, and incarcerated for nine years. When he was released, that sister sent him back home to live with the youngest sibling and her family. It was she who threw him out of the house because she had grandchildren and didn't want Verge to be around them.

"How's that medicine working for you?" Mike asked.

"Which one is that?"

"The one that's supposed to make you behave."

Verge rubbed his hands together. "I'm a good man, Mr. Detective. Mind my own business and don't ever have bad thoughts anymore."

"Even I have a few of 'em," Mike said.

Verge glanced over at Mike. "What do you do when you get them?"

"What do *you* do?"

"I'm telling you I don't get them. If I did, I'd hate myself." Verge sounded like he was trying to convince himself of that fact.

"So how can you hang around all those kids—those teenagers in the Park?" Mike waved the photograph of Angel in front of him. "Isn't it a great temptation to have them around you?"

Verge looked away from the picture, down at the floor, and shook his head.

"I don't mean to hurt anybody," he said. "I was on my own a lot as a kid, and even when I got older. Folks threw me out and wasn't nobody that would take me in. I know what it's like to be abused."

Don't start with the abuse excuse. I really didn't want to hear Verge say he was prompted to commit his crimes because of his own victimization.

"Do you remember spending time with this girl?" Mike asked.

"Yeah. She was in a group. She was with a bunch of other kids."

"Did you know the name of any of them?"

"No, Mr. Detective. I'm so bad at names, like I said."

Mike had one foot up on a chair, his arm on his knee, so he could get face-to-face with Verge Humphrey. "No offense, Verge, but you're three times the age of these kids. Why would you be spending time with them?"

"I never growed up right is what my sister says. I've always been around younger people."

"And these people in particular, what was your interest in them?"

"No interest at all. They were tomboys, weren't they?"

"What do you mean by tomboys?" Mike asked.

I thought of the foursome in the Ravine rescued by Verge, as Jo had described them. She and her partner were gay, the male run-away was transgendered, and the dead girl was an incest victim who may have concealed her sexual identity in the uniform of a homeless kid. Maybe Verge tried to keep a lid on his attraction to pubescent girls by surrounding himself with strays who wouldn't tempt him.

I put my BlackBerry in my pocket and walked toward the three men.

"You know what I mean. They were all kind of off, weren't they?"

"Gay?" Mike asked.

"You're making me uncomfortable with this talk."

"I want to show you some photographs," I said, approaching Verge.

I pulled up the pictures, one at a time, of the two statues from the Dalton collection. He looked at them with a blank stare and said he had no idea what they were.

Then I showed him the shot of the small ebony figure that had been found with the two others near the Lake.

"My angel!" he exclaimed, nearly tipping over his little chair. "Where'd you find her? Where'd you find my angel?"

"She was in the Park, Verge," I said. "The police found her last week."

"I was missing her for a while."

"How long?"

He was having a hard time containing his childlike enthusiasm. "I'm no better at dates than at names, lady. I don't keep a calendar."

"Do your best, Verge."

"Three weeks, maybe four."

"Did you give your angel to anyone, Verge?"

He shook his head vigorously from side to side.

"Think about it really hard," I said, grabbing the photograph of the dead girl and putting it in front of his face. "To her?"

He pushed my arm away and refused to look at the picture again.

"That would have been nice of you, Verge. Maybe you did it to protect her?"

He was too cautious to buy my suggestion. He looked at me like I had asked a trick question, and he knew enough not to volunteer an answer.

"I never gave it to anyone. It comes from my church."

"Your church?"

"Where my family worshipped, in Seneca Village."

"They've had it all that time?" I asked. "More than one hundred years?"

"No," he said. "No, no. I took her out of the church myself. Me and another guy."

Mercer raised his eyebrows as he looked over Verge's head at me.

"When was that?" I asked. "And who was the other man?"

"Two, maybe three years ago. Some people were all digging up the village. I used to go there most nights. Lots of folk did."

"What for, Verge?"

"They were digging holes in the ground. I was just curious. Then I saw them bringing stuff out sometimes. Broken dishes and things like that. Animal bones and tin cups. One night I went down into one of the ditches they dug. Saw all these tombstones and things."

"Tombstones?" I asked.

"From the churches in the village. There are still tombstones there, all covered over by the Park," Verge said. "That isn't right, is it? To bury over where people were laid to rest."

"Doesn't sound right to me. And the angel?"

"She was just there on the ground, near the foundation of the church. The man—the other man—he was picking up things from the ditch, at night while nobody else was around. He asked me if I wanted the angel. I told him yes, and he gave it to me."

There was always another man, someone to be blamed for a theft or a bad act. I was getting frustrated by Verge's selective memory.

"The other man, Verge," I said. "I don't suppose you know his name."

"No, lady, I don't."

"That's right, you're bad on names."

He caught the edge in my voice. I started to turn away, but he reached out and grabbed the sleeve of my blazer.

"But I've seen him before. I met him years ago. And every now and then I see him again."

"That's good to know, Verge," I said. "How do you know him?"

"I told you I worked at the garage, helping my daddy," he said. "From 1960 to 1980. That man recognized me from all that time back. Said we used to talk some and that my father was good to him."

"Where's the garage, Verge?" I asked. It sounded like he was bluffing me again—and I was just off my own bluff to Jessica Pell, so I didn't want to fall for it. "Maybe someone there can help us figure out who the man is. Figure out whether the dead girl had something to do with your angel."

"Amsterdam Avenue, near 77th Street, like I told you. It's an old stable, actually, that was made into a garage," Verge said. "It's the Dakota Stables. Called that after the apartment building it was built for. The Dakota Stables."

TWENTY-THREE

"What do we do with this guy in the meantime?" I asked. "I don't know if he's crazy as a fox or telling us the truth."

Mercer, Mike, and I were in the lobby of the rustic cottage, home to one of the last public marionette companies in the country. The cheerful décor of the children's theater was a sharp contrast to the serious subjects we'd been discussing.

Verge had gone outside in the company of four of the Park's anticrime cops who had helped Mercer find him early this afternoon.

"You can't lock him up, if that's what you're thinking," Mercer said. "Florida's got no hold on him, and he's not in any trouble here."

"But he knew the dead girl and he actually spent time with her. His little carved angel was found not far from her body," I said, struggling to put all that together. "He's got no idea where he was when she died."

"We don't know when she died, Coop," Mike said. "How can you expect him to alibi up?"

"The man has no home, his family doesn't trust him enough to want him. And our girl wasn't gay, even though she was with Jo and her friends. Let him go, and we'll never see him again."

"That's a little over-the-top," Mercer said.

"A convicted sex offender with a long history of hitting on teens?"

"A few hours ago you thought he was Angel's protector, when Jo was talking about him. He's sixty-three years old. He's probably aged out of the molesting business, courtesy of Florida's castration meds."

I started listing the offenders we'd handled together who had still been sexually violent in their senior years, some of them turning to blunt force or strangulation when they'd been frustrated by an inability to complete the physical act.

"Besides, the parkies who trusted him didn't realize Verge had a rap sheet, Mercer. But now he knows we know about it."

"You think the city will put him up for a night or two in a hotel?" Mercer asked.

"We're not quite at material witness status. I'll push McKinney to let us do it, if you think he'll stay."

"Let me ask him."

"Ask him about the Dakota Stables, too. Have you ever heard of them, Mike?" I asked.

"Never did. But it's my next stop."

"I'm with you."

We walked out the door of the cottage. Verge was entertaining the plainclothes cops with stories about the Park. He was holding a large object in his hands, but his back was to us and I couldn't make out what it was.

Mercer called out to him and he turned around.

"What the hell is that?" Mike asked.

"Damn," I said. "It's one of the marionettes, from the theater. It was in a box on the floor near the door when we went inside."

Verge was dangling a puppet that was dressed as Little Red Riding Hood. The cops were laughing with him as he made up his own version of the fairy tale, the two-foot-tall doll bouncing from the strands of string that controlled her movement. He was talking about walking her through the desolate Ravine, past the three waterfalls, when she was approached by the wolf.

"Where'd you get that, Verge?" Mercer asked. It seemed as though he didn't like the fact that the disarming nature of our "simple" friend could be so deceptive.

"I'm telling a story," the man said. "The police officers are my friends."

"The doll. The puppet. Where'd you get it?" Mercer knew the answer to my question as well as I did.

"Red Riding Hood? She was a gift to me. The people inside— the people who work the show—one of them gave it to me."

He was as straight-faced now as he had been when he responded to our questions just minutes ago.

"There's nobody inside the theater. You're not telling the truth, Verge," I said. "Who? Who was it?"

His head was weaving from side to side. "You know I'm not—"

"Good with names," I said, taking a step closer to him, holding my hands out to ask for the return of the puppet. "That doesn't work with me."

He jerked his right arm and Red Riding Hood flew up in the air, missing the side of my head by inches.

"Give it back, Verge," I said.

He was laughing hard now, spinning the marionette so that the strings became twisted around one another. "She's mine."

I turned to reenter the cottage.

"Where are you going?" Mike asked.

"To get someone from the theater. They'll be missing this doll. If he's not giving it back to me, there must be someone here who can reclaim it."

Mercer was trying to keep one eye on Verge Humphrey and follow my activity. "I'll get it from him, Alex. Don't knock yourself out."

"Do you get my point? Do you see that he just told a big fat lie, Mercer? So how can we believe anything he says?"

"He's mentally challenged, Alex."

"I can deal with that just fine. But what's the challenge? That's the issue. Is Verge just slow, or does he have problems telling the truth? How do we get him evaluated, Mercer? 'Cause he's useless to me—"

"To all of us."

"If he's a pathologic liar. And a serial sex offender."

"No signs of violence," Mercer said. "Not recently."

I went into the cottage, walked through the vestibule past the empty box in which the marionette had been resting when I first arrived. There was a door to the side of the stage, and I knocked on it. A young woman in jeans and a T-shirt, a paintbrush in her hand, opened it and asked what I wanted.

"I'm with the police officers who were just in here," I said. "One of your puppets was in a crate near the front. I'm just wondering—?"

"Red Riding Hood? She's fine there, thanks. We've got someone from the doll hospital coming to pick her up shortly," the woman said cheerfully. "She's got a broken arm, and we need her back for the Saturday matinee. Is she in your way?"

"Not at all. I just wanted to make sure she—uh—that she belonged here. We're leaving in a few minutes and I didn't want her unsecured, in case you thought we'd be hanging around."

"She's a definite crowd-pleaser. The surgery's on rush. Thanks for your concern."

So Verge had a problem with truth telling, perhaps a greater challenge for us than for him, especially since Mercer was in his corner.

I let the door slam behind me as I walked to rejoin the group. Mercer came toward me to cut me off. "Seems he's rejected your kind offer of a hotel room."

I tried to look around my friend's broad shoulders, but it was impossible to see Verge, who was still entertaining the cops and swinging the wooden puppet from side to side.

"That stinks. What's your plan?"

"These plainclothes guys say they can keep tabs on him for the next few days."

"24/7?"

"Be reasonable, Alexandra. They've got better things to do now."

"He's a liar. Flat out. Now, get the puppet back, please. Nobody gave it to him, and she's got to be picked up for repair."

"Understood," Mercer said, keeping himself between the old man and me as he walked over to ask for the marionette.

"C'mon, Verge," Mercer said, beckoning with his curled-up fingers. "We've got to put the doll back where she belongs."

"Not right yet," he said, starting to lope down the path leading away from the cottage. He was swinging Red Riding Hood like a cowboy showing off with a lariat. "She belongs to me."

One of the young cops started after Verge. "Hey, Pops. You gotta give back the doll."

"She's got a broken arm," I called out, thinking he might have a soft spot for the injured doll, like the way Jo described him responding to her friends. "She needs to get fixed before the kids come to the show this weekend."

"That can happen to little girls that go into the woods," he said, walking backward as he told the cop to stay away.

His laughter no longer struck me as the humor of a simple man. The tone had become more sinister.

"Stop right there," Mercer said.

Verge flipped the large doll over his shoulder, and when it landed—as he turned again to walk off—we could all see that she had become completely entangled in the long white strings that were suspended from the hand controls.

There was no point in my opening my mouth again. Mercer was on his way to reclaim the doll.

"Hand it over, will you?"

Verge lifted the marionette as though he was going to return it to Mercer. With a sudden movement he grabbed the doll's head between his hands and twisted it so hard I could hear the wood crack.

"She's beyond repair now," he said, smirking at me. "I think I just broke her neck."

TWENTY-FOUR

"Calm down, Coop," Mike said. "It's just a doll."

"But he's demented. I know Verge didn't kill anybody just now, but that was a sick thing to do, wringing the puppet's neck."

"There's got to be a psych history on this dude, Mercer. You looking?"

"I am now. I'll start with his sister in Queens and see what we get."

Mike had replaced the marionette—with her multiple fractures and a completely snarled set of strings—in the crate for pickup and repair. I watched with dismay as Verge Humphrey walked away from us, headed off the path into a grove of trees, and disappeared.

"I hate that he's roaming around on his own," I said. "Between him and Tanner, I feel like driving through the Park and scooping up all the girls who are out there tonight, thinking it's a safe place to be."

"Hold that thought. I don't think social work's your strong suit."

"Are you going to the garage?" Mercer asked Mike.

"Yeah. It's just a few blocks over."

"Taking Alex?"

"Yup."

It was after five o'clock. "I'm starving," I said. "And tired. Let's do that and make a plan for tomorrow, and maybe I'll have an early night."

Mercer wagged a finger at me. "Not so fast. How about dinner?"

"With you?"

"With us." He looked over my head to Mike and nodded.

"Something up?" I asked. It was one thing if Mike wanted to spend the evening alone with me, and if not it would be a smart idea to get some rest.

"It's a good time to organize where we stand," Mercer said, "what we need to do with the weekend approaching."

"Come to my place for takeout?" They both usually liked that idea. The bar tab was cheap, the digs were comfortable and private, and they could watch the Yankee game while we ate.

"We can do better. Call me when you're done at the garage. I'll get us a table."

Mike and I walked out of the Park and across 79th Street till we came to Amsterdam.

"You want to talk?" I asked him.

"We're on the clock, Coop. On the job."

"So it's going to be *that* way?"

"Course it is when we're working."

"You have any second thoughts about last night?" I asked.

"Nope."

"You just don't want to—?"

"Discuss it right now," he said.

"I don't either."

Mike turned his head to me, bit his lip, and laughed.

"Hey," I said. "I'm easy."

"Highest-maintenance broad I know, and you're suddenly easy? Sweet."

"So how do we make sense of Vergil Humphrey?"

"Let Mercer figure him out," Mike said. "I just want to understand why so many of these roads are leading back to the Dakota."

At the southwest corner of 77th Street and Amsterdam Avenue we came up to the drab old building bearing a beat-up sign: THE DAKOTA GARAGE.

There was a man in the ticket booth and two attendants, one young and one who looked older than Verge, sitting on wooden chairs with their feet up on the metal railing that separated the one-room office from the rows of parked cars.

"Mike Chapman, NYPD."

He had the attention of the younger fellow, but the older guy still stared straight ahead, gnawing on a toothpick.

"There's no trouble," Mike said. "I've just got some questions about the building."

"What do you want to know?" the kid asked.

"How long have you worked here?"

The older man spoke without glancing at us. "That's not about the building, is it?"

The kid answered anyway. "Me? Only eight months. Abe's been here fifty years."

"Fifty-six. But if you've got no trouble, why are you asking?"

"You must have started working before child labor laws," Mike said.

"Dropped out of high school, wiseass. One of our cars gone missing?"

"Nope. Maybe one of your horses."

Abe stood up and stretched. "Long before my time."

"That's what I want to know," Mike said. "Was this really a stable?"

"Certainly was. From here to 75th Street was called Stable Row. See those portals? Each one was an individual stall," Abe said, pointing his toothpick toward the warm orange brick arches that lined the long room. "This place was built to hold more than a hundred horses, and space for three times that many carriages on the second floor."

"But the Dakota apartments—they're a couple of blocks away," Mike said. "Why would the stables be built this far west?"

"Did you ever smell the likes of a hundred horses and all the slop that goes with them?" Abe asked. "This here couple of blocks was close enough to be convenient to the staff, but far enough away for the odors and the sounds of the animals not to bother the rich people who lived over on the Park. I have all that from the old-timers that worked here when I came on. Once upon a time, when it was built, the Dakota had horses right in the courtyard, and a special entrance in the rear so hay could be delivered without bothering anyone. But that's all ancient history now."

"When did this become a garage?" I asked.

"By the 1920s, I think." Abe's toothpick broke in half. He took both pieces and tossed them in a trash barrel.

"Do you know the name Lavinia Dalton?" Mike said.

"What's the problem now? The chauffeur claiming I dented one of the cars? I didn't think you guys were insurance adjusters."

"We're not."

"So if there's no trouble, what's the trouble?" Abe asked.

"I'm curious is all. Miss Dalton can't answer questions herself. Some property went missing from her home, and I'd like to look in her car, just to satisfy my boss we checked everywhere."

"Cars. Five of them. Suit yourself," Abe said. "I'll take you upstairs."

The elevator creaked its way to the second floor. Abe limped as he made his way down rows of automobiles until we reached the farthest corner of the building. An entire section was roped off, and four of the five machines in it were covered with blankets that appeared to be designed for each.

"These all belong to Miss Dalton," Abe said. "The Mercedes sedan here, that's not covered, that's the one her chauffeur uses. Does all the errands in it, takes her out to the doctor when she needs to go, and sometimes ferries guests back and forth."

"You mind if I look?"

"Don't belong to me. Do anything you'd like."

Mike opened each of the doors, looking under the seats and in the glove compartment, finding nothing except the registration and insurance form. He opened the trunk, but it was as clean as a whistle, with only a spare tire and a lap blanket folded neatly to the side.

Abe pulled the covers off the other cars. There was an SUV, two smaller sedans, and then an enormous car that looked like the stuff of royalty.

Mike let out a low whistle.

"The Dalton Daimler," Abe said. "A 1965 four-door saloon. A rebadged Jaguar Mark 2. You know cars? This one's a real beauty."

Mike was taking in every inch of the vintage luxury vehicle. It was the color of champagne, with black trim, a fluted grille, distinctive wheel trims, and a gleaming black enamel steering wheel.

"Good as it gets," Mike said as Abe opened the hood to show him the works. "Two-point-five-liter V8."

"I was just a kid when Miss Dalton bought this. My boss never let me touch the damn thing, but late at night I used to climb in and sit behind the wheel, just pretending."

"Not a bad fantasy," Mike said, looking at every interior inch, as well as the boot. "How often does the Daimler go out for a spin?"

Abe patted the roof of the car. "You know about Miss Dalton's grandbaby, don't you?"

"Yes," I said.

"This is the car Miss D had used to go out to her fancy ladies' luncheon the afternoon the baby was snatched. She's never allowed it to be driven since," Abe said. "She probably doesn't realize the chauffeur has to take it out every now and again—that it isn't good for it just to sit. And it has to be inspected and all that. But as far as her using the car? Time seemed to stand still once Lucy disappeared."

"The police," I said, "did they talk to you back then?"

Abe, with help from Mike, replaced the covers on the cars and then he slowly limped back toward the elevator.

"That would be too polite a way of saying what they did. We were all guilty, you know."

"What do you mean?"

"Wasn't a living soul who didn't think it was an inside job—the kidnapping, I mean. Any of us who had any contact with the grand lady's staff, we were made to look like lowlifes and thugs. Questioned and then questioned again. Rousted out of our beds in the middle of the night if anyone in the Dakota said they knew us. Half the cars parked here came out of those apartments. 'Course we all knew folks who lived there."

"Did you know Lavinia Dalton?" I asked.

"Never laid eyes on her. She liked to be picked up at the front door of the building and dropped off there as well. I doubt she had a clue where her cars were garaged."

"Did you know anyone on her staff?"

"I saw the chauffeur—sometimes two of them worked for her— just about every day. That one is dead now. Had a stroke ten years or so after the snatching. Been a few since. Good people."

"Any of the women in the household?"

"Not as I recall."

"Did you ever go to the Dakota apartments?" Mike asked.

We were out of the elevator, heading back to the ticket office. "Not Miss Dalton's. But certainly I went to the building from time to time. Some folks liked their automobiles brought to them right there. Sometimes I went to pick up a rent check or give a person bad news that I'd dinged a fender. You gonna lock me up for that?"

"No, sir," Mike said. "But that reminds me, Abe. You ever know a guy who worked here way back called Vergil Humphrey?"

Abe snorted at the sound of the name. "Verge? He was nuttier than a Snickers bar. His father was one of the supervisors here when I started. We could tell every time Verge got himself in a jam because the next day he'd wind up helping out with us."

"What kind of jams?" I asked.

"Verge couldn't keep his privates in his pants, if you understand me. Liked the girls a little too much."

"Young girls?"

"Hell, I don't know. He was a teenager then and so were they, from what I remember. I don't think he ever hurt anybody. Verge was slow. Got made fun of a lot. Guess that's called bullying today. His father liked to keep him around the cars 'cause we got so full of grease and sweat none of us had much time to think about girls."

"Was Verge working here when the Dalton baby was kidnapped?" Mike asked.

Abe thought for a minute. "Sure he was. Had a harder time with the cops than I did, probably 'cause he was black and 'cause he couldn't think straight or talk straight. Nobody ever knew when to believe Verge Humphrey."

"Did he have anything to do with Lavinia Dalton and her cars?"

"His father was too smart for that. Verge might have been the only person working here who had no connection to the Dalton staff. Wasn't allowed near the cars, you can be sure."

"Other young men," I said. "Would he have made friends working here?"

"More than any of us cared to have," Abe said. "These cars were like magnets for every kid in the neighborhood. Finest makes and models sitting here all shiny and clean and sparkling. Kids were always hanging out, eager to take a rag and help us polish them up."

"Any of them connected with Lavinia Dalton?" I asked.

Abe gave me an exasperated sigh. "You're pushing me now, young lady. Sure, Miss D had a staff the size of a small army, and a few of the ones who were married had sons who'd hang out around here. All the boys did. Could I name 'em now for you? Not a prayer."

There were three cars lined up at the entrance, waiting to be parked. The other attendant was calling to Abe to help him out.

"Did you ever hear of Seneca Village?" I asked.

"What's that? An Indian reservation?" Abe said. "One of those gambling casinos?"

"Not important."

"Have I answered all your questions, then?"

"Yes, you have," Mike said. "Thanks for your time."

"You keep Verge away from me, now, will you? Man never made a lick of sense. If you're relying on him for help, you'll be sorry."

Mike was quiet as we made our way back toward the Park, where he had left his car.

"That was a dead end," I said.

"Seems to be. I actually asked the lieutenant to send for the case file on Baby Lucy."

"Not enough on your plate, I guess."

"I'm just interested in the whole picture. It's odd they never were able to solve it after all this time."

"Start off with they never found a body," I said. "That didn't help."

"Most people who followed the Lindbergh kidnapping figure Bruno Hauptmann couldn't have pulled it off alone. Would have taken two guys—one to hold the ladder while the other took Charlie from his crib and out the second-story window."

"You're never been a conspiracy theory kind of guy," I said.

"I'm not. But Lindbergh's case just screams out for a mastermind behind Hauptmann."

"I guess there's always someone coming along to take a second look. Might as well be you."

Mike pulled out his phone to call Mercer. "Coop and me, we're ready to bag it. Everything in place?"

I wondered what Mike meant by that as he waited for an answer.

"Okay, that'll work. See you in fifteen minutes."

"What was that about? What did he put in place?"

"Mercer's the man. Scored us a table at Rao's."

"No wonder the secrecy," I said, high-fiving Mike for the good news. "How'd he do it?"

"The big man has his ways."

We got in the car and headed east. There was no place in New

York like the fabled eatery in East Harlem, a tiny building on the corner of Pleasant Avenue and 114th Street that was run more like a private club than a restaurant. Reservations were harder to come by than tickets to an inaugural ball. The owners, Frankie and Ron, didn't even list the phone number, and if you were lucky enough to get in their good graces, they would tell you when to show up—it was impossible to pick a date and reserve it.

Mercer was waiting for us in the first booth—there were only twelve tables—opposite the bar where Nicky Vest, whose nickname came from the 136 colorful jackets he owned, mixed the meanest drinks in town. Some regular had turned in his table for the night, and Mercer's persistence had paid off.

We were greeted by the waiters like long-lost friends—since we managed to slip in a couple of times a year—and were about to sit down beneath the wall-to-wall display of autographed photos of A-list celebrities, athletes, politicians, and authors when Mike reminded us that if we went into the back office right now we could catch the Final Jeopardy question.

As we waited for the category to be revealed, we caught Mercer up on our short visit to the old stable. He told us he had nothing to report either.

"Tonight's category," Trebek said, "is WEATHER."

He repeated the word three times as the contestants logged in their bets.

"I'm an automatic loser," Mike said. "Doppler Alex here is always on patrol for hurricanes and blizzards. Worst-case-scenario kind of broad."

"I am not."

"You'll get this one, girl. And the winner buys."

"I'm in," Mercer said.

Trebek stood beside the blue board as the final answer was displayed: "Intense dust storm carried on an atmospheric gravity current."

"What's a sirocco?" I asked.

"Yeah," Mike said. "A sirocco."

Two of the three contestants made the same guess, and Trebek told all of us we were wrong. "No, gentlemen, it's not that Mediterranean wind that blows off the Sahara."

"What's a haboob?" Mercer said.

"The correct question is 'What is a haboob?' A haboob, folks. They're commonly found in arid regions around the world."

Mercer smiled and patted Mike on the back. His knowledge of geography was unparalleled. He had grown up studying all the airline maps that his father had accumulated in his job at Delta, and knew as much about foreign cultures and customs as Mike knew about the military.

"They were first described in the Sudan," Mercer said as we walked back to our table, "and they often happen when a thunderstorm collapses. The winds reverse and become a downdraft, creating a wall of dust that can move at sixty miles an hour."

"A dust storm," Mike said.

"Same thing. That's what it's called out west."

"Then I would have gotten it right. Like Coop says when she trips over her tongue, it's just semantics."

Nicky brought our cocktails, and we clinked glasses. I was still thinking of the Arsenal rooftop when I looked across at Mike and said, "Cheers."

There was no menu at Rao's, and all the food was served family-style. We started with baked clams, roasted peppers—maybe the best anywhere—and a seafood salad.

"So what's the word?" Mike asked Mercer.

"Scully's got four teams from SVU out looking for Raymond Tanner. He's public enemy number one."

"In Central Park?" I asked.

"And all his old haunts. But the Park is still saturated. They've moved some anticrime guys to the North Woods, so he figures they have that covered."

"But a lot of those men will come out this weekend," Mike said.

"No question. The body in the Lake gets back-burnered."

I shook my head and counted on the Scotch to calm me down.

"What's tomorrow like for you?" Mike asked Mercer.

"I'll be at Verge's sister's house early. No call, just a knock on the door. Then they're probably throwing me onto the Tanner task force. You?"

"I feel kind of stalled," Mike said. "Did you get a chance to talk to Chirico?"

"I went to see him after you left for the garage. He was over by the boathouse."

"What for?" I asked.

"Did you forget about Jessica Pell?" Mike said, holding up his glass and shouting out to the bartender, "Nicky, how about a refill?"

"No, but—"

"Her deadline to tell Scully to bounce me if Chirico doesn't discipline me is tomorrow. I'm nervous about what she's got up her sleeve."

"She's not going forward with this, Mike," I said, stirring the ice cubes with my finger.

"Pell's a wild card, Coop. You don't know what she's up to."

"No, but—" I didn't want to tell him about my intervention in her robing room earlier today, but I was surprised that she hadn't yet walked back her complaint.

"But nothing. Did you tell Mercer she was staking out your driveway last night?"

I blushed. "No. No, I didn't say anything about it."

"What'd you do?" Mercer asked.

"Just rode around for a while," I said. "Why'd you go to Chirico?"

"To look him in the eye, so Mike didn't have to do it himself. Push the sergeant to do the right thing."

"What would that be?"

"Call Pell before she calls Scully tomorrow," Mercer said. "I want Manny Chirico to knock her on her ass, is what I really want."

"What does he say to that?"

"He needs ammunition to do it."

Now I had a way to start my day if I could figure out how to get involved without leaving my DNA all over Mike's problem.

"It's off the table for the moment," Mike said. "Enjoy the feast."

The guys ordered rigatoni Bolognese with a side order of the largest, most delicious meatballs in town; Rao's signature lemon chicken dish; a veal chop with hot peppers; and shrimp parmigiana. I didn't have room for the homemade ice cream, but it was impossible to refuse a spoonful as I washed it down with my second glass of barolo.

Mercer paid the bill, and we said our good nights to the kitchen crew as we went out the door. "I'll take you home, Alex."

I spun around and looked at Mike, puzzled by that decision. "But Mike's got to pass by my place to get home."

"It's all right. She can ride with me, Mercer."

The Triborough Bridge was spitting distance from the restaurant. Why wasn't Mercer just going on home to Queens, and why—after last night—wasn't Mike coming to my place?

"What's going on?" I asked.

"I've got some papers—some stuff—that Mercer's stopping by to pick up," Mike said as I got in his car.

We cruised down Second Avenue, and I could see Mercer's SUV in the rearview mirror. Mike still wasn't talking—nothing personal at least—and I attributed it to the distraction of Jessica Pell's threats.

By the time we reached the driveway in front of my apartment, Mercer had overtaken us and nosed into a parking place ahead of us.

I could see a patrol car parked on the sidewalk at the exit of the driveway, and when I turned to look into the glass-fronted lobby of my building, I noticed a pair of uniformed cops.

Mercer opened the car door just as the lights went on in my brain.

"Now I know what you meant when you asked Mercer if

everything was in place," I said to Mike, my eyes flashing fire. "The cool dinner at Rao's was just a distraction till you could set this up. I guess Scully's put a bodyguard on me."

"We convinced him that Mercer and I have got you covered all day," Mike said. "It's just at night; he doesn't want you alone as long as Raymond Tanner's out there with KILL COOP etched into his skin."

Mercer put his hands in his pants pockets and walked away to explain the situation to Oscar and Vinny, the two doormen—my good friends—who were on duty.

"What about last night, Mike? What was the point of that? The Arsenal, the rooftop, the—the rest of it?" I slammed the door shut behind me. "Was that just a diversion to keep me out of harm's way?"

"Look, Coop, last night had nothing to do with Scully's decision. He called the lieutenant today and ordered this detail put in place."

"My babysitters are waiting for me, Mike," I said, walking toward the revolving door.

"I'll call you later to check in."

"Don't bother. I haven't got anything at all to say to you tonight. As far as I'm concerned, you've just checked out."

TWENTY-FIVE

I made the two rookies as comfortable as I could in my den. I went into the bedroom suite, took a steaming-hot bath, and then slept fitfully till 6:30 A.M., when I awakened and dressed for the office.

By the time I emerged from my bedroom, one of the cops had brewed a pot of coffee. They tried to divert me by telling stories of the more bizarre cases they'd handled recently.

Mercer had texted that he would pick me up at 7:30 and that the officers would be relieved then.

When the doorman called to say that Mercer was in the driveway, my bodyguards brought me downstairs and delivered me to my next keeper.

"Good morning, Alexandra."

"Morning."

"We didn't mean to sandbag you last night. The commissioner's plan makes sense."

"I understand it all. I just wasn't expecting such an abrupt end to my day. It's so impersonal to have two armed strangers keeping watch in my home."

"But safer than not."

"Thank you."

"And it looks like Raymond Tanner has a bad case of recidivist rage, Alex."

"What now?" As Mercer drove to the southbound entrance of the FDR, I picked up the day's papers, which were between us on the front seat.

"Too late for the news. Tanner raped a young woman at two A.M."

"I can't believe it. Where did it happen?"

"This time in Brooklyn. In Prospect Park, just off the Midwood Trail."

"Dear God. This is our worst nightmare," I said. "Is she going to be all right?"

"Yeah. I went to the hospital to see her. Twenty-one years old."

"Homeless?"

"Out of work. Her parents, way out on Long Island, gave her a hard time. They didn't want her staying there unless she could contribute to the rent because they're struggling. So she's been living in Prospect Park."

Prospect Park was also designed by Olmsted and Vaux, using many of the same elements as they had created in Manhattan, on an even larger chunk of land. I'd jogged the Midwood Trail many times with my friend Nan Toth. Like the Ramble, it was a woodland area with the last remaining natural forest in Brooklyn.

"Are you sure it's Tanner?"

"No doubt, Alex. Same exact language, same order of the sexual acts. He threatened to split her head open with a lead pipe, and she felt the cold steel of the weapon when he pressed it against her ear every time she squirmed."

"And the tattoo?"

"It was too dark for the girl to read it. All she could say was that there were letters inked on his hand—two words, she thought. And the forensic exam yielded seminal fluid, so we'll have DNA."

"Good, 'cause Tanner's in the data bank," I said. "But how ironic that he moved to Prospect Park."

"Why?"

"In so many respects it's like a double for Central Park. The combination of great natural beauty, like the Midwood Trail, along with man-made lakes and waterfalls. Tanner seems to know both of them pretty well."

Many people don't realize that in the 1850s and 1860s, when Central Park and then Prospect Park were designed, Brooklyn was a separate city from New York, and the two were only connected by ferry service. It was not until 1898 that New York—then comprised of only the island of Manhattan and a small piece of the Bronx—joined forces across the river with Brooklyn, at that time the third-largest city in America.

"They'll be looking at him hard for Angel's killing. The Midwood's so much like the Ramble, and both girls were homeless, white, and about the same age."

"Impossible to know—with no ID for our vic—whether there's any connection between them. Did she tell you where she was living?" I asked.

"Do you know Elephant Hill?"

"Yes." The name referred to one of the highest points on the Midwood Trail, where a century ago there had been a menagerie that housed elephants and bears. Now there were towering trees that covered the landscape along the interweaving paths.

"She was camping out there, in sort of a shelter."

"A cave?" I remembered the story Flo had told about the small grotto behind the waterfall in the Ravine, and that Mia Schneider had promised to find out for Mike and me the location of the original caves that were part of the Park design.

"No. This one was made of logs," Mercer said. "Apparently it's a thing in Prospect Park, according to what the rangers told the cops, that when trees fall and begin to decay, they're left in place unless they block a path. This way the fungi and molds return nutrients to the soil."

"You're serious? She was living in a stack of moldy logs?"

"The first team in showed me the photos. They're all over the Park."

"How can we not take better care of the people in this city?" I said. "It rips me up to think of how vulnerable these kids are."

"I hate to tell you that today marks one week since Angel was found in the Lake. This Brooklyn rape will give Scully exactly what he needs to withdraw a task force from Central Park and beef up the patrols in Prospect."

"But suppose Tanner's playing a game? He's fully capable of switching up his location and then doubling back."

"Course he is. So don't be stubborn about letting us stay close to you."

"No comment, Mercer. I think he's moved on from thinking about me."

It was easy for Mercer to find a parking spot on Hogan Place so early in the morning. We picked up coffee and Danish at the corner cart and went upstairs to settle in the conference room with all the case reports. With every twist, like Tanner's new attack, and every bit of information about the evidence, like Vergil Humphrey's claim about the black angel statuette, we had to reevaluate each assumption we'd made earlier.

I left a voice mail for my counterpart in the Brooklyn DA's office—the chief of the Special Victims Unit—telling her that I would be happy to exchange details with her on our Raymond Tanner cases, and give her all the background on both his criminal and psych history. Then Mercer and I began digging into piles of police reports, talking over the significance of the developments of the last twenty-four hours.

It was just after 9:30 when Laura came down to look for me.

"It's the district attorney, Alex. He called on your hotline, so I picked it up. He wants you in his office right away."

"Tanner, you think?" Mercer asked.

"Probably," I said, pushing back my chair to get up. "It's not like him to call himself. At least Rose will tell me what it's about."

I walked down the corridor and crossed through the secured entrance to the executive wing. Rose barely looked up from her desk, her expression as tight as I'd ever seen it. That signaled to me that there was no point asking her about the district attorney's mood. I hadn't been summoned for a casual chat.

When I entered Battaglia's office, I was surprised to see Manny Chirico sitting across the table from him. "Good morning, Paul," I said, looking from one of the men to the other. "Sergeant Chirico."

"Sit down, Alexandra."

I did.

"I understand this character Raymond Tanner is on the street. A case you lost, I see."

"Yes, sir."

"One completed rape earlier this morning, one attempt earlier this week, and possibly a murder."

"That's right."

"What's he got against you?"

"That I tried the case against him, I guess. Who better to hate than the prosecutor?"

"But you did a lousy job," Battaglia said, with the straightest of faces.

"Thanks, boss. You might tell him that when you see him. I think he finds the psych hospitalization terrifically confining when he thinks he can get away with so many more rapes on the outside. Especially since he must think, like you do, that I did a lousy job."

"You okay with the bodyguard?"

"I guess it's necessary."

"Scully called me on it late yesterday. Wish I'd heard about the situation from you," the DA said, "but it seems like a sound idea."

"Then I'm okay with—"

"So long as it's not Mike Chapman."

I met his stare head-on. "It's not, Paul. Anything else you want?"

"Don't get up yet, Alexandra. The sergeant tells me he's been dealing with a problem of Chapman's all week."

"Just like you have, boss."

"Excuse me?"

"It's why you and McKinney were so happy to dump the Central Park homicide in my lap. Jessica Pell's on the warpath, she's obviously had your ear about me, and you're taking her seriously. Without the courtesy of letting me be heard."

"Don't ever forget who runs the show here, Alexandra. Why the hell shouldn't I be taking the judge seriously?"

"Because she's crazy," Manny Chirico said. "I'm telling you, Mr. Battaglia, she's dangerously off-balance."

I exhaled, realizing that Chirico was actually on Mike's side. Maybe he had a good purpose in coming here, forcing Battaglia to look at the two threats—one against Mike and the other against me—as a single package.

"What's your point?" the DA asked Chirico.

"I've had a week to think this through, puzzle the pieces, pull together some information before the judge meets her noon deadline and makes her demands of you and the commissioner." The sergeant was well respected by his men, with a great career as an investigator in the detective bureau. "I think I know how you feel about Alexandra, Mr. B, and there's no way I'm giving up Chapman to a lunatic, no matter how bad a slide his love life took."

He opened a file folder and placed a sheaf of photographs in front of Battaglia.

"What are these?"

"Raymond Tanner. They're eight-by-tens of all the photos of him, from the standing shot at the time of his arrest in the case that Alex tried to his most recent from psych city."

There were at least eight pictures in the pile. Battaglia studied each one and passed it along to me. I knew the arrest photo and had introduced it into evidence at the trial. It showed Tanner standing in Central Booking, next to the measure on the wall that recorded his height at six-foot-one. The tattoos that snaked down both sides of his arms from beneath his white T-shirt were already in place—a bodyscape of violence featuring guns of all shapes and sizes and knives that dripped blood from their tips.

But there was, as yet, no writing on the backs of Tanner's hands, which hung by his sides in the first photograph.

The next four were taken at the facilities in which he was incarcerated as a result of the NGRI verdict. One pair was from the infamous Clinton psych ward, in which Tanner stood—first a full-body shot from the front and then from the back—with his long-sleeved shirt on. The next was with the shirt removed, showing some of the art on his chest and his back, including a brightly colored dragon whose tail curled around his torso while flames shot out of its mouth.

Eighteen months later, at a facility midstate, the same photos—facing the camera and away—showed a new sketch across the span of his upper back. It was a crudely drawn pit bull, black and white, with drops of blood on his bared teeth. The word BUSTER was printed below the dog. But still there was no lettering on Tanner's hands.

The next pair of photos marked the prisoner's admission to Fishkill's mental facility, from which his brutal forays into the city began.

I looked at his hands, which again were unmarked. The first shot was unremarkable because of his clothing; the second showed that a red-caped black-figured drawing of a devil had been squeezed in between the pit bull and the old dragon. Some jailhouse artist had misspelled Lucifer—LOOSIFUR—under the tattoo.

The last photo was dated just days before Raymond Tanner absconded after his taste of freedom during work release. Battaglia looked at it without comment—I had no idea whether any of the images made an impression on him—and passed it to me.

"Here it is," I said to Manny Chirico. "For the first time you can see the words."

"What?" Battaglia asked. "What are you trying to tell me?"

"See that? See the words KILL COOP?" Chirico said, grabbing the picture from me and handing it back to the district attorney. "That's the tattoo on Tanner's hand."

"I'm aware of that."

"Look at the date, Mr. B. That picture was taken on May 8th. Did you notice that the image was not in any of the previous photos?"

Battaglia wouldn't acknowledge that he hadn't tracked that feature. He reached a hand out toward me, and I passed the stack back to him.

"They're taken periodically, Mr. B, to enter information in the databanks, whether it's about tattoos or scars or nicknames or prison events."

"I'm following you."

May 8th. I was frantically trying to attach a significance to that date. My birthday was April 30th—just one week earlier—and *that* was shortly after Mike told Jessica Pell he'd be spending time with me that night. I wanted to know where Manny Chirico was going with his theory, and I desperately wanted him not to trip up in front of an unforgiving Paul Battaglia.

"And May 8th," Chirico said, "was while Tanner was obviously still at Fishkill, but allowed to come into the city for work release."

"It's also the Feast Day of St. Victor the Moor, Sergeant. What's your point?"

Chirico extracted the next group of papers, half an inch think, from another folder. "Think about it, Mr. B. Assume that Raymond Tanner hated Alexandra, especially during his trial. She was the face and voice of the prosecution, standing in the way between him and a free ride."

"But she didn't get the verdict she wanted, Manny."

"Even worse. To the perp who hears the words 'not guilty,' he thinks he ought to walk out the door. Get out of jail free. Instead, he's freezing his ass off in a prison on the Canadian border. And who does he have to blame? Alexander Cooper. She's the reason he's there."

Battaglia stared at the photo showing Tanner's tattooed hand. "So you think it would have made more sense for him to have had the KILL COOP branding done when he was most enraged? When they slammed the cell door on him?"

"Makes much more sense, Mr. B," Chirico said. "He's had lots more people to hate than Alex since he went behind bars. So that's why I've run everyone who's currently in the psych ward with Tanner starting April 1st."

"Got it," Battaglia said, tossing the photo on his desk.

"There's thirty-six guys, but only three of them, according to admin, are into inking tats."

Battaglia lit a cigar, squinting at me as he struck the match to see if I was part of Chirico's plan or as mystified as he seemed to be.

"And one of them, Mr. B, had a competency hearing on May 3rd to determine whether he was fit yet to stand trial."

"So?"

"A competency hearing *at* Fishkill, instead of here in the courthouse. The perp's in the loony bin with Tanner 'cause he killed his landlady and stuffed her in the incinerator. He's up there pretrial—instead of at Rikers Island—'cause he's a parole violator from an earlier conviction."

"I know the case," I said. "Kerry O'Donnell has it. Trial Bureau 80."

"Exactly. And Kerry had to travel to Fishkill to do the hearing because the prisoner is considered too violent to risk the transport to Manhattan. Still incompetent to stand trial, Mr. B, but they had to go ahead with a hearing since it was mandatory. So they held it at the facility."

I could see a flash of daylight. "And who conducted it, Sarge?"

"Judge Pell," he said. "Judge Jessica Pell."

Battaglia rustled the cellophane wrapper of his cigar into a ball, squeezing it into his fist. "She have any connection to Tanner when you tried him?"

"No, Paul. None at all."

The district attorney leafed through the papers Chirico gave him. "Was she alone with Kerry's prisoner at any point in time?"

"No. But his artwork came up during the hearing. Not 'cause his lawyer wanted it to, but Kerry says the guy just rambled on about how he'd found God through the tattoo needle."

Battaglia held up his hands. "I'm missing the link."

"I interviewed Kerry on Tuesday, to see what went on while she was there at Fishkill. But it wasn't until Wednesday morning that Alex linked Raymond Tanner to a new case. Kerry recognized his name and called me back that afternoon. She told me to have the warden pull the log from the day of the hearing."

"Why?" I asked. I wished that Kerry had told me this, too, but we were good friends and she had put whatever information she had into the proper hands by telling Chirico. That was so much smarter than confiding in me.

"Kerry said that when her proceeding was completed and she was about to leave the hearing room, one of the prison guards walked in with a special request."

"For what?" Battaglia asked.

"Raymond Tanner—Kerry heard the guard say his name—had started work release. He wanted to get a relief from civil disabilities ruling," Chirico said, "which is required for some of the licensing needs in the nursing home industry."

"So he needed a judge to sign off on that application," I said.

"And there was Jessica Pell," Chirico said. "In the house."

"But she didn't know about my connection to him."

"The warden gave him the folder, with your name on the cover page as the prosecutorial contact, Alex."

"They couldn't possibly have left the judge alone with this Tanner animal?" Battaglia asked.

"Seventeen minutes alone, according to Kerry's timepiece. After all, Mr. B, he wasn't guilty. He was just insane, and he was already deemed safe to be out and about among the general population of this big city."

"Eight days after April 30th. Almost two weeks since Mike Chapman tried to get out of her clutches," I said. "And within the week, the words KILL COOP are inked on his hand, perhaps suggested to him by a judge out to get Chapman and me for her perceived slights, just minutes after she had presided over a hearing involving his cell-block mate and tattoo artist."

"April 30th?" Battaglia asked. "What's that?"

"My birthday, Paul. Mike says it was one of the triggers for Pell."

The embers on the tip of his cigar lighted up as he turned his head to me and puffed on it. "Sorry I missed it, Alex. Help yourself to a Cohiba. And she was set off because you were in bed with Chapman then?"

"Last time I'm going to address this with you, boss," I said, pushing away from the table to stand up. "My sexual relationships—such as they used to be—are none of your goddamn business. But if you have Rose check your calendar, April 30th was the day of the confrontation at Stallion Ridge Cellars. Luc Rouget was my lover, as you may recall. The rest of the bullshit that set Jessica Pell off was a function of her own paranoia."

Battaglia looked back at Manny Chirico. "You can't prove that Pell talked to Tanner about Alex, can you?"

"He doesn't have to," I said. I was ready to tell both Battaglia and Chirico about my conversation with Jessica Pell, and that I had audiotaped it so there would be proof to back me up.

But the district attorney continued to ignore me. "Sergeant, you think she put him up to the tattoo as some kind of threat to Alexandra?"

"It's not a threat," I said. "It's an advertisement. Pell had no idea Raymond Tanner would go AWOL. She's twisted, Paul. She was just trying to get at me any way she could at that moment. I bet she saw my name on Tanner's file and that set her off. She may have lit a fire under him without even knowing how far he might go with it."

Battaglia scowled at me. "You keep saying Pell's twisted and crazy. That's not the woman I know, and the mayor vouches for her like she's Sonia Sotomayor."

"You gotta trust me on this one, Mr. B," Chirico said. "She's smart, but this broad is off-the-charts whacko."

Supreme Court Justice Sotomayor had worked as a prosecutor in Battaglia's office before my tenure. The well-respected jurist and amazingly grounded woman was the polar opposite of Jessica Pell.

"You want examples, Paul? You don't think she's crazy enough to just want to put the fear of God in me 'cause she thinks I'm after Mike's ass?"

"Why? You've got ex—?"

"Buckets full," I said. "What would you like to know? Pell went to some Innocence Project program and did a panel with a three-time loser who was exonerated last summer on a murder charge. Hooked up with him after the show. You know what that means, Paul? Hooked up? She took him home with her that night and had sex with him. He blogged about it on his website—www.outandoverit.com—shortly before he was arrested in Queens County for throwing lye in the face of his ex-wife."

"Jesus."

"I'm not done. In the fall, when Dan Berner tried that triple homicide in front of her, she sent him mash notes before the trial was over. Happily married guy who's squeaky clean and she practically wanted to do him in the robing room."

"Why the hell didn't he—?"

"Tell McKinney? Of course he did. And defense counsel, too. There's a whole file on Pell that Pat must have."

"Calm down, Alex," Battaglia said. "You catch more flies with honey."

"I'm not a flycatcher, Paul. And Pell may have jumped on her moment with Raymond Tanner for sport—she's just that crazy—but now he's out of the blocks and running wild."

"Does Scully know what you've got?" Battaglia asked the sergeant.

"I'm on my way over to him now. I thought I'd show you first since it's Alex who's in Pell's crosshairs, in regard to Tanner."

"I'll talk to him later, Sergeant. Let's let Pell run her course."

"Well, that option is totally unsatisfactory to me, Paul," I said.

I couldn't control my anger. "That whackjob gives an ultimatum to Manny about one of the best detectives in the city—and about me, whatever that's worth to you—and you're going to let her play it out in two hours, no matter what Manny has to say to you? No matter what we've just heard?"

"You got a better idea?"

"I do," I said, walking toward the door. "You call the mayor right now and tell him he gets her resignation before six o'clock tonight. Hizzoner wants to know what a stalker's like? Well, his deputy mayor gave us one—and the mayor appointed her himself, put her in robes, with a gavel in her hand—and I'd like to serve Pell right back to him on a silver platter. He listens to you sometimes, Paul. You tell him she resigns by the end of the day."

Battaglia almost choked on the cigar smoke, he puffed so hard. "Or what?" he said, laughing at my show of temper. "What do you want me to tell the mayor?"

"Tell him to watch Brian Williams at 6:30. *Nightly News*."

"That's comical, Alex. You doing the weather this evening, are you? Is that your next gig?" He laughed again, but Manny Chirico's handsome face was frozen in a grimace as he watched me open the door.

"Yeah, boss. Storm brewing on the bench. Tropical-force winds. What the mayor ought to know is that I have an audiotape of Jessica Pell that's a bit incriminating. Made it myself, Paul."

Battaglia took the cigar out of his mouth and crushed it in the glass ashtray on his desk.

"Who the fuck signed off on a wiretap of a judge?" he shouted at me. Smoke even seemed to be coming out of his ears.

"It's not a wiretap, Paul, and I didn't need your signature," I said. "All I have to do is download the audio and e-mail it to one of the television producers. It'll make a great scoop on the news tonight. Especially the sound of the judge smacking me across the face."

TWENTY-SIX

"Rose is going to call you before I finish talking," I said to Laura as I stuck my head in, barely pausing on my way back to the conference room. "You don't know where I am, you don't know when I'm coming back, and you'll be happy to get a message to me if necessary."

The light on the first line of her phone lighted up. She put her hand on the receiver to pick it up, but I put mine on top of hers.

"And if the man himself walks over to talk to me, just tell him I've stepped out."

A second ring. I knew it was Rose Malone calling for Battaglia, who'd be looking for an apology first and then for more information about my taped conversation with Pell.

"Tell him I seemed very upset. That I flew out of here," I said. "And if Manny Chirico drops by, remember to tell him that I love him. I absolutely love him. Or maybe give that message to Rose, and tell her to be sure to pass it along in front of Battaglia."

Laura picked up the phone. "Alexandra Cooper's office."

She covered the receiver with her hand and mouthed to me that it was Rose. I shrugged and shook my head, and scooted down to the conference room.

"You look like you got hit by a truck," he said.

"We have to get lost for the rest of the day, Mercer. I may have just talked myself out of a job."

"C'mon, Alex. What's—?"

"Insubordination. Rudeness. Untimely display of my ill-managed temper. Threats," I said, sitting at the table with my head in my hands. "I think I just sort of threatened Paul Battaglia. And the mayor of the city of New York. Tell me I didn't do that."

Mercer walked over behind me and started to massage my shoulders. "I know you didn't do that."

"Quite sure I did. It's Friday. I'm just going to take off early for the weekend. Unless you'll hang with me," I said. "Can we take the most critical papers we need with us and go to my apartment and keep working?"

"I'll do anything you want. But let's get your head on straight."

"That feels good. Keep rubbing my neck."

"Will do if you tell me what just happened in there."

I got as far as Chirico's presentation of Raymond Tanner's prison photos. Mercer had been with us at Stallion Ridge on the day our last major investigation came to an abrupt end. He had helped to find a way to celebrate my birthday when my personal world imploded that afternoon, and so the timeline Chirico established made great sense to him.

"Jessica Pell and Raymond Tanner in the same air space up at Fishkill?" he said. "Mighty dicey. Being on her bad side's a dangerous spot."

"I think that tat is only about spooking me. Nothing more than that."

"So what's Battaglia's problem?"

"I didn't get to the end of the story, Mercer. I went up to court yesterday to see the judge, like I told you I was going to do."

"You *what*?" He let go off my shoulders and sat down opposite me. "Pick up your head, look me in the eye, and tell me you didn't do what I told you not to do, Ms. Cooper."

"I didn't mean to go against you, Mercer. There's just too much on the line here for this laissez-faire approach everybody seems to have about Pell."

"Spare no details, Alexandra."

Every word of my conversation with Jessica Pell was still fresh in my mind. I repeated the story for Mercer, whose expression never changed throughout the telling. Then he stretched his arms out on the table and bowed his head.

"Who's going to believe you, Alex? You think you're getting jammed up so you went to her one-on-one? I would have gone with you if I'd thought for a minute you were serious."

I pointed at the scratches on my cheek and Mercer reached across the table and held my chin in his hand to look at them.

"It's not about you, is it, Alex? You didn't crawl out on a limb for your own sake. You did this so Pell wouldn't pull the plug on Mike."

Tears welled up in my eyes. I shook my head from side to side.

"Damn, I wish I'd been there." Mercer stood up and started to pack several of the manila folders into one of my canvas sail bags.

"One more thing you should know," I said. "I had the guys from the DA's squad wire me up. It's not just my word, Mercer. There's a tape."

He dropped the file that was in his hand, and the papers spread over the floor. "Mother of—"

"Hey—it's legal."

"Ill-advised, Ms. Cooper. Risky but ballsy—and yes, legal. Where's the audio?"

"At my apartment. And a copy in the squad safe."

Mercer smiled at me. "Way to go, girl. Wait till Mike hears."

"No way. Blood oath on this one. When Pell gives the all clear, let him just think the madwoman came to her senses. He can't know I got into this battle."

"I can respect that for now. Pick the files you want," he said, bending down to retrieve the papers. "I've got mine. Now all we have to do is figure a way past McKinney's door, and we can hustle down the rear staircase."

"It's Friday. McKinney's shrink gets the first crack at him in the morning. We're good to go."

I called Laura from my cell. "All calm?"

"Not from my vantage point. Rose called three times before the DA came by. You do not want to cross his path today. He wants to hear from you as soon as I find you."

"In about three minutes, two people who look a lot like Mercer and me will slink past your door. Bury your nose in a file cabinet and then we're out of your hair. I promise I'll respond to all your calls and texts. I just blew out of here. That's all you know," I said. "And I will try to find some way to thank you."

"Stay safe, Alexandra. The radio says that Tanner bastard raped again last night."

"I'm with Mercer, and he's on top of that. Talk later."

With a small fraction of the case folders in our totes, we raced down the short corridor between the conference room and my office. Instead of the main elevator, we took the service staircase down to the street.

Once inside Mercer's SUV and headed uptown, I called Rose's number.

"Alex? Let me put you right through. You seem to have started a small war."

"No, no, no. I'm not in the office. I'm taking the day off. I'd just like you to tell the boss I'm sorry for the contretemps, and that I'll call him later. No point his waiting for me to come see him because I'm gone for the day."

"And if anything breaks on your murder case?"

"The detectives know how to find me. Sorry to be so disrespectful."

We were setting up our work space at my dining room table by 11:15, air-conditioning at full blast and summer sunlight flooding the cheerful apartment.

There was a knock at my front door half an hour later. The doormen never let anyone except Mike or Mercer up to my floor without calling first. "Did you—?"

"Yeah. I buzzed Mike when I was looking for a parking space. Told him to spend some time here before he heads to the Park. And hush, I didn't say a word about Pell, okay?"

I walked to the front door and opened it. "C'mon in, Mike."

"How's her mood, Mercer?" he said, practically tiptoeing past me, not even venturing a greeting.

"Better since I apologized for both of us last night."

"I get it. It was the right thing to do, and the cops were perfectly nice," I said.

"How nice?" Mike asked. "You get lucky?"

"Very. I actually got to sleep for a change," I said. "You've heard about Tanner in Prospect Park?"

"Yeah. SVU and Homicide are jumping all over the place." Mike was carrying a cardboard banker's box, which he rested on the mahogany table.

"What's that?"

"The Cold Case Unit pulled the Baby Lucy kidnapping papers for me. What's left of them."

The paperwork from cases that lingered for years—or decades— was often picked apart, unintentionally destroying the integrity of the investigation, while on the dusty shelves where it was stored. Cops would go back to them to review witness statements, or characters would reappear in a later investigation so their earlier questioning became relevant. Police reports sometimes vanished, and cases like the disappearance of Lucy Dalton would have generated mounds of documents and media reports, many of which wouldn't survive long stretches of inattention.

"That's it?" I asked.

"Six more like it. I just picked the first one up at 7:30 this morning. Sat in the squad room reading till you called, Mercer. I think

I'm still on day two of the investigation. What a manhunt this was," Mike said. "Why are you guys here and not downtown?"

"I'm exhausted, and it was kind of quiet at the office. Everybody ready to take off for the weekend. I just figured we'd be more comfortable at my house, and I'd be all set up to keep working over the weekend."

Mercer gave me a thumbs-up.

"Is this what you're doing today?" I asked Mike. "Reading ancient history?"

"That was the original plan. Peterson wanted to keep me on a leash, in the office. They were expecting fireworks from Judge Pell right around now."

I busied myself labeling folders with colored tabs.

"Don't go to the bank on this," Mike said, "but Manny Chirico called right after Mercer did. He thinks she's going to back off. He must have worked his charm on her is all I can say."

"Must have. He's got loads more of it than you do, and he's too smart to misuse it," I said. "So now what?"

"Fair game, kid. So I called Mia Schneider. Someone at the Conservancy is pulling out the original renderings of the Park from the 1850s so we can see if there are really any caves in it. That could set me up for tomorrow."

"I'm with you," Mercer said.

"Don't you guys want a day off?"

"Maybe Sunday. I hate that the Park presence will already be so reduced by the end of the day," Mercer said.

"And my next stop is the Dakota," Mike said. "See what I can wheedle out of Ms. Sorenson."

There was a manila folder on the top of the box, crisp and clean and new. Mike slid some photographs out of it and put them on the table. "Courtesy of Hal Sherman and his Panoscan man."

This was my second photo exhibit of the day. I was hoping that it would be half as productive as the first.

The digital camera had captured its characteristic fish-eye images, a full 360-degree photo record shot from Bow Bridge just hours after Angel's body had been pulled out of the Lake.

I started with the shots in order, scouring the ground around the Lake, spreading farther into the trees and bushes till it was too dense to see, hoping to find some jarring scene, something totally out of place, a clue that hadn't been visible to the Crime Scene crew as they worked within short range of the victim's corpse.

"Stumped?" Mike asked.

"I give up. Where's Waldo?"

Mike reached among the photos for the blow-up of the Dakota apartments. "Count up from the ground floor, Coop. Lavinia Dalton's got the entire eighth floor."

"Of course. You told me you saw a shadowy figure on nine, in one of the eyelid windows."

I went to my coffee table to take hold of a decorative antique magnifying glass and looked again.

I slid the horn-handled magnifier up to the tiny rectangular windows, which sat a flight above the grand long ones of the eighth floor but below the eaves of the roof.

"The servants' quarters," Mercer said, standing over my shoulder.

Directly above the living room windows of Lavinia Dalton was one of the openings. With my naked eye, I could see the outline of a tall object, maybe even a figure, framed in the narrow pane of glass.

I pushed the magnifier up and tried to focus the image more clearly.

"It's a person," I said, recalling the crush of cops and passersby who had huddled around Bethesda Terrace while the Crime Scene Unit was taking the pictures. "It's a man, I think, his palms pressed against the window, looking down at the homicide detectives doing their work."

Mike grabbed the photograph from my hand. "And I'm going to find out who he is."

TWENTY-SEVEN

"Are you expected, sir?" the young housekeeper asked when she opened the door to Mike, Mercer, and me.

"No, ma'am. I'd like to see Ms. Sorenson," Mike said.

"She's not in at the moment."

"We'll wait," he said, trying to charge past the petite woman.

"I'm afraid I can't admit you until she returns."

"How is Miss Dalton doing today?" I asked.

"Very well, thank you."

"Perhaps I could just talk with her for a few minutes? The gentlemen can wait in the living room."

The housekeeper didn't know how to respond.

"She invited us to stop back," I said. "She really did."

"But you're police, aren't you? You're not going to agitate her with talk about Lucy?"

"I won't do that. I promise."

Reluctantly, she pulled back the heavy door and let us in. I motioned to Mike and Mercer to stay put and let the housekeeper lead me through to the dayroom. This time, Lavinia Dalton was sitting in a wing chair, wearing a long-sleeved dress with a chenille sweater around her shoulders. Her cheeks were rouged, her hair had been curled, and the sapphire suite of jewels had been replaced by pink stones on her fingers and earlobes. She looked as though she might have been expecting the Duchess of Cambridge.

Again there were two nurses attending the elderly woman, one of whom had been working on our earlier visit. I introduced myself, and they offered me the chair opposite Lavinia's sunny window seat.

"Hello, Miss Dalton. I'm Alexandra Cooper." Although her eyes looked bright, it was obvious she had no recollection of seeing me just a day before.

"Pleasure, my dear. Is Archer keeping you waiting?"

"No, ma'am," I said, returning her warm smile with one of my own. "I just came to talk with you."

"How lovely."

One of the nurses spoke over my head. "Miss Lavinia's very happy today. After lunch, we're going to take a walk in the Park," she said, pointing to the wheelchair. "It's her very favorite thing to do."

"It's one of my favorite things, too."

I had just promised not to ask questions about the heartbreak of Baby Lucy's disappearance. But here was a perfect opportunity— without Sorenson's censorship—to see what nuggets Dalton's long-term memory had that might give us guidance.

"Where do you like to go inside the Park?" I asked.

"Gardens, my dear. I love the gardens. But they're so far away I can never get to them." She looked out the window so wistfully.

The nurse spoke. "Don't you remember, Miss Lavinia? We went with the car to the Conservatory Garden just last week. It was all so beautiful."

"Yes, yes, it was," Dalton said. But I had no good reason to believe her mind had been able to capture that recent memory.

"Do you like the Carousel?" I asked.

She lifted a hand—such a fragile-looking wrist, encircled by gold bangles—and pointed. "Since I was a child, dear, I've loved the Carousel. You can see it there, can't you?"

It was just south of the 65th Street Transverse, and I was able to see the roof of the building, which was more than a hundred years old.

"Do you know, dear, that the first time I rode that Carousel," Lavinia Dalton said, perking up as she talked with her hands, expressively and so clearly in the moment of a long-ago time, "it was powered by a live animal? And I couldn't see him anywhere, but I could hear the noises he made. The neighs of a real horse."

"How funny."

"You don't believe me, do you?"

"Of course I do." I had no idea what she meant.

"When Miss Lavinia was a little girl," the nurse said, "the Carousel wasn't run on electricity, like it is now. And in a hole beneath the platform where the beautiful painted horses sit . . . Am I right, Miss Lavinia?"

"You're exactly right. The poor animal was in a hole in the ground."

"There was actually a live mule, chained to a harness, which is what made the Carousel go around."

"And the operator who took our nickels, he would stamp his foot, and that's how the mule knew when to start and stop the Carousel," Lavinia said. "I bet you didn't know that, young lady."

"You're absolutely right, Miss Dalton." But now I knew she had a sharp image and details of something that had happened more than eight decades ago.

She reached for her cane and asked the nurse to help her to her feet so she could stand and look out the window, leaning her other arm on the windowsill.

"And there's the Lake where I used to ice-skate. And rowboats, of course. I was courted in rowboats, even though my father didn't allow it."

"That must have been fun."

"More fun than you can imagine. And worth the paddling I'd get from time to time. Come stand beside me, missy."

I moved next to her.

"This is my home," she said to me, looking up to make sure I was taking it all in. "And when I was a little girl, my father used to tell me that he built this Park just for me. The sheep grazed in the meadow right below my bedroom. At night, with my windows open, I could hear the noise from the band shell. John Philip Sousa and all his marches. There's an angel—a glorious angel right over there. Do you know her?"

"The Angel of the Waters," I said.

"She was there to look out for me," Lavinia Dalton said, grasping my hand in hers. "I believed that, you know? She's my very own angel."

A death angel, to be sure.

"I was glad other people loved the Park, of course. But I was so badly spoiled, missy, that I actually believed it was all designed for me."

Lavinia Dalton grew tired quickly. She reached out her arm to the nurse, who stepped her backward and reseated her in the chair.

"Did you ever play in the rooms upstairs?" I asked. "When you couldn't go to the Park, when the weather was foul?"

"The gymnasium?" she asked, clutching the ornate silver handle of the cane between her hands. "There's a wonderful gymnasium upstairs."

"No longer, Miss Lavinia," one of the nurses said. "It's not there anymore."

"There weren't many children in this building when I was growing up. And that was the only place to meet them. There's the croquet court and the tennis, too, downstairs."

"Gone a long time," the nurse said, shaking her head at me.

Lavinia Dalton was so firm in her insistence of describing the past that she tapped her cane on the thickly carpeted floor. "Papa objected to my doing sports, so it was hard for me to play with the others at croquet. But the gymnasium was on the tenth floor, and there was the great dining room up there as well."

"Dining room?"

"Oh, yes, missy. A grand hall where all the families could eat if it was their cook's day off, or there was company."

The nurse shrugged her shoulders and gave me a look that suggested she didn't know whether Lavinia's memories were sound.

"We hardly ever went there—public rooms—because Papa had such a fear of germs. Immigrants and their plagues, he used to say. Never wanted me mixing with other children, for fear they were being raised by foreigners who brought every illness with them from Europe."

"The tenth floor?" I asked. "I didn't know the Dakota had a tenth floor. I was hoping you'd tell me about the ninth floor."

She looked at me with a mischievous grin, almost whispering. "You won't tell Papa, will you?"

It was as though she had taken a literal step back into the past.

"It's wondrous up there"—talking in the present tense, as though she still visited the servants' quarters. "It's my happiest place to play, when I have to be indoors."

The nurses both seemed bemused, as though they had heard this all before.

"Why is that?" I asked.

"I'll take you up when I'm feeling stronger, missy."

"Tell me why you like it up there."

"Don't you always like best the places you aren't allowed to go?" Lavinia Dalton said, with a conspiratorial grin. "I certainly do."

"It was staff quarters, you understand," one of the nurses said.

"Papa doesn't like me to be with some of the common people," she said, then waved her hand in the direction of one of the nurses. "Not them, you see. These girls are professionals. Papa's nurses always have rooms in the house, don't you, dears?"

"But the cook and—?"

"And the housemaids and the laundress and the chauffeur, well, they've got all these wonderful nooks and crannies upstairs," Lavinia Dalton said. "And they're all wee and such."

"Wee?" I asked.

"The rooms are small, not all ostentatious like this, missy. Nothing in them a child can break or damage. Nobody to tell you to keep away from the porcelain or not to put your fingers on the windowpane. No one to remind you the carpet came from Kathmandu and the vase is Ming dynasty.

"Somebody always has sweets up there for me, and a child of their own sneaked in from home if they had to work a holiday or weekend. A child I could play with to my heart's content and then run downstairs to Papa the minute my nanny hears that Papa has come home."

"It sounds wondrous indeed, Miss Dalton. And who's up there now?"

That was a major gaffe. I wanted to know about the present day—about the figure in the ninth-floor window that appeared in the photograph—but Lavinia Dalton was in another place, happily reliving moments from her childhood.

"There's no one up there now, Ms. Cooper," Jillian Sorenson said, startling me out of my seat. Her footsteps had been muffled by the thick Oriental carpet, and I hadn't heard her approaching. "Nothing but a bunch of dark and dusty rooms."

"What, Jillian?" Lavinia asked, as though snapped back to today. "What's dusty?"

"Nothing at all to trouble you, Lavinia," Sorenson said. "Miss Cooper has to be leaving now."

"Yes, yes, I do." That was the first moment at which I noticed the older housekeeper, Bernice Wicks, standing behind Jill Sorenson.

"It's a beautiful day, Lavinia," Sorenson said. "Take a rest and then you'll go to the Park for an hour."

I was walking past Dalton's social secretary. "How rude of you to take advantage of Lavinia when I wasn't here to protect her."

"I wasn't trying to take advantage of her at all. A piece of evidence came to our attention this morning and—"

"Evidence about Lucy?" Sorenson asked.

"No, no. About the body found in the Lake last week," I said, but Sorenson's remark had done the damage.

"Lucy?" Lavinia Dalton said. She had heard the child's name loud and clear. "Where's Lucy?"

The brightness was gone from her eyes, as though a curtain had descended in an instant.

"You're going to rest for a while, Lavinia."

"Has she come down from the ninth floor yet? Is Lucy playing up there with Bernice?"

"I'm right here, Miss Lavinia," Bernice Wicks said, coming around me to comfort her longtime employer. "Been here with you all day."

The young housekeeper had been right to worry about Lavinia Dalton's agitation. In my brief visit, I had lifted her from the muddled perception of today's events to a happy series of memories from her childhood and now landed her in the heartbreaking territory of Baby Lucy's disappearance. The distress I had caused the kind old woman was conspicuous.

"Lucy must be upstairs playing with the children," Lavinia Dalton said, an exaggerated tremor now visible in the right hand that she held out to Jillian Sorenson. "You must bring her down to see me. I promised she could go with me to the zoo today."

TWENTY-EIGHT

"Whoa, whoa, whoa. Don't give us the boot," Mike said to Jillian Sorenson as she ushered us toward the door. "We'd like to see the apartments that Miss Dalton owns on the flight above this one."

"That's not possible."

"It's not only possible, it's necessary. You've got keys?"

"I neither have keys nor the lawyers' permission to give you access, Detective. We haven't used most of that space for years. In fact, Miss Lavinia sold several units off to other residents."

"Most of that space?" Mike asked. "What about the rest of it?"

"I misspoke. We've used none of that space recently. It's not like it was in the old days, Mr. Chapman. We have a very small staff now, and there's room for all of us here in the apartment. Bernice and I spend a lot of time here, along with the nurses and the other house-keeper. The men—the butler and the chauffeur—are only part-time now, so they go to their own homes."

"Where on the ninth floor are the units that were sold off?"

"I don't know exactly."

"Well, facing the Park? On the north end of the building or the south? Facing the courtyard?"

Bernice Wicks was at the far end of the room. She was standing in the archway, hands folded across her apron. She looked like she was about to burst with information. I remembered that she told us yesterday that she used to spend time in the quarters upstairs, even bringing her son to stay with her when she wasn't able to be at home.

"Miss Jillian," she said, "would you like me to answer the questions?"

"That won't be necessary, Bernice. You might help the nurse with Miss Lavinia's lunch."

"What do you prefer, Ms. Sorenson?" Mike asked. "A search warrant or a battering ram?"

"What's the evidence you're talking about?" she said without flinching.

"You answer a question with a question. Seem like the battering-ram type to me. Make a note of that, Mercer, will you?"

"And publicity?" Sorenson asked.

"I don't believe in it. No reason to alert the press."

"If you had enough evidence for a search warrant, you would have arrived here with it."

"I thought I'd try a courtesy visit first before letting everyone in the courthouse know we're doing a drop-in."

She licked her lips and adjusted her headband. "Which apartment are you interested in?"

"Maybe you didn't get my point. First I want to know which apartments are still owned by Lavinia Dalton and the family trusts. Then I'd like to know the lay of the land before I—"

Mercer was making his way to the front door.

"Where are you going, my man?" Mike asked.

"There's a management office downstairs," he said. "It's a much smoother way to get where we want to go. Floor plans, records, nobody with something to hide. Time is precious, my good Mr. Chapman."

"I'd prefer you don't go to the office," Jillian Sorenson said. "We don't need them meddling in our business. Bernice and I can try to figure this out for you."

"Better attitude," Mike said.

"Bernice, would you see if there are keys in the kitchen cabinet for any of the ninth-floor rooms?"

The housekeeper scurried off as though she'd been invited to a ball and needed to ready herself to go.

"It's been so long since I've been upstairs," Sorenson said, seemingly flustered by the thought that we were getting into the rooms one way or another. She began to describe the complex arrangement of rooms, and the sell-off of several in the last few years, with the soaring value of real estate property in Manhattan, and especially after the onset of Lavinia Dalton's dementia.

"Is there anything in the rooms that belongs to Miss Dalton?" I asked.

"I wouldn't think much. I believe we left the beds and dressers, that sort of thing. But when we put the silver collection in storage, Bernice and the butler cleaned out much of the property left behind in those rooms."

Bernice Wicks returned in several minutes bearing an assortment of metal chains with keys extended from them.

"Keys to the kingdom, Mrs. Wicks," Mike said.

"Oh, yes, sir."

"Your kingdom?"

She laughed at him. "Once upon a time, Mr. Chapman. It would never happen today that a servant had the best view in the city, but we did."

"Stairs or elevator?" he asked as we closed the apartment door behind us.

Wicks pointed. "There are service elevators around the corner on each end of the hallway—north and south. We're not allowed to use the ones for residents, at least not while in uniform."

"Let's take the stairs," he said. "Are you able?"

"It's good for me to do, the doctor says."

"Where are they?"

"See the wide door, the last one on the corridor on each end? That would be the staircase."

The southernmost door was directly opposite the room that once had belonged to Baby Lucy. Mike caught that, too. "Let's go to the one down there."

The heavy oak door opened easily. The steps were broad and deep, and we mounted them slowly so that Bernice—grasping the banister tightly, stopping to catch her breath—was able to lead us.

The ninth-floor corridor had an entirely different look than the residential hallway below. The ceiling was much lower than the fourteen-foot apartment height, the walls were a dark-paneled wood, and there was an endless lineup of doors on each side, much closer together than in the grand suites that comprised the eighth floor. There was a claustrophobic, almost sinister feel to the long, silent space.

Bernice stopped still as soon as she reached the first doorway. Jillian Sorenson walked past her, taking the sets of keys from her hand.

"So this line of rooms to your right," she said, "from this first one all the way to the farthest end—the ones which face Central Park—they were all the property of the Dalton family from the time the building opened."

"Every one of them?" I asked.

"As I've told you, the staff was rather large in those days, and until quite recently," Sorenson said. "The rooms on the left—well, that's a bit deceptive. A couple of them are apartments, am I right, Bernice?"

"You are, Miss Jillian. May I?"

"Certainly."

"The staff quarters, you see, are quite small. Just a few feet across, with a bed and a tiny cabinet for your things. A little sink in the corner. That's why there are so many more doors up here," Wicks said, taking a few steps. "Three common baths. All of us on the hallway had to share them, no matter who you worked for. I'll show you them as we go along."

"How many altogether?"

"Staff rooms? Probably twenty—and eight of them were Miss Lavinia's. The Park side, of course. Then keep in mind we had laundry rooms up here, over the courtyard. There were dumbwaiters down to the apartment."

"Dumbwaiters?" Mike asked.

"Oh, yes, and didn't the children love those?" she said. "Put in when the place was built so the help didn't have to carry all the cleaning supplies and heavy linens and such up and down the stairs. Ran all the way to the ground floor. My Eddie hid in one overnight, when he got bored with himself waiting for me to get off work. Scared the wits out of me till Cook found him sleeping there in the morning."

"Miss Dalton was telling me how she thought it was 'wondrous' up here," I said, looking directly at Sorenson to let her know the direction of our conversation, and that I had not been trying to upset the gracious woman. "Just like Mrs. Wicks just said, that it was a happy place for kids to play."

Jillian Sorenson almost smiled. "It has always been popular for that."

"A little too dark and gloomy for my taste," Mike said.

"We'll open a few doors and you'll see how magical it is."

"Thanks."

"The first three units on the right were sold to another building resident three years ago. This is a cooperative, of course, so the only buyers allowed are residents, who have already passed the scrutiny of the board. This owner is a well-known screenwriter—thrillers and that sort of thing. Miss Lavinia was very fond of him, although she didn't much enjoy crime stories, as you might imagine—and so when he inquired about purchasing some of the rooms to create a writing studio, Justin Feldman arranged the sale of these spaces to him."

"So some of this floor has been remodeled?" I asked.

"Most definitely. A number of the rooms have been gutted by their owners and repurposed. Several on the courtyard side and the back of the building remain big storage closets for their owners, which will all change someday. No one today would use this valuable property—you'll forgive me, Bernice—for their staff. The rooms may be small, but the Park views will take your breath away."

"It's not configured as it was in Lavinia's day?" Mercer asked.

"Not even the same as when Lucy disappeared, if that's what you're getting at," Sorenson said. "It was a maze of cubbyholes and passageways, staircases to everywhere and to nowhere in particular, hallways restricted to staff and other parts to residents. It was a place to stay when one didn't want, or need, to be seen, and it was a delightful escape when children wanted to play hide-and-seek with one another—or just be rambunctious."

The fourth door, Wicks showed us, was unlocked. It was a bathroom, recently renovated, that had the necessary toilet facilities and several shower stalls.

"Four more, is it, Bernice?"

"Six, Miss Jillian."

"Six more rooms still belong to Miss Lavinia."

She searched the bale of keys until she found one with a tag that corresponded to the brass number above the doorknob. The door opened, and she and Wicks waited in the hallway while Mercer, Mike, and I went in.

The room was tiny, spare, and almost monastic in appearance. Mercer's head nearly reached the ceiling. There was a single bed—a very old metal headboard painted white supporting a bare mattress with sagging springs. There was a plain bedside table and a primitive bureau, with two photographs of Dalton railroad cars hanging slightly ajar on the wall. The room had been stripped of all else, and a layer of dust covered all the surfaces.

But when I stepped to the window, it was as though the shabby room might have been within a palace. Spread out beneath me was most of Central Park, from a vantage point low enough to make out people on the ground, but high enough to see the great expanse of the magnificent green playground of the island of Manhattan.

The three of us took turns practically pressing our noses against the window, spellbound by the views it offered. Behind us, Bernice was apologizing to Sorenson for allowing so much dust to gather.

"So sorry, Miss Jillian. I haven't gotten up here in months. I didn't see the need, really."

"I didn't either. You've got nothing to be sorry about."

They waited until we'd had our fill of gawking and locked the door behind us. Sorenson found the key to the second room, and we peered inside, with identical results.

"Have you ever spent much time at the Dakota stables?" Mike asked her as she matched the third key to the lock.

"I've been there, Detective. And for a while I garaged my own car there, but the chauffeurs have always had the responsibility for dealing with that part of our life."

"Ever heard of an African American community called Seneca Village?"

"No, Mr. Chapman. Where is it? Why do you ask?"

The third and fourth rooms had stacks of cardboard boxes labeled BANK RECORDS and FAMILY CORRESPONDENCE—all dated from the 1940s and 1950s.

"Something else we found in the Park is all. A small object that might have come out of an old church," Mike said. "A guy who worked at the garage when he was a teenager claims it was his."

"Does it have any significance to what you're investigating?" Sorenson asked.

"Not likely."

The fifth room, which was much farther down the hallway, separated from the others by several units that had been sold and by another common bath area, was crammed with Dalton family sports equipment. There were a few sleds, half a dozen pairs of very old cross-country skis, snowshoes, tennis racquets, and croquet sets. It looked like the athletic division of a more modern King Tut's tomb.

"You mean the fellow who runs the garage?"

"No, no. Actually a homeless man who lives in the Park," Mike said.

"You don't mean Vergil Humphrey, now, do you?" Bernice Wicks asked.

I couldn't have swiveled around any faster to face her.

"In fact, I do," Mike said. "But you've always worked in the house, haven't you?"

"Bernice," Sorenson said, "there's no need to—"

But the words were already out of the older woman's mouth. "Verge worked in the Dakota when he was a boy," she said. "Helped the handymen with the trash and all that."

"The guy at the garage told us yesterday that Verge had nothing to do with the Dalton staff."

"He didn't really," Bernice Wicks said. "But he couldn't keep his hands to himself, that boy. He didn't last very long here. His father had them hire him over at the garage before he got fired from this job, so maybe that's why they didn't know he worked here first. It's not like they were ever going to get a good reference for him from the staff here."

"Is there anything you don't know about this building, Bernice?" Mike said. "I might put you on retainer."

"You're a flatterer, Mr. Chapman," Wicks said, exchanging her warm smile for a look of profound unhappiness. "I know most of the Dakota's secrets. The one I'd have given everything to figure out, though, that's never come to pass."

Jillian Sorenson wiggled the key in the lock of the sixth door.

I could see from the length of remaining hallway—one door left on this side—that the room we were about to enter was the one in which the outline of a figure appeared in the Panoscan photograph. Mike winked at Mercer and me, nodding as he did. The fingers of his right hand were already running through his hair.

"Bernice," Sorenson said, "did anyone change the lock? I can't seem to get this one to open."

"No, Miss Jillian. No one's been up here at all, to my knowledge."

She held the key up again and put on her reading glasses to check the number. "It's the right one, but it won't seem to turn."

"You mind if I try?" Mike asked.

"If you think you can get it to work, be my guest."

He twisted and turned his hand, but the lock wouldn't give. "This won't open it," he said. "Don't you have a master?"

"I don't think so," Sorenson said. "Haven't you seen enough? Or will you let me call one of the custodians tomorrow and see if we can get you in?"

"I'd really like to have a look," Mike said, turning his side to the door and throwing his weight against it.

Jillian Sorenson let out a yelp when she saw Mike's movement. "Don't!"

But he had already launched his assault. The dry wood cracked and split as the two women gasped. The lock didn't give, but Mike reached in through the hole he'd created in the splintered panel and opened the door.

The room was very much like the first three—a single bed, a nightstand, a bureau, and a window with a glorious view of Central Park.

But there were also signs of life.

There were footsteps—large ones—imprinted on the dusty surface of the floor. There were two cardboard coffee containers, both empty, resting on the windowsill, along with a wax paper wrap that looked like it had once held a sandwich lying open on the floor below the sill. It looked as though someone had nested here for a while, leaving a few pieces of yellowed newspaper and other fragments of a transient life resting on a paper bag in the far corner.

Mike held out his arm so that neither woman could enter the room. "Get a team up here," he said to Mercer. "Maybe there's something unique in the shoe prints. And there's certain to be DNA on the coffee cups."

Someone had stood in this very window, watching Angel's body being removed from the Lake, exactly one week ago this morning.

"I'm going to ask you again, Ms. Sorenson," Mike said. "Who's got access to this room?"

She held out both hands, dangling the chains. "I've got no idea. Someone's obviously changed the keys."

Bernice Wicks looked frantic. "I'm so sorry to make trouble, Miss Jillian. Last time this happened it was my fault."

"Let's not discuss that, Bernice."

"It was my Eddie, that time. I gave the key to him—"

"Bernice!" Jillian Sorenson's single-word reprimand echoed in the gloomy corridor.

"Who's Eddie?" Mike said.

"My son. Eddie's my boy."

The frightened housekeeper had talked about the fact that he used to stay here during his childhood when she had to work late nights or weekends. Perhaps he'd been back here more recently.

"He's not a boy, Bernice. Eddie's fifty-nine years old. Stop babbling, will you?"

"Can't be him who was here anyway," she said, trying to force a smile. "Poor Eddie's been away almost a year now."

"Away?" I asked, trying to calm her. "Where is he?"

"We had him committed, ma'am. Rather, I had him committed," Bernice Wicks said, looking over to Jillian Sorenson. "Civilly, that is. He didn't do anything to anybody but himself. He's in the psychiatric ward at Bellevue Hospital."

TWENTY-NINE

"Eddie Wicks has spent a good deal of his life in mental institutions," Jillian Sorenson said. "Private ones, mostly. Paid for, most generously, by Lavinia Dalton."

Mike and I were sitting in the living room of the Dalton apartment with Sorenson and Bernice Wicks, who was wringing a linen handkerchief between her trembling hands. Mercer had remained on the ninth floor, trying to get a Crime Scene crew to go over the small room, looking for evidence.

"The new lawyers are interested in conserving more of Miss Lavinia's money. This time Eddie's in Bellevue."

"Blue-papered?" Mike asked.

"Sorry?"

"An involuntary commitment?"

The form authorizing involuntary hospitalization had long been done on blue paper, and those two words had become synonymous with the process.

"Yes," Sorenson said.

"For what reason?"

"Must we do this in front of Bernice?" she asked.

"Bernice is more forthcoming than you seem to be. If her son had new keys made a year ago, then they might have been stolen by someone or passed on by him. I'm not looking to add to her woes—or to his."

Jillian Sorenson nodded. "May I tell them, Bernice?"

"Yes, ma'am."

"Eddie Wicks is bipolar, Mr. Chapman. Are you familiar with that condition?"

"Somewhat. Tell me about his case."

"When Bernice first started working here with Miss Lavinia, Eddie was an adolescent."

"Fourteen," the housekeeper said, her small body almost enveloped by the oversized wing chair. "I came here in 1968."

That was three years before Baby Lucy's kidnapping.

"His father—Bernice's husband—had taken his own life a year earlier," Sorenson said. "She told you yesterday that he had passed away. In fact he was a suicide."

"I'm so sorry," I said to Bernice.

"Nobody called it a disease back then. Just said it was depression. But he jumped out the window of our apartment in Queens, right in front of me and Eddie."

Not even the handkerchief could slow the tears that were falling.

"Miss Lavinia recognized that Bernice and her children needed help. Eddie most especially. She got him a wonderful psychiatrist, who diagnosed bipolarity by his midteens," Sorenson said. "Although experts still don't fully know its cause, there is certainly a view that it runs in families. That it's congenital."

"Did Eddie go to school?" I asked.

"My son's very smart, ma'am. He's very well educated and accomplished."

"Yes, Ms. Cooper," Sorenson said. "Eddie's quite intelligent. He was mainstreamed throughout school, at his psychiatrist's insistence, and he handled it well. Eddie got a Regents scholarship to one of the SUNY colleges. He's a mechanical engineer. Smart and accomplished."

But wounded, I thought. Damaged, like the people our murdered girl liked to collect.

"And why the institutionalizations?" Mike asked. "Did they start when Eddie was a teenager?"

"The behavior did, but nothing that required hospitalization."

"How did it manifest itself?"

Again, Jillian Sorenson took the lead. "The mood swings were extreme. Eddie's older sister couldn't handle him alone at home, of course, which is why he spent more and more time here. Upstairs, in fact, in that little room.

"When he was in a manic phase, he had enormously high energy levels. There were times he was extremely happy. He'd go out into the Park for hours on weekends, and we'd hardly see him. Or he'd roam about the corridors up here late at night, looking for things to do."

"That was a good thing," Bernice added. "There was always something for him to amuse himself with in all these little rooms. The other staff were awfully good with him, too. Except for the tantrums."

"That's the manic side of it," I said. "I've had a lot of cases with teenagers. The swings from the great highs to the irritability and temper tantrums of the lows."

"Yes, ma'am. Eddie sure had those."

"Did he ever act out sexually, Mrs. Wicks?"

"What?"

"A lot of the young men with a bipolar condition—well, they begin to use very sexual language, inappropriate language. Touch their own genitals a lot," I said, thinking of Baby Lucy and how she loved to play on the ninth floor. "They often come on to others in a sexual way."

"Not my Eddie." Bernice Wicks seemed shocked by the very idea. "Not my son."

"I want to know how Eddie wound up in Bellevue," Mike said, getting us back on point.

"It was often a problem of his medications, Mr. Chapman. When he was under a doctor's care and taking his meds, he had constructive periods in his adult life. But as smart as Eddie is, the disease prevented him from holding most jobs for any long period of time," Sorenson went on. "He's also struggled with alcohol abuse since his twenties."

"Living here?" I asked.

"No, no. On his own for most of the time when he was working. A small apartment in Queens, near where he was raised. Never in a significant relationship, so far as we know. I must say he was a real favorite of Miss Lavinia's—as is Bernice—so he was welcome here whenever he chose."

Bernice Wicks wiped her cheek with her hand. "Oh, yes. He'd love to sneak in up—"

"He didn't sneak, Bernice," Sorenson chided her. "We were happy to have him."

But it was hard to imagine that Eddie Wicks—or anyone else who could get through the servants' entrance at the rear of the Dakota—couldn't hide himself up here for days at a time.

"Was he ever arrested?" I asked.

"Never." His mother gave a firm response to that one.

"He was hospitalized a number of times against his will when he had episodes of bipolar depression. Usually, those had to do with threats to hurt himself," Sorenson said. "Once he got back on his meds, he was released within days."

"Was he able to support himself?"

"With my help," Wicks said proudly.

"And with Miss Lavinia's assistance, of course."

"Of course," I said. "And this time? Bellevue?"

Jillian Sorenson looked over at Bernice before she began to speak. "It's coming up on a year. Last summer, in July, Eddie had a major crisis, although I have no idea what provoked it."

"He was staying upstairs then," Bernice said. "And I couldn't have him here, around Miss Lavinia, constantly stinking of alcohol and being so aggressive."

"He threatened Bernice," Sorenson said. "She told Eddie that he'd have to leave the Dakota, late one night. And he threatened to kill her. He said it was her fault that his father had killed himself. He was extremely irritable and aggressive. Other people who'd seen him up here in the preceding weeks said he was up all night wandering around."

"So we called 911," Bernice said. "To get him out."

"I called 911."

"The police came?" Mike said.

"But they didn't arrest him," Sorenson continued. "We didn't want them to. We just wanted him out of here so that he didn't hurt Bernice any more than his words already had."

"They took him out?"

"Yes, Mr. Chapman. And I understand that they tried to calm him down. It was my mistake not telling them his history and his diagnosis. In any event, by the time they thought he was ready to be let go, and he convinced them he still had an apartment to go to in Queens, it was about four o'clock in the morning."

"Eddie left the station house," Mike said.

"He did. But then he went into Central Park and broke into one of the gate houses—the north one that's right on the Reservoir."

The north and south gate houses sat directly on the jogging path, jutting out into the Reservoir. The one that Eddie Wicks breached was closest to the West 94th Street entrance to the Park.

"How did he get into it?" Mike asked.

"This is someone who'd played in that Park since he was a kid, Detective. How did you knock down the door just now? Maybe he broke the glass, maybe he picked the lock," Sorenson said. "Eddie got inside and up to the roof. He jumped into the Reservoir."

The suicide fence, I thought, is what the chain-link structure that enclosed the Reservoir had been nicknamed long ago. In earlier days, the Reservoir had been a common place for people to try to kill themselves—the reason for the tall fence around its perimeter today.

"Not a sure way to die," Mike said. "It's not all that deep."

"It works, Mr. Chapman, if you don't know how to swim and you're wearing sneakers and long pants. Or at least it almost worked."

"There were joggers," Bernice said, "who saw my Eddie flailing his arms around. They called 911, and there were police close by who got him out. Thank the Lord."

"So the cops took him to Bellevue for a psych evaluation," Mike said. "Someone signed the papers confirming that Eddie has a mental illness and was in danger of harming himself or somebody else."

"Yes," Sorenson said. "After five days, Bernice and I testified at a hearing before a civil judge, a very kindly man, and Eddie was committed. That was the end of last July, and I believe the second time we testified was in September. But the doctors hadn't yet found the right combination of medicines, and Eddie was still being detoxed."

"A hospital's the best place for my son, really and truly."

"We'll be notified if there's a plan for release."

"Have you seen him lately, Mrs. Wicks?" Mike asked.

She bit her lower lip and shook her head. "The doctors prefer that I don't visit, Detective. Eddie— Well, I'm— What's the word, Miss Jillian?"

"Trigger, Bernice. You're his trigger," Sorenson said, turning back to me. "Eddie blames all his troubles on his mother at this point. Eddie's chosen not to see her anymore, and his doctors agree with that decision."

"Last time we saw him was at his hearing after the summer," Wicks said. "He's not the boy I raised, Detective."

"Not your fault, Mrs. Wicks. But if he's getting the care he needs, that's a good thing," Mike said. "Detective Wallace will stay with you till the Crime Scene guys go through that room and help us try to figure out who was there."

"Thank you," Sorenson said.

"In the meantime, I'd suggest you have your security system checked. Whoever got in there is capable of figuring out your other locks, too."

"There's been enough tragedy under this roof, Detective. I'll get on that right away."

THIRTY

It was two o'clock in the afternoon. I checked my phone when we got to the sidewalk and saw that I had a full mailbox, most of the calls originating from Battaglia's office.

"Where to?" I asked.

"Want to hit Bellevue?" Mike said.

"Exercise in futility."

"Why?"

"You didn't get enough double-talk from Vergil Humphrey?"

"Don't answer a question with a question," Mike said, opening the car door for me. "This guy isn't crazy like Verge."

"No. He's smart but self-destructive. He hates his mother."

"He's spent more time in the Dakota than Minnie Castevet," Mike said, referring to the eccentric old neighbor played by Ruth Gordon in *Rosemary's Baby*. "He's the maven of the ninth-floor corridor, and he's responsible for the last change of lock and key."

"You want to put a name on the shadowy figure in the Panoscan photography. I get it."

"Maybe Eddie Wicks can help me do it."

"Let's go."

Mike headed south toward First Avenue in the 20s, home of the oldest continually operating hospital in America, founded as a haven for the indigent four years before George Washington's birth.

"Is Battaglia looking for you?" he asked.

"Seems to be."

"Ease up on him, Coop. He's worried about you."

"He should know that if he can't find me, it's unlikely that Raymond Tanner can." I slumped down in the seat and put my feet up on the dashboard. "Any word from Manny Chirico about the love judge?"

"Nope. If you're not nicer to me, I might leave you at Bellevue."

"The place totally creeps me out." The hospital did great public service work, but the psych facility still remained the most substantial part of its daily business. "I feel badly for old Mrs. Wicks having to kowtow to Jillian Sorenson."

"She's got the staff on a short leash, I think," Mike said. "I wonder if it's Sorenson or the lawyers who've tightened up on the spending. If Eddie Wicks has been in private facilities for all his other hospitalizations, Bellevue might be its own form of shock treatment."

Mike had cut to the east on 34th Street. I recalled for him, from my English lit lessons, the writers who'd made it through Bellevue's psych services. Eugene O'Neill was sent there after a suicide attempt, Malcolm Lowry battled his alcoholism as an inpatient, and Norman Mailer had a stay after stabbing the second of his four wives.

We parked and entered the building, where I'd spent many hours doing competency hearings for defendants—like Raymond Tanner—who were in the prison wing of the hospital. I pointed to the sign for the administrative offices, and we walked down a linoleum-lined hallway until we reached the glass-paned door.

The secretary took our names and asked for our identification. When she came back, she told us that Dr. Hoexter, the director of the psychiatric unit, would see us.

Herman Hoexter's office was a large room, full of metal desks and file cabinets, without character or style but clearly the professional home of a busy man.

"How can I help you?" he asked. "I presume you're here about a prisoner."

"Actually, no," Mike said. "It's about a guy who was blue-papered last summer. No handcuffs, no penal law violations. We think he can assist us with an investigation that's stalled."

"Let me see if I can help," Hoexter said, turning to his computer. "What's his name?"

"Edward or Eddie Wicks. Male, Caucasian, about fifty-nine years of age."

Hoexter typed the name and waited for it to come up on the screen. I watched the doctor's expression change as he read the information.

"I'm glad all you needed was some help from him, Mr. Chapman. I'm afraid Eddie Wicks is lost."

"Lost?" I said. "You mean he's dead?"

"No, we lost him—quite literally—in what our staff call the Bellevue diaspora. The horror that was Hurricane Sandy."

"What's does that mean, literally?" Mike asked, tapping his fingers on the edge of Hoexter's desk.

"You may remember that we were one of the hospitals that flooded in the great storm. We had that massive evacuation, which began the night after Hurricane Sandy hit last October, and we had to move five hundred patients out of this building in several hours' time because our basement and ground floor were underwater. We were completely without power."

"So they scattered," I said, "like a colony of people living away from their homeland. Like a diaspora."

"Yes."

"I thought most of your patients were accounted for."

"Most were, Ms. Cooper. But Eddie Wicks? Eddie Wicks got lost."

THIRTY-ONE

"How do you lose a patient?" Mike asked. "A psych patient, no less, who threatened to kill himself and off his old lady, too?"

"If you calm down, Detective, I'll remind you."

The storm that struck the New York metropolitan area on Monday, October 29th, was the largest Atlantic hurricane on record, with a diameter spanning more than 1,100 miles.

"Water had flooded the streets in lower Manhattan that night, and flooded the hospital's basement as well. Our generator was gone, and we had a pretty desperate mission to make our patients safe. You're thinking of psych patients, Mr. Chapman, but we also do heart surgery here and deliver babies; we have people on dialysis and ER admissions with brain trauma and life-threatening injuries."

"I didn't mean to imply—"

"By the next day, all of our thirty-two elevators had shut down. We lost our ventilators, so we put portable oxygen equipment next to the patients who needed it We ran out of food and we had no drinking water, Detective. But if you stood still for a minute, you could hear a sound like Niagara Falls roaring through the elevator banks as the river water submerged all of our generators. Any of this sound familiar?"

Hoexter had silenced both of us.

"I began to urge that we evacuate, like the NYU and Coney Island hospitals had done before us. And you know what? I received resistance to that idea, even while sleep-deprived nurses were carrying newborns down ten flights, and two of my best docs were helping a triple-bypass patient navigate an unlighted staircase, dragging his oxygen tank behind him."

"I'm sorry I sounded so critical," Mike said.

"The NYPD was great. So was the National Guard." The silver-haired doctor seemed overcome by emotion. "I sat at my desk with a couple of flashlights but no phones, trying to figure out who should be saved first, while ambulances—ambulances by the dozens, organized by FEMA—lined up in front of my hospital and squared the block, two or three times over."

Those images had been shown on the national news over and over again that evening and in the days to follow. It was an unforgettable scene. Emergency truck after emergency truck, from every hospital and service and department anywhere within an hour's drive had responded, red lights flashing in the rainy night as they waited to take on patients while the storm surge continued to wipe out all the power in the city's southern grid.

"I had no idea where these individuals were going," Hoexter said, reliving the desperation of that moment as he retold the story. "All we knew is that they couldn't survive here. ICU, the nursery, the coronary care unit—those patients went first. Where we were sending them, God only knew.

"I'm told that when each stretcher arrived at the front of the line, a dispatcher—someone on our staff—had triaged the patient, and the corresponding ambulance made its own determination about which facility—Mount Sinai, Roosevelt, Lenox Hill, Cornell, Columbia Pres—about which one could take that particular person and treat his or her needs."

"And off they went into the night," I said.

"Most of them left Bellevue without medical records to accompany them. All of them left with uncharged cell phones because we'd been without power for so long. Neither they nor we had the ability to notify next of kin. And when they walked—or were wheeled—out the door, none of them had the slightest idea where they were going. Nor did we."

"So you lost patients, literally."

"Seven of them, Ms. Cooper," Hoexter said, dropping his head into his hands, elbows on his desk.

"All psych?"

"Yes. All civil commitments. The NYPD got all the criminally insane prisoners out. But Wicks was among the last patients evacuated. He had no urgent medical needs, like the others in his unit," Hoexter said, checking the notes on the computer. "He's quite intelligent and really hated being confined. Somehow, in all the confusion of that dreadful night, Eddie Wicks simply put on a rain jacket, followed the others out of the building, and walked away from his keepers."

Hoexter tapped a button on his keyboard and printed out a photograph of Eddie Wicks. He passed it across the table for both of us to see. I looked at it, then handed the paper to Mike.

I didn't know the significance of Wicks's disappearance. Clearly, it shouldn't have presented the threat to society that the escape of Raymond Tanner did. Wicks was a danger to himself, and possibly to his mother. And maybe Mike's concern about the figure in the window of the Dakota was legitimate. Maybe Eddie Wicks had returned to his favorite hiding place.

"How about his mother?" Mike asked. "Why does she still think he's here in Bellevue?"

Hoexter scrolled down through the file. "I don't know what she thinks."

"She's next of kin. Why didn't she get notified?"

"She may be next of kin," the doctor said, "but Mr. Wicks is fifty-nine years old. He didn't want any relatives notified about anything. The head of his team says a lot of his anger is directed at his mother. Bernice Wicks, is that her name?"

"Yeah."

"We had no obligation to tell her anything."

"Suppose he's still on the warpath?" Mike asked. "Part of the reason he's in this snake pit is because he threatened to kill her."

Hoexter put his reading glasses on and returned to the patient file on the computer screen. "That problem wasn't even referenced any longer by mid-August. I doubt he's a menace to his mother. It was all about suicidal ideation. All about Wicks's desire to hurt himself."

"So where'd he go, Doc?"

Hoexter leaned back and put his hands behind his head. "I haven't a clue."

"Where was he likely to go, given his condition back in October?" Mike sounded exasperated.

"We try to treat the human mind, Detective. We have no ability to read it."

"You just told us you don't think he'll hurt his mother."

Hoexter brought his arms down and looked Mike in the eye. "Eddie Wicks was diagnosed with this bipolar disorder when he was fifteen years old. It's a highly treatable condition, and it appears that Wicks accepted that treatment for long periods of time. He was in some pretty damn fancy facilities, as I skim his history."

"How does it manifest itself?" I asked. "The bipolarity?"

"The mania occurs when the patient's elevated mood exists with three or more classic symptoms for most of the day, for a week at least."

"What symptoms?"

"Feelings of euphoria, becoming restless and hyperactive, confusion and poor judgment."

"Alcohol abuse?"

"Frequently. And I see Wicks has a history of that."

"Increased sexual drive?" I asked.

"In a much younger man, certainly. In Wicks, it doesn't appear to be a serious part of the history."

"And the depressive episodes?"

"Characterized by negative feelings—intense sadness and hopelessness, withdrawing from others, feeling angry and unable to think clearly."

"Does Wicks exhibit any psychosis?" I asked.

Hoexter went back to the computer screen. "Yes. He was frequently delusional. Persecutory delusions."

"I guess it won't help that the police will be looking for him," Mike said.

Hoexter scrolled up again. "Looks like he's had these delusions since his late teens."

I thought of the way Lavinia Dalton's household staff—and their loved ones—had been subjected to interrogation and media scrutiny after Baby Lucy's kidnapping. A bipolar kid who'd witnessed his father's death must have been particularly vulnerable to feelings of persecution. Perhaps he'd been haunted by them his entire life.

"And never been cured?" Mike asked.

"We can't cure this disorder, Mr. Chapman. We can manage it with medicines and therapeutic intervention. That's the best we can do."

"And now Eddie Wicks is off his meds."

"Yes. He was being treated with lithium and with valproate, to which he was responding pretty well. But unless he's sought treatment somewhere more to his liking, he's off his meds, and that's a very difficult place for him to be."

"So what's at risk here, Doc?" Mike said. "I want to talk to this guy. He may know something I need for a murder investigation. Now that he's been out of here for eight months, he may even be a witness to events in the case. I don't want to start a conflagration, but I'd like to find Eddie Wicks."

Hoexter took a minute to reflect. "It's clear that he's afraid of the police, Mr. Chapman. He might find your manner a bit—"

"Overbearing?" I said, with a frisky tone in my voice.

"Better that you say it than I, Ms. Cooper. Wicks will probably respond more openly to questioning by you than by the detective. I doubt he'd find you—well, quite as intimidating."

Mike stood up, ready to go. "Then he'd better hold tight to his balls, Doc, 'cause Coop can break them faster than eggs in a frying pan."

"I don't cook, Dr. Hoexter," I said with a grin, "but I do enjoy breaking—"

"Where's a guy like Wicks gonna go?" Mike asked.

"He complained to his physician that he could no longer afford the rent on his apartment, and he had no family he was interested in staying with. I'm afraid this would all have fed into his feelings of hopelessness, his withdrawal from others. Wicks might have experienced a few manic days—some euphoria, actually—when we managed to hand him the tools for his own escape from Bellevue."

"We've got to check with the city's Department of Homeless Services," I said to Mike. "They relocated thousands of people after the storm."

"It was a perfect opportunity for many to create new lives for themselves," Hoexter said. "Folks were washed out of their homes without a chance to bring identification with them. Eddie Wicks had the smarts and ability to sell himself as a storm victim and start life over. You're right to look at that option, or anyplace in which he had a comfort level."

"He'd go back to someplace familiar?" Mike asked.

"Especially when manic."

The ninth floor of the Dakota, his childhood sanctuary. The vast backyard of his youth, in Central Park.

"And if depression gets the better of him?" Mike said.

"The biggest risk there is what brought him here in the first place."

"Suicide."

"Twenty-five to fifty percent of patients with bipolar disorder attempt suicide at least once, Detective. Six to twenty percent of them succeed," Hoexter said. "Seeing as how he has a family member who killed himself and having tried to do so previously, I'm almost surprised Wicks hasn't made his way to the morgue yet."

"Sobering words," I said. "Are there warning signs? Things to look for?"

Hoexter's fingers were templed now. "Constant talk about taking his life, which is a big part of his record here. Deep feelings of shame and guilt, which he's expressed, apparently, through most of his life. He blames himself for his father's suicide—or at least, since he was at home, for not preventing it. He blames himself for his mother's menial labor, and that he couldn't rescue her from that life. That sort of thing."

"Understood."

"Risk-taking behavior. I'd say heading off into the dark and stormy night last fall, away from his team and his lifeline, with no destination—that's a major risk. And things like putting his affairs in order, such as they are. Like giving away any possessions he might have."

"I don't imagine there are many of those," Mike said.

"Belvedere Castle and the Obelisk," I whispered to myself, more as an aside than a statement. "The black angel."

"What about them?" Mike asked.

"Maybe Eddie Wicks is somewhere in Central Park, or he's the figure you saw in the ninth-floor window, the day the body came out of the Lake?"

"How did he get his hands on pieces of the Dalton silver collection?" Mike seemed as puzzled as I was.

"Don't answer my question with a question, Detective. Somebody stole those two pieces of silver," I said. "Who's to say it wasn't Eddie Wicks?"

THIRTY-TWO

"Nobody's where they're supposed to be," Mike said.

"What do you mean?"

"Tanner and Wicks walked away from the nuthouse, you're AWOL from the office, I'm being held by my short hairs, and Mercer's out of cell range."

"Maybe he's still in the attic of the Dakota," I said, getting back into Mike's car with two hot dogs from a stand on First Avenue.

"Guess so."

"I just texted him to phone me."

We were halfway through our tube steaks when he called back. "Where were you?"

"Time traveling back a century, up on the ninth floor. No reception there. Sorry."

"So Eddie Wicks can't help us," I said. "Don't tell his mother or Jillian Sorenson yet, but he took a hike during the hurricane last fall."

"He *what*?"

"I think we need to make sure that once the department issues an alert for him—if Scully thinks that's necessary—there's a bodyguard at the Dalton apartment, for his mother's sake."

"We're fresh running out of bodyguards," Mercer said.

"So I have this idea," I said. "If it's okay with Vickee, why don't I spend the weekend at your house?"

Mike threw his head back and started talking. "Nightmare on Elm Street. There they were, planning a nice romantic weekend together, and you throw yourself into the mix."

"Don't choke on the dog," I said to Mike. "They've got a toddler. No such thing as a romantic weekend."

"We'll be fine with that," Mercer said.

"Frees up the two rookies who were sitting on me to hold Bernice Wicks's hand if we flush Eddie out of hiding. Meanwhile, I'm safe and sound with you two."

"How can you just invite yourself to their home?" Mike asked.

"Because the department thinks I have to be protected against Raymond Tanner, and because I have no plans for the weekend, Mr. Chapman," I said, covering the phone with my hand. "Care to change that?"

"Not in the stars right now, Coop," Mike said, chewing on the hot dog. "I'm a eunuch for as long as Manny Chirico wants me to be. Ask Mercer if Crime Scene got anything out of the room."

Mercer heard Mike ask me the question and responded. "The coffee cups are going to the lab for possible DNA in the saliva. They've done imaging of the footprints, which appear to be an adult male—not a sneaker but some kind of rubber-soled shoe. Size twelve. Newspaper fragments from late May, early June. Snack food wrappers."

"Generic debris," I said.

"Except for one little slip of paper," Mercer said.

"Oh?"

"Stuck in the fold of one of the newspapers was a ticket—like a large manila tag you'd use to label something—from a storage warehouse on Second Avenue: Day & Meyer, Murray & Young," Mercer said. "Ever hear of it?"

"Of course. It's on 61st Street, just north of the Queensboro

Bridge." My friend Joan Stafford's grandmother, one of the wealthiest heiresses in the city, used to roll up her most valuable Oriental carpets and take down her collection of Old Masters every summer, before moving up to Newport, to be stored at Day & Meyer. The carpets were shelved in cedar to repel moths, and the paintings kept in climate-controlled vaults. "It's where the richest New Yorkers have stored their most precious possessions for a hundred years."

"Would you guess Lavinia Dalton?"

"It wouldn't surprise me."

"The tag has no name, but it does have a number. Surely they can track that."

"Have you asked Jillian Sorenson about it?" I said.

"No need to tip my hand to her," Mercer said. "I just don't trust her. But I'm going to take a run over to the storage place myself."

"We're a straight shot up First Avenue. Meet you there in ten minutes."

"Meeting where?" Mike asked when I clicked off the call.

"61st and Second. That monolith of a building that straddles the block on the east side of the street."

Millions of New Yorkers passed the Day & Meyer neo-Gothic tower every day, most never knowing the treasures that were housed behind its mostly windowless façade were as valuable as the contents of the Metropolitan Museum of Art.

"Have you been there?"

"Never inside. But they used to pick up all of Joannie's grandmother's most precious belongings and—"

"Pick them up? What do you mean?"

"I remember being at Grandma Stafford's home—that incredible duplex on the river—when the men from Day & Meyer came to collect her living room one time."

Mike pulled out into the uptown flow of traffic. "What in her living room?"

"I told you. The living room. Every piece of furniture she'd bought in Europe's finest antique markets over the years, the baby

grand piano, the rug all those things were sitting on, the Delft porcelain that lined the walls, the family portraits as well as the Mary
Cassatt and the minor Van Gogh. And on and on. When the men
were done, the room was absolutely bare."

"And they moved that stuff how?"

"Ah! What they're famous for at Day & Meyer is the Portovault
system."

"Panoscan I know. What's a Portovault?"

"Think of each Portovault unit as a steel safe—about eleven
feet long and as tall as the ceilings at the Dakota, and weighing
about a ton."

"Like a shipping container?"

"Pretty much. Except that these are on wheels, and they're im-
penetrable. They're loaded onto an armored truck—armored,
okay?—and taken to the client's home, where the men pack them up,
lock them—so that the owner can watch—and return them to the
building on 61st Street."

"Where they're unloaded again?"

"Or not," I said. "The building has an interior rail system—
that's why the units are on wheels—so each one goes from the loading dock to a freight elevator and right into an assigned space, like
the most gigantic safe imaginable."

"Locked and loaded. And then the whole room just sits as it is,
waiting for its owner to send for it someday."

"When the season at Newport ended, Granny Stafford used to
call for her vault, and everything was dusted off and put back into
place."

We reached 61st Street before Mercer did. My cell mailbox was
full, and I was happy to ignore everything incoming, most of which
had to be from an angry Battaglia. I dialed Nan Toth's office number and was pleased that she was at her desk and picked up.

"Glad you're still there," I said. It was almost four in the afternoon.

"Yeah, but where are *you*?"

"Field trip. Don't ask."

"I am asking. Laura's tearing her hair out with worry."

"I'll explain everything later. Will you be there a while?"

"Yes, unfortunately. I have a witness on my d.v. case who can't come in until after work at five."

"Great. Can you hammer out some creative subpoenas for me while you wait?"

"How creative?"

"I'm meeting Mercer in a few minutes," I said, leaving Mike out of the mix in the event Battaglia or McKinney pressured my good friend Nan on my whereabouts.

"A break in the case?"

"To be honest with you, I don't know what it is. We may be chasing rainbows—or shadowy figures in windows and shoe prints in dusty rooms—but that's all we've got to do at this point."

"Okay. What do you need?"

"Mercer's got a receipt for something that's in storage. You know Day & Meyer?"

"The Fort Knox of storage facilities. I've heard of it."

"We're about to go in to try to access a particular container."

"Because?"

"Some guy who had the receipt may have been watching the police remove the dead girl's body from the Lake in the Park. We have a picture of him checking out the crime scene at seven A.M. last Friday morning, the time the body was bagged and the guys were scouring for clues."

"Go on."

"And there were several items of value—stolen items which are part of a larger collection—that may be connected to the girl's death. We're betting this storage container holds the key to connecting the dots to the killer."

"So you want me to draft a search warrant for the container?" Nan asked.

"That will take way too long."

"And no judge in his right mind would sign it."

"That, too," I said. "All I'm asking you for is a grand jury subpoena. No judge's signature required. There's an open investigation. It's all legal."

"And that subpoena would be—?"

"A 'must appear'—to the manager of Day & Meyer, to show up on Monday, before the grand jury, with the contents of the container. As soon as Mercer gets here, I'll give you the number on his receipt."

"On the theory that it will be way too much trouble for the manager to get inside the storage vault, and he couldn't possibly bring the contents—whatever they are—with him to the courthouse, so he'll just roll over and let Mercer have a look."

"Something like that."

Nan paused for several seconds. "Alex, how far out on a limb are you going to go?"

"Probably not much further. Battaglia has a chain saw, and I can hear him buzzing while he tries to cut me off. I get it if you can't come along."

Nan sighed. "Just a subpoena."

"Thanks. I'll call you once we're inside."

Mike was out of the car, directing Mercer to a parking spot across the street from ours. As he made his way to us, he showed us the large manila ticket, bearing the name Day & Meyer, which was in a small plastic bag.

"Let's get inside before they close," Mike said.

The building was about fifteen stories high. The walls were solid to the rooftop, except for a double row of windows that formed a strip down the middle. The Portovaults were probably parked on both sides of that. Many prisons looked less forbidding than this private fortress.

Once inside, a security guard directed us to the manager's office. When the three of us entered, he raised his eyes from his desk to ask how he could help us.

"NYPD," Mercer said, showing his blue-and-gold shield and introducing each of us.

The man was unperturbed. He pushed his reading glasses to the top of his bald head and listened to our request. The plastic sign on his desk said WILL JARVIS.

"I'm trying to get some information about Lavinia Dalton's account," Mercer said.

"Then you should speak with Ms. Dalton. We're not in the business of giving information."

"It's about a homicide investigation," Mike said. "You might be aware that Ms. Dalton isn't able to help us."

"You should talk to Ms. Sorenson, then," Jarvis said.

"We've done that."

"She's given permission for me to answer your questions?"

"No need to ask her permission. She's a witness in our investigation. She doesn't get to call the shots."

It was obvious the man was quite familiar with the Dalton account, seeing as how he had Jillian Sorenson's name at the tip of his tongue.

"She's a witness to murder?"

Mike leaned both arms on the manager's desk. "We're not in the business of giving information, either."

Will Jarvis reached for the telephone on his desk, opened his old-fashioned Rolodex, and started to dial a number. I assumed it was Lavinia Dalton's home.

Mike put his finger on the button to stop the call from going through. Then he turned to me. "Ms. Cooper, you got that subpoena you were talking about?"

"If Mr. Jarvis will kindly give me his fax number, I can have it sent through in a matter of minutes."

Jarvis wasn't happy to hear the word "subpoena."

"A search warrant," I said, "will take five or six hours longer."

"We close at six."

"The warrant won't get done until night court," I said. "We're used to waiting it out."

"And the subpoena?" Jarvis asked after slowly reeling off the fax number as I wrote it on a Post-it from my tote.

"Much easier," I said, stepping back near the doorway to call Nan and tell her what to ask for and where to fax it.

"What's the information you want?"

"Basic stuff," Mike said. "I'm not looking to break chops. It's not about you, Will."

"Like what?"

"Like how many storage units does Ms. Dalton maintain here?"

Jarvis's computer was on a table behind him. He swiveled his chair and logged on, searching the database for the accounts while I whispered to Nan.

"The accounts are held by the Dalton trust, actually," Jarvis said. "And there are eight vaults."

Even if all the Daltons going back to Lavinia's grandfather had been collectors, that was still a massive amount of possessions to hang on to.

"How many does the building hold?" Mike asked.

"Five hundred vaults," Jarvis said. "About fifty per floor, and then we have special areas climate controlled on other floors for things like paintings. The eight Dalton units are together on the twelfth floor. Archer Dalton was among Day & Meyer's first customers in 1928. We take their family business very seriously, if you get my drift."

"I'm drifting with you," Mike said.

I stepped closer. "That fax should be coming through momentarily."

Mike and Mercer continued to ask questions about the building—obviously impressed by the level of security offered to customers—warming Jarvis up enough that he offered to tour them through to show them how the rail system worked.

Three minutes later, his fax machine lit up and set its gears in motion, and a copy of the subpoena rolled out of the printer.

Will Jarvis picked it up, read it, and lost every trace of good humor Mike and Mercer had just lured out of him.

"You've set me an impossible task. There's simply no way I can produce all the Dalton records, all the receipts of entry for the Dalton vaults—and it's preposterous to suggest that I can take out the contents of a locked vault that belongs to a customer."

"Stay calm, Mr. Jarvis," Mike said. "By all means don't get all herky-jerky here."

"This document says I have to appear before the grand jury on Monday. That's not an option, Ms. Cooper."

"Options," Mike said. "I like options. Prosecutors can be so damned unreasonable. You want to discuss the options with us, Coop?"

"I certainly didn't mean to impose a hardship on you, Mr. Jarvis. Let's take this one step at a time."

Jarvis was fuming. He eyes darted back and forth between us. He reached for the receiver again, and again Mike tamped down the button. "Let's leave Ms. Sorenson out of this."

"I'm calling our lawyer, Mr. Chapman. He'll have something to say about this."

"That's fine. Go right ahead."

The number rang five times before going to voice mail. Jarvis slammed the phone down without leaving a message.

"What about the record keeping you do here for each account?" I asked. "Perhaps if you explain it to me, we can put that issue to rest."

Will Jarvis was on high alert and reluctant to trust me. He thought his answer through before speaking. "We've been computerized for twenty-five years, Ms. Cooper. Before that, everything was done by hand."

"So you can call up the Dalton account right on your computer?"

"If I chose to do so, yes. It would give me a quarter of a century of information."

"So a family or individual with eight vaults, would the contents of those vaults be listed?"

"Never. Do you tell the bank what's in your safety-deposit box?"

"Is there a date when each vault was rented?"

"Yes. Yes, of course."

"And a record of every time the Portovault leaves this building to go to an account and make a pickup?"

"Or a delivery," Jarvis said. "Yes."

"And a notation when an account holder comes to this building to get access to his or her vaults?"

"Just like a bank, Ms. Cooper. A record is made, signed by the holder or his representative, and countersigned by one of our agents, too."

"And what if something is added into a vault during one of those visits?"

Will Jarvis took a few seconds to answer. "That wouldn't be information we'd know. That's our client's right."

"How about if something is removed?"

He scratched his head. "Removed from his or her own vault? You don't seem to get my point, Ms. Cooper."

"So you don't issue receipts for that kind of thing?"

"We're very discreet, you understand. The customers entrust their objects to us—everything from moose-head mountings to Queen Anne furniture to solid-gold Krugerrands. If they want to pay a visit, we ask them to sign in—we have a signature card with assorted permissions for family members or trustees—and we provide an armed guard to secure their visits, their transactions," Jarvis said. "We don't issue receipts, Ms. Cooper. This isn't a pawn-shop."

Mercer removed the plastic bag from his jacket pocket and put it on the desk, under Will Jarvis's nose. "Now, what do you call this little tag?"

The middle-aged manager's face reddened as he leaned forward to look at it.

"Day & Meyer, right?" Mercer asked. "Sure looks like a receipt to me."

"This—this would be a different sort of circumstance," Jarvis said.

"Exactly what?"

"It would mean that someone authorized on the account paid a visit—a visit to one of the vaults." Jarvis paused, moistening his lips as he struggled for an explanation. "Someone authorized, I remind you. He or she removed something from the Portovault—I couldn't possibly tell you what that was—and stored it with us for a period of time in a safe. A small safe. A service we offer our clients for smaller objects and short durations of a hold. It's occasionally more convenient for people to put items here—securely—without going through the trouble again of opening an entire vault. That's why we offer the alternative of smaller safes."

"And this receipt?" Mercer asked.

"That would have been used to retrieve the object from a safe. There should be a stamp on the back of the tag," he said, reaching for the plastic bag.

But Mercer got there first. "There is a stamp on the back. And a date," he said. "The date is May 10th."

"So the only thing missing is for you to tell us who signed for this receipt," Mike said. "Who had access to one of Lavinia Dalton's vaults in the weeks or months prior to May? And is that the same person to whom this receipt was issued?"

Will Jarvis didn't budge.

"We want a name, Mr. Jarvis. We want to leave here with a name."

"If I give you this information, I don't have to appear before a grand jury?"

"That sounds fair," I said.

"And you won't tell Jillian Sorenson about this?"

"We have no reason to." Although I was interested in what his relationship was with Sorenson and why he seemed so fearful of her reaction to our visit.

"Then would you please read me the account number on that receipt, Mr. Wallace? It's the first set of figures."

Will Jarvis turned his back to us to face his computer. He entered the numbers, and results appeared on the screen. He printed out several pages of paper.

"In the spring of last year—during the month of April—the trust commissioned two Portovaults to go to the Dakota. Four guards escorted the trucks, and they were returned at the end of the same day. They were added to Lavinia Dalton's account as vaults number seven and eight."

That might have corresponded to the storage of the Dalton silver collections—one vault for Archer Dalton's train set and the second for Lavinia's Central Park.

"At some point in May," Jarvis said, "Jillian Sorenson signed in to our facility. She spent the better part of an hour on the twelfth floor. The two newest containers were opened for her. There isn't any more information than that, as I would expect."

Jarvis studied the paper from which he was reading to us—and signature cards that appeared to have been scanned into the system.

"Then in June, one year ago," he continued, "a visitor came to the building and spent an hour or so here, also signed in to the newest vaults. Both were opened for her, but one was closed immediately. She spent time in the other one."

"She?" I asked.

"Here's the signature card, Ms. Cooper." Jarvis was nonplussed now. "I don't know the woman personally, but she must be the one on the list of proper signatories, you can see that for yourself."

He slid the paper across from me. The name on the line for the June 8th visit of the year before was Wicks, with simply the capital letter B after it. The authorized list of signatures, which Jarvis also showed to me, had Bernice's full name printed out and signed.

The person who'd written her name on June 8th had a much firmer hand than Bernice.

"Bernice Wicks," I said, "is one of Lavinia Dalton's housekeepers."

"Then that makes sense," Jarvis said.

"But the signatures don't appear to match, Mr. Jarvis. And no one seemed to require Mrs. Wicks's full name on this June 8th record." I passed the record to Mike and Mercer.

"It must have been a busy day. Mistakes happen. Let's see what the signature is when the items on that receipt were picked up. That will be the numbers in red, Mr. Wallace."

The next paper printed out.

"So, the receipt shows," Jarvis said, "that the items were claimed on November 5th."

"One week after Hurricane Sandy," I said. "And who signed for them?"

He looked up from the paper. "B. Wicks once again."

Of course Eddie Wicks would have known that his mother was a trusted signatory of the Dalton properties. He had probably seen the dramatic arrival and departure of the Portovaults many times while staying at the Dakota since his youth.

"Mr. Jarvis," I said, with renewed urgency, "how about the video surveillance you have inside this place? There must be cameras everywhere. There would have to be."

"That's not something we advertise, Ms. Cooper."

"I understand, but it would be stupid to think you didn't need them in this day and age."

Jarvis didn't know whether to give it up or not. "We have other measures of security that are quite sufficient. Our clients prefer privacy—and a great measure of discretion. There are no video cameras to record their comings and goings."

Mike was practically on top of him. "Do you take photos of people who come through your front door?"

"No. That would be ridiculous. We get deliveries and service people and inquiries that have nothing to do with—"

"Go back, please, to that November 5th sign-in sheet, will you?" I said. "I'd like you to print out a copy of the signature."

Will Jarvis didn't lift a finger.

I picked up the plastic bag and waved it in his face.

"The number again, please?" he said.

I read the four digits that were handwritten on the bottom of the tag. "8521."

"What? That can't be right," Jarvis said. "Our identification numbers are longer sequences than that."

"Not those handwritten numbers on the tag," Mercer said to me. "Give him the figures in red print."

I found them and read them aloud while Jarvis entered them in his computer. The printer groaned again and rolled out a copy of the signature of a B. Wicks.

"Maybe Eddie Wicks came here right after the storm of the century," Mike said, "to pick up something he must have wanted pretty badly."

"He's one possibility," I said. "That's for sure. But why is Jillian Sorenson so arch about all this? She certainly didn't want us up on the ninth floor and in the room where this receipt was found. If she didn't want to be caught with her hand in the till, what better than to sign Bernice's name?"

I looked to see whether Will Jarvis reacted to my speculation about Sorenson, but he was stone-faced.

"You both seem to be ignoring the fact that Vergil Humphrey has known Eddie Wicks—and Bernice—for a very long time," Mercer said. "And he claims to have been the keeper of the black angel."

"What about it?" I asked.

"Well, the angel was found in the Park with both of the silver pieces. I'm just sayin'—because a man is toothless doesn't mean he can't write."

THIRTY-THREE

Fifteen minutes later we were on the twelfth floor of the massive storage facility.

Will Jarvis had acknowledged the giant security breach and admitted that whoever signed B. Wicks's name had forged it. He agreed to let us eyeball the contents of Dalton Portovaults number seven and eight, in light of the subpoena, and because whoever visited a year earlier had been unauthorized to do so.

"You can physically get into the vaults without the owner, can't you?" Mike asked.

"Certainly. We have to be able to do that in case of a fire or an emergency like that. We've had two or three abandonments as well, when owners died without heirs."

Four workmen had followed us up in the service elevator, and Jarvis pointed them to the units we wanted to view.

One of the men stationed himself near the control switch. When Jarvis gave him the signal to start, the system generated a noise that was frightening in its volume and intensity.

The huge steel vault shook awake like a hibernating bear, whatever motored it growling at us in the dark space. Suddenly, Portovault number seven lurched forward on its rails, coming toward us in the middle of the floor, then chugging as the man at the controls was able to regulate its speed and bring it to a stop.

A pair of wheeled jacks, operated by two of the men, helped them spin the container around to reposition it. Will Jarvis explained that only one end of the giant vault had a door that opened. We stood to the side as he used the master keys—a duplicate of Lavinia Dalton's set—to unlock the fist-sized bolt, while the foreman disengaged the Day & Meyer backup lock.

It took two of the men to slide open the heavy metal door, chaining it in place on the inner wall of the vault.

Jarvis handed each of us a battery-operated flashlight so that we could look inside the black hole that was the mouth of the vault.

"Watch your step," he said to Mike. The steel rollers on which the container had been moved were slippery. One of the workers walked over with a stepladder that had been leaning against the far wall of the large room.

Mike and Mercer climbed up onto the platform and stepped into the vault. They were on either side of the container, beaming their lights downward, and I could see the reflection of the many shiny objects inside.

"It's Archer Dalton's train set," Mike said. "An entire silver city of railroad miniatures."

I saw him squat and pick up one of the cars.

"The originals?" I asked.

"Gorham and Frost. The real deal."

"The Park?"

"No need to jump up here, Coop," Mike said. He replaced the train and walked farther into the dark void of the vault. His flashlight's beam and Mercer's crisscrossed each other as they examined the contents of the space. "There's nothing from the Park in here. The railroad tracks take up the entire thing. Grand Central Terminal, the old Penn Station, and every kind of train you can imagine."

"All in silver?"

"Like Jillian Sorenson said, it must be worth a king's ransom."

They took their time examining the entire vault before stepping onto the platform and down the ladder.

"Satisfied, Detective?" Will Jarvis asked.

"For now," Mike said. "Let's see number eight."

It was a difficult job for the men, once they had resecured the locks on the Portovault, to wheel the jacks back into place, push the weighty container into alignment with the rollers, and position it to be docked back into its berth.

There was a slight incline to the floor—perhaps from decades of wear by the loads it bore—and when the motor roared on again, two of the men got behind the vault and steadied it while they shoved to get it moving. Mike and Mercer added their strength to the crew's manpower, each throwing a shoulder against the giant-sized container.

"Okay, guys," Jarvis said. "Let's bring out number eight."

The foreman never left the controls to help the other men on his team. He was out of sight, near the elevator, and responding to orders from Jarvis.

Mike and Mercer followed two of the workers across the set of rails from the vault they'd just examined and got into place on either side of the transfer platform in front of which number eight would come to a stop.

The rollers beneath number seven stopped humming and vibrating as it was shut down, while its neighbor started to make noise.

The behemoth of a container nosed out of the darkness and headed our way.

Another sound, behind me, made me turn my head. The elevator door was opening, and a shrill voice was calling out for Will Jarvis.

"Where are you, Will? What's going on?"

It took me a couple of seconds to place the voice, but I recognized it as Jillian Sorenson. Jarvis had managed to call her after all, to alert her to the fact that he was taking Mike and Mercer up to the vaults.

The metal rollers were grinding as the number eight container came barreling down toward us.

Mike had heard the voice, too. "Yo, Ms. Sorenson," he called out, trying to cross the rail track. "This is police business. You'll have to wait down—"

I watched in horror as his foot caught between two of the rollers and he fell to his knees.

"Stop it!" I screamed. "Stop the damn thing."

More than a ton of steel—a Portovault on a fast track—was aiming straight for Mike, ready to crush him against the concrete-reinforced pillar that separated both sides of the vast storage space.

I charged toward Mike as he tried to free his right foot from the roller, praying that the foreman would brake the system, although he couldn't see what was wrong.

Jarvis had also yelled to cut the power, but the vault kept coming.

Mercer's back had been to Mike when he fell—looking to see who had gotten off the elevator—but he was still closest to our fallen friend.

The big man bent over and lifted Mike beneath his shoulders, dragging him to safety a moment before the speeding Portovault mashed Mike's loafer into the spinning rollers and came to a screeching halt.

THIRTY-FOUR

"Accidents happen, Coop," Mike said.

He rarely showed emotion, even when rattled. We were both sitting on the edge of the loading platform, and I was clearly more shaken up than Mike.

"We can do this another time," I said. "Is it your bad ankle?"

"I don't have a good one."

"He's fine, Alex. Last thing you want to do is baby this dude," Mercer said. "He needed a new pair of shoes anyway."

Mercer wouldn't let Will Jarvis have any time alone with Jillian Sorenson. He'd asked one of the workmen to take her down to Jarvis's office if she insisted on waiting.

"You do understand this was an accident, like you just said?" Jarvis asked.

"Ms. Sorenson's arrival? I don't believe that for one minute."

"I'm talking about the vault, Mr. Chapman."

"I got no problem with that. I slipped. Not the fault of your men."

"I can run to your place and get another pair of shoes," I said, looking at Mike's bare feet. No socks in summer was another of his telltale traits, and his apartment was only a block away from Day & Meyer.

"There are driving mocs in the trunk of my car," Mike said, flexing his right ankle and standing up to put weight on it. "Two Tylenol and a six-pack of Grey Goose and I'll be a new man."

"Ready to take a look?" Mercer asked.

"Let's go."

Two of the workmen brought the vault around, opened the door, and chained it back in place.

Mercer stepped up first to give Mike his hand, and I followed behind, each of us with our flashlights.

The sight was dazzling. The entire Greensward, the magnificent vision that was Manhattan's great public space, was laid out in its entirety—in the original silver version—upon a landscaped green suede base, with bright blue paint shimmering as we lighted it, in all the places in the Park that were filled with water.

"Can you imagine the value of this?" I asked. "All locked away where no one can see it. It shouldn't be this way."

"Maybe it won't be for long," Mercer said. "Maybe Lavinia made plans for these before she became ill."

"Do you mind if I—?" Will Jarvis wanted to step up with us.

"Stand back," Mike said. "Just keep away from the door."

Our voices echoed, but we had no interest in letting anyone else know what was going on.

We were standing at the south end of the faux Park, along the gray stone walk that represented the 59th Street border.

Mike squatted again and picked up the replica of the Simon Bolivar statue, which was closest to him. He turned it over and confirmed that the Gorham and Frost hallmark was engraved in the silver base. "The originals, I'd say."

Mercer turned left. "Coop and I will take the west side. Why don't you go east?"

We each used our flashlights to search every inch of the vault. Last year's visitor may have taken some items—which is what we assumed—but also may have moved others or dropped something along the way.

All three of us were working from memory, since we had no map of the Park. I was running my light back and forth across the surface of the background, checking against my recollection of landmarks that should have been represented.

The Maine Monument was in place at the southwest entrance, so I started north, parallel with Mike, who was on the far side of the vault.

Each of us called out significant markers as we could see them. I reeled off the names of gates and arches that were still in place, just as Mike did from the east-side perspective.

It was Mercer, with the advantage of a head more height than I had, who noticed the first missing piece. "The Carousel's gone."

"One of Lavinia's favorite places," I said.

"Every kid's favorite," Mike said. "Probably Baby Lucy's, too."

"Well," Mercer said, "it's missing."

"The Indian Hunter's here. So are Shakespeare and Balto."

"The Falconer's in place," I said, looking north from the 70th Street parallel. "Daniel Webster, too."

Mike spotted the 72nd Street roadway first. "The angel is gone."

"Why am I not surprised?"

"But just the angel," he said, stooping down to examine the base of the fountain. "The top part screwed off. Whoever took these things just wanted the angel."

And seconds later, when Mike stood by the 72nd Street Cross Drive, he pointed to the gaping holes where both Belvedere Castle and the tall Obelisk used to sit.

Farther along, at 106th Street, I noticed that the so-called Strangers' Gate to the Park had been removed.

The north gate house—a significant site in Eddie Wicks's tormented life—was also gone. And as Mercer and I circled to the far end of the Park, it was clear that several other statues, the Warriors' Gate at the 110th Street entrance, and the remote Blockhouse had also been stolen.

"What do you think?" Mike asked. "Ten pieces missing? A dozen?"

"Easily," I said.

"Anything left behind?"

"Pretty careful," Mercer said. "I didn't see a dropping."

"Then let's check out the storage locker that matches the receipt," Mike said.

Mercer eased himself out of the vault, extending his hand first to Mike and then to me as he helped us down. Then he took the receipt from his pocket and dangled it in front of Jarvis.

"We'd like to see this locker now."

Mike put his foot in his surviving loafer and limped along.

"But someone was here to empty it," Jarvis said.

"I've got a feeling," Mercer said, "that whoever it was got this receipt back because the unit wasn't completely cleaned out. The person was stamped in for one visit but left here still holding the ticket, so we'd like to see what's in there."

Jarvis dismissed the workmen and took us down in the elevator to the fourth floor. He had given up wrangling with us and submitted meekly to our request. The foreman, who had all the master keys, accompanied us down.

Again, Mercer showed him the tag with the number on it, and the now-docile man led us to a locker that was about two feet square, resting on the floor with two rows of similar containers above it. Mike asked him to unlock it and step away, along with Jarvis.

Mercer shined his light in, and it immediately caught the glare of a shiny object inside.

"Got a pair of gloves for me, Mike?"

Mike pulled them from his rear pants pocket, and Mercer put them on. He reached into the space and came out with a pair of silver gates.

I read the words engraved on the silver slab. "Strangers' Gate. How appropriate a name for this investigation."

"What's with these?" Mike asked. "They look like stones, not gates."

"That's the whole idea. Olmsted and V—"

"Vaux. Like hawks. You only have to tell me things once, Coop."

"They didn't want iron railings around the Park—so as not to break up the pastoral look of it, and also not to make it appear to shut out the poor—so they just created these stone sculptures and gave each one a name, like a gate, so people could know where to meet one another."

"So our guy leaves behind Strangers' Gate, okay. You know where it is?"

"106 on the west side."

"Wonder if there's some significance to that," Mike said. "Anything else, Mercer?"

Mercer reached his arm in again. "Yup."

When he brought it out and opened his hand to us, there were two very small silver figures—miniature marionettes like the ones in the Swedish cottage, strings and all.

"Damn. I wonder if that was Eddie's idea," Mike said, "or Verge's."

"You've got to get this to the lab," I said. "Let them try this FST DNA testing on it."

"What'll that do?"

"I thought I only had to tell you things once, Mike. It can pick up mixtures of genetic material, so if two people touched these miniatures, or even three, we can prove who they are."

"But neither Wicks nor Humphrey is in the data bank," he said. "We get a DNA mixture, and who do we match it to?"

"If we get our hands on them again—and I assume that day will come—it's a way of putting this all together."

Mercer had bagged the tiny puppets and passed them along to me.

"I'm with you, Coop, if you'll just—"

I heard the shrill voice before the light footsteps of Jillian

Sorenson, approaching through the dimly lit hallway. "Put those things down right now, Ms. Cooper."

By shutting Will Jarvis out of our investigation, we apparently had sent him scurrying back down to his office. Sorenson must have gotten him to tell her where we were. She was steaming mad as she demanded we return the silver objects to her.

"You're a little bit late for that, Ms. Sorenson," Mike said. "They're evidence now."

"You'll be sorry you did this, Detective. Harm seems to come to everyone who touches Lavinia Dalton's prized possessions. Deadly harm."

THIRTY-FIVE

It was after eight P.M. on Friday evening—past *Jeopardy!*—and the three of us had lost all sense of time when we pulled into Mercer's driveway in Douglaston, a handsome neighborhood of private homes in Queens.

Vickee was at the front door, and the moment she opened it four-year-old Logan Wallace ran down the steps in his pajamas—which were printed with brightly colored dinosaurs of all varieties—flying into Mike's arms and begging for bedtime stories. I got the second-best greeting and held the child's hand as we walked inside the house.

I stopped short at the sight of Manny Chirico sitting on the living room sofa. Mike was behind me and did the same.

"It's okay, Mike," the sergeant said, getting to his feet and walking toward him. "It's only good news I've got. Jessica Pell stepped down from the bench tonight."

Mike wrapped his arms around Chirico, grabbed his face between his hands, and planted a kiss on his forehead. "Why the hell didn't you call me?"

"Peterson told me you were in the middle of something serious," Chirico said. "Besides, I wanted to deliver the news in person.

I heard about the plan for Alex to stay here and texted Mercer to drag you along."

"Bar's open," Mercer said, slapping Mike on the back.

"How'd you do it, Manny?"

"Believe me, Mike, I don't really know. It didn't hurt for Alex to go to bat with Battaglia."

Mike turned to me, but I held up my hands in protest. "Keep me out of this one."

"Did you—?"

"Nothing," I said. "I didn't do anything."

Vickee was trying to get Logan upstairs, but he was too excited by all the backslapping and high spirits to leave the company. "You hold on to your godson, Alex. I'll make the drinks."

I picked him up to give him a hug.

"Why are you crying, Lexi?" he asked.

"I'm not crying. I'm just—um—I'm just so happy to see you. It's been a month or two."

"But there are tears in your eyes."

"Then wipe them away, sweetie. You, Master Logan, have the power to make me smile anytime you want to."

I walked toward the screened-in porch that faced the backyard, staying in earshot of everyone but staring off into the night. The rooms were only separated by a tall archway. The guys were talking about how crazy Jessica Pell was and what balls Battaglia showed in getting the mayor to twist her arm to step down. I rocked Logan back and forth in my arms.

I didn't think tonight would put an end to the problems Mike's dalliance with the madwoman had caused.

Mike was toasting Chirico and Mercer for their friendship and support, and I sat down on the porch sofa with Logan, who was still asking for a story, even willing to accept one from me.

"Here's your drink," Vickee said. "I'm going to order some pizza. You cool with that?"

"Absolutely."

Logan stood up on the sofa next to me and started tugging at Vickee's hand. "Lexi was crying, Mom. She was crying, but I made her stop."

"That's my boy," she said, patting both of us on our heads. "Ten more minutes and you are history, young man. Way past your bedtime."

The child pouted a bit and then curled up next to me, resting his head on my thigh as I started to make up a story for him.

"Where's Coop?"

"Out on the porch," Mercer said.

Mike came to find me and clink glasses. He started to say something to me, but I put my fingers to my lips. Logan looked up, and any thought I had that he might have calmed himself down was gone in a flash. He jumped up and reached out for Mike to pick him up.

"I'll be back for that," he said, pointing to the vodka martini that Vickee had mixed.

He walked off with Logan, headed for the staircase to the boy's bedroom, undoubtedly telling another of the tales about how he and Mercer tackled a Tyrannosaurus rex in Central Park when they were rookie cops.

I carried my Scotch into the kitchen and helped Vickee set the table for the five of us. Mercer took the opportunity to come in and embrace me, asking if it was okay if he told Mike about my confrontation with Pell.

"No way," I said. "At least not yet. Let's let him think this was resolved on its merits."

"Whatever you say, Alex. You've earned it."

The pizzas arrived, and the five of us were having a cozy celebration. At the heart of the matter, though, I was still peeved that Mike had left himself open to such a dangerous liaison.

At ten, while we were still gabbing and eating, Mercer got up to switch on the local news.

"It's ten P.M.," Manny said, laughing as he mimicked the old public service message about knowing where your children are. "Do you have any idea where your favorite stalker is?"

"Looking for work, I hope," Mike said as he uncorked another bottle of wine.

The anchor led with a car crash in Times Square that took the life of one driver, followed by the drowning of a teenager in a public pool on Staten Island.

"There's just no good news anymore," Chirico said.

"I got all the good news I could want for one night," Mike said. "I'm going home soon, and I expect to have pleasant dreams for a change."

"Home?" I asked.

"Yeah."

This wasn't the right time or right place to take our relationship to the next step, I knew, but it was such an odd thing to be celebrating the end of Mike's hookup with Jessica Pell with him going home alone after our night together on the Arsenal rooftop.

"It's the summer solstice, you know?" I said. "Longest night of the year."

Mike leaned over to refill my wineglass and whispered in my ear. "Think of it this way, kid. I owe you two short ones."

The commercial break was followed by a story about a domestic stabbing, then another about a child abuse case in the Bronx. The body in Central Park was last week's headline and didn't even merit a mention.

A picture of Jessica Pell flashed on the screen. "In news that seemed to take City Hall by surprise this evening, rising judicial star Jessica Pell—a favorite of the mayor's staff—tendered her resignation from the bench. Reporters followed her to her home, but as you see in this clip, the former judge began ranting at them—language we can't quite use in prime time—and sped off in her car just a couple of hours ago."

"Maybe some of those reporters got a hint of her potential for rage," Mike said, reaching for another slice.

"Sources tell New York One that Pell has been under a lot of pressure recently because of threats she received, connected to her work in the courts. When she complained about the denial of police protection, one of her friends at City Hall green-lighted her application for a gun permit two weeks ago."

The anchor spun away from his teleprompter, making an effort to inject a bit of humor into his commentary. "So a warning to all you reporters and paparazzi out there looking to get in the judge's face like we tried to do tonight, Jessica Pell is armed and extremely angry.

"Now over to you for the weather forecast," he said to the woman standing next to his desk.

"Lucky to be out of that one," Mercer said, clicking off the TV. "There's no taste like bad taste, Mike. I hope she's on to her next target."

I put my fingers against the scratches on the side of my face. I was thankful not to be alone tonight.

THIRTY-SIX

I was down in the kitchen at seven A.M., noshing on toast and Froot Loops with Mercer. The bright sunlight streamed through the window. The almost-suburban sound of birds chirping and kids already honking bicycle horns on the street in front of the house was so relaxing, so unlike my high-rise lifestyle.

"Did you sleep okay?" he asked.

"Best night in weeks. Any news?"

"I'm meeting Mike in the Park this morning."

"May I?"

"Don't see why not. No ballet class?"

"I'll make up for it by hiking with you. What's he after?"

"Peterson got orders to pull his men out of the Park. Uniform will do the same, for the most part. Mike wants to explore the caves, although I really don't see any mention of them on my map."

"Mia Schneider of the Conservancy was going to get him some of the original Park plans," I said. "How come it's so quiet around here?"

"We just got Logan a bike with training wheels, and he's pumping away out on the sidewalk with his mama."

"So we can slip out? Stop by my place for some jeans and stuff?"

"Anytime you're ready."

We drove out of the quiet street and made quick time to Manhattan. Mercer waited for me in the driveway. I went upstairs and changed into jeans, a short-sleeved cotton shirt, and driving moccasins, and wrapped a cashmere crew neck around my waist in case the weather turned later in the day.

"Mike wants to meet us in the parking lot behind Lasker Pool," Mercer said. "That's near 107th Street, about midway between east and west. Thinks we ought to spend some time walking through the Ravine."

It took us another fifteen minutes to get there. Unlike the southern end of the Park, with tourists constantly pouring in from midtown Manhattan, or the Reservoir, with its steady traffic of runners, the North Woods was quiet on this warm Saturday morning.

Mike was waiting for us when we drove up and parked against the wall that backs the pool, which turns into a skating rink every winter. "Welcome to the Ravine," he said. "Ready to get down and dirty?"

"You bet."

"This area is like the Ramble," he said. "It's meant to look like a nature retreat in the Catskills, just doesn't have quite the same elevation."

"But it's got caves, I'm guessing."

"So the Conservancy folks tell me. All but one or two of the caves in the Park are man-made, like most everything else. Built in the 1860s, but once bad things started happening in them, they were covered up."

"What do you mean by 'bad things'?" I asked.

"You name it. They faxed me over some of the old renderings of Park plans," Mike said, "along with copies of newspaper clippings, some of them more than a hundred years old. When the landscapers started clearing brush for the Park, down on the southern tip, there was one rock formation that had been a hiding place for skeletal remains. Animals mostly, but some dead folk, too. But that's the only cave that was in place at the time Park construction started."

"Where are the others?"

"Scattered pretty much throughout, south to north. The problem is that nobody has a record of the locations now, because as things happened over the years, the caves and grottoes were covered over. They were thought to be too dangerous even a century ago.

"Then thirty years would go by," Mike said, "and some hiker would stumble across a rock that had been rolled away from an opening in the ground. The history of bad things was lost to a new generation, so someone in the Parks Department would arrange to reopen that particular formation or cave. Five years later, a stabbing or a violent sexual encounter would occur, and a new rock pile would be formed. There's no telling what's out here without turning over every rock, as they say."

Mike took his map out of his rear pants pocket. Rolled up in it were some of the design sketches of the land and copies of the old news stories. He read off the headlines as he handed them over to Mercer and me.

"Fifteen-year-old runaway lived in a cave, near 72nd Street on the west side. That's a press clipping from 1897, can you believe it?"

"People have always lived in caves, man," Mercer said. "No surprise there."

"In 1904, a young man shot himself to death on the steps leading to a cave, this one in the '80s, farther to the east side. And here's a police blotter entry about an artist who was sentenced to three months in the workhouse for assaulting another man on a bench inside a cave."

"A bench?" I said. "There are caves in here large enough to hold a bench?"

"That was 1929, Coop. I guess there were. The last piece is about a couple—a married couple—who lost their home in the Great Depression. The guy and his wife lived in one of the caves for a year. For an entire year. Living off berries and panhandling and drinking from the streams."

"Scary stuff," Mercer said.

"That's why the city ended up closing all the caves. Covering the openings over with boulders and redesigning every last one of them. By the 1940s, no one involved in the original landscaping was around to worry about the plan for a return to nature. All they cared about was safety for people using the Park."

"So if there are cave entrances left," I said, "we'll have to find them ourselves."

"That's what I got for you," Mike said. "A walk on the wild side."

"Wild?"

"The Ravine is considered to be forty acres that are the wild heart of the North Woods. More remote than the Ramble. The surrounding buildings outside the Park are completely hidden from view because the elevation here is depressed—unlike the Ramble—and then this stream bubbles all through it, with three waterfalls and several arches."

"Are there grottoes?" Mercer asked.

"Yeah. And you know what you said about where Tanner's rape victim was living in Prospect Park the other night? Well, in the Ravine, the fallen trees are treated the same way as in Brooklyn. So there are homeless people who make shelters out of the dead logs, just like the Brooklyn rape victim on Elephant Hill, and who camp out inside the log structures."

"And maybe Angel was one of them," I said. "This is the end of the Park where that homeless girl Mercer brought in to see us—"

"Jo," he said.

"Yes. Jo claimed she stayed up here somewhere until Verge led them away. Took them farther south to Muggers Hill."

"Now why the hell would he lead them away?" Mike asked.

"Jo said he didn't think it was safe enough for them."

"I get that. But what if he had something up here he didn't want her to see? In a makeshift log hideaway, or in one of the small caves. Anyway, the commissioner isn't interested in anyone else digging around anymore. Might as well give it a day."

We left the cars and started due south on the narrow path that led from the parking lot. In just a few yards, it joined with one coming in from the east, and they merged to lead us directly to the Huddlestone Arch.

"I hope this all wasn't just a plan to get me to Tanner's hunting ground," I said. "This is a magnificent structure, but it's the perfect crime scene, too."

Even as we stood twenty feet in front of its gaping mouth, the blackness of the opening was unwelcoming. It was a long tunnel, the walkway against one side of the stone wall and the streamlet running against the other. I thought of Flo entering this very spot a few nights ago, with Tanner waiting to pounce on her when she emerged on the far end.

"I wanted to see it the other night, when we were at the Conservancy," Mike said, "but you reined me in. I hear it's one of the great construction marvels in the city. You probably know who Huddlestone is, right? Some rich dude who wanted a rock pile named in his honor?"

"I have no idea."

Mercer pointed up at the massive boulders that created the semicircular foundation of the arch and the bridge it supported. "I got the info when I came here the morning after Flo was attacked. So the arch got its name," he said as we walked toward the entrance, "because the stones, as big as they are, are just huddled together. No mortar, no binding material of any kind."

"And I'm walking inside it? What holds them up?" I asked. "It doesn't seem possible."

"It's an architectural principle as old as the Romans. Keystone foundations, they're called. That huge rock directly overhead—it weighs a hundred tons—it's the keystone of the entire arch. All the other boulders press against it and against one another. Been doing that since 1866, even with all the automobile traffic that drives over it. It's ingenious."

I quickened my pace to get through the dramatic underpass. I paused at the spot where Flo was attacked, uneasy at the thought that this was a comfort zone for Raymond Tanner.

"Which way?" I asked. One trail continued south. The other crossed the stream and led deeper into the North Woods.

"Let's follow the water. There are three waterfalls in the next half mile. Flo was talking about a recess in one of them. About a place she used to sit in."

The growth around the path was dense and lush after all the spring rain.

"The Park lost almost one thousand mature trees to Hurricane Sandy," Mike said. "So there are lots of dead logs all over the woods. Scully left a small detail of uniformed guys here to look through them in the North Woods, on the theory that potential vics—like the Brooklyn girl—may be shacking up."

"Not to mention a Tanner or Verge or Eddie Wicks," Mercer said.

We walked up the muddy incline, encountering only a handful of people along the way. The first waterfall was the one to which Flo had been heading when Tanner struck her down. Mike balanced himself on the slippery rocks that led to it from the side of the stream. He ducked behind the falls, getting doused with water as he did, and then called out to us.

"It's sweet in here," Mike said. "Flo's right."

"How big?" I asked.

"Just a stone seat. Three, maybe four people could sit on it. I wouldn't call it a cave 'cause it doesn't go any deeper. But it's just as Flo described it to you."

Mike came out from beneath the overhang and shook himself off.

"You're all wet," I said.

"Hardly the first time. Let's keep going."

At some points the path hugged the edge of the stream, while at others it meandered off into thicker woods. This was so densely forested and so peaceful, a part of Manhattan that most New Yorkers didn't even know existed.

The second falls was constructed in an entirely different manner. The boulders used were longer and flatter. The distance in the drop from the running stream to the water below was much shorter than the first one, creating its own distinct sound—apparently part of the Olmsted and Vaux plan.

Again Mike made his way over the rocks as water gushed around him and disappeared.

"Can you see him?" I asked Mercer.

"Nope."

"Mike?"

"Be right out," he called, his voice echoing from a hollow space within. He was on his hands and knees when he emerged, and stood up when he got right behind the curtain of water. "A bear could hibernate in there."

Mercer extended a hand to help Mike back onto solid ground. "Anything inside?"

"Empty. Empty and cold and damp in there, but it's about four feet deep. I wonder whether it was built that way specifically to have an effect on the sound of the water dropping on the rocks. Wouldn't seem to have any other purpose."

We continued southwest, where the stream narrowed and curved around a stand of tall trees. I felt as though we could have been lost in these woods, were we not in the middle of Manhattan. The only noise I heard was the sound of branches crackling as we stepped on them and the amazing variety of birdcalls overhead.

"Here's another tunnel," Mike said. "Glen Span Arch."

It, too, was an imposing stone structure that shrouded the pathway in total darkness when I entered. I hurried through it, noting the small grottoes built into the walls on its side but anxious to escape the dank interior.

When I came out on the other end, there was an even larger cascade than the others. Water pounded down onto layered steps of rocks.

"Where's that coming from with such fury?" I asked.

Mike came up behind me. "It's the Pool."

"Not the Pond, not the Lake, not the Reservoir."

"Nope. It's the Pool."

I climbed up on the rocks that topped the waterfall and looked out over the body of water, surrounded by weeping willows on its grassy banks—another setting, another type of vista altogether.

"All artificial," Mike said. "New York City tap water gushing out of here, the Conservancy guy told me. Take a peek, Coop. The whole length of the stream we just walked is fed from that Pool . . ."

"Which is pumped-in water from upstate New York." I stepped down onto the top of the flat rocks that created the formation. Here, unlike below, there was a wide opening, and the waterfall flowed over it, so I could actually kneel on the inside without getting wet.

I handed my sweater to Mercer and got on all fours while he shined a flashlight over my head.

"How far back does it go?" he asked me.

"I've seen smaller studio apartments in the city," I said. "Can you give me more light?"

"You see anything?"

"There's some paper a few feet ahead. I'll keep going. And two frogs who are moving a lot faster than I can."

The rocks that bordered the gushing stream were more slippery to the touch than the ones outside the cave opening. They were coated with a layer of something slimy, soft, and green. I moved forward a bit more and reached for the papers, picking them up and shoving them in the rear pocket of my jeans.

"Any more light, Mercer?"

He must have ducked down behind me and aimed his beam right over my back.

"I've got a pipe, guys. No kidding, I've got a pipe."

I could hear Mike laughing. "Those dudes built the pipes in a hundred and fifty years ago, kid. That's what makes the waterfalls run all the time, even in a drought like we had this spring."

"Not that kind of pipe," I said. "Give me a glove."

Mercer crawled forward, and I reached back to his hand.

"What kind of pipe?" he asked.

I sat up and pulled on the vinyl glove, reached for the foot-long length of metal pipe.

Even in the darkness of the small cave, with only the shaft of light from Mercer's flashlight, I could see a dark-red stain—the color of dried blood—on the cold cylindrical object.

"The kind Raymond Tanner uses to attack his victims. That kind of pipe."

THIRTY-SEVEN

"Let's walk up to the West Drive," Mike said, referring to the vehicular roadway, closed to automobiles on weekends, that coursed through the Park and ran right across the Glen Span Arch. "I've got no cell reception down here."

"Who are you calling?"

"The ranger in charge. He can find someone in uniform to pick this up and voucher it. Let's get it to the lab and see if this stain is human blood. See if they can get any prints off it."

"I'm thinking Raymond Tanner."

"I know you are. And I'm thinking Angel, with her head bashed in. Good find, Coop."

The pipe looked absolutely lethal. The idea of swinging the sturdy piece of metal against a human head made me shudder.

We reached the top of the incline, and Mercer pulled on a pair of gloves while Mike gave our location to the park ranger. "Let me see those papers you picked up, Alex."

I handed him the wad that was in my pocket, and he squatted down to separate them and spread them out on the slats of a wooden bench.

"Food wrappers," Mercer said. "Empty chip bags and cellophane from cookie packages. And this scrap of lined paper."

I leaned in over him. It looked as though the ink had been soaked in water at some point and had run. "Can you make anything out?"

"It's pretty blurry," he said, passing it to me.

"Reads like part of a description of the Park," I said. "How the Ravine is— Maybe the word is 'fluid'? A fluid line. But the Ramble is a scrabbled— Scratch that. A *scrambled* maze. Some words just washed out completely, but I can make out 'remote' and 'no one will find me.' Something about a brother— No, no, it's 'not bother me,' I think."

"A journal."

"And Jo told us that Angel," I said, thinking of the dead girl whose real name we didn't know, "kept a journal with her that might unfold her life to us."

I flipped the torn piece of paper over, but there was nothing on the other side. The writing was an even script, where it hadn't bled onto the page, and appeared quite feminine.

Mike hung up, and I showed him the fragment. "See if you can get the cops who come for the pipe to take another look in that cave. We need to find the rest of this book, okay? It may be the key to what happened to your girl."

"Whatever you say, Coop. I think we're looking at our own manpower, though. The ranger just told me there's a commotion in the Sheep Meadow. I've got to hold on to the pipe till they clear it."

"What's that about?" Mercer asked.

Before Mike could finish saying that he didn't know, an RMP with lights flashing and siren blaring came speeding up to us where the roadway intersected with the 102nd Street Cross Drive.

Mike was grinning as he walked toward the patrol car to greet the uniformed sergeant who let himself out on the passenger side. He was holding the pipe out in front of him. "That wasn't so bad, was it? You got here pretty fast."

"You're Chapman, right?"

"Yeah. Mike Chapman."

"You want to get in the car with us?"

The driver made a U-turn and was ready to head back east.

"Nah. Just voucher this pipe for me. Got a manila envelope in the trunk?"

"Shove the pipe, Chapman. Get in the car. We got a situation right in the middle of the fucking meadow, which is covered with naked bodies like a love-in's about to happen, and then appears this—"

"What kind of situation?" Mike asked.

Mercer stepped closer to the car.

"An EDP," the overweight sergeant said, huffing from the exertion of getting out of the car. He was trying to tell us about an emotionally disturbed person who had picked one of the most populated parts of the Park in which to implode.

"Who told you to get me?" Mike asked. "Grab a uniform up in the North Woods, Sarge. I don't do—"

I thought of the three unstable men we were trying to track— Eddie Wicks, Vergil Humphrey, and Raymond Tanner. "Maybe you should go, Mike."

We all seemed to be talking over one another. Mike sighed with annoyance and gave me a backhanded wave to stay out of it.

"It's not a job for a rookie is what I'm hearing from headquarters. You'll do this one yourself is what they tell me, Chapman," he said, turning back to the car. "It's a good-looking broad with a pistol, threatening to blow her brains out in the middle of the meadow unless the commissioner comes to the Park to listen to her demands."

Mike covered his eyes with his hand and dropped his head.

"The deputy commish said to forget about Scully, but that you'd be somewhere around here today and to bring you to the scene *stat*. So get your ass in the car."

Mike turned his back to the sergeant to face me. He put his

hand over his heart when he started to speak. "I am so very sorry to drag this mess into your orbit, Coop. I'm—"

"This isn't about me, Mike. You've got to get this done before Pell hurts herself or anyone else out there."

Mercer stepped between Mike and the patrol car. "I'm going with you, Sarge. He's the wrong guy to deal with this. You've got to trust me on that."

"Don't, Mercer. It's all my doing."

"You're a lightning rod for her, Mike," Mercer said, putting a hand on his shoulder. "You go? She gets exactly what she wants. A public humiliation of you, no matter what happens to her. The broad's crazy, and we all know it. I'm more likely to be able to talk her down than you."

The sergeant had maneuvered himself back into the RMP. "One of youse. I don't care who, but I'm not looking for a bloodbath on my watch, guys."

Mike shook free of Mercer and pulled on the rear passenger door of the car.

"Mercer's right," I said. "He's a hostage negotiator because he has the patience and calm and grace to talk people down off ledges and out of danger. Sorry, Mike, but you don't have any of those traits."

"Don't let Jessica Pell make it personal today," Mercer said. "She wants a shot at you, pal. She wants to aim that gun and pull the trigger. No doubt in my mind."

"And you think you can stop her?"

"Go off in the woods with Coop and get lost for a while," Mercer said as Mike stepped aside so he could get into the police car. "I can do this so much better than you."

I jumped back as the sergeant turned on the sirens at full force again.

Mike slammed the door. "You watch yourself, man."

"Go find yourself a killer," Mercer said. "Let *me* get this monkey off your back."

THIRTY-EIGHT

Mike seemed shattered and totally distracted. We walked down the steep incline from the roadway to the secluded path at the foot of the arch.

"It'll be noon by the time we retrace our steps to your car," I said. "We can take a break."

"Why?"

"Because your head isn't in this."

"I just let Mercer go off to clean up my mess. What else would you expect?"

"You want to walk to the North Woods?" I asked. "See whether the guys are turning up anything?"

"They know how to find me if they do. Just follow the trail."

I tried to keep up with Mike, but it was impossible. The path was narrow, with branches and rocks in the way, but we made better time going back than on our exploratory trip through the Ravine, and it was clear to me that he didn't want our trek to become an intimate walk in the woodlands.

Mike locked the lead pipe in the trunk. Before we got into his car, knowing we had cell service out of the woods in the parking lot, he phoned the squad. The lieutenant had the day off, but Manny

Chirico was working. From Mike's end of the conversation I could tell that Manny knew exactly what the situation was at the Sheep Meadow.

"What's with Pell?" I asked.

"Still ranting. They've cleared the area and given Mercer a vest, and he's going to work. She's agreed to talk to him."

"She likes an audience," I said. "Where to?"

"Back to the Ramble."

"Okay. But why?"

"'Cause the powers that be have given up on it. But Raymond Tanner likes it, and Verge knows it well, and Eddie Wicks—well, he's a crapshoot," Mike said. "And they tell me it's got caves, or used to have them. Caves were built into that whole area before they were covered up with boulders."

"And because it's so close to the Sheep Meadow, you can get there—to Mercer's side—in a flash if need be."

"That, too."

Mike reversed the car to back out of the parking area and make the long loop west and south around the Park, to reach the lot behind the boathouse at the Lake, where we had entered the Ramble early in the week.

"Feel like talking?" I asked.

"I'm just trying to breathe, Coop."

"I understand." After he let me get so close to him on Wednesday night, it didn't seem possible that the week's events had conspired to put this much distance between us. But Mike didn't have a better friend than Mercer Wallace, and I appreciated his deep concern for this dreadful set of circumstances that he had put in motion.

We made the ten-minute ride in silence, the police radio crackling with reports of responses to a variety of locations around the borough. Mike parked the car and we got out, the bright sunlight directly overhead.

I pointed at one of the vendors whose cart was near the entrance to the trail. "Want some lunch?"

"Not hungry."

I walked over and bought us each a bottle of water, handing one of them to Mike. I drank half of mine as we started up the hill together, leaving the paved path for the rocky road that wound through the Ramble.

As we began our ascent, I noticed that the area was far more populated than the Ravine. There were lots of couples behind us, many of the men shirtless on this early summer day. Young women wore bikini tops or halters. Birders and dog walkers were intent on their missions. Each and every one who passed us by seemed to have a destination as he or she branched off at the forks that appeared at every turn of the way.

"You're walking with purpose, Detective Chapman," I said.

"There's a lot of territory to cover."

When we reached the top of the hill, Mike turned left, moving south to the Point, which overlooked the Lake and was directly opposite the statue of the Angel of the Waters. This was one of the most remote sections of the Ramble, beloved by birders, and where the Austin sisters had encountered Raymond Tanner.

I had a hard time keeping up with Mike. Despite the shade offered by the dense tree growth in this area, I was sweltering from the oppressive midday heat.

I finally saw him ahead of me, standing on one of the giant boulders left behind by glaciers in another age. Now his purpose became clear: He was trying to get a line of vision to the Sheep Meadow.

"How'd you get up there?" I asked.

"It's a guy thing, rock climbing. Not good for ballerinas."

"Give me a hand, will you?"

"I can't see a damn thing."

We were both looking across the Lake, right over the graceful arch of the Bow Bridge, where the girl's body had come to rest. There was way too much foliage at this time of year to see to the Sheep Meadow.

"I'll drive you over there," I said. "As long as you just sit in the car with me and don't do anything foolish."

Mike flashed me a look as he started to find his way down from the glacial rock.

"Sorry," I said. "I know you would never do anything to jeopardize Mercer."

"C'mon. There's a whole bunch of rock formations to look at. We'll stay right here."

For the next two hours, Mike dragged me from one huge pile of boulders to another. We poked and prodded—though it would have been impossible to budge any of the glacial erratics that had been deposited so many centuries ago.

Occasionally we stumbled over cave-like openings, some large enough for a human to crawl into for temporary shelter, but none that brought to life the tales we'd heard of people who lived in them.

At three o'clock, I found a shaded spot next to Willow Rock and rested myself against its cool surface. Mike flipped his cell phone open to call Chirico, but he had no reception, which was as typical in the removes of the Ramble as it had been in the Ravine.

He carried a walkie-talkie in his pants pocket and used that to reach one of the park rangers.

The stand-off with Jessica Pell was still in progress. She wasn't being aggressive toward Mercer, the ranger said, but clinging to her demand that the commissioner himself appear.

"That's a relief," I said. I had taken off my moccasins and was rubbing my feet. "She'll get worn down."

"You quitting for the day?"

"Not if you aren't."

"Those puppies of yours hurt?"

"Not enough to stop me."

He put the walkie-talkie back in his pocket and tossed me a protein bar. "Here's lunch, kid. That ought to hold you until cocktails."

The path led us deeper into the woods before it twisted to the north. There was a charming array of rustic benches and foot-bridges as we walked. I was separated from Mike from time to time, usually able to spot the bright aqua color of his collared polo shirt among the green leaves. He'd go off on a trail to explore a dense patch of bushes or to lift a fallen log that lay across a pile of similarly decaying wood.

Ahead of me I could see the Gill, the man-made stream that tumbled through the Ramble, looking as natural as though it had been there since the beginning of time. Its source was a few dozen yards to the north, in the artificial but beautiful Azalea Pond, and it ran down into the Lake below us.

"I'm just going to soak my feet for a few minutes," I called out to Mike. "Do you think the water in the Gill is safe to drink?"

"Safe as your kitchen sink. Same stuff."

I was terrifically thirsty. I knew I could refill the empty water bottle I had crammed into my pants pocket. I left the path and spotted a crystal-clear section of the stream at one of its widest points—free of leaves and very tempting to restore me.

I was looking for a grassy slope on which to make my way down to the Gill, but the area on both sides was lined with huge rocks. Gingerly, I sought out the flattest surfaces and began a delicate advance—avoiding the one on which three large turtles were sunbathing. It took me a full minute to get down to the stream, but then I sat not far from the turtles and dipped my empty bottle in the water.

I took off my shoes again and slid forward, dangling my feet in the stream. The only sound I could hear was the noise the water made running over and around the rocks. It was as though I had retreated to another time and place, apart from the violence of the last ten days.

The cool water refreshed me instantly—as both a drinking source and a soothing footbath.

To my right, the stream wandered to a turn in the bend before disappearing up to Azalea Pond. To my left was a pair of perpendicular boulders that stood like silent sentinels, unusual in how even and flush they were compared to all the rocks that had been piled in place beside them.

On the far side of the stream, almost completely concealed by the massive boulders and an overhang of leafy trees, was a sequence of flat rocks, each set back beyond the next like a primitive series of steps in a Mayan ruin.

"Hey, Mike," I called to him. "Check this out."

I thought I heard him return a shout to me.

I stood up, leaving my moccasins behind, and carefully made my way into the stream, steadying myself on larger rocks that jutted out from the shallow bed. I got across it, pushed back the limb of the tree that was partially covering the moss-laden staircase, and yelled again, "You've got to see these steps."

I heard him say "What?" or maybe it was "Wait." In either case, he couldn't have been far behind me.

I grasped on to a large stone that was perpendicular to the boulders, set almost like a banister beside the steep formations. Step by narrow step I pulled myself up, seeing only dark heavy rocks above me.

When I stood on the fifth of eight stacked stones, I was surprised to find a gap—a space between the layers of horizontal rock that appeared to be about two feet high.

I continued to climb, and when my waist was about even with the gap, I leaned forward and peered into the black space—standing on my tiptoes—so that my upper body was enveloped by the cool, dark atmosphere of the cave.

I thought I could see light inside. I blinked and adjusted my eyes to the inky blackness, trying to determine if the brightness was in fact another opening six or eight feet away from me.

But it wasn't daylight at all. I began to see a radiance from inside the black hole, something that was shiny and gleamed from within. As I grew accustomed to the dark, I became aware that it was several objects together that were reflecting the bit of sunlight that flickered in over my head, between the tree branches.

I could make out the round lines of a bright silver carousel, and beside that the iconic image of the Angel of the Waters, her topaz decorations shining like cats' eyes in the dark.

Before I could pull myself out and call to Mike again, a cold hand grabbed me by the back of the neck and smashed my face against the dirt floor of the hidden cave.

THIRTY-NINE

There was so much dirt in my mouth that I couldn't speak. My eyes were bleary as well, my vision obscured by the large particles of earth clustered on my lashes.

My captor was inside the cave. He had one foot on the ground—I could see his rubber-soled shoe—while his other knee pressed against my neck to hold me in place. He pulled back my head by grabbing a handful of hair, lifting it just high enough to slip a strip of cloth across my mouth, tying it behind my head.

Once the gag was secure, he moved from my side to in front of me, grabbing me under the arms. He dragged me over the top of the rocks that formed the mouth of his retreat and slid me deeper into the cave. Then he flipped me over, like a piece of meat on a cutting board, and tied my hands together with a similar strip of cloth.

I was staring into the face of Eddie Wicks, the man I had seen in the photograph at Dr. Hoexter's Bellevue office.

"Who are you?" he asked.

That may have been the only advantage I had at the moment. I knew my captor, but he had no idea there was anything unusual about his prey, except that I had invaded his territory.

My answer—"Take this off"—was muffled, and I doubt he understood me.

Wicks put his hands in the pockets of my jeans, front and back, rolling me from side to side. My ID was in my wallet in the glove compartment of Mercer's car. In my effort to travel light this morning, I had nothing on me with my name or professional credentials. There was only half a protein bar that he removed and tossed aside.

"Who were you talking to out there?"

I shook my head from side to side.

I didn't know much about psychiatry, but all my amateur instincts kicked in. Eddie Wicks was bipolar, and if he was indeed living in this cave, he was likely to have been off his meds for an extended period of time. He appeared to be agitated and jumpy, and from the deep rings beneath his eyes he looked as though he had not slept well in days.

He was literally twitching with indecision. He wanted to find out who I was and why I was there, but he didn't dare release the gag. Meanwhile, the clumps of dirt in my mouth were pushed toward my throat every time I tried to speak. I knew that if I panicked I would have even greater trouble breathing.

"Why are you here?" Wicks asked, prodding me in the side with his foot.

"Birds," I said.

"Words?"

I didn't want to upset him by speaking more loudly and cause him to hurt me. I was beginning to choke on the dirt particles, and my chest was heaving up and down as I tried to urge myself to say calm.

I spoke the word again. "Birds."

"Birds?"

I nodded my head up and down.

"Atlantic Flyway," I said, having no idea what that sounded like through the gag but hoping that the bits the park rangers and Commissioner Davis had taught us would sound like birder talk.

Eddie Wicks understood what I had said. He muttered "Flyway" as he stared at me. He didn't seem any happier to have me in his space than I was to be here.

"Birds don't live in caves."

I was biting at the gag, trying to moisten it with my saliva to make it move, to bring it down off my mouth so that I could engage with Wicks. "Swallows. Cave swallows."

"And that's why you were climbing out of the stream, looking for swallows?" He was standing almost upright in this black hole. The silver objects were behind my head, out of sight. I was on my back, struggling to keep an airway open, and all I could see around me was the darkness, and Eddie Wicks's pale, pasty face looming over me. "I don't think so."

I knew better than to try to play the homeless card. My jeans had been laundered and pressed, my cotton shirt bore a designer label, my nails were manicured, and there still might have been a whiff of my favorite scent if fear had not consumed all of it.

"What are you looking for, miss?"

Wicks's eyes were bulging. His paranoia was on full display, even though I was shaking my head from side to side in the negative.

I started coughing because of the dirt that was going down my throat. "Sit me up, please."

He was pacing the floor behind me. I had surprised him in his lair, and he was obviously concerned with what to do about me.

"Why should I listen to you? Why should I care if you choke to death?"

I used my tongue to move the gag even lower. "Look, mister. I don't know who you are or why it freaks you out to see me. I'm not from around New York. I'm just exploring the Ramble and looking for birds and glacial rocks—"

Half of him wanted to hear me, and half of him looked like he wanted to put me out of my misery—and out of his way.

"If you just let me out of here, you know I'd never be able to find this hole again. I'm turned around as it is, I—I'm lost and—"

There would be no reasoning with Eddie Wicks. He was so strung-out looking—dirty and disheveled, stinking like someone who hadn't bathed in weeks, and always that crazed, bug-eyed look about him as he stared down at me like I was an animal in a cage.

"Shut up!"

"Please let me sit, sir. I can't breathe."

I was clinging to what I knew from his mother, from Jillian Sorenson, from his Bellevue records—and to the hope that Eddie Wicks didn't have a violent history. If I could reach him on some human level, if I could find some chord to connect with him, then maybe I could talk my way out of the cave.

He walked away, several steps at least. I was tallying any advantages I might have, and added that he was close to sixty years old to the fact that I knew more about him than he could hope to guess about me. Surely if I could work my way out of the material that bound me, I would be faster and stronger than he could possibly be.

Now Wicks stepped closer to me, one foot next to each of my ears. He leaned over and again reached under my arms, dragging me across the floor of the cave—over rocks and sticks that scraped my back. He stepped out of the way as he propped me against the uneven stone wall, so that my head bobbed and struck against the pointed end of a boulder.

He knelt beside me and tried to adjust the gag to fully cover my mouth, then thought better of it until he found out more about me.

"Tell me why you are here, damn it."

"I've told you, it's just a mistake."

Wicks slapped me across the face. My head rocked back and forth, and my cheek stung from the smack.

"Think about it while you have some time to yourself," he said.

He stood up, walking across the cool, damp space until he was almost out of sight. Then he returned, carrying a huge rock that caused him to bend practically in half as he positioned himself to place it in front of the hole through which I had entered.

Half the daylight—and most of my hope of somehow stagger-ing safely down the steps—disappeared. Four more loads of rock and it was entirely dark around me.

Then Eddie Wicks disappeared, too, in the same direction from which he'd moved the rocks that formed his portable door—there must have been some other kind of exit. I squinted and fo-cused my eyes on that area, and as it came more clearly into view, there appeared to be an incline—not an opening to the outside—that curved around the corner of the largest interior boulder.

Suddenly above me I heard noise. He was walking just over-head, the rubber-soled steps of his footwear only made audible by the echoing nature of the cave. Surely there was another way of egress, which meant an alternate opening for Mike to find a way in to me.

I leaned my head back and tried to make myself go through my options. Eddie Wicks wasn't a killer. He was mentally ill, in desper-ate need of treatment, unlikely to trust me no matter what I said. He seemed to have abandoned his plan to hurt his mother. And now, if all the psychiatrist's predictions were to be believed, what he was most at risk to do was to kill himself.

I didn't want Wicks to hurt himself, nor did I want to be an ac-cidental casualty of his paranoia and self-loathing.

I looked to the right and saw the shiny silver figures that had been stolen from Lavinia Dalton's storage vault. Had Wicks been giving his possessions away, as the Bellevue shrink suggested yes-terday, in preparation for taking his own life? Had he been getting his things in order? Or had the homeless girl who wound up in the Lake stumbled upon something that distressed him—something that caused him to hurt her?

My wrists were tied in front of me. I knew that if I had enough time, I could work loose the binds. The material was no stronger than the gag in my mouth.

I glanced again at the Carousel as I wriggled my hands. And then at the miniature form of the Angel of the Waters—or the death angel, as Mike had called her just a little more than one week ago. I shivered as she stared back at me with her icy-blue eyes. I didn't want her to claim another victim.

Five minutes, maybe ten went by. I didn't hear any noise above me, and not a sound from outside, not even the stream whooshing below this solitary spot.

At last the cotton material started to give slightly as I pulled on it. I got up on my knees, faced the sharp-edged boulder that made up the foundation of the cave's wall, and rubbed the strip against the edge, slicing it in two.

I kept it in one hand, figuring I could pretend to retie it if Eddie Wicks came back before I could get out of here.

I rushed to the pile of rocks he had stacked to cover the opening and lifted one off the top. It was so heavy, it practically fell out of my arms to the cave's floor. I let it down and made no effort to get it out of the way.

I heard a noise above me. I stood still for a few seconds, not able to tell whether Wicks had said something or whether he was moving in my direction. I'd never be able to redistribute the large rocks fast enough to escape if he was on his way back down to me.

I turned and made my way over to the silver objects across the room, if that was what one called this claustrophobic site. I picked up the carefully carved stone that represented the Warriors' Gate and stuffed it in one pants pocket.

The Carousel horses caught my eye. Each one was small, but their legs were long and sharp and might be useful to me in fighting off my enemy. I pulled two out of their bases and put them in the right pocket of my jeans.

And then I saw the box. Right next to the Carousel, and much larger than the miniature objects.

It was made of wood—homemade, it appeared—and perhaps had been used to store or steal the valuable pieces from Lavinia's collection.

Maybe there was a tool inside—a screwdriver or a hammer or something with which I could arm myself.

I lifted the lid.

The only thing in the box was bones. Human bones.

I was looking at the skeleton of a small child. I was looking, I guessed, at the skeleton of Baby Lucy.

FORTY

I was engulfed by a wave of nausea.

More than forty years had passed since the kidnapping of Lucy Dalton—most likely by someone who knew her, by someone who knew his way around the home in which she lived, by someone who knew his way in and out of all the service entrances and design anomalies of the luxurious Dakota apartment building.

I needed to get out of this burial vault before Eddie Wicks came back for me. I needed to find a way to return Lucy Dalton's remains to the grandmother who had lived four decades with the uncertainty of the fate of this beloved child.

I closed the lid on the box and went back to the stone wall, redoubling my efforts to clear the blockage and escape. Two of the oversized rocks were out of my way, but there was still not enough room for me to climb up and over the others.

When I reached for the third small boulder and swung it around, I wasn't able to hold it up. It was much heavier than I'd anticipated and it slipped out of my arms, landing with a thud on top of another one.

Now I could hear Wicks moving above me, padding on his

soft-sole shoes in my direction. I was certain he'd heard the commotion I'd created.

I pulled at the next-to-bottom rock but could barely budge it, so I climbed up on it and started to stick my right leg through the opening. I was over the top of the pile, and I was stretching to make contact with solid ground below, but Eddie Wicks had me by the neck.

"Mike!" I screamed. I thought the noise could be heard for miles around. But it was the last thing I got to say before Wicks clamped a hand over my mouth, shoving more dirt inside as he pulled me back onto the floor of the cave.

"I didn't think you'd come alone."

"It doesn't matter what you think. If my friend was still around, he would have followed me in here by now," I said, spitting out dirt as he tried to keep my head from moving. "We got separated hours ago."

"Don't move or I'll have to hurt you."

I was struggling against him, pushing at his chest with both arms. I could feel blood trickling down the backs of my legs where they had scraped against the rock surfaces when he dragged me inside again.

Eddie Wicks was about my height and outweighed me by a good thirty pounds. He kneed me in the abdomen this time, more worried now about my flailing arms than about my mouth.

"Let me out of here," I screamed.

He had more of the same material: a pale-pink gauze that he wound around my hands in a crisscross motion, and then another length that he loosely wrapped—despite my kicking—around my ankles. He knew as well as I did that it couldn't hold me very long, but I didn't know what else he had in mind to do to me.

Then Eddie Wicks stood up to assess his handiwork. He backed up, keeping an eye on me, while he refortified his fallen wall. He was so used to this dark interior that he didn't seem to need anything to illuminate his way around.

That's when he caught sight of the wooden box, the makeshift coffin that held the child's yellowed bones. He saw—as I just realized now—that I had not replaced the lid properly, and that it was slightly ajar on top of the box.

He went into a rage, screaming at me—his words bouncing off the walls of the cave—until finally he knelt beside the box and lifted the lid off it completely.

"Why did you have to open this?"

"I—I didn't open it."

"You moved it. The box wasn't open like this before."

"I didn't touch it. Maybe I backed into it when the rock fell," I said, trying to keep my voice steady, on an even pitch. "All I want is to get out of here. Out of your—your life. You have no reason to hurt me, and I have no reason to hurt you."

I was trying to stretch the gauzy fabric he'd tied me with by pressing my legs apart while Wicks was preoccupied by the thought that I had seen the bones.

He was rocking back and forth on his haunches. "You saw her, didn't you?"

"Her? All I can see are those silver things and a box. I just want to go home. I didn't see anyone."

"You saw the child, didn't you?" Wicks rose up to full height, turning back to me.

"What child? There's no child here."

"My friend," he said. "That little girl was my friend."

I didn't want him to talk. I didn't care why he had Lucy Dalton's remains in a box in a cave in the middle of Central Park. I just wanted to see daylight and run as far away from him as I could.

"Don't tell me anything about it, sir. I don't—"

"Nobody ever calls me 'sir,'" he said, smirking at me.

"I'm very squeamish. I—I just want you to let me out of here before I get sick."

"You're the only one, then, that doesn't want to know about the child," Wicks said. "Why is that?"

"Because I don't know what you're talking about. I don't know anything about a child—and I'm so tired and hungry. Let me out of here and I'll run and I'll never look back. I promise you that."

"The girl was my friend," Wicks said, coming closer to me. He had picked up another length of the pink gauzy fabric somewhere across the room—perhaps from behind the wooden box—and he squatted beside me, wrapping it around both his fists. "I didn't have many friends when I was a young man. Do you?"

"A few. Only a few," I said. But I knew they would do anything for me if they could only find me. I tried to stay confident that they would come back before too long, unless I could get this unhinged madman to let me loose.

"There was someone you called out to when I grabbed you."

"Not a friend. Just a guy I met on the path today. He loaned me his field glasses to look at the birds."

"If he's your friend, he'll try to find you, won't he?"

"I'm very shy, really. He's not my friend. I'll never see him again."

"I was seventeen when Lucy died," Wicks said, jumping around from subject to subject, as though he was unable to hold a thought for very long.

"You were a kid yourself," I said, trying to be empathetic.

"You've heard of her, of course. Lucy Dalton?" he asked.

"No. No, I haven't. But I'm not from here. I'm—I'm from Wisconsin. I'm just visiting. That's why if you just—"

"You must be ignorant, young lady. She's a very famous little girl," Wicks said, his bug-eyed sneer seeming so sinister in the dark surroundings of the cave. "She was kidnapped a very long time ago. More famous than the Lindbergh baby, people say."

I couldn't tell if he was getting madder because I claimed not to know the story of Lucy Dalton, but there was no going back on my decision to play dumb about her.

"Are you the one who—?" I asked. "Did you hurt your friend?"

"That's a stupid thing to say, isn't it?" Wicks said, raising his voice as his cheeks reddened. "She was just a little girl, only three years old. I had no reason to hurt her."

I picked up my head to look at him. "But she died, and—"

"It was an accident. All the brilliant reporters and the police investigators and even the servants who knew me as well as they knew Lucy, they all got it wrong. And I couldn't tell them the truth because Lucy was with me when she died."

Eddie Wicks sat on the floor of the cave, just inches away from me. He started to stroke the fabric that was wound around my legs—not my legs themselves but the gauzy cloth. And then he began to cry as he continued to talk.

"We loved this place—this Park. It's what Lucy and I had in common. The zoo, the Carousel, all the playgrounds. And one day she asked me to take her with me to the Park, to play there in the afternoon."

The crying stopped. He was angry again. The mood swings were violent and abrupt.

"We lived in a big house, in a great big house, right near the Park. It was Lucy's house, and sometimes I felt like it was my house, too. I thought it was the safest place in the world," Wicks said, now winding the gauze more tightly around his own hands, holding them up in the air like he was playing a game of cat's cradle.

"I don't want to know any of this," I said. I wanted to buy time by talking about almost anything, but I feared that if he disclosed too much to me about Lucy's death, he would become more determined to do me harm.

"But you can't go now, dear. That wouldn't be right. There has to be someone to tell the truth to people after I'm dead, don't you think?"

"You're very much alive. And you've frightened me horribly. And if the child's death was an accident, then just let me go and you can tell them that by yourself."

"I might not be alive for long," he said. "It's a terrible burden to live with this."

"With what? To live with what?"

"Lucy's dead because of me," Wicks said. "My father's dead because of me."

"How do you mean?"

"I was thirteen when my father jumped out of the kitchen window in our home. I was sitting at a table ten feet away from him, and I didn't stop him. Do you understand how that made me feel? Do you understand how people blamed me for that—my mother? My sister? How they told me it was my fault?"

"But you were a child yourself. I doubt you could have stopped him," I said, trying my amateur psychology on a man who'd been through years of treatment, most unsuccessfully. "If he was intent on killing himself—if those were his demons—then he would have succeeded another time whether you stopped him that day or not."

"But I didn't even try."

Survivor guilt, I knew, was a powerful paralytic.

"But the child— Is her name Lucy?" I asked. "You said her death was accidental."

"Do you think anyone would have believed me at the time? Do you think anyone would have believed that if they had found her little body?"

"I don't know what people would have thought. You're a very intelligent man. I'm sure someone— Was your mother alive then?" I asking, feigning lack of knowledge. "I'm sure someone would have believed you."

"My mother was a housemaid," he said, baring his teeth as he snarled at me. "Nobody cared what she thought. Even *I* didn't care what she thought."

"I'm sure—"

"It was a day in June when the accident happened. A much cooler day than this one. I was staying in a room above Lucy's home because my school year had finished. And because I didn't have any friends to keep company with."

"Why are you—?"

"Shut up," Wicks said as he pulled on my restraints. "I told

Lucy I'd take her to the Park. I promised her, even though no one would have allowed me to do that. To them, you see, I was damaged. I was my father's boy, and too damaged to be around that happy child.

"After her nap she came upstairs looking for me. We had all these wonderful rooms in the house where we could hide from the adults, where I could amuse her and do magic tricks that made her laugh."

I thought of the endless string of rooms we had seen yesterday at the Dakota—the quirky layout, the labyrinth of spaces, some private, some public—all removed from the living quarters where Lavinia Dalton and her pampered grandchild were cared for.

"Lucy had a dress on—a smock, really. Pink-and-white gingham, because her grandmother always insisted that she was dressed in pink."

Then Wicks stopped and adjusted his position to get closer to me, to look me in the eye to make sure I was listening to him.

"And Lucy had *this* on, too," he said, holding his hands out to me.

"This?"

"This beautiful material that her grandmother had ordered for Lucy from Paris. And my mother had sewn into a party dress for the child."

It was the gauze that he had bound me with, the gauze he had primed in his hands for use on something—or someone.

"Pretty, isn't it?"

"Lovely." I had nothing else to say.

"So pretty and so much of it that my mother made a shawl out of it for Lucy, too. A long strip that the child used for dress-up, that she liked to put around herself when she was pretending to be a princess," Wicks said. "She wanted to wear it out to the Park, even though I thought that was kind of silly. That it was too warm to wear it. But she insisted on it because it was so light and filmy, not warm at all, and so I couldn't disagree."

"But how were you going to take her out if no one in the household would allow that?"

Eddie Wicks rocked back and forth again, never taking his eyes off me as he told me what happened—testing me, perhaps, to see how his story went over.

"I had a plan, of course, so that we wouldn't be seen. No one would miss us because they'd all assume we were playing in the attic, that Lucy was happy to be with a friend who was part of the household.

"There was a dumbwaiter," he said. "It could go all the way from the top floor of the building to a service room on the ground floor. Nobody used that room anymore, and nobody really used the creaky old machine."

I thought of the archaic device, and even what an attractive nuisance—almost a game—it might have been for an inquisitive child.

"Lucy? Well, the dumbwaiter was her favorite place to hide. It wasn't meant to fit people—just loads of laundry or cleaning supplies or dirty dinner service—so it could only hold a child at best. We decided together—" Wicks said, pausing for a moment before he went on.

We decided, I thought—a damaged teenage boy, possibly sexually charged during one of his manic phases, and a three-year-old child who was his favorite companion.

"Lucy got in the dumbwaiter, in her gingham smock with her princess shawl wrapped twice around her shoulders and neck like a scarf, as she always wore it, smiling and laughing about our secret trip," Wicks said. "That's how I left her, how I always want to think of her."

I tried to conjure up that cheerful image but brought to mind only a wooden box full of bones.

"I pressed the button to send her to the ground floor, and then I ran down the servants' staircase—the rear staircase—just as fast as I could, so I'd be there to help Lucy out, so we could go on our way, through one of the back doors."

Eddie Wicks stood up and started to pace back and forth.

"But when the doors opened, there was this helpless little child—she'd been strangled to death—whose knees were bent beneath her, hanging from the top of the tiny elevator car."

The image was chilling and repellent. I bit down hard on my lip.

"The tail of Lucy's shawl caught in the door when the dumbwaiter closed, many flights above, choking the baby, before the material ripped apart as the machine carried her down to me."

I recoiled against the wall of the cave, shuddering at the picture of the dumbwaiter beginning its descent, slowly asphyxiating the vibrant three-year-old, who was on her way to an adventurous afternoon in the Park, wearing her princess-like shawl wrapped around her shoulders and neck.

I thought I was going to be sick. "Please don't—"

"Don't tell you any more? I live with that image of Lucy every day of my life. It's more than I can bear, so don't tell me not to say it, now that you've found her broken little body."

"Didn't you try to get help?"

"She was dead, young lady. No question about it. Her face was blue, her neck was mangled, and though her body was still warm, Lucy was dead. And I knew I'd be blamed for her death."

"But you didn't leave her there," I said.

"In the dumbwaiter? Of course not," Wicks said. "I brought her here. I knew this place well. The Indian Cave, they called it when the Park was designed. But then there was trouble inside it from time to time, and it had to be closed up. I found a way in—the same way that you did—when I was just a boy. It's where I came to get away from people who were mean to me."

I didn't say a word.

"There wasn't a speck of blood. There was nothing to mark the place where Lucy died. No one had to know," he said, in a conspiratorial whisper. "I found a laundry bag in one of the washrooms, and I put Lucy inside it, as gentle as I could be, and I carried her out in my arms, past all the workmen near the back door. It was a big building, you know, and an important one, but everyone there was used to seeing me come and go. And there wasn't anybody who cared to talk to me. Not that day, not ever before."

"And you came to this—this cave?"

"I know every inch of this Park, every last inch of it. I wanted Lucy to be somewhere safe. I wanted her to be somewhere I could see her and watch over her."

What a sick idea had taken over Eddie Wicks's mind all those years ago.

"And most of all, I wanted to die beside her. I wanted to kill myself, miss, but I found out that I was too much of a coward to do that."

"That's not being a coward. That's—"

Wicks was walking toward me, holding out the same gauzy fabric that had been the instrument of death for Lucy Dalton.

"I've tried to kill myself, and I've even failed at that. I've tried four times, maybe five," he said, and I knew the most recent one had resulted in his Bellevue hospitalization, "and I haven't been able to do that right, either."

"Let me take you out of here and get you help," I said.

"I've got a better idea, although the last person I tried to enlist in this endeavor wound up dead herself," Wicks said. "An impetuous girl, actually, who should never have made it her business to tell anyone about Baby Lucy."

I thought of the body in the Lake—the homeless girl who thought she was best at helping wounded people, damaged people like Eddie Wicks.

"I know about her, I think. I read it in the papers last week," I said. "The girl who was found at Bow Bridge."

"I'll make a deal with you, Wisconsin," Wicks said, his eyes bulging as he tightened the ties on my legs. "All you have to do is kill me. Make me know the pain that Lucy knew in the minutes the life was sucked out of her. Maybe that will be the way you can get out of this burial chamber alive."

FORTY-ONE

"Why don't we give Lucy a proper burial?" I said.

I needed to get Wicks to stop talking about his death—and mine—and focus him on the child he loved, maybe as a way of getting us both out of the cave. I was revolted at the suggestion that I help him kill himself.

"I did that once already," he said. "Now you're going to have to stand up. You're going to have to come with me to see what I've prepared."

"But—but this box looks—well, it looks practically new."

"I didn't have a coffin when Lucy died. I kept her here with me for several nights, sleeping right beside her, until I was able to bury her in a cemetery."

Wicks grabbed my arm and started marching me—since I could only take small steps—toward the far wall and up the ramp that led to the higher part of the cave.

"How did you do that?"

"There's a cemetery in the Park," he said, squeezing my upper arm with his hand.

I couldn't let him know that I was pretty well up to speed now on almost every corner of the Park, and there were certainly no cemeteries here.

"I've got a map. I—I didn't see anything like that."

Wicks had a tight grip on me. I was stumbling on the steep incline of the cave's floor as we turned a corner and continued on.

"Move faster."

"Untie my legs if you want me to go faster," I said. "Where are you taking me?"

"Nowhere."

"But—but it's pitch-black ahead."

"It's a cave, Wisconsin. Don't you have any of them back home?"

"I don't know how you can see. I—I can't see anything."

Eddie Wicks was like a feral creature, accustomed to the cool dark space that no light seemed to penetrate, pushing me forward farther and farther away from the only opening that I knew existed.

"You don't need to see, young lady. Only I do."

"But Lucy," I said, trying to appeal to his professed devotion to the child, "you're leaving her alone back there. What cemetery are you talking about?"

"You wouldn't know it, Wisconsin. There are three cemeteries in the Park, and nobody knows they're even here."

"But where?" I asked, tripping on a rock and falling to one knee.

Wicks grabbed my shirt collar and pulled me to my feet. "You can't see the graves any longer. Nobody respected the dead, even though they've been there for two hundred years. The city built this Park right on top of all those lost souls, but that's where I put Lucy to rest."

Of course, I thought. All Angels' Church. Three cemeteries for the three churches that once made up Seneca Village. The church buildings and houses had been razed to the ground, but the cemeteries of each had been left on-site and covered over when the Park was originally landscaped.

"I'm so thirsty," I said, stopping in my tracks and trying to put Wicks's story together. "Can't I please have some water?"

"You can't have anything," he said as he pressed me to shuffle along.

"If you buried Lucy in the cemetery, why is she here? That doesn't make sense."

"You weren't even born in 1971, were you?"

"No."

"The whole world was looking for Lucy Dalton. The cops, the FBI, everyone at the Dakota," Wicks said. "Did I say that name before? The Dakota is the place that Lucy lived."

"I didn't know."

"The police treated me—they treated all of us in Miss Lavinia's household—like criminals."

He was indeed a criminal, and little wonder that Dr. Hoexter spoke of Wicks's noted history of feelings of police persecution. Hoexter had called them persecutory delusions, but there was nothing delusional about them. Eddie Wicks, like the Dalton staff, must have been interrogated over and over again.

"But they were all so stupid they had no idea how to find Lucy."

"Because you had buried her," I said softly, trying to shake off his grip.

Wicks had turned around, facing me and moving backward, my wrists in his hands. His eyes were on fire now, the only thing I could see as I haltingly walked along with him.

"I wrapped her in a sheet that I brought here from the house, and I tied it with some of her favorite ribbons. In the middle of the night, I walked from this cave, holding Lucy in my arms."

"And no one stopped you?"

"It was the '70s, dear. You had to be crazy to be in this Park at night," Wicks said. "And it isn't far to the cemetery. It's near 85th Street, just west of here."

8521. I almost said the numbers out loud. I remembered the first day we had walked in the Ramble with the park rangers, and the reminder that every lamppost bore the number of the street location nearest to that point.

8521 was the number written on the Day & Meyer receipt that Mercer picked up from the dusty room on the ninth floor of the Dakota. It must have marked the place in the Park—in the very middle of what used to be Seneca Village—where Eddie Wicks had buried the body of Baby Lucy Dalton.

"I can't walk anymore," I said. "The ties on my ankle are too tight. And it's cold in here. I need something to stop my chills."

"You won't be cold much longer," Wicks said. "You shouldn't complain so much."

"But why is Lucy here?" I asked. "I don't want to leave her alone."

"Because someone had the bad judgment to dig up the area around the cemetery, to dig up the little village and churchyard."

Nan Rothschild and the Barnard-Columbia project—the dig to examine Seneca Village a couple of years ago—must have unsettled Eddie Wicks completely.

"I had to go back and rescue Lucy—"

"Rescue?"

"I didn't want anyone digging up that poor child, disposing of her somewhere else."

Profilers and shrinks were going to have a field day with Eddie Wicks, if I could get both of us out of this godforsaken place alive. Behavioral scientists would claim that Wicks's mind-set was shown by how he treated Lucy's corpse. They would tell us that wrapping her in a sheet, decorating her shroud with her favorite ribbons, and burying her in a proper—if out-of-sight—churchyard demonstrated a degree of attachment to the child. The Lindbergh baby was tossed to the side of the road in the Jersey woods—a point often underscored—to be scavenged by animals.

"So you brought her body back here, before that dig?"

"Well now, there isn't much of a body, Wisconsin, is there?"

"Let go of me, please. I can walk faster if you loosen the ties on my legs."

"You looked in the box, didn't you? She's only just bones now. But I'm going to bury them with the proper respect, too. Right there, in the floor of the cave. And Lucy will be surrounded by the things she loved most."

The Carousel, the Angel of the Waters and other silver pieces from the Dalton collection must have been part of what Eddie Wicks stole from the storage unit after his escape from Bellevue. Some of the other treasures—Belvedere Castle, the Obelisk, and even the ebony angel that undoubtedly came from underground, from somewhere in the churchyard that was once Seneca Village—must have become separated from this cache.

My thoughts flashed to Vergil Humphrey. He told us that the black figurine came from the churchyard that he and another man— a man he had known since his childhood—found when they were digging at Seneca. Had Wicks relied on the unreliable storyteller to help him retrieve the remains of Baby Lucy? Did Verge pilfer the black angel when he helped his old friend with the grim task of moving Lucy from the old churchyard?

I couldn't help but wonder whether our Angel—the dead girl— realized that both men had something to do with this heartrending box of bones.

I had no doubt that Wicks was creating a shrine for the child he claimed to have adored.

"Please tell me where you're taking me."

"Almost there."

"But I can't help you hurt yourself. I'd never do that. Take me out of here with you and I'll explain all this to the police. We'll convince them that Lucy's death was an accident."

Wicks pulled on my hands again, and as I shuffled forward I kicked against an object that almost sent me flying over it. Something low, on the ground, that obstructed my path and scraped my shins.

I looked down and saw a platform of some kind, also wooden, as far as I could make out.

"You don't have to hurt me, actually," Wicks said. "You can just be my canary in the coal mine."

"What—?" He was wide-eyed now and agitated. The canary was what miners sent ahead of them to test for deadly gases. What had his diseased mind conceived of as my fate?

"Step up on this, Wisconsin. Let's see if I've got it right this time."

"Got what right?"

"You step on this. Come, come. It will hold your weight quite easily."

When I didn't move, Eddie Wicks walked behind me and lifted me onto the improvised stand. That's when I saw the pink gauze.

The metallic strands of gold in the precious fabric glittered above my head. I craned my neck to look up at the odd display.

While I'd been wriggling against my binds earlier, Eddie Wicks had come up here, to this second level of the vast man-made vault, and wrapped lengths of Lucy's sparkling material around the tip of one of the boulders that jutted into the cave.

Wicks had fashioned a noose from a long piece of heavy rope and covered it with fragments of the pink-and-golden gauze that had crushed the life out of the little child. He was determined to kill himself this time, but he was more determined to kill me first.

FORTY-TWO

"What have you stuffed in your pockets?" he asked. He was standing in front of me again, reaching for the noose. "They're bulging."

Wicks patted me down, finding and removing the small silver objects with which I'd hoped to defend myself.

He dropped them on the ground, then stood squarely in front of me and smacked me across the face. "They belong to Lucy, you fool."

I tried to lift my bound hands to my cheek, to lessen the sting, but Wicks grabbed them and held them directly in front of me.

"This is going to be painful for you, I know."

"And what is it about watching me die that you're looking forward to?" I asked. "Will that excite you?"

"Nothing about watching you excites me. I want to see how much it hurts you so I'll know how much it will hurt me. The slower it is, the better," Wicks said. "I'd kill my mother, too, if I could."

"Your mother?"

"She made the scarf for Lucy. If she hadn't made the damn thing in the first place, the child would still be alive."

Wicks looked down to see why the platform was shaking so violently on the uneven ground of the cave floor. He leaned over and put his hand on it to steady it for his coup de grâce.

The moment he did—just as he started to straighten up—I lifted my hands over my head, seizing the noose and launching myself in the air, bringing my knees up behind me and then kicking my legs forward with all the strength I could muster.

Eddie Wicks doubled over. I swung back and forth, clutching the fabric-covered rope between my fingers—pumping my legs like a child on a swing—and this time I brought my feet up, scoring a hit directly in my captor's groin.

He howled in pain, falling to the ground and rolling onto his back.

I lowered myself onto the platform. Although my hands were still tied, I was able to pull apart the binds on my legs, the ones I had been stretching before Wicks came back to get me.

I walked to the rock wall and rubbed the restraints on my hands against it for several seconds, till they tore in half and I was loose.

I guided myself back to the lower floor, running my hand along the cold stones. I had to try to uncover the entrance again, though I didn't know how long it would take Wicks to get to his feet.

I ran back over to the silver pieces on the floor beside Lucy's bones. I picked up the statue of the Bethesda angel and stuck her in my waistband.

Then I turned to the business of trying to move the boulders.

I was frantic and had no reason to be quiet. I reached for the one on top and dislodged it after pulling on it for almost a minute, stepping out of the way so that it fell to the ground with a loud thud.

I heard a noise and looked over my shoulder, but I figured it was Wicks still moaning, still recovering from my powerful kick.

The second and third rocks were somewhat easier to move. I pushed and pulled on them until both fell outside the cave, crashing down against other boulders, splashing into the stream of the Gill.

The hole was too small for me to exit easily. It was still light outside, so I took deep breaths, wiping the dirt from my mouth as I tried to calm myself. The last thing I needed was to get stuck trying to make my escape.

I struggled with the next two rocks—both very large—and seemed only to be making progress with one of them when I heard Wicks, coughing, coming down the incline.

"Don't come near me," I said. My hands shook, slowing me down, but nothing could dampen my determination to get out of this dank space.

There was still fabric wrapped around Wicks's hands. I was sure he would try to bind it around my neck if he could get close enough.

"You'll die here with me," he said, reaching out both arms to me.

I stepped up onto one of the boulders that had tumbled to the ground. He tried to grab me, but its surface was so uneven that I slid backward and he missed.

When I found my balance seconds later, I reached for the silver statue, tucked under my shirt in the waistband of my jeans.

In a single motion, I swept her up above me and brought her down squarely on the top of Eddie Wicks's head. He screamed out in rage—not words, but like a beast that had been felled by a hunter. I smashed it against his skull again, knocking him to the ground and opening a wound that bled freely onto the dirt.

I didn't care about making the hole in the rocks any larger. I hoisted myself up onto one of the higher boulders and pushed out onto the ledge leading through the opening.

I screamed for help as loudly as I could while I lowered myself headfirst against the rough surface of the cave's exterior. When the large tree limb seemed within reach, I grabbed it and clung to it with both hands, righted myself, and came to rest on a small precipice to the side of stone steps—the ones that had first appealed to my curiosity.

Barefoot and bruised, I made my way down that primitive staircase, crossed the stream, and stepped back into my driving moccasins.

The path was empty, and my scream hadn't drawn anyone to my aid. Mindful of the lampposts and the guidance they provided to get me out of the Ramble, I ran as fast as I could downhill to extricate myself from this deadly maze.

FORTY-THREE

"You know better than to think I would have left you out there on your own," Mike said. He was sitting in the stern of a rowboat, in front of the boathouse on the Lake, as the last moments of twilight were giving way to darkness. "I figured you were pouting 'cause I wasn't talking to you about anything personal. You said you were tired, and I thought you'd just walked on back down to the street."

I was sitting on the grass next to the boat, my feet in the water. Mercer was on a bench behind me, rubbing my shoulders.

"How often have I quit on you?" I asked.

"I thought it was different this time," Mike said. "You know, different since—"

"Yeah, I know."

"Then I heard on the walkie-talkie that Mercer had talked the six-shooter right out of crazy Jessica Pell's hot little hands, and I flew out of the Ramble and across to the Sheep Meadow like I was Usain Bolt."

"That probably puts me next on Pell's hit list," Mercer said. "After she gets discharged from lockdown."

"I just assumed you'd be with Mercer," Mike said. "Not a good day for spelunking alone, kid."

"Sorry?"

"Spelunking. Isn't that French for cave exploring?"

"It's not French for anything. Drop it there, okay?" I said. "I didn't plan on going into a cave alone. I didn't know it was a cave, and I thought you were right behind me. I counted on the fact that you'd see my shoes and sweater on the ground beside the stream, if nothing else. That you heard me calling to you."

"I did. And I told you to wait."

"You need to see a doctor, Alex?" Mercer asked.

"That toothbrush took care of all my medical needs." The Loeb Boathouse had become the hub of all the police action again, as it had been on the Friday morning that Angel's body had been found. One of the rookies had been dispatched to buy some toiletries for me so that I could clean up. I wasn't leaving the Park until I had answers to most of my questions.

The Emergency Service guys were setting up floodlights so that Crime Scene could do its work above us, in the Ramble. Mike had been allowed to question Eddie Wicks before an ambulance took off with him to New York Hospital, cuffed and under arrest for the bludgeoning death of Janna Dixon, the homeless girl whose journal had been found in the cave, next to the box with Lucy's bones.

I had been debriefed by Manny Chirico and two other homicide detectives from Mike's team. I told them everything that Eddie Wicks had said to me.

"What did Wicks tell you?" I asked Mike.

"I read the diary first," Mike said. "That's what got the girl killed."

"Jo was right, then," Mercer said, referring to the homeless girl he'd brought to my office to be interviewed.

"Yeah. Janna's life was pretty much all there, in her own words."

"Where was she from?" I asked.

"Payson, Arizona. Nineteen years old."

"Did you find her father? Have you called him?"

"I had no interest in speaking to that bastard," Mike said. "She has an aunt who seemed to be Janna's only lifeline. Her mother's sister. I reached her an hour ago. We'll fly her in tomorrow to make the ID and take the body home."

I wrapped my arms around my legs and rested my chin on my knees. "It was all true, about the sexual abuse by her father?"

"Way too true. Years of it."

"There's so much help we could have given her here."

"Wait till you read her words, Coop. The thing that Janna Dixon knew best was despair."

"What a heartbreak. And why did her words get her killed?"

"It was Verge who introduced her to Eddie Wicks," Mike said.

"Verge." I straightened up with a start. "Have they found him?"

Mercer leaned me back to rest against his long legs. "He's in the boathouse. Verge showed up in the Sheep Meadow while I was sweet-talking the judge, to see what all the ruckus was about."

"And now?"

"The guys are inside, trying to make sense out of him. Seems he and Wicks knew each other way back as kids. Saw each other dozens of times over the years."

"And the black angel?" I asked.

"It really did come from the graveyard of one of the churches in Seneca Village," Mercer said.

"Verge helped Wicks take Lucy's bones out of their resting place," Mike said. "I don't exactly think he knew what Wicks was doing, but he helped himself to the ebony carving while Wicks was up to his own business."

"What about Janna?"

"She and Wicks got along at first. There are sketches of him in her journal. Stories about him, too, and how he showed her some of the Park's secret places. He told her about the Indian Cave himself. That it had nothing to do with Indians, but it was just designed to be a mysterious part of the Ramble, with two entrances."

"Two?" I said. "I'll be damned if I could find a second one. I was counting on Mike to do that before he ran off on me."

"Commissioner Davis just told me there used to be an inlet off the shore of the Lake, and you could row right up to it."

"That must have been the part of the cave that's on higher ground, where Wicks set up his noose," I said.

"Yeah. Then there's that steep flight of stairs that you found, kid. The lower chamber. But Davis said this cave in particular was such a hot spot for men harassing women back in the 1920s that the entire thing was blocked off—both entrances—as though they had never been open. The Park records suggested to him that no one would ever be able to penetrate it without getting a bulldozer up there."

"They were certainly wrong about that," I said. "It's a pretty sinister place."

"There are Indian caves—really ancient ones—in Arizona, not far from Payson. Janna wrote about how they fascinated her, and so when Wicks told her about this one, she wanted to see it. He even let Janna stay there, sleep there a few nights. None of the other kids in the homeless crew, just Janna."

"Without—?"

"No sexual overtures, Coop," Mike said. "At least nothing she wrote about, although there were plenty of references to what her father had done to her. But then Janna found the box with Lucy's bones, which Wicks had hidden in a corner, under a blanket."

"And he went berserk, I'm sure. Did she write about it?"

"It looks like she never had the chance to do that. She sketched a picture of the box, and then one day she must have looked inside it and seen the bones. She drew those, too."

"Then Eddie Wicks must have found the drawings and knew Janna had seen Lucy's bones. That's what set him off on killing me, too," I said. "Did he admit anything to you?"

"Yeah. In his own way. He killed Janna because she was afraid she was going to tell someone about the bones. That they didn't belong in a cave."

"He said that to me, too. Called her 'impetuous,' though I don't know who he thought she was going to tell. Do you figure it was Verge?" I asked.

"Wicks doesn't seem too worried about Verge and his stories. He said he knows no one takes the guy seriously. That's why no one believed him about people living in houses in the Park or finding the angel in a churchyard."

"That's why no one would have listened to Verge if he said they dug up a body together," I said. "What did he kill her with? Janna, I mean."

"It's been a long day, Coop."

"Give me the rest of it, please."

"He hit her with the same piece you used to crack his skull."

I lifted my head and looked across the Lake at the regal figure of the beloved statue on the Bethesda Terrace. "Death angel, Mike. You weren't wrong about her."

"Well, the silver miniature of her is on its way to the lab. Maybe we'll get some of that mixture DNA you've been talking about."

"Janna Dixon, Eddie Wicks, and me all over that precious little statue."

The water gently lapped at the edge of the Lake. It hardly seemed the same deadly site that it had a week ago. But the Park was treacherous that way, pulling you in with its beauty and betraying you with the dangers that lurked in its darkest recesses.

"Maybe it's true," I said. "I mean, the story he tells about Lucy and how she died."

"Yeah, but if you're saying he didn't kill her, he was still a mutt way back then—and a despicable criminal—for taking the body and disposing of it. Think how it tormented Lavinia not to have any idea what became of the child for the rest of her life."

"I'm not on his side, Mike. Do you get that? I'm the one who just spent a few hours in a spider hole with the man. He's as responsible for Lucy Dalton's death, in my view, as if he put his hands around her neck instead of the scarf. It was totally reckless of Wicks—even though he was only a kid himself—to put that little girl in a dumb-waiter and send her off to her death. And now there's Janna."

"Janna wrote about the silver objects, too," Mike said. "She had no idea they were valuable, but she had a habit of stealing things—food, clothes, and maybe things she thought she could cash in. She tried to barter with Wicks—brought him food and stuff, and then she asked for one of the pieces—but he said no. She wrote that two days before she found Lucy's bones."

"Did Wicks carry Janna's body down to the Lake?" I asked.

"He kept her in the cave for a while. He wouldn't give it up to me completely," Mike said, "but I'm betting Verge helped him do that."

"Is that what Verge is saying tonight?"

"He's doing his rope-a-dope, make-no-sense dance for the detectives right now," Mercer said. "I think we're going to find out that Wicks trusted Verge to help him dispose of Janna in the Lake. Maybe promised to give him back the black angel. Janna claims in her journal that Verge did give it to her. Like a talisman, a spirit to watch over her. I'm thinking once he was in the cave and saw that statue again, along with the silver pieces, he tried to steal them out from under Wicks's nose."

"You're probably right," Mike said. "Maybe Verge carried them with him. Got as far as the bushes near the Lake when Wicks went after him. Then couldn't go back for them because of all the cops around the Lake when Janna's body was found. I'll have you that news by morning."

"Morning? I'm ready to go to work on those other cold cases you have from the Park," I said. "Will you let me in on them?"

Central Park was the most seductive place in New York City. It offered the magnificent vistas, public thoroughfares, private pathways, and natural scenes of great physical beauty. But it wasn't a place to enter alone in the dead of night, and I had seen far too much evidence of that fact in my decade as a prosecutor.

"I don't think Battaglia'll be too keen on that idea. But I like your style, Coop. All cred to you for that crater you put in Eddie Wicks's head."

"My footwork was even better."

"I'm not surprised."

Mercer pushed me forward and stopped kneading my shoulders. A uniformed cop was coming toward us, and he was carrying things in both hands.

"What's up?" Mercer asked him.

"Sergeant Chirico sent this out to you."

The boathouse was an elegant restaurant as well as a police staging area. The officer had two bottles of white wine and three glasses, along with an opener.

"Thank him for us, will you?" I asked.

Mercer uncorked the bottle and poured us some of the chilled wine. I reached out to Mike with one of the glasses. He took it from me, eased off the seat and put the oars inside the boat, then sat down on the bottom of it. He rolled up the legs of his jeans and hung his feet over in the water.

"Now all we need to find is Raymond Tanner, and we'll have a trifecta," Mike said.

"Let's take a couple of days off, guys," Mercer said. "Let the task force deal with Tanner."

"But—"

"Not to worry, Alex. I'm on the task force. You'll know everything the minute that I do."

"But I've got ideas about him, Mercer. I bet his next hit is Van Cortlandt Park."

"What's your hunch?" Mercer asked.

"He's doing parks in each of the boroughs. Manhattan's over for him. Too many cops on his tail here. He's tried Brooklyn. I'm guessing the Bronx is next. I wish I could warn every young woman in town not to venture in after dark."

"Listen to her, Mercer," Mike said. "Coop isn't wrong till she's wrong."

"I've been listening to her for years, Detective. Time for you to tune in."

I got up and gave Mercer a hug, then stepped into the boat. I sat facing Mike, my back against the other side of it and my feet up on the gunwale. I sipped the wine and rested my head back.

"Will you take me home tonight?" I asked.

"I'd like to, Coop. I really would. Didn't Mercer tell you?"

"Tell me what?"

"I got a twenty-one-day rip. Suspended without pay for three weeks."

"You're kidding me."

"Scully got the order directly from the mayor."

"For—?"

"Crossing the line with Jessica Pell. I've sworn off crazy broads for the moment. That goes for you, too."

I picked up my foot and poked Mike's thigh with my toes.

"Three weeks from now and no paycheck? You'll be back. Even my kind of crazy might start to appeal to you."

"Don't get too cocky, Coop," Mike said, combing his fingers through his hair while he grinned at me. "Old ways are hard to change."

"I'm your escort tonight, Ms. Cooper," Mercer said. "Detective Chapman has a lot of paperwork to do on his big arrest. Let me top off those glasses, will you?"

Mercer reached over to refresh both of us. Then he put the bottle down next to me and with one strong shove, he launched our rowboat onto the Lake.

"We'll be leaving here in half an hour, Alexandra. In the meantime, don't make waves."

ACKNOWLEDGMENTS

"Who was the author of the wise scheme to turn the waste lands in the centre of the island into a city park?" John Punnett Peters, the early chronicler of St. Michael's Episcopal Church, asked more than one hundred years ago. Scholars and politicians have suggested many answers to that question over time, but none argue with the necessity and brilliance of creating the glorious design that became Central Park, in the heart of Manhattan. It is, as Kenneth Jackson of the New York Historical Society has said, "the most important public space in the United States."

I am grateful to everyone at the Central Park Conservancy and the New York City Department of Parks and Recreation—employees, donors, and volunteers—who have been entrusted with maintaining this magnificent work of art.

I was fortunate to spend hours in the Park in the company of Sara Cedar Miller, Central Park historian and photographer, as well as a thoroughly delightful guide to the pathways and hidden beauties of the land. Sara's book, *Central Park: An American Masterpiece*, is one of the most glorious volumes to grace a bookshelf. My thanks, again, to Susan Danilow, who opened doors and made introductions with her characteristic generosity, wisdom, and friendship.

The research for *Death Angel* took me everywhere from the earliest nineteenth-century reports of the Board of Commissioners of the Central Park to Roy Rosenzweig and Elizabeth Blackmar's *The Park and the People* (1992) to Joe Mitchell's *New Yorker* piece about "The Cave Dwellers" (1938) to *Cemetery John* by Robert Zorn (2012). The finest and most powerful writing about homeless youth in New York that I have ever read was in Rachel Aviv's *New Yorker* essay entitled "Netherland" (2012). As always, the *New York Times* articles about this city and its history—past and present—have been an invaluable source of information. Most especially fascinating and useful were articles by Mark Lamster, Liz Robbins, Danielle Ofri, Anemona Hartocollis, Nina Bernstein, Christopher Gray, Lisa Foderaro, Elizabeth Harris, Michael Wilson, and two pieces without bylines—from 1857 and 1897—about caves in Central Park and their inhabitants.

Then there are the real-life heroes who have provided inspiration: Manhattan District Attorney Cyrus Vance; the women and men of the great Trial Division—and all its Special Victims Units—of that office; the women and men of the New York Police Department (and former Crime Scene Unit expert Hal Sherman); the women and men of the OCME Forensic Biology Lab, including Theresa Caragine and Adele Mitchell; Nan Rothschild of Columbia University and her co-workers on the Seneca Village project.

Commissioner Gordon Davis (he really *was* the New York City Parks Commissioner once) wrote of Central Park in 1981: "Of all its great achievements and features, there is none more profound or dramatically moving than the social democracy of this public place." I was introduced to the Davis family by my husband, Justin, and those friendships have been among the most meaningful of my life. My thanks to Gordon—gently nudged by Peggy—to let me recommission him and put words in his mouth. And to my summer

ACKNOWLEDGMENTS

family of Davises—Allison, Susan and "goddaughter" Jordan—it's impossible for me to express the joy I have when spending time with you.

In addition to my very sincere thanks to my Dutton friends, I must add gratitude for your patience. Brian Tart, Ben Sevier, Christine Ball, Jamie McDonald, Jessica Renheim, Carrie Swetonic, Stephanie Kelly, and Andrea Santoro—you are all a class act in a very tough business. And the same to David Shelley and his team at Little, Brown UK.

Esther Newberg has long had my back, and that's the way I like it.

Family and friends—all the usual suspects—who have been a rock for me throughout the last few years, I remain in awe of all of you.

To Karen Cooper, who has been a devoted friend for almost thirty years—since the first evening you walked through my front door on the arm of the *real* Alex Cooper—you have inspired me every day of the last six months with your fortitude, courage, beauty, and strength.

And always to Justin, who remains my trusted muse and guiding spirit, and who believed in me when Coop was just a creature I dreamed about, fifteen books ago.

ABOUT THE AUTHOR

Linda Fairstein is America's foremost legal expert on crimes of sexual assault and domestic violence. She led the Sex Crimes Unit of the District Attorney's Office in Manhattan for twenty-six years. Her fourteen previous Alexandra Cooper novels have been critically acclaimed international bestsellers, translated into more than a dozen languages. She lives in Manhattan and on Martha's Vineyard.